"The Silent]   xteen;
hilarious, sul   ft for
the Snapchat   ance,
friendship is technicolor, and there are few things more pleasurable than roaring down the highway in a living truck. Do not read this at night. Do not read this alone. But read it. Now."

—**SEAN BEAUDOIN**, AUTHOR OF
WISE YOUNG FOOL AND *THE INFECTS*

"Imagine if Halloween had been written by The Kids in The Hall instead of John Carpenter and you start to understand the wild, mesmerizing mash up that is *The Silent End*. Monsters and monstrous fathers, missing mothers and young love—somehow all of this and much more fits wonderfully into this book. It manages to be scary and sweet and very, very fine. Sam Sattin is a talent and this novel is a joy."

—**VICTOR LaVALLE**, AUTHOR OF
THE DEVIL IN SILVER AND *BIG MACHINE*

"I dreamed I climbed into a 1950s sci-fi rocket ship with Thomas Pynchon, Charles Dickens, H.P. Lovecraft, Jonathan Lethem, Rabelais, and the crew from Monty Python. The ship didn't launch—we went nowhere—but by the time they let me out, my hair gone white and my face looked forever in a skeleton's grin, I'd had so much fun and terror and tragedy and delight, I was ready for the booby hatch. You can't dream my dream, but you can get everything it gave me. All you've got to do is read Samuel Sattin's *The Silent End*."

—**D. FOY**, AUTHOR OF *MADE TO BREAK*

THE SILENT END

SAMUEL SATTIN

CRESTVIEW HILLS, KENTUCKY

THE SILENT END
Ragnarok Publications | www.ragnarokpub.com
Editor In Chief: Tim Marquitz | Creative Director: J.M. Martin
The Silent End is copyright © 2015 by Samuel Sattin. All rights reserved.

The characters and events portrayed in this book are fictitious or fictitious recreations of actual historical persons. Any similarity to real persons, living or dead, is coincidental and not intended by the authors unless otherwise specified. This book or any portion thereof may not be reproduced or used in any manner whatsoever without the express written permission of the publisher except for the use of brief quotations in a book review.

Published by Ragnarok Publications
206 College Park Drive, Ste. 1
Crestview Hills, KY 41017

ISBN-10: 1-941987-54-0
ISBN-13: 978-1-941987-54-4
LCCN: 2015948341
First Edition
Worldwide Rights
Created in the United States of America

Copy Editor: Amanda Shore
Editor: Tim Marquitz
Publicity: Melanie R. Meadors
Social Media: Nick Sharps
Cover Art & Design: M.S. Corley
Map: Jacob Magraw-Mickelson
Interior Layout: Shawn T. King

For my mom, RIP.

"Thus the explorations of space end on a note of uncertainty. And necessarily so. We are, by definition, in the very center of the observable region. We know our immediate neighborhood rather intimately. With increasing distance, our knowledge fades, and fades rapidly. Eventually, we reach the dim boundary — the utmost limits of our telescopes. There, we measure shadows, and we search among ghostly errors of measurement for landmarks that are scarcely more substantial."
—Edwin Hubble

PART ONE

ON TRICK-OR-TREATING AND A MONSTER IN THE WOODS

ONE

Have you ever heard of an airplane vanishing? A set of engines, rumbling into fair weather, a moment later eaten by atmosphere? Well, that's how Mother's disappearance was for me. A traceless beacon. A silent end. It was as if she dematerialized from her bedroom as a midnight sacrifice, something for the monsters Father now hunted.

I'd just met up with my oldest friend, Gus Mustus, for what he swore would be our last Halloween in town. I often wondered if he thought about the disappeared. We never spoke of it. But Mother refused to leave my mind; while she had departed, her memory had not. I envisaged her sailing into the cicada orgy of Graywood Forest, her mouth open wide and her eyes black and empty. The real reason she'd vanished, almost a year ago, depended on who you talked to—adultery, suicide, homicide. But Father blamed it on beasts. Creatures that needed killing now more than ever. No matter which answer was correct, however, I knew one thing and one thing alone: that she was gone. Gone and finished like the end of a story.

Gus asked me the night it all truly began: "Is she coming?"

Though it was a predictable question, it caught me off guard considering who I'd been thinking about.

Gus's dark, nimble hands were snapped tight into white, cotton gloves, and he used one to punch my shoulder amicably. He was dressed as some breed of magician, in a hot pink tuxedo jacket with a penguin tail, ribbed white shirt, and magenta top hat that could have been retrieved from an insane asylum's lost and found box. Gold monkstraps fastened his tuxedo shoes, and a silver cummerbund crossed his waist. His idea of an illusionist was nothing I found familiar, but it was obvious a lot of thought had gone into it.

"It's not like I keep track of Lexi's schedule," I said though in reality, I sort of did. She'd been spending a lot of time with us over the last few weeks, and I couldn't say I wasn't enjoying it.

"I hope she shows up."

"Why?" I flashed a smile in his direction. "I don't have enough Halloween spirit for you?"

"No, asshole." Gus checked his hornet-yellow Casio, a little too big for his wrist. I assumed it was close to 7:30 based on when I'd left my house to meet him at his. "She promised to bring me Tesla Blue, Blood Mahogany 2, and a jar of Bonecrusher White…" He sighed. "She got them from Ronald, I think. I don't even know how."

"He probably owed her something." I hoped I didn't sound jealous. Even if the idea of Lexi alone with Ronald Peterson made my mouth feel dry.

"Whatever. I just hate it when people are late. I mean, why even make plans?"

"What did you expect? You think she gives a damn about us? You know she hangs out with us because she's bored, right?"

"Shut up, Eberstark." He tilted his body with un-delicate poise as he said my name (my last name, actually—it was what everyone had called me since middle school). Gus, while lithe, had a kinetic personality. A confidence so inbred it made me doubt my own. "You think everybody pities us. Which, you know, makes me think you really just pity yourself."

"No, I'm just sick and tired of being branded an outcast because of your need to be so blatantly public about your hobbies."

"*My* hobbies? Are you kidding me? I seem to remember someone *crying*, yes, CRYING, when his Techno-Lorque Legion got crushed in the Attactix tournament last year. Don't try and under-nerd *me*, man. It'll be an uphill battle." He noticed my costume then, as if for the first time, and gave a double take. "What are you supposed to be, anyway?"

"A shadow."

I hated Halloween for a lot of reasons, but the principle of all of them was dressing up. This year, I had, in a last ditch effort, painted my face black, covered my arms and legs in clothes of the same color, and sneaked out the front door before Father or, Odin-forbid, his cohort the Hat, kept me from doing so.

"That's fucking racist," Gus said.

"What? Why?"

"How am I supposed to feel about that?"

"Oh, come on."

"Why don't you just put on a minstrel's jacket, huh? Or better yet, Eberstark, *I'll* go find a yarmulke and go around asking the neighbors for their firstborn—I'm sure you'd like that."

"All right, fine. I'll change, okay?"

"There's no time for that, you idiot. Just keep out of sight. My mom will kill you."

"Fine."

"And she'd be justified."

"I like your costume. It's colorful."

"You're still a dick."

Gus was right…and not only about the "dick" observation. He was smarter than me, for starters, organically speaking. Even though I'd caught up with him in some ways in the last couple of years, I'd stopped trying to dispute he was just better at understanding things than I was. Ultimately, I was thankful he maintained the upper hand. Many times, I'd found myself preparing to fuck up my entire life, and many times, I could count on him to cut me down to size before I went the distance. Just short of eighteen months ago, when Mother was still around but was becoming "unwell," as Father liked to say with his fingers crunched into quotations, I landed myself in a rough patch involving pyrotechnics and psychedelics. Almost all the evil P's you can think of, really. Gus, he'd practically made it his civic duty to straighten me out. He offered less terroristic outlets—the main involving space warfare and twenty-sided dice—that kept me out of juvie but, in exchange, put my social life on lockdown. Maximum clearance.

Since the two of us were about as attractive as you'd expect members of an organization called the Myers High Sword Star Society to be (which, yes, we did now co-sponsor along with Ajay Kapur and Ronald Peterson, the latter also a co-sponsor of the Manga Society and owner of three samurai swords that his mom had, wisely, neutered with cable locks), it could be argued that I never stood a chance in the first place. Though I also liked to think that, on some level, I'd actually wanted to become a better person.

It was just over four years ago that my family moved from Cleveland to this small, sleepy city. It was called Mossglow, a name more fit for the English countryside than the Pacific Northwest. Born and reared in a big(ish) city, Mossglow was unlike anywhere I'd been before. Quiet. Sparse. Private in that scary way. It had been perfect for Father's business plan, and when we'd moved in, things hadn't seemed quite as fusty as they were now. Then again, that was before Mother's depression. Before Father started raving about the thickening mists and the neighborhoods hollowing out. Though I'd begun to see strange things myself in recent weeks, Father had been ranting on about them since Mother disappeared.

"Somewhere between that fetid bay and Mossglow proper lies the key to revealing the penumbra," he liked to say of the phenomenon. But only when he emerged from his underground bunker where he practiced what he insisted on calling "science." "Makes me wonder what sort of alive we are."

The bay he spoke of was known to the rest of us as the Horn. Some old mining families had named it that a century or two back. Its gateway was marked by the townie neighborhoods—places best stayed clear from—and I'd never been down to the shore. From above, I'd heard it resembled its namesake, a bony curve of land with a fat beginning and sharp end. The waters weren't welcoming, the temperature slightly more hateful than the waves, which were rumored to snap crab pots off their cables. Though since the majority of citizens, my family and Gus's included, had settled on the other side of town, I didn't think about it much. Until a few weeks ago, that is, when I saw a swell of mist so large and solid-looking that, as it passed across my front yard, I wondered if it were alive. For that reason and others, I'd begun to worry I had been infected by Father's paranoia, that soon, I'd be suffering from the same disease that sent him spiraling into mania. When it gets so dark at noontime you can't see across the street, and when the mist grows thick enough to consume you whole, you can't help but worry something's going on that even madness can't explain.

"Those dark patches light creates, they work against us." Father, again, this time on the subject of "evil penumbras," a term he coined after he'd spent the first month looking for Mother, camping out in Graywood Forest and getting lost in the caves of Goon's Cove. The man I'd come to know as the Hat sat beside him, his eyes under Ray Bans, his mute lips pursed, a white fedora perched atop his head. "At least in this city. That's why I say, 'Never trust a man until you see he's asymmetrical. And if you can't tell from his body, check the eyes.' Light can't hide in the eyes, you see. Not the kind I'm talking about… not inside that kind of darkness."

The last thing I wanted to do was validate Father's babble. But my gut wouldn't let it slide. When Mother disappeared, it was one thing… Though she'd been missing about ten months now, she might as well have faded away a good few before then. People asked me about her for a while, curious about whether she'd skipped town, the relationship between her and Father, and the like. Old Sherriff Nichols even stopped by the house once and put my balls to the wall on the subject. But when two more girls, teenage twins from the Upper Thicks, went missing a few months later, it was as if I, and Mother, completely faded from view. I'd even begun to think things could go back to normal for a little while after that. Of course, the town had its problems. Jobs were becoming scarcer than ever. Sometimes, the townies would drive around looking for kids to clobber. When that happened, the city seemed to shift in character, become something eviler than it knew itself to be. But people still had their barbecues in Graywood Forest in the summer, and school started in the fall. Nothing improved when things got bad, and nobody seemed to care about how they'd gotten that way to begin with.

"God, Eberstark," said Gus, saving me from my own thoughts. "Don't try and look too excited about tonight."

"Settle down. I was just thinking."

"Next thing I know, you'll be reading books."

"Screw you."

"Touchy, touchy."

Gus's father, a heavy-gaited archeologist named Marshall who, for reasons unknown to me, refused to relocate after he got offered a big university job on the east coast, opened the front door of his freshly remodeled home and allowed us a joyless, "please shut the hell up" wave.

"You two still here?"

Marshall's eyes looked bleary from the black cherry pipe tobacco he liked too much. He held a book titled *Lithics* in his hand, one chapped finger down the middle. He'd recently found work teaching online seminars at a Midwestern university, and I knew that was a good thing. Marshall had been experiencing a creative drought in writing his new book over the last couple of years to the point where his ability to secure academic work had diminished. I couldn't understand why he hadn't just taken a tenure offer he'd received, picked up the family, and skipped town. But I'd also seen what happened when he sat on his back porch and gazed into the mist. How he drifted off. How he lost himself.

"We're just waiting for someone," said Gus.

"Don't be back too late." Marshall arched his neck to see behind his son. Keeping in mind what Gus had made me realize about my getup,

I tried to find cover. But Marshall's worried eyes saw me crouching behind their mailbox, the hull of which had been fashioned out of a papaya-shaped geode he said he'd brought back from a cave in Utah.

"What in the hell are you dressed as, Eberstark?"

I brought myself up from the ground.

"A shadow?"

Marshall scrutinized me from head to toe.

"Asshole."

"Told you," said Gus.

Marshall coughed and closed the front door of his well-tended home, leaving us alone on the driveway. I was grateful he'd only given me the cold shoulder. The last time we talked, he'd asked me about Father, and I'd stammered so much I was sure I'd given something away. In the spinning of so many tales over the last year, I was afraid the weave would jostle loose, though for some reason, it hadn't yet.

We'd stashed the majority of our Sword Star battle terrains in Gus's basement and prepared all our strategies for the upcoming tournament there. Though it wasn't easy, I'd managed to keep Gus away from my house since Mother went missing, and as for Father, he stayed in his bunker most days, sometimes for weeks at a time, and skulked often to the forest at night, fading into the fog like a passing supposition. In truth, the man's occult preoccupations made my life easier. I preferred for him to leave me be. The way his eyes crossed made me nervous.

We heard a motor grinding up the incline to the west of Gus's home. A tub of nuts and bolts *gnarring* so harsh it sounded like it was dumping out its innards. It climbed the hill from the bottom of the Lower Thicks, where I lived, and approached us at a crawl. Headlights kneaded over the willows at the peak of the incline. Tires hammered as they came level to the road.

"Lexi?" Gus's costume turned a scintillating shade of pink in the headlights.

"Can't be." Though I hoped I'd be proven wrong. "The Shepherd's in the shop."

"That thing's always in the shop."

"Everything they own is."

When an old, green Jeep Cherokee climbed into view, we knew immediately it wasn't Lexi, whose treasured vehicle was an old Bronco she'd named the Shepherd. As I began to see through the windshield, mucky from tobacco, I glimpsed the contours of two people. Teenagers, like us. One had a mangled cigarette in the corner of her mouth, pushing yellow smoke to the roof. The other, chin down, head bald, cheeks sickly white, worked the transmission and steered.

"Garbage," I heard him mutter through the open window as the Jeep appeared to stall for a moment.

"I can't believe your dad makes you drive this shitbox," came the other voice, growly and vaguely female. "Why are we even down here? You know Jesse's throwing a shindig up in Crowstone."

"Did you just say shindig?"

The bald one started the engine again, and the Jeep lurched forward. The one with the cigarette turned to watch me as the tires scraped past Gus's driveway. Fear crept from my groin into my stomach the second I saw who they were.

"That's Joe Ross driving," I shuddered.

Again, the motor stuttered to a halt.

"Fuck you." Joe smacked the dash with his fist.

"And the other one, that's Charlene Poughkeepsie."

"Just take it easy," Gus said, sensing my fear upon seeing what might have caused some at our resident school, Myers High, to climb the nearest tree. Someone like Gus, who ignored popularity games, wasn't on the radar of adolescents like this that didn't believe in the existence of consequence. I liked to hope I wasn't on their radar either. That I'd stayed far enough away from being a campus personality to not warrant notice. Gus and I—and to an even greater extent, Lexi—sat apart from the others. Not because we were different but because we were invisible, like shadows at dusk. Since Mother's disappearance, I preferred it that way. It seemed to keep me safe.

Joe Ross revved the engine. Charlene, a bulk of a girl with painfully tied-back hair and a red track suit two sizes too small for her body, glanced at me again briefly as she lit another cigarette. She was snickering at Joe, saying something like, "Fucked him up real good, didn't we?"

When the Jeep growled to life and lurched onward, I trembled with relief. The bumper sticker right above the left brake light reading TOWNIEZ caught my eye as the vehicle trailed up Geraldine Lane, towards Crowstone Heights and away from the Thicks. It screeched around a corner in a burst of speed and a babble of laughter from Charlene.

"They're gone," said Gus. "See? Nothing to worry about."

"Did you see her look at me?"

"What's her name again?"

"Good God, Gus. Charlene? Charlene Poughkeepsie?" His face was blank. "The girl who broke Danny Feld's ribs?"

Gus chuckled. "Who cares what she looked at, Eberstark? Why would she have anything against you?"

"Do you even live on planet Earth?"

"Do you even know how big planet Earth is? In metric

centimeters?"

"I hate how the two of you talk to each other." A voice from behind caused both of us to jump. "Like two dolphins trapped in a bucket."

"Balls, Lexi." Gus held his hand to his heart though you could tell he was mostly relieved. "Why don't you ever make noise?"

"I brought your paint." Standing primly before us, she was dressed as a prom queen covered in blood. The dress was frayed around the ankles and somewhat colonial-looking save for the ruffled bust and corn syrup spatters. She stood duck-footed, per usual, with her knees angled outwards, her shoulders exposed and her jet-black hair tied up in a messy, blood-stained bun. She shoved a paper bag into Gus's hands, which he snatched and peered inside. Just watching her long, muscular arm stretch out to do so filled me with a combination of what I could only describe as desire and mild nausea.

"Aren't you lovely." Gus ogled the jar of Bonecrusher White as big as his fist, which he would soon use to lend necessary highlights to his newly minted Demigods along with an Order AFT bequeathed by Jim Muller, who'd been hospitalized with Leukemia and could no longer play. Since I knew I'd be using it to spruce up my Techno-Lorques too, along with other reasons, I couldn't keep from smiling. "I am going to make my Crow Seraph shine with you…you sexy, sexy pigment."

"Gross," said Lexi with an apparent lack of emotion. She retracted her hand and used it to scratch her crimson eyepatch—not part of the costume. I couldn't even believe she was hanging out with us on Halloween. School was one thing, but this was the outside world. For an almost insane moment, I wondered if that could mean she actually liked—*like* liked—one of us (and by one of us, of course, I meant me). I saw the contempt in her eyes as she watched Gus molest his paint and struck the possibility from my mind. Though I still didn't understand why she'd come out with us.

Gus eased the paper bag into his faux-magician's faux-leather satchel. "Now, we can go."

"Go where?" said Lexi.

"Trick-or-treating. I told you on the phone."

"I know what you told me. I forgot to remember."

"You're dressed up."

"So are you."

"But why then…"

"I still don't know why you want to do this," I said to him. Fucking Halloween. I'd seen enough blood and darkness in my own life to be interested in celebrating it. It was really only because Lexi agreed to go that I'd not fought harder with Gus to stay ditch out. "Aren't we getting a bit old for—"

"Who gives a damn how old we are?" he yelled, which for Gus meant raising his voice an octave above stern. "This is our last year before we go to college. Doesn't that mean something to you?"

"College." It was as if I was guessing the wrong answer on a game show. "And no."

"We've been trick-or-treating the Thicks since freshman year. It was the first time you stayed over at my house. Remember, when we watched Akira and you got all freaked out?"

I remembered the evil teddy bear leaking milk and uttered some sort of affirmation. But I really wished he hadn't brought it up in front of Lexi.

"Well then, you should know that for us, trick-or-treating isn't a pastime. It's a sacred tradition. A mark of friendship. Call me a purist, but—"

"We should go to the forest," blurted Lexi.

"Halloween is a holiday that puts us in touch with our pantheistic selves. A gem of American paganism. And that's reason enough to celebra—wait, the forest?"

"One of the girls I hate in Spanish class told me her brother saw a monster out there in Graywood."

"And you believed her?"

"Yeah?" I sniggled uncomfortably at the mention of monsters. "You believed her?"

"No." She kicked at the ground with her battered dance flat. "But I still think we should go."

"Why?"

"Because trick-or-treating's lame."

"So lame," I blurted. I hated how I got around Lexi. It had been the same ever since the first time she appeared, a little over six months ago. When for some reason she pulled up a chair and sat next to Gus and me in the cafeteria. She hadn't even introduced herself. Just sat there, eating in silence day after day as Gus and I went on about Sword Star and whatever else crossed our minds, occasionally checking to see if she was still around. She basically became our friend without us realizing. A peripheral friend, sure, but now a member of our tribe. In the last few weeks, she'd become more vocal, though, which I wasn't used to. The more she spoke, the more her voice, harsh and intelligent, stirred something inside me. I tried to make myself look relaxed when I felt whatever it was coming on but instead stumbled to do so much as speak. And now, she was talking about going into the woods with us. A place where she and I might have found a moment to be alone had Gus not been here and had we not been in danger of becoming pawns in one of Father's plans.

"Anyway." Her eye narrowed. "There's got to be something in there that's not happening out here."

"What type of monster?" I tried not to sound nervous. I'd become good at keeping secrets from others but not so good at keeping them from myself. Since Mother disappeared, I'd adapted shades of loneliness that always seemed to linger in the Mossglow sky. Whenever I heard any mentioning of the M word, I was forced to accept the existence of Father's lab. I was forced to guess at the strange goings on beneath that hatch in the backyard where I was scared to venture. Just yesterday, I'd overheard him with the Hat downstairs, whispering about high-grade explosives, a scheme for catching what he called "big game." If he was out tonight, he was up to no good, probably in the forest, and I couldn't say a word about it.

"I don't know what type," said Lexi. "A big, scary one. Let's find out."

"I don't know," said Gus.

Lexi smiled at me in a way somehow both dangerous and inviting. "You know you want to, Eberstark."

"But I was kind of thinking we could all go to Gus's house. You know, paint some Prodlings?"

"Why are you guys such shut-ins?"

Gus frowned. "I'm not a shut-in."

I thought about the haggard expanse of Graywood. I watched Lexi's eye flicker between the two of us and thought about what it would be like to reach out and touch her cheek. I thought about those things until I remembered Father. Then, the word "explosives" took over, and all I could see before me were flames. Lexi injured in some unholy blaze.

"Fuck it, Gus." I put my hands in my pockets. "Let's just go."

"You kidding me?"

"It'll be fun," I lied. "And no."

"Look…all right. We hit the Lower Thicks first, and then we can go to the forest. Okay? For like twenty minutes."

Lexi grinned victoriously.

"Ridiculous." Gus hated the forest. With good reason. "Of all the things to do in Mossglow…just a bunch of beer parties and wasted ambition."

"You don't like beer parties?" Lexi took a pack of cigarettes from her bloodied cleavage. She popped one in her mouth and swanned her neck toward a blue Bic lighter with the barcode scratched off.

"I don't drink."

"Never?"

"I don't like to lose control."

"You've already lost control…" I said. "Of your ability to get laid—am I right, Lexi? Am I right?"

"Your costume's racist." She exhaled smoke over her pink lips until it turned kindred with the mist. "Now, let's go get this over with before I reassess my company. I'm interested in monsters, not men."

TWO

OUR TRICK-OR-TREATING BEGAN slightly after eight-thirty during a rare lull of autumn fog. In infrequent times like these when the night sky cleared, I made sure to steal a look at the moon. It was almost full. The blue of it filled my eyes with a geriatric feeling for a few seconds before the clouds returned to smother it. Mother appreciated the moon and celestial bodies in general, thinking of them like hazard signs on a darkly lit mountain road. Even as she began to wither, she maintained the stars withheld secrets we on Earth were too small to grasp. Since she'd gone missing, I'd more often found myself clumsily looking skyward. Ignoring the fact that Mossglow was probably the worst place in America to go stargazing, I was frightened by what they might tell me.

We turned onto Mather Avenue, two blocks east of Gus's house, remaining in the wealthier end of the Upper Thicks. This was the nicest part of Gus's neighborhood and, though some townies would punch you for saying so, probably the nicest part of all Mossglow. It consisted of a small and pretty patch of three-story houses filled mostly by families who either struck gold off the snow mobile factory—known as Hinterlord, closed now after a fire—or wealthy loners from cities down south who'd bought here with the intent of tasting small town life. They glimpsed the Horn and deemed it dramatic, which was true if you were just passing through, seeing for the first time a swarm of orange, black, and purple clouds, twisting together in awe-worthy patterns. But the rest of us were perplexed at how anyone with money to spend would relocate to a place so deprived of opportunity. Families like Gus's did all right because his father remained in the friendless quiet of his office, corresponding with people across the country and even ocean. But for folks like Lexi and me, it wasn't that easy. We were less like people and more like mice hiding beneath a kitchen stove. I couldn't count on Father anymore. I had to make sure I not only took care of myself but that no one else knew I was doing so. It was exhausting, and sometimes when I walked around Mossglow, I found myself crouching in the shadows, looking into the windows of happier people's homes, trying to steal their warmth.

Gus led us to a street he thought would be bursting with Halloween bounty: Juniper Boulevard, a beltway of kempt homes where we'd normally have been unwelcome save for on All Hallows' Eve, when charity abounded. Windows blazed with electric candelabras. Jack o' lanterns twisted with candlelight on the sidewalks. Metal cutouts shaped like black cats and witches stabbed up from the grass. Whereas the Lower Thicks had come to resemble a scrapyard, Juniper prospered like an open-air market.

"This is impressive." I had to admit.

"This place is full of five-year-olds," said Lexi, pulling out another cigarette.

"Because that's where the good candy is." Gus readied his candy satchel. "Why do you think I brought us here? And would you please put that cigarette out?"

"Why?"

"Because this place is full of five-year-olds. Do you even have a bag?"

"I don't like candy," Lexi said with enough gravity I had to agree.

"Me neither." I knew how out of place we must have looked.

"Here." I unshouldered my navy backpack and tried to give her my most charming smile, the one I'd practiced in the mirror but which now, I suspected from the way she was looking at me, made me appear as if I'd swallowed a turd. "You can use mine."

"I don't like chivalry either."

"But...what?"

Lexi brought me into her vision. Her uncovered eye was dark, the iris so brown that it was almost black, and the lids were ringed with translucently thin lashes. An eyepatch had been with the girl ever since I'd known her. The result of a seizure brought on by infectious encephalitis, I learned, when she finally told us about it a few weeks ago. She'd been twelve at the time, with braces and Nike shoes, on a trip to the Philippines, touring her mother's village to see her grandmother in the weeks before she passed away. The symptoms didn't hit until they were over Chicago—they forced an emergency landing at O'Hare, where she was hospitalized for a full week. Partial, almost total, blindness in the right eye. Her mother, as far as I understood, avoided guilt by placing blame on Lexi herself for playing too closely with her cousins in still water. Her father had moved to somewhere in New England a few years back after a lengthy affair was unearthed, and since then, as the girl was deigned beyond refinement, Lexi assumed control over her household in a manner her mother saw fit. Unlike Gus, she never had to ask to come or go. I think she smoked her mother's cigarettes, an unfiltered foreign brand that always appeared to be in ample supply and whose smell stuck to all our clothes. She had a flat, pervasive way of speaking. Her mannerisms were devoid of inhibition, and it lent her importance—and had a particularly transformative effect on me. Transformative in that I become the mental equivalent of a (very horny) bowling pin.

"Your genitals produce stupid chemicals that make you want to serve me," she said. "My genitals produce stupid chemicals that make you *think* I want you to serve me when I don't. I hate thinking about the fact that our genitals produce chemicals at all, so I prefer not to accept any favors. Does that make sense?"

Gus looked shocked.

"And besides." She produced a crumpled up plastic grocery bag in her left hand. *Stumart—The Right Start!* it read in the lavender lettering I recognized all too well. "I've got this."

"I'm sorry." I was simply unable to continue as the word "genitals" bounced around my head. Lexi always "got" everything. Even the things that were impossible to get. Decision-making was in her biological make up. She was born with her foot already put down and was equally as ready to take that foot and shove it far, far up your ass.

Gus unfolded a stub of paper into a complex map outlining our candy-hunting route.

"What does that even say on it?" I tried to peek over his shoulder as he tore it away. "Over there are a bunch of houses." I pointed. "And we're over here." I pointed in a circle toward the ground. "So we should just go from here over to there, right?"

"You talk much, Eberstark, but understand little. Without this map, which I labored over for your benefit, we'd be roaming the streets for hours. This way, we move fast and easy."

"This doesn't seem fast and easy."

"Says the genius dressed up like Jim Crow's wet dream."

My pocket rumbled.

"Fuck," I whispered.

Bzzzzzzzzz, bzzzzzzzzzz.

"Western Juniper then Jorgsen Ave. Followed by Curtis Ave…" Gus went on.

I reached into my corduroys to pull out my old Motorola flip phone. A yellow light buzzed on in the display screen.

1 new message –Father

My stomach lurched, and I flipped the phone open.

T-Minus 15 minutes.

My palms grew wet.

T minus 15 minutes. T minus 15 minutes until what? Until Father came crashing down Juniper Street with a medieval lance and the Hat at his side, screaming, "Find a weapon, and follow me to the cove!" It *was* possible. The last few weeks, he'd been getting worse. From morose and paranoid to flat out manic, demanding that I carry mechanical "talismans" with me to school (which I dropped in the trashcan by the gas station) and trying to teach me "Antithetic Psychic Routes" to avoid contact with malevolence. I even thought I saw him crouching in the treetops outside my homeroom class a couple weeks ago, spying on me at my desk through a pair of binoculars and chewing on a stick of turkey jerky, accompanied, on a limb above him, by the Hat, who was blowing bubbles with a giant hunk of gum.

After Mother disappeared, Father disappeared in a sense as well. Apart from roaming the outskirts of town like a madman, when home, he ranted on and on about the evil living beneath our city having been exposed, that it intended to claim our innards as its own. At that point, he'd still been in charge of our grocery store, which had been the reason for us moving from Cleveland. "A new start," he'd called it. "The ground zero of ambition." Whatever that had meant.

Initially, he'd called the store Eberstark's and asked customers to treat him as if he were their personal pantry. He'd special order items based on the patron's preferences and tried to know everyone by name. But when he received an acquisition offer from Stumart, a corporate affiliate of a West Coast grocery chain, All Fine, he decided to accept the offer and its prefab store layouts in exchange for higher profits. He even talked about moving again as money came in, about taking our family somewhere south like Portland or even San Francisco to open up a second store. But by the time he got home at the end of the day and sat at the kitchen table, staring out the window into the mist like a holy man deciphering signs from the gods, the notion was flung from his mind. According to him, our family had left Cleveland for a reason. Mossglow was not a trap we had landed in. It was an escape. He'd come here to live his dream as a successful entrepreneur and, to an extent, succeeded. A part of me still trusted and admired him because of it. Or a part of me still wanted to anyway. Mother was gone, and he was all I had left.

Mother had trusted Father too and I wondered if it had destroyed her. At the beginning of his venture, as money from the store flowed in, her sleep hours, and her happiness, diminished. By the time we'd recorded our best annual earnings yet, her fingernails were bitten down, and her voice sounded like a hair-filled drain. Father kept working at the shop, chalking her problems up to lack of sunlight and a refusal to take the medication a local psychiatrist prescribed. He eventually got her to start working again at the store, but that only led to her first attempt.

When she finally disappeared one night, the full spectrum lamp he'd bought her shattered by the bedside, he started referring to what he claimed was a monster, a beast of intentions so interminably evil it threatened to drive the world mad. His eyes began to crisscross; he could never look at you straight. Soon enough, the Hat came around, the mysterious mute I couldn't figure for friend or foe, and that's when things really started to get weird. These days, the one Stumart employee who could stand working sixty-hour work weeks—a local stoner named Cory Bladenbelt—along with me on the weekends and a part-timer named Cherry who had been with us since the early days, were the only ones keeping cash in the register. The store remained open, but as far as everyone was concerned, Father had ceased to work there in person. The official line was that he was working from home or traveling the country in search of expansion. Though he was highly concerned with keeping his conspiracies a private matter, in me he occasionally confided Mossglow's horrors. In me, I came to understand, he'd discovered an unwilling test subject for his theories.

"Can we be done soon, Gus?" I said as we started out again, Father's message flashing through my mind. I tried to think about Sword Star to distract myself, about the new figurines sitting in my room that required painting before we could bring them to next week's tournament for our first shot at league play. "Those Prodlings won't paint themselves—*oof!*" A nine year-old in military fatigues rammed an army helmet into my stomach. I hoped Lexi wouldn't see me grasping my fat gut as the kid ran away. But moreover, I couldn't keep from fixating on the number 15, which had by now surely turned into 5.

"You okay, Eberstark?" Gus yanked me by my sleeve. "Come on, man, don't get in one of your moods. I have a system, okay? I worked it out at home. We'll be done in no time."

"Did you hear, Eberstark?" Lexi said. "Gus has a system. Surprise."

"Can it, lung cancer," said Gus.

Lexi coughed.

Gus tried to guide me along with a palm on my shoulder, but my head was drawn to the sidelines of Juniper Street. There, under the light of a street lamp, I saw a man I knew, or more of a ghoul I knew, in a seersucker suit and Ray Bans. Even though when I focused my eyes he was no longer there, I could swear I'd seen Father's associate, the Hat.

Run, I thought right then. *Pick up your fat legs, and get the hell out of here. Out of Mossglow altogether, you clumsy rhinoceros, and never come back.*

"If we get these houses first with the kiddie crowd, we won't be recognized when we come a second time around," Gus said. "Then, we can get back to my place and get to work on the Prodlings, okay?"

"After we go to the forest," Lexi said.

"After we go to the forest," Gus repeated darkly.

Bzzzzzzz, Bzzzzzz

I looked at my phone again. I didn't want to open it but ended up doing so, flipping the screen up near my pocket so that no one else would see.

Better hold on to something.

"I'm taking candy quality ratios into consideration, trying to maximize our Kit Kats intake; who gives big, but cheap, small, but big, etc." Gus droned on. "So in this initial phase, stand to the periphery. Let's sneak up here around this group here. You, Eberstark, get between the robot and whatever the hell that kid is supposed to be. Lexi, you follow him. Hold out your bag. You don't even have to say trick or treat if you don't want to. Just try and not look like a racist, okay?" He gave me a double take. "Eberstark?"

"What are you doing, dude?" asked Lexi.

"Nothing." Though I'd really been trying not to draw attention to the fact that I was wrapping my arms and legs around an oak tree in someone's front lawn.

"Eberstark?" Gus took off his magician's hat. It revealed his close-kempt hair, the sides of which had been going prematurely gray. "Get off that tree."

I let out a nervous moan. How could Gus begin to understand? A part of me knew how crazy I must have looked. Another part of me knew that crazy didn't always mean stupid.

"Please?" said Gus.

"You guys just go on ahead without me." I clung harder to the tree. "I'm just going to hang back a sec."

"Maybe we should listen to him," said Lexi.

"*Shh...*" Gus tried whispering but I could still hear him. "Let me handle this."

Gus walked over to me with his palms outstretched.

"Hey, buddy," he smiled. "I know you don't like Halloween and that you're dressed up like an idiot, but let's just get off the tree."

"Does this happen a lot?" Lexi asked.

"Look, guys." I saw my phone had another message in it. I didn't dare to let go to open it up. "I know this sounds...uh...I just think you should hold on to something too?"

"Hold on to something?" Gus's voice was as soothing as a suicide hotline as he took my hands from the trunk.

"Whoa," said Lexi.

"I don't think that's a good idea." As I warned Gus away from my fingers like a caged animal, I realized that I'd been duped again. Duped again into buying into another one of Father's ravings, dragging me into hyper-paranoia in front of the only people who saw me as semi-normal.

"It's okay, Eberstark," Gus said. "Let go. We'll be done with all of this soon." He gave Lexi an 'I've got this' nod as I detached myself from the trunk and hung my head in shame.

T minus 15 minutes. What a load of crap. And now, Lexi had seen me clutching a tree like a drooling psychotic. I had the feeling that Gus attributed my "attacks," as he called them, to losing Mother. In part, he was right. Her disappearance made it harder to cope with things that had been easier before. But he didn't understand the extent to which Father's sanity had plummeted. The extent to which he could convince me at times that something was truly out to get us. If I decided to tell Gus about all of that, I didn't know what he'd think. Whether he'd pity me, be afraid of me, get angry, or turn away. And as for Lexi? That wasn't even an option.

"I'm all right," I reassured them. "Let's go."

"We'll be done soon," said Gus as he began to lead the way.

As I followed him, sniffling from the cold, I looked down at my cell phone. Feelings of rebellion washed over me. Yeah, I'd check Father's next message. And I'd send the bastard a response too. A big SCREW YOU in capital letters for him to chew on one by one.

I flipped open the phone and looked at the display screen.

1 new message –Father

"What have you got to say now, you son of a bitch?" I mumbled to myself as I pressed the access button.

Oops. Make that 20 minutes.

I looked up at Gus and Lexi, my mouth contorted in delirious fear. "Mra!" I attempted as a *BAAARRROOOOOOOOM* shook the earth, throwing all of us off toward mailboxes and jack-o-lanterns as the street erupted into screams. In the distance, I heard an evil howl. The inhuman portent of our futures. And for a moment, my vision shook between light and darkness, unsure of which one it would choose.

THREE

A HEAVINESS SETTLED ON MYERS HIGH the next morning. Normally, the halls would have been flooded with sound as the entire student body, 600 large, traded insults and gossip over each other's shoulders. But this morning, twelve minutes before the start of first period, all was snuffed out in a whoosh of conspiracy. If someone, particularly someone not native to Mossglow, had passed through the main atrium at 8:48 a.m. on this chilly November 1st, he or she would have picked up on something injurious, like the school had slipped a disc. People associated us teenagers with noise. Not this nervous chatter and unease. An unease in part that could be traced back to me and Father in an instant should someone manage to connect enough dots.

"My dad says it was one of those government drones dropping bombs," I overheard Ronald Peterson slur through his spit-covered braces to Ajay Kapur, a boy that played Sword Star with us whenever an exam wasn't on the approach (which for Ajay appeared to be more often than anyone else I knew—even Gus). The two of them were picking through their lockers a few feet away from mine. Ronald acknowledged my presence by upturning his chin, exposing what was practically a billiard-sized Adam's apple. His neck was long too, and since he was a sucker for video games and bad posture, it stretched down low.

"That's ridiculous," Ajay said. His body, unlike Ronald's, appeared boxed in and packed tight as if preparing to surge upward at any moment. "Why would the government waste its time on Mossglow? We're not even on all the state maps." "Well, that's exactly why they'd come here." Ronald flopped his neck from side to side like a big, sweaty noodle. "Because no one would notice. My dad, you see, he says this country's becoming a police state. Like Nazi Germany. They're trying to create the next generation of worker bees by making us fall in line without even knowing what hit us. Soon enough, you won't be able to take a drink from the water fountain without putting a quarter in it. And that'll be just the beginning."

"If that isn't a load of utter bullocks," said Ajay.

"Hey. That's my dad you're talking about."

"It was probably an earthquake," said Ajay calmly. "Small towns have been wiped out in the blink of an eye by less. And it's certainly a more likely explanation than being targeted by the military industrial complex."

"Gentlemen." Gus arrived a little later than usual. He slipped between Roy and Ajay and began spiraling the dial combination on his locker, which sat next to mine.

I greeted him along with the other boys before they returned to conversation. I looked over his shoulder, hoping to see Lexi digging in her locker, which was right across from mine. But no, for the first time I could think of since she'd started hanging out with us, she wasn't there. After the blast last night, she'd still wanted to go into the forest—even more than she had earlier. Insistent to the point of rage when we refused, mashing her cigarette filter to a slimy pulp, she called us cowards for "being afraid of a bunch of trees." We tried to explain to her that we weren't afraid of trees themselves as much as we were of what we'd seen happen above them (and who had *caused* it to happen, in my case). The crackling claw of light that uncurled from Graywood Forest into a collusion of yellow and red in the night sky. Maybe it had excited Lexi, carried the scent of discovery. Though Mossglow had become an increasingly strange place, it wasn't known for eventfulness. Something like this was probably the closest we'd come to excitement in years.

As the light had trailed into dust on the horizon, it spewed forth a silt red color. Then came the howl. And the screams that followed as children and parents regained their footing and ran to their children. Neighborhood pets who happened to be outside cut wayward and terrified through the streets. And then, for a moment, all was peaceful. The three of us hadn't been hurt save for a scrape here or there. But that only seemed to encourage Lexi. We were able to calm her down after a few minutes, convince her to go home by saying we could go to Graywood after the source of the explosion was revealed. She ended up agreeing but, before we parted at the Octopus Fountain, gave me a withering look I didn't think I'd ever forget.

I asked Gus if he'd seen her yet while still keeping a lookout.

"Nope." He was so quiet I almost didn't hear him. Ronald and Ajay continued their debate as they shut their lockers and made their way from the atrium.

"See you in there," they said.

"She didn't call you or anything?" Gus asked.

I shook my head and looked over my shoulder as I watched them leave. "But has she ever?"

"Good point." Gus shut his locker. "And it's not like she misses class. Girl's crazier than I am with her studies."

"No way." I'd always pictured Lexi as so rebellious that she shredded up her homework to arrange hate mail to her teachers.

"I'm not supposed to know this, but Mr. Schmidt told me she's poised to become school valedictorian if I don't ace all my classes this semester."

"You've got to be fucking kidding me." I wanted to laugh. The idea of Lexi speaking to students and their families on the merits of good study habits was nothing next to insane.

"Would certainly make me happier if I were being that the closer she gets, the harder I've got to work." He canted his chin toward the ground and grew stormy. "Man, if it wasn't for—"

"I know…" I cut in. "The A minus you got in Mrs. Pasilla's class…"

"If it wasn't for the A minus I got in Mrs. Pasilla's class, this wouldn't even be a discussion."

"You do suck at Spanish."

"I'm going to put a rattlesnake in your bed."

"*Que dolor?*"

"If she's not here by third period…" Gus took on that serious look that meant he would lay down the law. "Then we worry. But she could just be running late. I mean, a few houses collapsed last night in the Lower Thicks. What if she's pulling the shepherd out of a mud trap?"

"I've never seen her be late before."

"Third period." Gus held up three fingers. "Then we worry."

I pulled the book we'd been reading for Intro to Modern Lit from a quarry of filth I'd been accumulating over the last two years and shut the locker lightly behind me, afraid of making too loud a noise. I noticed others, including Gus, were doing the same, sneaking from their lockers toward their classrooms like prey on watch for a wolf.

Mrs. Duncan began lecturing the second we sat down. The big hand on the clock over her desk hadn't yet snapped over the hour, but our homeroom teacher, a sturdy, sharp-tongued woman with eyes so big it was as if one of her parents had been a cartoon, was infamous for starting early. It was her method for catching students off guard who might have been getting too comfortable. Students like me, who'd spent all their spare time painting Sword Star figurines.

Even after last night's explosion, when I returned home to an empty house, a kitchen filthied by what must have been twenty blackened pots and a smell like wetted dog, the first thing I did was uncap my paints and get to adding layer after layer on my newly acquired Prodlings, trying to forget about Lexi. There was no sign of Father in the house, and the bunker was dark outside. But I locked myself in my room anyway by shoving the edge of my dresser against the doorknob (one could never have too many ways to bar entry when it came to Father) and stayed up until 3 a.m. making micro-stroke after micro-stroke under a mounted magnifying glass. I gave meticulous consideration to every Prodling, Hofarth, and Gorn. I was still trying to teach my fingers not to shake. The book we were assigned to read to chapter eight, called *The Trials of Xerxes*, sat unopened on my dresser. And now, it lay unopened on my desk in Mrs. Duncan's class.

Mrs. Duncan began by moving toward the front of the classroom as she tended to do now by matter of habit. She swung lightly back and forth on her heels and pushed her tortoiseshell glasses up the short, generous bridge of her nose. "So I know the entire town's in a panic. But I also know that panic is subject to control. Franz Kafka once said, 'God gives the nuts, but he does not crack them.' So, we must crack our own nuts. Do you not agree?"

Gus nodded avidly while most everyone else seemed not to understand what the hell Mrs. Duncan was talking about. Ronald snorted.

"Today," she continued, "we will turn to questions of immediate import. As in why this book is called *The Trial of Xerxes*?" She took a couple of steps back to sit on the edge of her desk, holding the novel in her left hand. It was stuffed full of post-it notes. The cover had a painting of a stack of burning chairs and the author's name, Hazel McNairy, emblazoned in ruddy lettering along the bottom.

"Anyone?"

Gus raised his hand, but Mrs. Duncan ignored him.

"Here we have a novel about a woman raised in upstate New York at the turn of the century. A woman who ends up giving birth to a child at seventeen after a pregnancy that came out of nowhere..."

As Mrs. Duncan spoke, each of her words so well-chosen, so pointed, I stopped being able to concentrate. My eyes followed the movement of her mouth, my ears registered the tone of her voice, but my brain was elsewhere, hovering over Mossglow, searching for Father, searching for Lexi, searching for the man known as the Hat.

"Does anyone know what the virginal conception is?" Mrs. Duncan had put a special emphasis on 'virginal.'

Gus continued to raise his hand, his fingers outstretched to the point of pain.

"Mr. Peterson." She nodded her head to Ronald, who was clearly trying to do a last-minute skim through chapter three.

"Um…" Ronald's heavy lower lip uncurled to reveal a bottom row of long teeth. "It's, um, it's when a woman forgets to have her period, I think, and she—"

"Mr. Kapur." Mrs. Duncan shifted her attention to Ajay, who raised his hand to save Ronald from destroying himself.

"In the Catholic Church, it's the belief that Jesus Christ was conceived by the Holy Spirit while his mother Mary was still a virgin," Ajay said.

"Oh yeah," said Ronald. "That's right—God Junior."

My classmates' words floated over my head, rising above me like helium balloons. I tried to listen but instead just ended up watching Mrs. Duncan's mouth as she spoke. Her teeth were straight and long. Her lips were so red they could have been made out of candy.

"Ms. Valdez." Mrs. Duncan pointed to a quiet wisp of a girl named Melinda with thin, red hair, narrow cheeks, and a severe brow. "What happens in chapter eight?"

"She…she lied, right?" said Melinda.

"Did she now? If so, what did she lie about?"

"Well." Melinda looked around at the rest of the students in her vision as if for approval. "She lied because she knew the baby's father. A boy in town."

"What do you mean by 'she knew him,' Ms. Valdez?"

"She, well, she, you know…she…"

"Had sex with him?"

"Uh, yes." A couple giggles bubbled up from around the room. Ronald Peterson guffawed, "That means screwing!" But was quickly quieted by Ajay, punching him on the arm. Everyone but me seemed to proceeding as usual, assuming their roles as class clown and class dignitary.

"That part with the guy at the gas station was horrible," said Ajay.

"Somebody's reading ahead," said Mrs. Duncan with a faint grin. "Let's circle back to my initial question. Why is this book called *The Trial of Xerxes*? Hmm…" She surveyed the room, clucking her tongue like a metronome, one which seemed in sync the dripping of someone's kitchen faucet. "Mr.…Eberstark." Her gigantic eyes came towards me. "What do you think?"

"Sorry?"

"Why is this book called *The Trial of Xerxes*, Mr. Eberstark? As opposed to the Trial of Gisele, for instance? Or the Trial of Matt?"

I flipped the book over and over in my hands. I opened it, tried to catch a phrase or two, while feeling Mrs. Duncan would rip any answer I gave her to shreds. I came clean. "I…didn't have time to finish. With the explosion and everything."

"You mean you didn't have the foresight or commitment to start when you received the assignment a week ago?"

"Right."

"Mr. Mustus." Mrs. Duncan sulkily turned her head to Gus in resignation. "Why is this book called *The Trial of Xerxes*?"

Gus's hand dropped with a grateful slap onto his knee.

"I appreciate you calling on me, Mrs. Duncan." He looked around at the rest of the students, disappointed in their flaccid intellects. "Xerxes was one of the greatest, if not *the* greatest, king in the Persian Empire. His name translates to 'Ruling over Heroes,' which is ironic, acknowledging his role in squashing revolts all over the ancient world and invading the Greek mainland. I'm bringing this up because, if you notice on page 133, Gisele has a run-in with her drunken father in which the subject of heroism and conquest come into play, as in whether one can truly exist alongside the other. Also, there's the matter of Christianity to take into account and the father's problem with the fact that Gisele, as a Catholic, has to study the Persian Empire. I don't want to give much away being that I've read to the end already, but the title does become more relevant after she presents her report..."

It was about that time that I started to drift away from the classroom altogether. Around me, I imagined the rest of the students drifting too. I imagined Ronald Peterson, to my left, slowly alighting from his desk and pulling it up with him by the tip of his sneaker until his head touched the ceiling with a light, painless *thump*. I imagined Melinda, Ajay, Stephanie Kirby, and Allan Faust all doing the same, untethered one by one from gravity so they could float, dazed, toward a place above Myers High they never would reach. I imagined their heads going *thump…thump…thump…* against the ceiling panels, over and over again, their eyes black and empty. All save for Gus, who was tethered to the ground.

Just as class got out, Mrs. Duncan called me over. Gus gave me a piteous look as he trotted ahead of me out the door toward our next class, US Politics. Mrs. Duncan closed the door after him and paced back toward me with her hands before her knee-length, maroon skirt. I felt like I was watching a movie of myself, a familiar story of disaffected youth. I looked down at my feet as I lingered in front of her desk, my red and black tennis shoes kicking at the rug.

Mrs. Duncan brought around two chairs in front of her desk. "Why don't you sit down."

I obliged, easing into the closest one. She sat down opposite me and crossed her legs.

"Mr. Eberstark." She let her words settle for a moment. "What's going on with you?"

"Me?"

"Yes, you? I know you've had your problems in school. A little preoccupied here and there. But I've never seen you forego homework like this. It just isn't like you."

I looked at the floor. "I won't do it again."

"Has everything been okay at home?"

I could have laughed or cried at that one.

"What do you mean?"

"Your family life, Mr. Eberstark. Is there anything you want to tell me? Is everything okay?"

I shook my head.

"I'll do better. I promise."

"Mr. Eberstark…" She leaned in toward me. Her voice was a little hoarser than usual. "Don't be afraid of me. I'm here to help. I just want to make sure you think about your life. I mean really think about it. I don't mean to insult our lovely township here, but do you really want to spend another year bumming around after you graduate? After all your friends are gone?"

She looked at me for a response and, when I didn't provide one, continued.

"I for one would rather never see you again. No offense, of course, you're a lovely boy, but this town, it's too sleepy. Too small. Too… forgetful."

I looked at her for a moment, thinking of Father and the text messages, the explosion in the forest. I found I was unconsciously fingering the Motorola in my pocket. When you looked at Mrs. Duncan face to face, you noticed that she had something disquieting about her. An unusual beauty that could conceal tremendous anxiety. My eyes kept on drifting toward her breasts, I found, though I tried to keep them from doing so. I was drifting toward them like I'd imagined the other students drifting toward the ceiling.

I bit my lip hard so that I'd avert my eyes. "I…I know what you mean."

"I just don't want you to become another…" She hesitated for a moment, weighing what she was about to say. "I don't want you to become another Mossglow kid, a Mossglow kid who becomes a Mossglow adult. I know I shouldn't say things like that, but when I think about those folks up in Crowstone, doing whatever they want whenever they want…it just breaks me. Whether they think they own this town or not, they'll never really have anything but that little outcrop of houses. A cold, black bay and salty air."

"I'm not going to become a townie, Mrs. Duncan."

"I know you won't." She forced a smile. "I don't even think they'd let you become one, would they. But just to be safe, I want to make sure we get you set up for college next year. So you won't even have to think about it."

"College?"

"There are plenty of options. For the time being, just listen to what I have to say. Read the books I assign. Get a good grade. Ask me all the questions you want. Get good grades in all your classes, and you'll be ready. Some minds don't evolve in isolation. I've learned that over the years. If a plague settles in, you can board up your windows and bar your doors, but as Edgar Allen Poe once wrote, 'Even with the utterly lost, to whom life and death are equally jests, there are matters of which no jest can be made.'"

Her eyes fluttered as if in response to a tic. As if she'd forgotten something important yet again. I looked out the window. Rain sprayed the pane, and through the downpour, I saw the mist swelling over Goon's Cove in the near distance. We'd have a bad storm tonight.

FOUR

WHEN I MADE IT INTO Mr. Kraft's US Politics class, it was just about to start. Gus turned around at looked at me from his desk in the front row and gave me a 'what happened?' shrug as I sat down two places behind him.

"Later," I mouthed.

Mr. Kraft was a handsome man. Unnaturally handsome for Mossglow. Here, diabetes, gout, and emphysema were like endemic species of wildlife. A smiling, chisel-jawed man like Mr. Kraft, then, with manicured nails, a French-cuffed shirt, and a cashmere sweater vest looked extra-galactic. He also happened to be a recent transplant, which I was sure caused some to question what had drawn him here to begin with. Then again, what had drawn Father here from across the country? How had he even discovered this place?

Some of Mossglow's citizens left after they graduated Myers High, escaped the polar pull the town had on them. But more seemed compelled, even cornered, into staying. The town itself seemed able to prune its population organically, never rising or falling above or below 20,000, or so that's what Father said when he was first scoping it out. It ended up being one of the main selling points on us leaving Cleveland. Small town. Quiet and stable right down to its annual census. If the numbers ever began to drop, then they got filled back up. And the opposite occurred when they increased. Mr. Kraft was one of those who had moved in without clear reason, all on his own, showing up at the beginning of this school year without much of an introduction. He was rarely seen about town save for in the halls of Myers High. But the same, or worse, could be said for mine or Gus's father. Mr. Kraft was probably a man who'd tried his luck elsewhere in a bigger, brighter place and not succeeded. And that was something a Mossglow resident could appreciate.

"Hey there, champ," Mr. Kraft said as I made my way toward my desk. I was taken aback. This might have been the first time he addressed me directly. He usually roped me in with a sweeping "you guys" and avoided eye contact during lectures.

"Oh, hi, Mr. Kraft." I sat down in my desk.

Our US Politics teacher's amber eyes were scored at their edges by crow's feet. His gaze was so sharp and intelligent returning it almost felt uncomfortable. I did it, but it was like looking at Mrs. Duncan's breasts.

"I was thinking about you," he then said. A couple of students snickered. I saw Jesse Maroon was the main culprit, snorting through his tiny nostrils. I shrunk in my seat. I didn't like being singled out. Particularly with someone like Jesse nearby, who was an errand boy for Charlene Poughkeepsie and Joe Ross, who had been kicked out of Myers, readmitted, and kicked out again for repeated acts of violence.

Since their parents were from Crowstone Heights and had friends in the administration, they could skew the system.

"Your father owns the grocery store over on Miller and Main, right?" Mr. Kraft's voice was so sweet it could have been sold at a candy store.

"That's the one." I noticed Gus was writing down something in his notebook, presumably copying some notes on the judiciary system that had already been drawn out on the blackboard.

"I don't mean to be so enigmatic." He laughed. When he did so, Bethany Cho, a slight girl who became more outgoing whenever she sat next to her friend Heather Mathis, began whispering about what I knew was Mr. Kraft's good looks. "I was just thinking about the building it's in. It used to be an old fort, didn't it? Something to do with the founding of the township a while back?"

"I think so." I remembered Father saying something about maintaining building codes to preserve the property's historical value, but I hadn't listened close. I just worked there on the weekends to ensure it didn't fall apart.

"I wonder..." Mr. Kraft took a sip from a coffee mug with an imprimatur of Andrew Jackson tattooed into it. "If you wouldn't mind, do you think you can ask your father if I can stop by sometime and have a look around? I'm just so fascinated by the early history of Mossglow. There's not a lot of information available in the public archives, and I do happen to teach an online college course on this region's governmental history."

At the mentioning of Father, Gus turned around and looked at me. I could tell he was concerned. Not because he knew the truth behind Father's current predicament but because he suspected something more or less just as debilitating. Morrison Eberstark was a man who'd been thought to retire to the very same shadows that surrounded his wife's disappearance. They didn't know about his backyard bunker or that he might have been responsible for yesterday's explosion, but they did know he had faded into obscurity. It made sense that Mr. Kraft, new to the area, may not have heard about this, but if he understood enough about the history of Father's store, it was strange how little he knew about the family that ran it.

"I'll ask him."

"That would be lovely." He tossed me an avuncular wink before turning to the blackboard.

I found myself gazing through the windows into the hedgerow across Myers Lawn about halfway through Mr. Kraft's class. The lawn acted as a good eating and study area whenever it wasn't raining and was sprinkled with wooden benches. Mr. Kraft's class was on the opposite side of the main Myers High building than that of Mrs. Duncan's. I preferred it. The seaside of Goon's Cove was constantly tumultuous. I felt as if sometimes the waves would rip through the glass and my throat would be sliced to ribbons. On this side, facing east toward earth and grass, I sometimes thought that I could just start walking and end up in a place where the sun shined for at least two hours a day.

It was as I attempted to follow Mr. Kraft's lecture on federal regulations that I caught a glint of movement in the taller hedges outside, a section of the row backed by maple trees. I shifted my shoulders toward the window. In the crown of the highest tree, wrapped in a tangle of branches and leaves, I knew sat Father, staring in my direction with a pair of binoculars. I don't know how I was able to recognize him exactly. Instinct, perhaps. The quickening of my heart.

"May I be excused?" I asked Mr. Kraft, breaking his trajectory mid sentence. "I have to go to the bathroom."

"I have to go the bathroom," Jesse Maroon tittered.

One of his friends, a ratty, big-cheeked boy named Tony Hemster, whispered, "Faggot," quietly at my back.

"But of course," Mr. Kraft said. "We'll be here when you get back."

"Pussy," I heard Jesse Maroon hiss. "Dick sucker."

I jogged down the hallway toward Myers West. My shoes pattered on the linoleum. I decided to head out the southern exit near the smoker's hill, where students congregated to smoke cigarettes and, at night, trade drugs. Normally, it wouldn't be the best route to use to sneak away from the main building, but today, everyone was shaken up enough to miss a thing or two. There was always the possibility of running into Dean Veltry, almost seven feet tall and conspicuous as a tree panther. Trying to avoid him was like trying to avoid hunger. He found you when he wanted to.

I ran fast over the smoker's hill (which was more of a dirt ramp), my feet collecting mud, trying to stay under the cover of a couple of service building awnings and interspersed trees to keep dry. It was really coming down now, and the entirety of Mossglow pulsed with a vibrant purple. The vegetation seemed drunk and exhausted.

When I came upon Father, he was enshrouded in leaves. After the smoker's hill, I snuck behind a storage shed and from there followed an ivy-wrought stretch of cyclone fencing. On the side I stood was the hedgerow, before a line of trees. On the other side hummed a power generator with wicked antennas. From my vantage now, my head reaching tall enough to peek over the hedgerow, I could see Mr. Kraft lecturing away. Gus furiously jotted down notes, and Jesse Maroon fiddled with something beneath his desk. The sarcophagal face of Myers High rose taller than it ever needed to. The first floor hosted classes, but the second and third, each of which was narrower than the previous level, were rarely used except for faculty functions and storage. Light brimmed from windows along the first floor, but darkness festered overhead.

The second I tried to pick Father out of the branches, a heavy body tackled me from behind. I wrestled with it in the way molasses might wrestle a pancake as my hoodie and corduroys slopped through the mud.

"Pfffft!" I wiped more mud into my eyes as I tried to clean my face. "Hey! Stop it!"

I struggled to my knees. Standing above me with perfectly polished Ray Bans, a bone-white derby hat, and a finger to his lips, stood the Hat. His seersucker suit was unblemished and pressed. The air around him could have been charged with static.

"Quiet, you despoiler of strategy," whispered a familiar voice: Father's. He was poised above in the branches of a tree like an arboreal lizard, wearing army camouflage fatigues and covered with a dark sheen of mud. A sheen of mud that seemed unnecessary considering the brightly dressed mute companion who, shaking his head, took a pen from his breast pocket and scribbled on the notepad he always kept with him. He tore out the sheet and held it up.

We rely upon your silence.

"Hat," Father whispered, his head barely moving as he lowered the binoculars. His eyebrows, I noticed, had been partially seared, and he'd shaved his already balding head so that it looked slick. "Ready the cannon."

"The cannon?" The Hat shot me a condemning glance as I spoke.

"You wet your bed a lot as a child," Father said without turning his head. "All the goddamned time. You do it once, twice, three times; it's normal. The body has to get used to its functions…"

From behind the tree Father was nested in, the Hat dragged out a Kevlar duffle bag. Unzipping it, he drew forth a weapon of obscene dimensions, nine inches taller than the man himself. Bifurcated by a belt of hammered steel, it featured two see-through tanks that curled above the rear shaft, spiraling outward like rams' horns. One sloshed around cloudy, yellow liquid, the other a midnight blue. Below the rear sight hung a copper cylinder rotating six messy capsules of wire and tubing. To the rear of the trigger sat a black button with a lightning bolt applied to the plastic. The second the Hat pushed it, the entire machine beamed to life. The liquids in the tanks bubbled.

"But you. You wet it nearly every day for six months. Like you were trying to turn your bed into an inflatable raft. A flotation device for a sea of your own urine. Hat, calibrate the cannon to 236. And give me another anti-penumbric. Or two. Fuck it, three. Things are getting shaky in here."

I assumed "here" meant Father's head as he paused to rub it with his gloved fingers. The Hat began to adjust a dial above a digital interface at the butt end of the cannon. As he calibrated it to 236, the tank liquids emptied a fraction of their supply into a corridor beneath the metal strip. The blue one seemed to empty more. The muzzle then began to rattle, as if alive.

"If you're not ready to admit to yourself that you're a bedwetter," The Hat tossed up a pair of what looked to be goggles, followed by a specialized utility belt equipped with three metal vials. Father caught both without even looking. "You're not ready to admit that your entire reality has been usurped by the penumbra. And it has been usurped, I tell you that. You belong to him, and you don't even know it. That's why your breath stinks."

"My…breath stinks?"

THE SILENT END

"I can smell it from here. Like you mistook your mouth for a pig's ass."

The Hat turned, sniffed, nodded, and withdrew a small tin of mints from his jacket, which he tossed to me. I almost dropped them. It was a container unlike any I'd ever seen before. It looked like it could have come out of a different decade, a different century, with Nazis and Kamikaze bombers. If that wasn't odd enough, its lid had what appeared to be an art deco illustration of the Hat himself imprinted in the aluminum. He was in a boxer's stance with his hands balled into fists.

"Careful with those," Father said as I uneasily fit them into my pocket. "That's dream food right there."

I didn't know how to respond to that, so I remained quiet as he wrapped the pair of goggles around his head—a center strap fit over the middle. Fixed to the top of it was a rubber antenna. Pushing a button below it, two red embers glowed where his pupils would have been. He then drew the first vial out, which was more of a metal canister. Taking the lid off revealed a needle, which he depressurized into his neck. His long, hooked nose drooped over the scruff that both covered his upper lip and the rest of his face. "Ah," he cooed, injecting the second and third canister. "Much, much better."

"Dad." I was attempting to be quiet. "What are you doing? Gus—you can see him—Gus Mustus, remember? He's sitting in the front row. Please, you're not going to hurt anyone, are you? This is my school."

"School," Father sniggered.

The Hat scribbled on his pad and held it up.

You should know better.

"You're not ready to see the truth, son. It's all around you, everywhere, but you're hiding behind your weenie. That's right, your little, shriveled weenie—Hat." The antenna on his head sprouted radar fins. They were coated with a milky blue layer of chalk. The clock face made out of a digital kitchen timer below the antenna began to blink Z:7u. "Note photospheric resistance, moving in from the west."

The Hat took the pen from his breast pocket and began scribbling on a pad, holding it up to Father when he finished.

-16 Timetudes/₁Mag(orphan) = 230.62 Apparetoids
73.22 Grz

"Fine math, Hat," Father said. "Now, calibrate the cannon accordingly. You'll have to upload two hundred and thirty additional Toids to make it through all that Ambiphoteric resistance. Two hundred and thirty-one, just to be safe."

"Please, can't you just tell me what's going on?"

"I've tried to tell you many a time." The Hat finished tuning the cannon by toggling another dial and, with a *hup*, sent it flying up toward Father, who captured it in his large hands and slung it over his shoulder so that the scope aligned with his goggles. "But you didn't listen. When evil infests our planet, none of us do. Mostly because it's always been there, lurking, waiting, becoming a part of the picture. And when it infests your town, you don't notice either because it's not yet entered your backyard. But when evil steals your love away, and when evil comes for you, well, if you're lucky, that's when you notice it."

The Hat scribbled another note and held it up before his Ray Bans.

Mr. Blue can see you in the mirror.

"He can, indeed," said Father, somehow picking up what his cohort had written without so much as a glance. "Hat, prepare Archefaratic count down. Five." He flipped the first in what I noticed were five switches. "Four." He flipped the second. "Three. Two." The conduit in the middle of the cannon began to rattle, and at the machine's rear, a gaseous, green light began to swell and bubble. Father's finger then hovered over a button near the cannon's grip. "When your shadow comes alive, son. Well by God, you've got to murder it."

While contemplating how I might stop Father from firing the monstrosity slung over his shoulder, I saw something out of the corner of my eye. A dark shape moving through the rainy courtyard. I turned towards it, wiping the water from my vision, and blinked in disbelief.

"Mr. Veltry. Mr. V-vu-vu-Veltry. He's...he's looking *right at us.*"

But before I could even get the words out, Father had thrown himself over the fence with the cannon in tow. The Hat had gone as well, leaving behind only one slip of paper from his pad, which floated face down in the mud. Before the hedge row, about thirty feet away, stood Mr. Veltry. His raincoat billowed over his uniform of black from slacks to tie. His buzz cut silver hair was uncovered, and in his eyes was something I found unsettling. A sort of emptiness. His skin looked gray, almost blue, and his tie whipped over his shoulder.

"Hey there, son," he bellowed without moving a muscle. I could tell he was trying to focus his eyes through the rain, not seeing exactly who I was. "Is there a reason you're out here in the rain?"

But by that point, I had already been running. I only looked once over my shoulder to see if he was behind me. But he wasn't.

Nobody was.

FIVE

MOTHER LOVED CHARM BRACELETS. THE cutesy kinds. With horses, covered wagons, stars, thimbles, all tiny and detailed and silly, as if each one could have been plucked from a Monopoly board.

They had disproportionate representation in her wardrobe. This obsession with charm bracelets was a sick turn of fate not because of the childlike nature of the jewelry itself but because of how they mocked Mother's desolation. When she sat in her armchair chewing her fingernails, her tea cold and untouched, the little ballet slippers, Raggedy Ann dolls, and twinned cherries appeared to laugh at her from a childhood that collapsed long ago.

A charm bracelet with dolphins and starfish sparkled on her wrist when I found her in the hallway a little over a year ago, on September 13th, which was not only the day before my birthday but the day of her near-death. The corners of her mouth were caked in vomit, her skirt had split open in a fall, and her eyelids were nightshade purple. She'd taken all of the pills Father had had prescribed for her—something she'd later admit she never thought herself capable of doing. "I think there's a part of me that didn't even know I was taking them at all," she'd said after she awoke in the hospital. "I saw something, like a face in the mirror…the face I've been talking about…oh, how crazy I must sound. Your father, he thinks I'm finished in the head. But it's true. There was a man—always a man. A young one. He's…handsome, in a way, like an old boyfriend of mine. But there's always something wrong in his eyes. Like they want to have me for lunch. And this time…this time was even worse. I looked down for a moment. Then, I looked back up, and he was holding my hand and, well, I really have lost it, haven't I?" Her eyes, weighed down by bags, drooped. "I guess it's true that mental illness skips a generation. Your great-grandmother, she died alone. No one found her for two months though because she'd already chased everyone away. Is that where I'm going to end up?" She clasped my face in her palms. The wrist tag from Mossglow General bunched up against my cheek. "Rotting in a basement apartment? If I do, just please forgive me, okay? Remember who I used to be, and show people the pictures from my early days when they ask. The good ones from my wedding? Or your fifth grade graduation?"

After she came home from the hospital, her condition seemed to improve for a while. For a few weeks, color returned to her skin, and she began eating regularly. Three square meals a day and even desert too. I saw her gobble up a cherry cobbler one night before I could even finish pouring my milk, and the sight brought me joy I was afraid to hold on to. She was smiling more often and not in a forlorn manner I'd seen before. One day, she even made me her specialty for breakfast, French toast, and I cried. Father, who had regarded her illness with an electrician's need to resolder faulty wiring and get the machine working again, was pleased, thinking that her attempted suicide had shattered a ceiling in her mind. I think he was even convinced on some level that he'd been responsible for the breakthrough. A part of him always attributed her improvements to circumstances he had created.

"What the hell happened to you?" Gus found me after 8th period. I pretended to have just opened my locker, stowing away some yogurt I'd grabbed from the cafeteria I knew I wouldn't eat it when I bought it. All I could think about anyway was Father running around Mossglow in army fatigues with the Hat.

After the hedgerow, I'd fled to a single bathroom for the disabled, attempting to wash the mud off my clothes and make myself look as I had before I went snooping. I then sat in the stall for two hours drying off, holding my breath every time someone knocked at the door, which wasn't often, and feeling guilty for doing so. But I had to wait. If I came outside drenched and muddy, Dean Veltry would know it was me he had seen. Thankfully, Father was too high up in the tree to have been noticed even with the eight-foot-long bazooka. And the Hat, I sometimes suspected he, like Veltry, only revealed himself to others when he chose to do so.

I decided to cut class for the rest of the day, emerging from the bathroom only to hop by the cafeteria for a Myers High quintessential (chalupas and tater tots) before huddling away in our club office, which we shared with Ronald Peterson's Manga Society. To calm myself, I re-read the updated Sword Star 4th edition manual until the last bell rang.

No matter how much I pored over pictures of Lorques and Xenos enmeshed in battle, I couldn't shake the feeling that something terrible was going to happen. *Thank God the dean had been there,* I began to think. If he hadn't, I couldn't begin to imagine what would have been unleashed.

"I wasn't feeling good," I told Gus. "Think I caught a stomach bug."

"Really?" He pursed his lips. "You look pretty good right now."

"That's because I feel better. Which is what happens after you puke all day."

"Fine, fine." He put up his hands. "Take it easy. Damn."

"Did Lexi ever show up?"

Gus unshouldered his backpack. "Not that I saw. Are you still worried?"

"I mean, I guess."

"Yeah. Me too."

We stood silent for a moment.

"She'll be fine," said Gus. "I know she will. This is Lexi Navarro we're talking about. Anyway, let's change the subject. Check these out. I've been waiting to show you all day."

Gus pulled a hard plastic case from his backpack. It had five compartments, each about three inches tall and two and a half inches wide. In each one sat one of his Demigods, as they were called. Battle leaders in the Sword Star universe that were required for league play. Each had been painted resplendently down to what was surely his prizewinner's—the Crow Seraph—very last feather. He'd even shaded them with extra thin black paint and applied a Citadel wash to highlight the details. Somehow, he'd achieved this in addition to reading all of *The Trial of Xerxes* and, I soon learned, acing a quiz in Mr. Schmidt's chemistry class. Looking at the figurines made me love Gus. It also made me hate him and his unflinching focus. He was Adderall-free, improved at everything he did, and not only did he improve but he improved quickly.

"I'll, uh, show you my Prodlings later," I lied. "They're really coming along."

"Can't wait," Gus said with genuine aplomb. "Want me just to come by your place? That would be easier, wouldn't it? Since you've got everything over there?"

"Today's no good for that." I couldn't remember the last time he'd asked to come over. "My dad, he works nights now from home."

"Oh."

"Maybe over the weekend."

Gus was half smiling. He knew what "maybe over the weekend" meant. "Well, let's at least walk to the bus."

We left the building and meandered through a sea of students pooling into queues for their respective shuttles. Ours stopped in front of the main steps that led into the school, right before the massive likeness of Mickey the Bullfrog, our mascot. The fifteen-foot-tall stone amphibian, for as long as I'd known it, sat fatly at the lee of the Myers High front steps, greeting students upon entering or leaving with its meter-wide simper. Apparently, another statue of equal size but varying characteristics could be found on the very top of Myers High, but no one I knew had ever glimpsed it.

Mickey squatted over a raised podium with a bronze plaque. Bolted into the stone, the engraving read, "Dedicated to Thomas Hellwidth Myers, 1826." Sometimes, I wondered who would have designed such a thing with its ghastly mouth and leathery hide rendered to such detail. I didn't know shit about Thomas Hellwidth Myers himself apart from the fact that he had something to do with the town's founding. But whenever I saw the statue itself, I couldn't help but remember when someone ripped off a cat's head and stuffed it in its mouth last year. An algebra exam with no name on it from Mrs. Greenly's class had been balled and shoved down the poor feline's throat. The girl who discovered it, Melinda Valdez' sister Nadia, fainted, and a brief investigation was launched. The culprit was never found, but it was suspected that Crowstone Heights townies were involved.

As if in response to my inner thoughts, I saw Charlene Poughkeepsie and Joe Ross boarding the bus two spots away from our own to Hunter's Ridge. Charlene's hugeness weighed down the entire vehicle as her left foot met her right on the front step. Her mouth grinned to span her entire jaw. The back of her shirt, stretching to accommodate her legion of back and stomach, had the words DUKE ON YOU scrawled in yellow cursive.

She stood still for a moment, admiring her command of gravity. Joe Ross, meanwhile, his bald skull shining almost as white as the bone beneath, raised his porcine nose to snort with laughter from behind her. Jesse Maroon, passing by the two of them on a way to another bus, said, "Poughkeepsie, Mogadishu? Yo yo yo!" He saluted the two of them, referring to Joe by his nickname, earned because the capital of Somalia was the only question he got right on a quiz in Geography class his freshman year (and only because he'd copied it from someone sitting next to him). Charlene turned and made a show of her bus-rocking for Jesse. The bus driver finally put an end to the spectacle by ordering them both to get on. Joe flicked a cigarette to the curb and followed Charlene's lumbering bulk, shaking the bus side to side before she took a seat.

Our bus driver, one of the thick-necked, gray-haired women who could be easily interchanged with the other thick-necked, gray-haired women who drove buses without anyone noticing, opened the door, and students began to file in. This bus would be stopping in Lexi's neighborhood, the Lower Thicks, near the dried up fountain shaped like an octopus and the Lucky Start gas station. Gus would have a longer walk ahead than if he took the bus to his part of the Thicks, but he usually accompanied me to the stop closer to my house. The two of us had us had a lot in common, but our fears couldn't be more different. He didn't worry that one day he'd be dragged up to Crowstone Heights, selected for an old-fashioned Mossglow arm breaking by those who thought he didn't belong here. Perhaps this was due to being unconcerned with the shallow social implications of high school. He was on a trajectory altogether his own. Whether that was naïve or not, I couldn't say. But it kept him focused.

"*Pssssssssst,*" we heard from somewhere to our right just as we were about to board the bus.

I grabbed Gus's backpack.

"*Pssssst.*" A hand beckoned us from around the corner of the Myers High main building.

"*PSSSSST!*"

"Oh no," Gus said.

"Let's go." I dragged Gus towards the voice.

Gus looked back at the bus.

"Come on, man!"

When we ran over, we saw Lexi crouching against the brick on the western side of Myers High, a few feet away from a power box. There was something immediately wrong about her. Normally upright and fuming smoke like something inside her was on fire, she was now shivering and filthy. Her hair was matted with mud and leaves, and her costume from yesterday, her bloodied prom dress, had been torn in some places—ripped to shreds in others. And was that…blood? Real blood? Real blood mixed in with the fake blood from the night before? A black-brown fluid had been spattered along her neck, bust, and legs.

"Lexi?" Gus gasped.

"*Shhhh,*" she said, holding her filthy hands up to us. "You need to come with me. Right now."

"But." Gus pointed towards the buses. "They'll leave without us."

"Fuck them. I've found something… Something that you both need to see."

"What did you find—" I tried to ask.

"JUST COME WITH ME!" Her right eye bulged with bloodshot insistence. She quickly quieted herself down, breathing heavy. "You… you won't believe me if you don't see it. You just won't, okay?"

"Okay," said Gus. "Okay."

"Where are we going?" I asked.

"Follow me." With a suspicious look, she darted off across the western patch of grass between Myers High and Goon's Cove, fading ever-so-slightly into a yellowing mist that drew up from the coast.

I looked at Gus, whose trepidation I could sense. "We can't let her go off by herself again."

"I don't see why not," he growled before starting off after her.

It was hard to keep up with Lexi. Her legs were muscled, lean, and dynamic in contrast to mine, which could have been filled with cottage cheese. Gus could keep up without too much effort, just like he could climb trees or hop fences without much effort, but I could tell he didn't want to, pausing every few seconds to shoot me a ridiculing look, convinced that Lexi was leading us to a ditch filled with half-empty liquor bottles or intravenous drugs.

But when we arrived at Nigh'Sow Road, on the edge of the Lower Thicks, the girl banked down a rocky path near one of the now-shuttered Hinterlord satellite factories and led us into a woodsy darkness. Soon enough, I realized where we were going. Graywood

Forest. The green-brown weald that stretched on for miles north, to the point where, if you followed a compass, would lead you to snowy mountains outside of state lines. Lexi hadn't gone home at all last night.

As soon as Gus noticed where we were heading, he stopped in his tracks. I was beyond grateful, hands on my knees as I gasped for breath.

"Just hold up," Gus huffed. "Where the hell are you taking us?"

Lexi's shoulders dropped as she skidded to a stop. She marched up to Gus in her battered flats. She still wasn't smoking, which was odd, and her eye held a sleepless, violent tinge. I noticed for the first time that what I'd thought had been dirt splattered across her face was also blood. Or something like it.

"You won't believe me if I tell you. To be absolutely honest, I don't believe myself yet either. I need you guys— I need you guys to tell me I'm not crazy, okay? We're close now."

"This is absurd! I have homework due tomorrow. You should just get back to your house, and then, we can talk about what happ—"

Lexi grabbed Gus by the collar of his button-up, navy-blue-pinstriped shirt and dragged him off its feet.

"One more word. And I swear to God I'll feed you to it."

Gus nodded, and we both quailed at what "it" could be.

Graywood Forest came on like an old fable where drooling inbreds chopped up children's bodies for pig feed. Though alluring to the point of enchantment at first, you could sense danger ahead. I was haunted by traces from whatever happened last night as we trekked under the trees. I wondered if the air was tainted. Had the quake been felt elsewhere? Had anyone beyond our local police department been notified? I imagined representatives of the underfunded (and overfed) Mossglow PD, led by Sheriff Earl Nichols, at the forest's edge, scratching their heads and stomachs. Some around town might have been carrying out their own search; it was front page news on the *Mossglow Sentry* anyway—*BLAST OVER GREYWOOD*.

While others tended to stay out, townies liked to explore the forest. They felt a kindred with the place and were known to booze over fire pits and smoke what they could, any leaf or crystal. They buried secrets; they made each other bloody; if they came upon someone from the Thicks, they made that person even bloodier. At least one cocksure thirteen-year-old would get lost there every few months or so only to reemerge a few days later busted up and crazy, talking about how the forest was like a puzzle you had to solve. Some had gone permanently missing as well, but no one really talked about that.

I was so tired from running that I almost fell to my knees when Lexi came to a halt. Looking toward the forest canopy, she arched her back elegantly and moved her hand to her rear. A second later, she'd unfolded a shimmering butterfly knife and held it before her. It was grease-slicked and menacing.

"A knife? Really?" Gus said.

"Shhhhh…" She tossed the blade into her other hand with a command that seemed practiced. My cheeks went flush as she did so. Watching her body tense, her exposed muscles twitch, lust traveled up my spine like a warm stream of wind and when it reached my skull diffused into something cold and shameful.

"This way." She motioned us forward with the knife.

She moved aside a tall pine bush and disappeared into a thicket. Gus and I followed.

"I wonder what she found," I whispered.

"I honestly don't want to know," said Gus.

We eventually emerged into a small clearing. The smell of recently burned wood tickled my nostrils. I put my hand on a trunk to stabilize myself as I moved into the open and felt that the surface was warm. No, not warm. Hot. I removed my hand partly in reflex and saw that the bark had been charred nearly black. The front portion of the trunk had been blown to shreds along with the front half of the crown. The same thing was true for all the rest of the trees that surrounded the clearing. It appeared as if a near perfect circle of death had incinerated all inside its radius, filling the span with a fire so contained it hadn't spread. This must have been where the explosion hit last night.

In the middle of the clearing, which had also been scorched to ash, Lexi had stopped next to what appeared to be a massive, black rock. It looked cold, was more than five feet tall and eight long. As I eased toward it, legs trembling, Lexi bent toward the ground. She pressed her ear against the object's surface.

"It's still breathing," she said as she sat down in the mud.

It was then that I saw that the rock was not a rock at all.

SIX

Though mother was better for a little while after she returned from the hospital, subtly, sleepily, the frost crept back in, crackling through her body until she appeared to grow an actual limp.

To Father's protest one night, she frantically covered all the mirrors in the house, claiming, after she'd drained a half bottle of Schnapps, they were watching her. She tried to retire them to the basement a week later, which caused Father, in the heat of a secondary Stumart acquisition deal, to lash out, threatening to put her back in the hospital. Their battle raged through the house for days, each blaming the other on topics from the food we ate to the way I'd been raised. Though realizing any war against Father couldn't be won, Mother soon gave up, relegated herself permanently to the living room where there were no mirrors, and blacked out the windows with plywood as a sort of compromise. She practically set up her own separate living space in the middle of the first floor. She'd skip meals and flip through grocery store paperbacks, tearing at the page corners and sleeping most of the day. We never knew whether she actually read any of them. She substituted her regular clothing for robes and nightgowns. The only thing she continued to wear consistently from her former life were her charm bracelets. She even changed them up, rotating motifs diligently every morning. When I came home from school in the middle of my junior year, I'd hear them clink occasionally as she thumbed through a paperback. If I happened to cross her path (though I tried to avoid it), she'd pause to stare up at me, stretch her neck long, and ask, "Will you bring me another book, sweetie?"

When I'd ask her which one she wanted, she usually answered, "Anything as long as it's different."

A few weeks before she vanished, I came home from working checkout at Stumart and found her crouching in the shower, her arm ripped open and gushing blood down the drain. She'd put her hand through the bathroom mirror. I knew so immediately even though when I asked her what happened, she remained silent, her expression self-satisfied, as if she'd just solved a puzzle. When I came to her side, I whispered, "Okay, okay," through my quivering lips so she'd drop a shard of glass that was slicing her palm open. The ambulance came soon after. Almost two liters of blood were lost by the time she got to the hospital. Father made me go to school the next morning, reasoning that "appearances aren't essential but important." And I pretended nothing happened for the days that followed.

Mother didn't check out until one week later. She came to pick me up at school with Father, rolled down the parking lot quad in a wheelchair. She wore an old wool sweater with stitched elk patterns. Her dark brown hair had grayed a bit, and I tried to shrink away from her so no one I knew would see us all together. When we got home, she appeared briefly happy again to have spent a few days away. But those emotions soon passed, and she returned to talking about mirrors again. Mirrors and anything with speakers on it too, which was a new development. "That's how it hears me," she said. "I figured it out. The mirrors are how it sees, but the speakers are how it hears. Even your headphones. It listens to me through you. That's why I have to be quiet. If I'm not careful…it'll be able to step inside me."

From that point on, I hadn't been able to look at myself in the mirror or turn up the volume on a stereo or television without thinking about them as eyes and ears. That was what Mother had left me with. A feeling that I was being recorded on a reel. That one day, I'd be forced to watch my silly life replay before my eyes.

My ears rang as Lexi put her switchblade horizontal and, with her other hand, motioned us forward. There was pressure on the sides of my head, and I shook off the sensation. What I'd thought to be a large obsidian rock was actually moving before me, rising up and down with slow, labored breaths. I heard the sound of its exhale. Stuttered, pig-like. And a smell…like burnt rubber.

"It's okay," Lexi said. "It won't hurt you, I don't think."

Gus and I gave each other a familiar look, one that implied we shouldn't be where we were. But Gus—it was always Gus—took the first step.

"What am I looking at, Lexi?" he said almost calmly as he came to her side.

"How am I supposed to know?" she said.

"I assumed you had some idea."

"You assumed wrong. I just found it here."

"Were you alone?" I asked.

Lexi nodded.

My pocket buzzed with a message notification on my Motorola, but I ignored it.

In the center of the clearing was a midnight-black mound of monster. Or at least I thought it was black at first. When I sidled around, I realized it was actually draped in a cloak of slick fur that covered the entire body. The cloak ended in a cowl that flopped over a bony snout unlike any I'd ever seen before. A snout, I noticed, whose tip had been dipped in something's blood, perhaps the same blood that stained Lexi's dress and face. Above it, two yellow, swollen lids concealed what I was sure were a pair of eyes.

The body itself, a rubbery expanse of chalk-white skin, was mostly naked beneath save for a set of paisley drapes that could have been stolen from someone's kitchen window. The creature had folded itself in a fetal position and was clutching its ribs like it was a child sleeping through a fever. Sharp-looking pieces of metal protruded from its arms and legs. They appeared to be part of the creature's biology. Under its chin, though, was the oddest part of all. Erupting from the bone was a massive, flickering light bulb. Filament intact, it fizzled and buzzed, giving off a cold, white light.

"He's hurt," said Lexi.

"He?" Gus said.

"He's been wounded by something. Here, right above the left leg."

"By something," I whispered to myself, thinking of Father.

"This has to be fake," Gus said, trying then to laugh. "Like one of those summer festival floats."

"Do summer floats have internal organs?" Lexi said. "Do they fucking breathe?"

We drew up upon the creature's knees, careful not to actually touch the skin. Above the left leg, as Lexi had said, was a hole. Or a gash, rather. Something had ripped through the creature's groin, almost clean to the other side.

"Come on," Lexi said. "Look through it."

"Fuck no," I said, my eyes drifting to the beast's jaws no more than five feet from my head. "How are you so calm right now? Do you realize what we're looking at?"

"Do you?" said Lexi. Gus nodded as if she'd made a worthwhile point.

Though the mouth was closed, the teeth jutting from the bottom lip were jagged and tipped with a sticky, black liquid. I imagined the second I followed Lexi's orders that the head would rattle to life and chomp down with a crunch. But then I saw Gus peering through the hole, his brow so furrowed that his ears perked up.

"Great Fenrir's pelt," he said. "It is alive. Or something like alive."

"Glad you finally noticed," said Lexi.

"How on earth…?"

Now, Gus, too, was asking me to come closer. Trying to look away from the creature's jaw, I inched behind him and Lexi, leaning forward on my toes. The beast's skin surrounding the gash billowed, blown by a warm wind. There was no blood dripping from the wound. There was something more unusual. Crystalline structures glimmered with light. Structures that at first looked to be mounds of crystal, like rock candy, but living rock candy. Organisms writhed under layers of ice-blue rime. They wriggled, they spasmed. And were they…making sounds? I thought I heard a soft sort of chuffing. I leaned in to listen and was so transfixed that I lost my footing and, with a shout, fell toward it, my left arm plunging into the wet, glimmering hollow of the beast.

ALLLLLLLoooooooLLLLLOOOOOOOOOOOOOOO

The monster moaned and thrashed as Lexi threw me clear. She

THE SILENT END

and Gus dragged me to the edge of the clearing, and we watched the monster whip its massive head blindly side to side before it crashed back down to the earth.

"Goddamnit, Eberstark," said Lexi. My face had been lodged in her armpit. After pulling me to my toes, she threw me back to the ground.

I held what looked to be a small handful of the beast's innards in my hand. A chattering lump of flesh I hocked away. I then turned toward Gus.

"Whoa, whoa, be careful," Gus said, backing away. "Who knows what the hell that stuff is."

"You didn't seem so concerned a minute ago?" I inspected my hand. I wiped off what was left over from my fingers, which reminded me squeamishly of insect guts.

"That's because I wasn't going to touch it," said Gus. "Not without a pair of gloves."

"I'm sure he's fine," said Lexi.

"Let's hope so." Gus brushed dirt from the sleeves of his pea coat. "Anyway, what the hell are we going to do now? I'm no expert, but my instincts tell me it would be best to bring this…thing to the authorities."

"The authorities?" whined Lexi, like a child told she couldn't stay up past her bedtime. "What, like Sheriff Earl Nichols?"

"What else are we going to do?" said Gus. "Take it home to my parents?"

"We could hide it," I said inexplicably, propped up on my arms. "Yeah, we could hide it. I know a place. On Goon's Cove."

"Sure," Gus snickered. "Hide a 2000-pound fucking monster on Goon's Cove. Great idea! I'll just grab one of its feet, and we'll drag it across town."

"That's actually a good idea," said Lexi.

"Are you kidding me?" shrieked Gus.

"Not the dragging across town part but the hiding."

The monster groaned a little.

"Who knows what this thing is, Gus?" I said. "Do you seriously want the Mossglow Police down here? Or worse, federal agents? Men in suits that turn our town into a military zone and end up conducting some crazy CIA mind wipe?"

"Please." Gus shook his head. "This isn't fucking Hollywood."

"You are an idiot, Eberstark" Lexi said. "But you've got one thing right. I don't think we can trust Mossglow with something this big. People around here…they aren't the worldly kind. They get freaked out real easy… I could see someone getting hurt."

"Why would anyone get hurt?" said Gus.

"Call it a hunch."

"You guys are crazy. This makes no sense. And besides, how the hell are you going to move something of this size? Are either one of you an alien from a dying planet?"

"No," said Lexi, "but I've got the Shepherd."

"I thought it was in the shop," Gus said.

"Just got out." She could have been talking about a relative who'd made parole.

"Sounds like we've got a plan," I said.

Gus glared at me with what looked to be betrayal. "I suppose we do."

The monster opened one of its eyes, shadowed beneath the hood, and looked in our direction as we left. Its pupil swirled with purple and yellow. Its creaky jaws opened, the eye closed again, and I saw something sparkle in its mouth. Something familiar that I couldn't

THE SILENT END

quite place wrapped around one of its teeth. But Lexi slapped me on the back to get moving, so I fled from the clearing with her and Gus. I didn't look back, but I realized as I left that my skin felt warmer, right where the innards had touched my fingers. I studied them again to see if there were any marks or discoloration, but it looked healthy enough. The warmth seemed to emanate from inside my skin. And I liked it.

SEVEN

Lexi called her truck the Shepherd. It was a black 1989 Ford Bronco with white trim, gated headlights, and bed-side steps. It got fourteen miles to the gallon, had a rear seat row installed for extra passengers, and found its parts replaced almost as quickly as they were installed. But that didn't matter to Lexi. She had an attachment to the creaky vehicle that had nothing to do with function. She revered it not only as a family heirloom but with a prickly sense of guardianship. She actually let slip once that in a frightening situation with a couple townies in Graywood, the Bronco had somehow saved her life. She'd never said much beyond that and refused to recall details when Gus and I pressed her. But when I made a joke about her truck talking to her like something out of cheesy science fiction cop drama, she shoved me on my back and didn't talk to me for a week. The Shepherd may as well have been a member of her family. It was also, I gathered, the only thing Lexi's father had left behind when he abandoned them for the east coast. An oil-stained stand-in for Christmas presents, birthday cards, and summer vacations. Whether by an extramarital affair or a midnight abduction, gone was gone. It was the same reason I kept all Mother's paperbacks and polished her vinyl records even if I was scared to read or play them. Because I knew she'd valued them in some way or another, and it reminded me that she'd once had a presence in the world.

Lexi's mother, a short-haired woman built like a pro wrestler and named Pinky, came out the front door of their home with a jug of antifreeze as we opened the garage. We'd had to hoof it from Graywood to Lexi's, but thankfully, her house wasn't as far away from the forest as mine. On the way, Gus voiced predictable concerns about what we were about to do, but Lexi didn't appear to register them. She just ran silently ahead at a pace that demanded we keep up. Her mother regarded us with a bit of suspicion as we panted toward her. Her face had a weary look to it, but her body moved with deceptive velocity. She was smaller than Lexi by a good four inches and slightly thicker as well. She wore a sweatshirt with the words "Fish Alaska" stamped in cursive over an a hook-snagged trout along with a pair of black pants; green, backless clogs; and a US Army cap.

"Load it up, Ma," said Lexi without even looking toward her mother, to which the middle-aged woman, nodding, dragged a wooden stool from the side of the garage with her other hand, climbed atop it, smacked open the hood, and let the Bronco drink deep of coolant. As she poured, she looked over her shoulder at us. She didn't even seem to notice or care that her daughter was spattered in blood.

"How's your father?" she yelled. Some of the words she had a harder time pronouncing she tried to conceal by cutting them completely.

"Things good over at the store?"

"Yes, ma'am," I chirped. "Good as they can be."

"Things always can be better," she said, putting the cap back on the coolant and tossing the plastic jug into an open garbage can without looking. "You've gotten fat."

"What?" I said.

"Last time I saw you, you were fat. And now, you're fatter."

Gus snorted.

"Sure, laugh," she said to Gus, wiping her hands and, a second later, tossing a cigarette in her mouth. She lit it with a kerosene lighter from the folds of her sweatshirt and kept it between her lips. "But you're too thin. A big brain doesn't matter if your neck's too small."

This was my chance to chuckle.

"Enough, Ma," said Lexi, not angrily but diffident. She flicked her fingers toward her while making clucking sounds with her mouth, and her mother tossed her a cigarette. She then made a louder cluck, and her mother threw her the entire pack.

"I'm surprised you can catch that," said Pinky. "Captain One Eye. You can't wear a pink eyepatch with Hello Kitty or something? And what happened to your dress?" she finally noticed. "You messing with that knife again? Never mind; I don't want to know."

"Jesus," Gus said as the uncomfortable nature of the exchange began to settle in.

"That guy's a motherfucker," Lexi's mom blurted to Gus, making me remember that, as Lexi had told me was uncommon, Pinky reserved a special odium for Christ. In the days after her husband left her for what turned out to be another family in a different state with three children—two of which were a year older than Lexi—she'd started to look a lot like the broken heart you imagined she carried in her breast.

THE SILENT END

In many ways, she reminded me of my own mother. Of someone who'd been poisoned by deceit.

"You hungry?" she said and then, looking at me, or around me, with purple-mascara eyes, "Not you, Butterbean. How about you?" she looked at Gus. "You look like you're about to die."

"We're leaving," said Lexi, cigarette in mouth, as she hopped onto the step beam and hurled herself into the driver's seat.

"Fine, I didn't cook anything anyway." She sped back toward the front door. Before she disappeared into the house, she yelled, "Pick up milk."

Lexi grunted as she started the engine. The Shepherd roared to life. Lexi backed it out of the garage and brought it down the driveway into the street so we could climb in. Crossing in front of the massive truck, with its secondary floodlights and steaming grill, I could have been in the presence of another monster. A dispirited creature of the road. When I got into the front seat and scooted toward the gear shift, belting in between Lexi and Gus, the engine shook the blood through my body.

We entered Graywood Forest from the eastern side, near the Upper Thicks. Lexi drove with no regard for rule of law, gliding from one side of the road to the other and rushing through stop signs. That's how driving was done in Mossglow, knowing that police were few and far between and that if you knew someone in the right way, you might be able to negate a speeding ticket with a smile. In the past year especially, what had formally been somewhat regular patrols had gone scarce. The department was in a state of exponential shrinkage. Sheriff Earl Nichols, who made sure to stop by Stumart every day for Little Debbies, I only saw rarely now, driving around like a man pretending he still had an important job.

Getting back to the circle where the monster lay proved difficult. The Shepherd made a variety of labored maneuvers, grunting into gullies and creeping through groupings of trees. It was dark now, and the fog had gathered. The floodlights pierced it nicely though because, as Lexi explained, they'd installed a powerful new battery. Still, I could barely see a thing. Lexi turned on the windshield wipers to squeak the moisture away, and her one eye narrowed.

A heavy branch swatted at the right side window, and I shrieked.

"Need you drive like a maniac?" Gus growled as Lexi took the Shepherd down an incline with punishing speed and smacked it into the earth. The shocks creaked but held, and she flipped hair from her eye.

Lexi only revved the engine louder. "He could be dead already. Can't waste time."

"Lexi, we don't even know what the hell *he* is," said Gus. "Or whether we can keep it—let's call it *it* okay?—from dying. I mean, I feel like I'm losing my mind. My parents are probably at the Sherriff's office already… What is it now, 8:30? Oh for fuck's sake, I'm not even going to be able to finish up next Tuesday's chem homework."

"Something tells me you'll survive."

Gus turned to me. "I can't believe you're condoning this. It's not like we don't have enough going on already, and you promised me that you'd keep your head straight. We agreed we'd concentrate on two things: school and—"

"Sword Star," I said. "Yes, I know."

"So what are we doing out here? What do you think three Myers High students are going to do about some hellbeast in the woods?"

Lexi slammed on the brakes before a tree, and my forehead hit the rear-view mirror. Gus's head narrowly missed the dash.

"Look," said Lexi. "You can bitch and moan all you want when you get home, but in the Shepherd, you keep it the fuck down."

"Sorry." I rubbed my nose.

"I just don't understand why you're doing this," said Gus.

"Gus," Lexi said a little hoarsely. "I know this is going to sound crazy. But I...I saw something."

"The monster," I said. "I know. We saw it too."

"Fuck, Eberstark. I mean that I saw something *else*. Not just the... what are we calling it? Monster? Alien?"

"Demon?" said Gus.

"I didn't just see *it*...I saw something in its eyes."

Lexi paused for a second as if waiting for us to understand. But when we didn't, she continued on.

"I was with it all night. Wondering what I should do. When you find something that crazy, you either run away screaming or start making decisions. So I put my hand on its wrist for a second—not only to see what the skin felt like but to check for a pulse."

"Well," said Gus. "Did you find one?"

"I don't know if you could call it a pulse. It was more like a chorus of pulses. Like hundreds of little fists, banging against walls. I know, it doesn't make much sense. And who knows if it even has a heart? But when I touched its wrist, it opened its eyes and stared right at me. It didn't seem like it could move its body, but I was scared. Those things...they looked hateful. Like they wanted to murder me. Either that or like they thought I was going to murder it. I backed away. I thought it was going to try and tear my head off or something. Which who knows, it might have wanted to. But from where I was, I sat on the ground, and we just looked at each for a few minutes. Genuinely just looked at each other. Then, its eyes closed again."

"So that's what you saw?" Gus said, less than interested.

"Let me finish, okay?"

Lexi thumbed her cigarette butt through a crack in the window, tossed another into her mouth, and pushed down on the car lighter.

"I don't know how to explain it any way other than this," she said. "But it was like it...recognized me."

"Recognized you?" I asked.

"That's ridiculous," said Gus, turning around to glance at me.

"Is it?" she growled. "I thought about what to do for a while. Where I should go." The car lighter clicked, and she held the glowing coils to the new cigarette. "I decided that you two were my...best option."

"How kind of you," Gus said. "Most of the time, it's like you're our ghost friend. I think tonight was the second time I'd even seen your house. And now you're saying we're you're 'best option?' I don't know...seems desperate to me."

"Gus," I said.

Lexi hammered the accelerator. Gus gasped. She veered right, and we drove down a steep incline. I could see that in her right open eye was a glimmering wetness. Maybe it was just from the smoke although her voice sounded strained.

"I have a hard time trusting people."

"But you trust monsters?" Gus said.

"A monster hasn't hurt me yet." Lexi frowned a little. Not her normal frown but something darker. Something she didn't want us to see.

EIGHT

WHEN WE ARRIVED BACK AT the clearing, the mist had saturated it so fully I couldn't see the beast. I searched for movement, and claustrophobia closed in. Why had I wanted to help hide this creature? Why hadn't I just listened to Gus and agreed to go tell someone who could actually do something about it? Father, I thought. That was why. Because I was afraid that if we weren't too careful, our actions would bring the madman out of hiding. And then, my life would really collapse. In all possibility, the grocery would fold, and Father would be snapped into a straightjacket and dragged off to a mental facility down south, probably in Ozark. I'd have to move to Massachusetts to stay with a member of Mother's family (who, since they never liked Father too much, never liked me too much either). Although I wanted to leave Mossglow more than many, this monster needed to be hidden away for now.

As Lexi flung open the door and I followed her into the clearing,

I saw that the creature in fact hadn't moved an inch. Its form swelled into view as the mist dispersed. We'd come in from the opposite direction before; the trees grew sparsely to the west of the clearing and made our entrance easier. The creature now faced us on its side and continued to breathe into the scorched earth, twitching ever so slightly as if fighting a fever in its sleep. I noticed the innards visible through the gash were brighter now. They glittered with not only blue but yellow and orange.

"Eberstark, over here," said Lexi. She was already uncoiling the chains from a hefty tow on the back of the Shepherd. There were two of them, each capped with a metal hook and attached by the opposite end to the tow. She took one, I took the other, and we trudged toward the monster. The chains slapped the dirt, and the beast snuffled a little.

"So then, we're just going to drag it out of here." Gus was casually observing our movements.

"You got a better idea?" said Lexi.

Gus looked at the Shepherd and then to the trees. "Of course I do."

A few minutes later, Gus had fashioned (or directed Lexi and me to fashion) a levering device. He instructed me to rope the chain under a fallen tree lodged behind two standing, half-burnt oaks on the outside of the clearing. I did as I was told, shoving the hook in between the log and the ground and pulling it up and over the top. Gus then had me pass the chain off to Lexi so that she could climb up into a larger tree that hadn't been as harmed by the blast. She slung her body up the trunk with the chain wrapped over her shoulder and under her armpit. Her hands were scraped, and her ripped dress clung to her sweaty body. She barely made a sound. When she landed on the crown, huffing, she shoved the chain over the strongest branch. It swung downward and slowed to a sway as it touched the ground, creating a crane-like device. Gus, though annoyed, couldn't hide his happiness with the results.

"Now, you've just got to hook the top of the cloak," Gus said. "And we're in business."

I looked at him like he was crazy.

"Do it, Eberstark," spat Lexi from the tree top. She was filthy in her perch among the leaves and almost blended in.

"But?"

Lexi stared at me, her body still and hard-looking. A moment later, I found that I had the hook in my hands and was edging toward the beast. When I arrived and saw its body rise in a suck of breath, I laid the hook on top of the fur gingerly and backed away.

"Eberstark," warned Lexi, "if you make me come down there, it's you the Shepherd will be dragging home."

I shuddered and approached the monster again. Its body heaved as I moved the hook and fumbled for a snag. I tried to nudge it into the fur, but it wasn't catching. Each time I touched it, a muffled moan escaped its mouth. The shards of metal protruding from its flesh wobbled. The cloak, like them, was part of its anatomy. When I looked closer, I found the fabric actually disappeared into the flesh above the collar bone. Its skin overall, though it felt hard, looked soft. The snout emerging from the center of its face was long, wolfish, and comprised of bone. The light bulb was embedded on its underside at its very end. The creature was an amalgam of things, all of which seemed to hold together firmly without sense.

"You're going to have to work harder than that," said Gus. "It's fur. Not a paper bag."

Shaking my head, I raised the hook over my head and focused. With a grunt, I brought it down with all my strength and drove it through with a moist-sounding rip.

AALLLALALALLLLLLOOOOOOoooOOOOOOO

The beast thrashed. I rolled away toward the Shepherd, smacking into the rear tire.

"What the hell, Eberstark?" Lexi hopped down from the tree. When she landed, she tripped, and her knee scraped the ground.

"I didn't touch its body," I said. "Swear!"

Gus came toward me and knelt down to where the hook had torn through.

"He's right." Where the sharp end had gone through the cloak, bits of the same blue crystals we'd seen in its stomach crept around the edges. I heard that noise again, like a chorus of tiny creatures screaming inside a cage.

"Whatever," said Lexi, dusting yet another layer of filth from her palms. She regarded me with disappointment. We were all acting loopy, and I was cold. "Let's just get the hell out of here."

Lexi climbed into the Shepherd and drove about ten feet forward, hoisting the beast messily into the tree tops. She edged forward in abrupt spurts and soon had the body high off the ground. Desperate sobs emerged from its open mouth, but it didn't appear to wake either. Its eyelids remained closed. Some of the insides from the wound dripped out of its abdomen and onto the forest floor. When they hit, they lost their luster and went dark.

Gus directed us to secure the chain suspending the beast around the fallen trunk. After he tested the sturdiness, he gave us the go ahead to detach the weight-bearing chain from the Shepherd's rear. The beast then hung by force of the chain and the trees alone, strung up like a great white shark being hoisted for a dockside photograph.

Lexi then positioned the Shepherd beneath the beast. We

reattached the chain to the tow and, slacking little by little, lowered the creature onto its top. When it landed, it whimpered in what seemed like relief. Its massive arms and legs flopped over the sides of the truck. One of them snapped the right rearview mirror clean off, and Lexi hissed, picking it up off the ground and tossing it in the cab. She hissed even louder when she noticed that a thick piece of metal protruding from the creature's back had put a large dent in the canopy.

We spent the next thirty minutes looping the chains over the creature's body and beneath the undercarriage. Lexi and Gus, climbing up the bed-side steps, made an effort to fold its arms across its chest. They then folded its hood over its face so that we'd have less of a chance of being noticed across town. Finally, we removed the hook from its cloak and looked at the blue cartilage sucking away at the edges of the hole.

"One second," Gus said. Poised on the hood, he removed a little plastic square box reserved for a Sword Star figurine that had not yet been filled, and, with the rear of a ballpoint pen, lifted a little of the crystalline sludge from the gash and tipped it into the container.

"Can't you do that later?" said Lexi as Gus put the box in his backpack.

"If I'm going to collude in this insanity, then I will do as I please."

"You know where we're going, right, Eberstark?" she said.

I nodded.

Lexi shut off the floodlights and took the back roads along the edge of Graywood Forest toward Goon's Cove. As we drove, I could feel the creature's listless presence above us. I was in the back seat, and when I looked behind me, I saw some of its cloak folding over the back windshield. Though I assumed anyone who saw us would suspect we were carrying a tarp on the roof, the light bulb flashing under the creature's chin could have drawn attention. Gus shivered in the front seat, wrapping his pea coat high around his neck and buttoning it over his face. He was gripping a cellphone in his hand that he hadn't turned on. He typically refrained from using it being that his parents had given it to him for emergencies only.

"Don't even think about it, Gus," said Lexi.

Gus, sour-faced, put it back in his coat pocket.

"I still don't know what I'm going to tell them."

"Them?"

"My parents, Lexi. Not all of us teenagers have carte blanche when it comes to making plans on a school night."

"Just tell them you were studying and lost track of time."

"Because that's so like me," Gus sniggered. "Not like I wouldn't if the library didn't close at 5. My dad's an academic, you know. He doesn't buy bullshit like that."

"People will buy anything once. No matter how smart they are."

"Not my parents."

"Tell them you met a girl."

"I don't…I don't think they'd believe me."

"You're probably right."

"Screw you."

"It has less to do with what you look like than what's in your brain. No one in high school thinks like you do."

"And how, exactly, do I think?"

"I'm trying to give you a compliment."

"You're not doing a very good job."

While they argued, I decided to check my message from earlier, when I was on my way to the woods. I flipped open the Motorola between my knees. I expected to see an indicator flash from Father.

But instead the sender came up as "Unknown." I flinched and pressed the green button.

You're gonna get stuck, piggy.

I read it again.

You're gonna get stuck, piggy.

I thought about laughing, thinking for a second it was some fucked up joke from Ronald or Ajay. But no. Peterson didn't even have my number, and Ajay wasn't a prankster. If either of them were to try and freak me out, it would likely involve switching one of my Lich Mariners for a Xenomarph five minutes before a game. Suddenly, the Shepherd felt a lot meeker than it had. I looked down at my swell of a stomach and imagined it being sliced open. I imagined blood and slick organs and squealing. I remembered Jesse Maroon and Tony Collette whispering "faggot" at me in Mr. Kraft's class.

"You okay, Eberstark?" said Lexi with something like a smile on her face. "I'm...not used to you not talking."

I wiped sweat off my forehead. "Fine. Just nervous."

My stomach rumbled audibly. Apparently, I was hungry too.

"Here." Gus tossed me a handful of Kit Kats from his backpack, some of his Halloween bounty.

We passed the small, dimly lit quadrant of downtown Mossglow from a distance, the Main Drive, where Father's store stood. As I gobbled down the Kit Kats, I wondered where the man who owned it was. The illuminated signs above the stores and a billboard advertising tractor tires were obscured by a thickening fog. The stadium lights were on at the Myers High Field about a half mile outside of downtown, and three bleacher sets of white-hot bulbs seared into the night.

Goon's Cove could be good for sturgeon fishing, if you sat on top of one of the rock formations leading down to the surf. But more

THE SILENT END

importantly, I knew of a place here, a cave I'd explored years ago with a couple of kids from before I met Gus. It was open to any vehicle daring to drive down the muddy causeway. There were many caves like this along Goon's Cove. Most were small. The one I'd explored, the one I was leading us to right now, was not. Inside was a shallow embankment, and at the end of it ran a stream of water that trickled into the earth beneath Mossglow through a large crack in the rock. When I was fourteen, just a few months after the move, I'd gone down there with two kids that would end up emigrating from Mossglow with their families later that year. Before they knew they'd be leaving, we decided to explore the cave in the spirit of outsiders attempting to claim their new home.

I'd gone a good twenty feet into the darkness myself when I started to get scared. The trickling of water had made me feel safe for a short while. But then I heard things. Like chattering. Like breathing. Like reptile whispers. In all likelihood, it had been the echoes of our own groping hands and snorting noses, but we decided to run anyway, run like the children back toward the light outside. The second we got out, we promised never to go back in again. And I'd kept that promise until now.

You're gonna get stuck, piggy.

I directed Lexi down a slight decline near the beach.

"How did you know about this place, Eberstark?" Gus whispered as, finally, the Shepherd sputtered into the cave.

"Word of mouth."

"Weird you haven't told me about it."

"It's not a big deal."

Lexi stepped out of the front seat and surveyed the environment. Wet clay. Silt and algae. A few years of maturity had shooed away some of the shadows. But still, there was that passage. The long darkness beneath the cove from which blew a deviled wind and ran a small stream. *I would have a hard time fitting inside it now,* I thought. I'd had a hard time fitting inside it then.

"This will do." Lexi gave me a nod of respect that cut my anxiety in half.

We slipped the monster's chains off. Tired and frustrated, we tried to nudge its body from the truck's roof in a gentle fashion onto the mud bank next to the stream. It proved harder than anticipated. The body was too heavy to unseat, and there were no structures with which we could create a lever like we had in the forest. Lexi thus suggested we all gather on one side and, on the count of three, shove. We could then run over to the other side and stop the beast's fall. But when we heaved into the beast, placing our hands on its right buttock and pushing with all our might, it toppled off wildly, dropping toward the ground. As it did so, one of its legs swung out in a livid arc, and a scrap of its body metal sliced my shoulder right through my shirt. The pain was hot and swift.

"Shit!" Lexi shouted as I dropped to the wet ground. "Are you okay?"

I rubbed the wound, which was more of a graze. "I think so. It stings."

"Are you current on your tetanus shots?" Gus asked.

"Yes, Mom."

The beast was now planted face down in a shallow stream that ran through the cave. Bits of yellow, blue, and red innards from its wound leaked into the water. The bulb on its chin buzzed with a faint, purple light.

"So...now what?" I asked, but Gus and Lexi were still fixated on my shoulder. "I'm *fine*. Let's just figure this out, okay?"

Lexi cut off a piece of her dress with her knife, a strap of fabric from the lower part, near her knees. I stared at her dirt-covered thighs. She then bent down and indicated that I should take off my sweatshirt. I didn't like the idea of her seeing my stretch-marked stomach, so I rolled my sleeve up as far as it could go. She gave me a ridiculing glance and dipped the cloth in the cave water before washing the gash. I watched a little bit of blood trickle out as she repeated the motion a couple of times. Then, concentrating on my shoulder as if it wasn't even attached to a body, she wrung the fabric clean and cinched it tight.

"What next?" she said, walking away.

"We go home," said Gus. "That's what's next."

"We can't just leave it here like this."

"I don't see why not. The goal was to get this thing out of the forest, right? Well, we did. So let's go home."

"He's right, Lexi," I said, rubbing my shoulder. "Nobody's going to find it here. We can always come back…"

"Not me," said Gus.

Lexi lowered her gaze. She didn't argue. Instead, she just said, "One second," and went to the back of the Shepherd. Opening the back hatch, she tugged out a massive wool blanket at least as large as the girl herself. It was triple-folded, thick, like something used for mounting saddles. It was so heavy she nearly collapsed under it.

"Little help here?"

A few seconds later, we'd shoved the blanket into the beast's wound to plug it, grabbed a set of bungie cords from the trunk, connected three together and made a tourniquet. By now, the creature was barely breathing. It wasn't even groaning anymore. Its mouth sagged open, and an oily tongue slopped onto the ground. But at least its insides wouldn't be washed away into the darkness of the cavern. If that was, in fact, a good thing.

"Can we please go now?" said Gus.

"Fine," Lexi grumbled.

As the two of them turned around to get in the car, I passed the beast's snout. It was all bone and teeth without blood or skin. But as I looked closer, I finally saw it. What I'd glimpsed earlier, a shiny piece of jewelry wrapped around one of its teeth.

"I'm going to be up all night," lamented Gus.

My shoulder burned as I bent down and removed the object from the slickened tooth. It was a charm bracelet…just like Mother's… with seashells and dolphins. Quickly, I dropped it in my pocket before Lexi and Gus noticed.

"You coming, Eberstark?" said Gus, sounding not just tired but weary.

I climbed into the back seat and buckled my seat belt. The Shepherd's headlights slid away from the monster, lying in the dark where we left it.

NINE

I ASKED LEXI TO DROP ME off a quarter mile away from my house in front of the Lucky Start gas station. I wanted to pick up a Coke, I told her. Something to wash down the fear. She offered to wait while I did so, but thankfully, Gus groaned at the idea, so I didn't have to provide more excuses for why I didn't want them pulling up to my front door. The Shepherd rumbled off toward the Upper Thicks as I pretended to go inside the store, a kiosk attended by an elderly man from the Lowers with a handlebar moustache and a lip full of chew. When they were gone, I ducked behind it to the sidewalk on the other side.

My house was dark when I arrived. This wasn't unusual. If I didn't get home after school, no one would bother to make our-two story shingle home look like anything but an abandoned husk. Father had other places where he liked to spend his time. If he did come inside, he did so in the dark and without announcing his presence. It could be likened to living with a poltergeist, an after-midnight menace that savaged the kitchen. Though he hadn't anticipated he'd turn into a lunatic when he and Mother purchased it on a short sale weeks before we moved, the house was sequestered enough from the rest of the neighborhood to allow a man like himself to devolve in private.

Instead of being situated on the actual street with the other homes, the path to our house was marked by a mailbox with a placard reading *712 Hagan Road*. From there began a dirt road sided by trees that crooked around a bend. The entrance to the road itself was guarded by a swinging metal gate, upon which hung a small, wooden sign with our last name carved into it. Our neighbors were two recently transplanted families that hadn't been able to sell off their homes after the fire at Hinterlord a few years back. Now, apart from commuting to Ozark for work, they mainly kept to themselves.

I checked the mail, found none, and pushed the gate aside. I hurried down the path, coming upon the house, jaundiced with neglect. I creaked up to the front porch and wiped my feet on the rug, looking down at a series of ceramic planters filled with cracked dirt. I wondered if there'd be food in the refrigerator. I'd picked up some supplies from Stumart three days ago, but that meant nothing, knowing who, or what, I was dealing with. I crept to the side of the porch where the backyard was visible to check the hatch. The house was situated on four acres of land, and the underground facility where Father burrowed had come with the house when we purchased it. It had been built as an underground wood and storage cellar but now emitted a poison-yellow glow, seeping from a small crack where the hatch was held ajar by an outturned lock.

Hoping I hadn't been noticed, I tiptoed back to the front door and creaked it open, entering our foyer. The wood floors were polished but lusterless in the dark. I flipped a switch, and a ceiling light clicked on. Mother had had everything removed from the walls from mirrors to pictures and clocks. There was a cavernous, hollow feeling to every nook and cranny now. It was as if a vacuum had sucked out all traces of what we'd been, leaving behind vague clues like a leather chair. A coffee table. A stack of rumpled paperbacks.

Passing the staircase that went up to the second floor, I went into the kitchen with thoughts of eating. It was entirely trashed. The sink was piled up with pasta pots, dishes, glasses, mugs. Father, who'd never had a flare for domestic niceties, had stacked his used receptacles into a mountain of mess that felt like it would topple should one be improperly removed. Disemboweled food boxes and half-eaten bananas littered the black and white tiled floor. The bottom of a pot was still smoking on a low-flame burner. Nothing was inside it but a rank, metallic smell filled my nostrils as I turned it off. Father didn't use the rest of the house, but he was still fond of the kitchen. He ate there like a wolf on the edge of starvation and ripped through groceries with what might as well have been claws.

I went to the fridge to see what had survived his ravaging and found four empty boxes of instant macaroni and cheese. Alongside these was a bottle of ketchup, an almost finished jug of milk, and three economy-sized bottles of vodka, one of which was half-drunk. We'd been cleaned out. Maybe I'd have to go back to the gas station after all for microwavable nachos and pineapple slush.

I turned on the hot water and got to washing the dishes. I didn't mind. Chores helped me maintain order these days.

As the pipes rattled with heat, I picked up the boxes on the ground and tossed them into the trash can one by one. The hanging kitchen lamp swung slightly overhead, and fog matted up against the window pane as I returned to the double-troughed sink, filling one side with soapy water. What had happened to us in the forest? What had we seen, exactly? The entire evening was becoming a blur of fog and teeth, and I couldn't make sense of any of it.

After washing a few dishes and stacking them in the drainer, I paused to draw the charm bracelet from my pocket and placed it on the mantle above the sink. Bubbles rose and popped around it. My dumb reflection gazed back at me in the background. Purple sacs weighed down my eyes, which were puffy and thick-lashed like Mickey the Bullfrog's. My spongy chin was pink-tinged and had the consistency of baby fat. My stringy hair, the same weak wig I'd inherited from Father, was matted down with sweat, and my outfit, a hoodie and green khakis, made me look large and formless. I was an unhealthy blob of a teen, surviving on fast food and impulse. And worst of all, I'd stopped caring about fixing it.

The charms on the bracelet—dolphins, starfish, two crabs and a clam—were still slick. When I tried to separate them from each other, dark, viscous strands of saliva stretched between. It wasn't the same blue stuff that had come out of the wound and had an oily feel to it. The bracelet itself seemed indistinguishable from the one I'd seen Mother wear on the night of her near-suicide. But surely this was just a coincidence? I wasn't willing to assume she'd been the only woman in Mossglow to collect them. And even if it was hers, what did that mean? Had she been chewed up and swallowed by the thing we'd gone out of our way to help?

The bubbles continued to pop, and the steam thickened. I plunged my hands into the hot water and clenched my teeth.

"You're home late," I heard Father's voice say. I knocked a dirty ceramic mug into the other side of the sink. It cracked nearly in two when it hit the porcelain. I flashed around, concealing the charm bracelet on the mantle. There, in the swinging light of the kitchen lamp, stood the man, stuffing his face with macaroni and cheese out of a giant, red plastic bowl. He heaved forkfuls of the yellow noodles past his gums and chewed them with his mouth open.

"What were you doing?" His smile was sadistic.

"Hanging out with Gus." I turned around quickly to turn off the sink. As I did so, I managed to swipe the charm bracelet from the mantel into the suds.

"That right?" Father used his fork to regard me up and down. Though still dressed in his army camouflage pants, he was wearing a long-sleeved, black turtleneck that had been turned inside out and backwards. "Looks like you've been hanging pretty hard. You're filthy."

I looked over my dirt and oil stained clothes, pretending not to have noticed. Thankfully, I'd covered the gash on my shoulder. "I tripped on the path."

"Ouch." Father smiled. His shaved head glistened, and crow's feet squirmed at the corners of his eyes. He looked right past my lies. Or at least I thought he did, pausing for a few seconds so he could soak in my deceit.

"Well." His gaze dropped to his macaroni and cheese—all five boxes of it, I assumed. "We all trip sometimes. No matter how much balance we think we have. Macaroni?" He offered the bowl forward.

"I'll find something after I get these dishes down."

"Come on. Just a bite. Can't eat all this myself. And I know you like the stuff. Ever since you were a bedwetter, you've been asking for macaroni and cheese. Shit, even before you were supposed to be eating solid foods. 'Macwoni,' you'd cry. 'Macwoni and Speez!' Your mother," he chuckled, "she never approved. But mothers don't approve of anything, so I just filled you up with the crap. Kept you quiet."

The more I looked at the bowl, the hungrier I got. I had brought it home from the store anyway. I gave up and motioned toward it with my chin.

Father, smiling with his mouth open, stepped toward me. Chunks of macaroni slipped around his tongue and teeth. As I reached out to take a hold of the bowl, however, my hand passed right through it. As if it weren't really there at all.

Father began stamping his feet and screaming with laughter. Yellow clumps flew from the bowl and disappeared as they neared the floor. "Would you look at that?" He was cawing. "Oh man, Hat is going to be ecstatic when he sees this sucker in action. You have no idea how long he's been waiting. You have no idea how long *I've* been waiting."

He walked three steps toward me and, holding the entire bowl of macaroni and cheese, emptied it upside down over my head. I tried to fall back, expecting the worst. But nothing touched me.

Father stamped his feet even harder and guffawed.

"Oh boy, oh boy, oh boy. Come on outside to the hatch. You've got to see this."

I stood still in awe. Not only at what I'd seen but at the fact that Father never invited me down to the hatch.

"Come on, don't be frightened. Nothing's that remarkable once you see what it's made of. And besides, I'm where the food is. You must be hungry."

"I, uh…"

"Come down to the hatch."

I nodded, and Father reached out toward me to tweak what could have been my left nipple. But when his fingers twisted, he vanished from the earth.

I stood in the kitchen with my back to the faucet. Reaching into the dishwater, I retrieved the charm bracelet, less oily than it was before. Feeling it between my fingers made me recall Mother's touch. Something I remembered from the "before" years. When she could look you in the eye. She'd had dark, shoulder-length hair that reflected light like shined-up leather. Even when she began to drift into depression, it remained thick and lustrous. Though a small person, a little less than five feet tall, her body was well-proportioned and healthy, not too thick or thin. But her eyes were what I remembered most. They were large, expressive, the kind of eyes that couldn't lie. The kind of eyes that never hid whether they were sad or angry. When she stopped being able to look at me altogether, that's how I'd known she was in trouble.

The hatch now lay open to Father's laboratory. A flood of yellow-green light unfurled into the backyard. I stepped toward the entrance and started down the narrow ladder leading in. Each step was worse than the last. Near the top of the descent was a satellite with two antennae fixed to the wall. It beeped quietly, rotating from side to side. Multiple monitors featured radar displays and charts. One had what appeared to be some sort of seismic tracker, pulsating with a wavelength that, at the present moment, slacked. Circular, green, fluorescent ceiling lights lined the primary entranceway into the ground floor. I'd been down here once before, right before all the trouble began following Mother's disappearance. But it hadn't looked anything like this. It had been an ordinary, creepy, dingy cellar, filled with old junk and cracked concrete, not this hyper-technical control center that could have come right out of Sword Star.

I came to the bottom of the stairs and saw Father filling a second red plastic bowl with macaroni and cheese that he was spooning from a larger blue bowl, which sat on an aluminum stool in the corner of the room.

"There you are," he said. "Here's your Macwoni and Speez." He marched across the room and handed me the bowl and threw a fork into it. "Your mother used to make it from scratch, but I can't even remember what that tastes like anymore. I just know it was better than this. Anything's better than this. Not that I'm complaining. In my line of work, you can't waste a second. Food becomes function. And without function, you break down. If you break down, the shadow seeps in. And if the shadow seeps in…"

He looked at me for a moment, his eyes implying I should take a bite.

So I did.

"Scared you shitless, didn't I?"

"Where's the Hat?" I was oddly unnerved not to see him at Father's side.

"Reconnaissance mission." Father dipped his head. He looked jittery. "Nothing you need to be concerned with."

He paused.

"Come with me; I'm going to show you something that'll murder your emotions."

I gulped down another spoonful of macaroni and cheese and followed Father down a set of narrow stairs that led us to an even deeper part of the bunker I hadn't known existed. At the end was a steel vault door he'd left ajar. With unusual jauntiness, he nudged it open with his shoulder and brought us into a room clamoring with what appeared to be armaments. It could have been the garage of some future public enemy or backwoods militia preparing to fight a war for the end of days. Grappling hooks, tent poles, and fishing spears were interspersed neatly amongst shotguns that had been run through with wires and outfitted with diodes. There was a series of canisters that resembled fire extinguishers, each of which were a different color—red, yellow, magenta, green—neatly fastened into brackets on one wall. But what sat in a glass cage with a halogen light inside was strangest of all: a small pile of black, slimy tentacles. They weren't moving a lot but were certainly alive.

"Oh, don't mind those," Father said. "I've been frying the hell out of them over the last two weeks with anti-penumbrics. Resilient little shits always come crawling back."

I saw the cannon he'd brought out with the Hat by the hedgerow at school on a pair of hooks. Surrounding it were other pieces of arcane technology, gadgets I was amazed that Father had created. He'd never been an inventor as much as he'd had a keen eye for business. The son of a WWII veteran who ended up in a back brace after tripping over a telephone cord at work, he'd grown up with a combination of working class grit and a burning desire to get rich. Science just wasn't in the blood. Not until, that is, Mother disappeared. When he pursued her, vanished for days, and returned soon after with the Hat, he developed a flair for tinkering and a mind that seemed suited to the pursuit. I can't know what he discovered when he went missing, but gazing upon the fruits of his labors filled me with a strange sense of pride. I hadn't been down here since Mother's disappearance. And since then, Father and I had turned our backs on each other like two men walking five thousand paces to eventually turn and face each other with sniper rifles. The fact that he'd invited me down here at all struck me as suspicious.

"You made all these, Dad?" I said.

"The Hat's mostly responsible. I'm just the idea guy."

The something he'd wanted to show me turned out to be a mirror. Seeing it in the middle of this war room, about six feet tall and three feet wide amongst the abundance of tech, I didn't think much of it. It did bring back memories of the handsome man in the mirror Mother had tried to smash with her fists. But it also looked drab and ordinary.

"You saw me today outside your classroom," Father said. He'd turned serious, with dark black eyebrows that arched over his nose. "I didn't mean for that to happen, you know. I wouldn't have hurt you—at least I don't think I would have hurt you. One can never know what'll happen when you're cooking in this kitchen. But now that you've seen what wasn't meant to be seen, I have no choice but to make you understand what's at stake."

Father removed a small, metal canister from his pocket. He uncapped it, and from within shone an ice-blue light. With a pair of tweezers, he picked up what I immediately recognized as the same material as was inside the monster we'd hidden in the cave. Or at least a similar material. Crystalline and glimmering, it twitched on the tip of the tweezers.

"Beautiful, isn't it?" Father grinned.

"Where did you get that?"

"This?"

I nodded.

"From the belly of the beast, of course."

The bald man turned to the mirror and crouched down. On the frame's back was a small motor with exterior gears and a small, yellow hatch. Father flipped the hatch open with a finger from his free hand. He then wiped the sticky material inside the hatch and carefully shut the lid. Pausing briefly to put it back in his pocket, he said, "Try and keep an open mind."

He twisted one of two dials on the motor's side, and the engine began to emit a flapping noise. It grew in intensity, increasing in pitch. Father stood with hands on his hips as the mirror glass began to transform. Its surface, while not moving outside the frame, liquefied.

"If you're going to fight monsters." Father stepped toward the mirror and plunged his hand into it. The surface seemed to eat everything up to his wrist. "Then you have to find out why they came here in the first place."

He drew his hand forth and, cross-eyed in that horrible way, twisted a second dial on the side of the motor to the fourth of six notches. When he did so, his exact duplicate appeared ten feet away, near the vault door. It was the exact same in every regard as the man himself and mimicked his movements.

"Heh!" Original Father, the one in front of the mirror, snickered. "My very own shadow. Come over here, bedwetter. Have a gander."

As he spoke, so did the doppelganger. It was like being in an echo chamber.

"Your fear. I can feel it, son. And that's good. Me, I live in a world of perpetual terror. Nothing I see doesn't fill me with dread. But instead of fighting it, you see, I let it trickle into every fiber of my being until it negates itself. Until the animal takes over. Come over here and join me in embracing horror. See what it is that keeps me up at night."

Wary of the doppelganger, I stood still, gripping my bowl.

"Don't be nervous. It's just a simple…supernatural…copy machine."

Grunting my approval, I came to stand a few feet behind original Father and faced the mirror. We were looking at the same room we stood in but from a different vantage point. That of the doppelganger. A second set of eyes that were both Father's and not Father's. As he moved his chin up and down, the room in the mirror, the weapons and fish spears and tentacle cage, traveled with it. He had control over the manifestation as if linked to his own psyche.

"How?" I said, thinking about how amazed Gus would be to see something like this.

"Come on." Father shuffled out of the way. "You try it."

When he stepped aside, his copy disappeared. I cautiously approached the mirror in his place. When I got about four feet away, I saw out of the corner of my eye what I quickly understood to be me. A perfect copy. Stepping as if from a portal between worlds. I stopped and stared at myself. I looked meek and meaty with cheese on my lips. The red bowl I held before my stomach. My neck was turned away, and a twin striping of hair ran from the back of my ungroomed skull into my sweatshirt. I moved my hand, and so did it. I took a step, and so did it. I could sense there was an art to controlling the avatar that could be mastered. Like all games, it was a matter of periphery coordination.

"Now, here's the kicker," Father said. "Stay right there."

He walked over to an aluminum countertop and carefully picked up a small box with a funneled scope attached to its end. It looked like an old-fashioned camera. Something you'd see in a museum. As he moved it, aiming the lens around the room, my replica also moved. The mirror itself went wild, jumbling through space like the window of a carnival ride. Father treated the box like a projector, and I saw my form's position shift from the floor to the ceiling.

"My God," I said.

"God has nothing to do with it," Father said. "But if you're wondering about earlier, I put one of these in the kitchen."

He walked over to where I stood and shut off the motor. It slowed to a stop and, as the mirror returned to its normal surface again, my copy faded. I tapped the surface of the mirror just to make sure it had hardened and felt the glass snap against my fingernail.

"So what do you think?" He picked up his bowl of macaroni and cheese and heaved five forkfuls rapidly into his mouth. "Not much, I observe. Here we are together, father and son, facing each other directly for the first time in months, and still, the way you look at me... You think I've lost my mind, don't you? That losing your mother coincided with a psychotic break, and now, you're trying to hide me from everyone you know. The Eberstark family's dirty little secret... whatever allows you to wake up every day and think that tomorrow will come just the same. Well, gaze upon what skeletons dance in the closets of the deranged. Miracles are fashioned from clay. Miracles used to fight wars, infractions against nature so perverse the world could be swallowed into paradox."

I pushed one palm out toward Father. My words nearly stuck in my throat. "I don't think you're crazy."

One of his eyes bulged as it examined me. He stepped so close that I could smell his imitation cheese breath. "Strange if so. Has something changed in my wayward son? Has some arachnid of reason ensnared him in its web? Questions that perhaps can't be answered as of yet. Questions that will though. Questions that will."

"Nothing's 'ensnared' me. I just can't translate...you, to be honest."

"Ah, but what is insanity isn't subject to translation? Ever since your mom went missing, you've been hiding under your pillow like a rabbit in its warren. And now that I've finally figured out—or started to figure out—what's going on in this labyrinth of a town, you're extending your trembling hand in diplomacy. And why? Because you don't have anyone else that will touch it but me. Because I am the hero of this story and you the tragic unbeliever."

I was getting angry. "Put yourself in my position. Imagine your father talking about monsters and shadows and ditching work to hide away in some…underground bunker."

I knew my voice was full of self-doubt because self-doubt was my makeup. If it was true that I thought Father had a grasp of what was happening in Mossglow beyond what I'd previously believed, it didn't negate the fire in his eyes. He was on the verge of doing something terrible. He'd undergone a transition over the last few months from paranoid to manic. Regardless of what had happened to him, was any of it even reversible by this point? A part of me felt like if I told him about the beast, he could explain everything. But another part of me felt like he could strangle me just as well. Misconstrue me for an agent of evil and stick me in a halogen tank with those black tentacles… whatever they were.

"I'm ready to listen," I chanced. "That's all I'm saying."

"Now you want a teacher?" His sweat-filmed forehead narrowed into an almost perfect V. "Of course you do. And what would you like to learn? What will this lunatic in his bunker stepping through mirrors teach you about the ways of the world?"

I glimpsed a chance.

"The sticky stuff you put inside the machine? It looked alive. It was moving."

"Sticky stuff? Sticky stuff is what you put into a tube sock, bedwetter. What you saw… No. What you saw is something that can only be created by itself. Created by itself and, I believe, only destroyed by itself."

He paused.

"The Hat calls it Murje," he said.

"Murje?"

"And he'd be one to know. But never mind that. The mirror device is what's important here. Our shadow copier. It's still limited in its function, and I can't seem to figure out how to optimize its usage." He began pacing back and forth, gesturing wildly. I felt like I couldn't curb the conversation anymore. "I now understand how he gets out of the mirrors, you see. But what I want to know is how he gets *into* them."

"Who is him?"

"Ah, yes." Father laughed. "You still don't know, do you? You're still peeing yourself in a dark corner of your room, soaking sock to chin, lining up two of every animal to board your mighty ark? You still think you'll just keep on waking up and going to school and going on and on like nothing's wrong. Like this whole city isn't preparing to be sucked down into the Earth when his sick desires are finally fulfilled." He turned to the mirror. His lips were flecked with spit and cheese, and his eyes bulged with rage. He held the sides of the frame and screamed into it, "Where are you hiding? WHERE? Come out of there, you coward! Show me where you slink you slug, so I can squash you under my shoe!"

I backed away. "Who are you yelling at?"

"Mr. Blue," Father croaked, looking all of a sudden like a small child. He crouched on the ground and turned to me, eyes filled with tears. "Mister. Goddamned. Blue. He has your mother. He has her; I know he does. But where did he take her? Where? Please tell me."

I felt like running away but instead put an awkward hand on his shoulder. His head was in his palms, and he was sobbing. This man had never been a trusted moral force in my life, more interested in expanding his miniature business empire than in me. But he had been mythic, holding his back up against a dam of misfortune.

THE SILENT END

A sound sprung up. A high-pitched horn noise that wailed throughout the bunker.

"Hat!" Father snapped his neck toward the noise. He bolted for the wall and withdrew a holster fit with two bulbous-looking pistols. He also grabbed what appeared to be a spear and clomped into the next room. I followed him.

I saw him squint into his monitors, his eyes jumping from signal to signal. The high-pitched beeping was originating from the round satellite near the hatch; he reached out and smacked it with the side of his hand to turn it off. The screen with the seismic strip had started oscillating wildly. The circular radar next to it whirled in a circle. One monitor blinked in green letters: THREAT LEVEL: A3.

"I'll be damned," he said, staring at it.

He turned one last time to look at me before opening the hatch and holding it above him. As he spoke, he tightened his holster around his chest and drew the same pair of goggles I'd seen him with in the tree over his eyes.

"Go to your room," he said. His crazed expression suggested he was entering a situation that promised success or doom. "And go to school in the morning. But remember; that place is a den of wolves. Don't be afraid of starting a fire to keep them away. And make sure to keep it burning. Keep it burning bright."

TEN

THE NEXT MORNING, I WOKE up with my face smeared across my keyboard. After I came out of Father's underground bunker, I'd returned to my room. It was a mess, the aftermath of a battle between new and discarded hobbies. Sheets of foam poster board covered my bed, and upon each one lay a Sword Star legion for the upcoming tournament. Only half of the figurines were actually painted (which meant I'd only halfway passed the requirements for entry), and I knew that Gus would be furious if I didn't have the rest done by next week. Since I could feel my eyes closing, however, I went to my desk and took each school book from my backpack. Thinking of the discussion I'd had with Mrs. Duncan, I set each out separately before my old laptop and looked at them for a few minutes as a series, studying their covers. I thought that sitting up would keep me awake and tried to open *The Trial of Xerxes*, but by page three, eyes drifting back over and over to the beginning of a sentence—*She couldn't understand why he'd painted the wall green, of all colors*—I'd already drifted into something worse than sleep. Something like a dead state. I woke in my clothes, inhaling snack debris from between the space bar and the comma, realizing I'd already missed the bus.

I speed-walked for a mile and a half and trampled into Mrs. Duncan's class ten minutes late. When I did so, she paused from her lecture and said, "Welcome, Mr. Eberstark. I hope you won in your fight against what appears to be a wheat thresher."

A couple of the students chuckled. Ronald Peterson howled. But Lexi and Gus just turned back and shot me two vicious glances for drawing attention. I smiled stupidly as I sat into my seat and fumbled *The Trial of Xerxes* onto the desk.

"No matter though," Mrs. Duncan continued. "I'm sure you can borrow a classmate's notes if need be. We were just discussing a quote, actually. By Pablo Picasso. Do you know who Pablo Picasso is, Mr. Eberstark?"

I took a second to catch my breath. Pairs of eyes turned toward me. Gus and Lexi continued to stare at their desktops. I thought about a packet we'd been handed last week that discussed the man she mentioned. "He was a painter?"

"I don't know." She raised her reddish brown lips. It appeared I wasn't the only one to come to class disheveled. Though she concealed it well, I could tell Mrs. Duncan had had a hard night as well. Her gigantic eyes were veined with red, and the bags beneath them bled through a heavy layer of concealer. "Can you confirm that, Ms. Navarro?"

"He was a painter and a sculptor," Lexi grunted. "An all-around artist."

"What type of 'all-around' artist specifically? Surely, you know.

And not only because I told you five minutes ago…"

I noticed Gus had raised a hand, as was tradition. It might have already been raised when I came into the classroom or since the day I'd met him three years ago.

"Ms. Navarro? I'd like to hear from you," said Mrs. Duncan.

Lexi murmured something through the hair that half-covered her face.

"I didn't hear that." Mrs. Duncan put her hand to her ear.

"Cubist." Lexi brushed back her hair. "He was a Cubist. He invented Cubism."

"Good. And what is Cubism? Let's see…Mr. Peterson? You should know this, being that it was in last week's assigned reading."

"Pssh," Ronald said. He'd been rummaging through his backpack but had been caught off guard before he could get his notes. "It's, like, Cuban studies, right? CIA operations in the fifties?"

"My God. How you are even alive, Mr. Peterson, boggles the mind. Mr. Eberstark, can you answer the question?"

"No," I said. "I mean, maybe." I flipped aimlessly through *The Trial of Xerxes* as if it would provide the answer. "It's an abstract way of making art, right?"

"I can't say no," mused Mrs. Duncan, one hand on her desk for support. "Abstract. Avant-garde. Paradigm-shifting. There are better words. But don't worry, it is okay if you don't know the exact definition. I don't know if Picasso knew exactly what he was doing either. But perhaps the quote we're talking about can help us understand better. Who can repeat it for us…Mr.…" She scanned the room. "Kapur?"

Ajay, looking especially dapper today in a dress shirt with metal buttons tucked into a starched pair of corduroy pants, cleared his throat.

"Everything you can imagine is real," he said, reading from what

I noticed was the chalkboard, where the teacher had scrawled it in large, yellow letters.

"Thank you." Mrs. Duncan spent a moment clearing her throat. She then turned around, took a tissue from a box, and blew her nose furiously. "My apologies. I woke up this morning, and my front door had blown—*achoo!*—open."

She honked one more time into her tissue and sniffled up what remained.

"Anyhow, Pablo Picasso famously said, 'Everything you can imagine is real.' Before we get into what this means in relation to *The Trial of Xerxes*—which you should all be close to finishing, by the way." She gave me a hard look. "What was Picasso talking about? Let's define. Ms. Valdez. Shoot from the hip?"

Melinda squirmed in her seat. She was dressed in an orange sweater, red pants, and pink wool beanie. "It's like if you can imagine something, then, then it might be real?"

"Is that so?" Mrs. Duncan's voice was lower and more nasal now. "So then if you can imagine a unicorn for instance? Or Bigfoot, or the Loch Ness Monster, it must be real?"

Melinda's knees wobbled. "I think so."

"Wouldn't that be a feat?" Mrs. Duncan sniffled again. "If by simply thinking about something, it could come to life. If that were true, then I could fly my magic carpet back in time to tell myself not to become a teacher. But no, Ms. Valdez. Unfortunately, I do not think that's what Picasso was talking about. Not by a long shot. He wasn't talking about elves or fairies or Kris Kringle. Nor was he evoking that tired idea that if you only believe in something it will come to be. No. You must travel deeper. From the realm of the physical to the realm of critical thought. Mr. Mustus, you look like as if your arm is preparing to shoot off into space. Why don't you try and enlighten us?"

"Thank you for calling on me, Mrs. Duncan."

"Get on with it."

"Well, I think…" He looked tired too. I could tell he'd be grumpy for the rest of the day. "That Picasso was talking about ideas. Not things."

"Ideas? And not things? Well, that's more interesting than what we've heard so far. Care to elaborate?"

"Of course. Just because an idea is intangible doesn't mean it doesn't exist. Or that it can't be true in a certain sense. Unicorns, for example, are fantasy. But even though they aren't real, that doesn't mean thoughts of them aren't. After an idea is created, then it is alive whether or not it happens to be true or not."

"I am so confused," said Ronald, his fingers pressed against his temples.

"Well, if your essays are any indication of your thought process, Mr. Peterson, there's no reason why you shouldn't be," said Mrs. Duncan.

"Ouch," someone said.

"What Mr. Mustus said is absolutely correct." Mrs. Duncan's short heels clicked quietly against the floor as she moved around the room. "Not that I'm surprised. And yes, class. Listen carefully. An idea doesn't have to be tangible, or even feasible, in order for it to exist. It just has to be able to have been thought. Does this make sense to everyone?"

Lexi's hand went up.

"Yes, Ms. Navarro," Mrs. Duncan beamed. Lexi rarely spoke in class unless she was forced to.

"I have a question."

"It's good that you can ask it then."

"What if something you thought was impossible." She paused,

looked at Gus, and then to me. "Actually turns out to be possible?"

Mrs. Duncan sat on the desk and nodded her head toward the door. "Are you asking what would happen if a unicorn walked through the door right now? Because if so, the answer is easy: It won't."

"In a way, that's what I'm asking. And I guess it's also not. Maybe a unicorn is a crappy example. I hate unicorns. What if..." Lexi's face darkened. Flames could have risen around it. "A monster. A monster, Mrs. Duncan. Something with teeth and fangs and a lust to kill walked through the door right now? What would that mean?"

Gus and I looked at each other.

"That's a bizarre question. And really off topic. But fine, due to the fact that you typically possess the tonal character of a piece of wall tile, I'll play along. Are you asking in a strictly personal sense? As in how I would react to a monster coming through the door? Or are you asking in relation to chapter 11 in *The Trial of Xerxes*, when Delia has night terrors?"

"I'm asking in terms of Pablo Picasso?"

"As in, what would *he* think about the existence of a monster?"

"Let me try and say it differently. So here we have this artist—he was a modern artist, right?"

"Well, a 'modernist.' Although for the purpose of this class—"

"Right," Lexi interrupted. "So here we have this artist whose entire life is about trying to create new ways of looking at the world."

"Right, but you'll have to explain—"

"Well, my question is what would happen if an idea Picasso attempted to get us thinking about actually ended up growing legs? How do you think he'd react if he had to look the results of his imagination right in the eye as living, breathing things that can't be unmade? That can't be killed?"

Mrs. Duncan was silent. She looked a little angry.

"I'm not exactly sure how to answer that. Being that I believe you're speaking about things that are way over this class's head. Maybe even over my head. But since you don't seem ready to lay off until you get an answer, does anybody else want to chance to answer Lexi before we move on?"

Gus raised his hand. His eyes were full of venom.

"Mr. Mustus?" Mrs. Duncan said uneasily.

"I think that Lexi should be wary of leading the class off topic. We all know that monsters don't exist. So why should we be talking about them like they do? This discussion is about the currency of ideas."

"Noted," said Mrs. Duncan. "Let's move on then—"

"I disrespectfully disagree with Gus," Lexi fired back. "In his efforts to silence discussion. I'm sure that Picasso thought it was impossible for humans to talk to each other via satellite towers and circuit boards. What would have happened then if he saw a cellphone? What if it's the definition of 'tangible' that's problematic? What if an imaginary thing, a monster, for instance, could be made real by advancements in technology? What would it look like?"

"All right," Ronald said, throwing his arms up. "I have NO IDEA what anybody's saying."

"I think we should stop talking about monsters," I said quietly, tapping the edge of my book against the desk. "And get back to *The Trial of Xerxes*."

"You would want to stop talking about monsters," Lexi said with an eye a poison dart could have sprung from.

"That's *enough*," snapped Mrs. Duncan. She tilted her head and leaned back against her desk. "Funny. If I didn't know better, I'd say this conversation is wearing a mask. Wouldn't you agree, Mr. Peterson?"

THE SILENT END

Ronald shrugged.

"But since this class is not a costume party, I'm going to recommend we return to *The Trial of Xerxes*. Now, Ms. Valdez, if you wouldn't mind…"

The heavy wood door to our classroom opened, and a small rake of a woman, an office administrator and wearer of floral dresses, Kathleen Walton, peeked her head in. Before her, nineteen students sat in stunned silence. Ajay passed a note to Ronald. Ronald opened it and nodded.

"Mrs. Duncan," Kathleen whispered. "Is everything all right?"

"Just fine, Kathleen," said Mrs. Duncan. "Thank you."

"Oh, good, good." The woman's voice was tiny and timid. "I just need to grab one of your students."

"Oh?" Mrs. Duncan's tired anger gave way to concern. "Well, grab away, I suppose."

Kathleen Walton looked directly at me. Her circular spectacles were caught up in her mousy, brown hair, and she smiled with a mouth full of lipstick stained teeth.

"Please come with me."

I pointed at myself. My heart quickened as Kathleen nodded.

Gus and Lexi gave me anxious glances as I got up and went toward the door.

"Kathleen," Mrs. Duncan said as I left. "Try to bring him back quick, okay? I don't want him missing too much."

"Okey dokey."

I followed her outside of the classroom. Kathleen walked at a brisk, administrative speed, and I made myself keep up as we passed by the opening of the Myers High cafeteria. It was almost deserted at this hour, with a couple of students with early break periods snacking and studying quietly at round, yellow tables.

"Is everything okay, Mrs. Walton?" I asked as we took to turn toward a corridor that led to the eastern portion of the building.

"Dean Veltry wants to see you."

"Dean Veltry?" I coughed. "But...did he say why?"

"No, sir. I'm just an office assistant. Knowing why isn't my business, truth be told."

"And he wants to see me now?"

Kathleen nodded vigorously as we entered the administrative end of Myers East, where most of the faculty offices were, including the office of the principle, a woman I'd never seen named Geraldine Masterson. Through sets of grubbed up, scabby windows, the ocean at Goon's Cove sizzled with green loam in the distance. The main hallway leading up to Dean Veltry's office contained various Myers High class photographs and trophies going back to the early 1900s. I'd only been down here once by accident during my sophomore year when I'd mistakenly been searching for Anders Gym for a team sports class. The photographs that lined the halls, I'd noticed at the time, were unusual not in their arrangement but because the class sizes tended to remain the same as the years went back. Maybe it was a few students larger in some years than others, but throughout, the number seemed fairly uniform from 1922 on, when the first gum-faced crew of rural Northwesterners posed before the camera. Now, as I hurriedly followed Kathleen down the corridor, I felt each set of tiny eyes trained on me, every tiny mouth spitting and whispering. A glass case filled with various trophies—mostly earned by our baseball team, which had fared well in regional championships until four years ago—twinkled where dust hadn't settled.

Dean Veltry's office door was overshadowed by a stone mantle.

THE SILENT END

Upon it, a wart-headed bust of Mickey the Bullfrog grinned down. Its veiny cheeks stretched, and its vocal sac puffed out. The door itself was made of wood with a fenced glass window upon which the words Dean Faustus Veltry were printed across it in black lettering. Kathleen Anderson toggled the knob, and as she opened the door, its bottom scraped against the carpet.

"Mr. Eberstark," I heard a heavy voice boom. "Please do come in."

ELEVEN

THE MAN WAS MASSIVE BEHIND his desk. Some people simply loomed above life in general, like they'd devoured a growth serum as children. Dean Veltry was one of those people. A gray-skinned mammoth with hair buzzed to a silver rind and ears that clung to the sides of his face as if frightened they'd fall off. He would have passed for a well-manicured corpse if he wasn't so muscular and well-shaved.

As he bellowed, "Welcome," his hairy-knuckled fist strangled a pen into scribbling down something on a notepad. He then looked up at me and smiled. One corner of his mouth went up higher than his left, and I could see that he was missing teeth in that side. The rest filmed over with a ghoulish yellow slime that altered the look of his sports jacket, silver tie, and French cuffs, all so meticulously assembled. "Please sit down."

"Is everything okay, Mr. Veltry?" I stammered as I sat on a narrow chair.

"Is everything okay?" The great man tapped his pen lightly against the notepad, and his steady, pale green eyes settled on me. "Why would you ask that?"

I swallowed. "You took me out of class, so I thought…"

"You thought you must be accused of wrongdoing?" The dean leaned forward from his leather backed chair as if to commiserate. Behind him was a wall filled with accreditations and photographs. It was as if each one were taunting me into believing there was nothing intimidating about this man at all. That he was just as typical as the rest of us. A community pillar with a family and a small rowboat with which he took his son fishing on Goon's Cove. Though he'd only moved here two years ago from who knew where, he seemed to have adjusted well. I never saw him around town, which I supposed was strange, but maybe he lived in one of those hill houses in the Upper Thicks? Surely, he hadn't set up in Crowstone? Pictures aside, the only thing I could handle examining was a letter opener on his desk. Its head was a bronze likeness of Mickey the Bullfrog and had the letters T.H.M. below it in cursive.

"I'm not going to fault you for your assumptions." The dean still tapped his pen. "But you do know more than you lead on, Mr. Eberstark. I've come to understand that about you."

I realized I'd begun holding my breath.

"Pretender, pretender, so young and tender…how I wish you saw what I see."

He paused and brought forth a file. My file. He opened what I imagined to be the record of my life at Myers High and scanned through three and half years of adequate to middling academic performance, contact information, complaints, teacher assessments, and maybe, just maybe, a paragraph or two about Mother's attempted suicide and subsequent disappearance. Fat, motherless, mediocre Eberstark, the file could have read. Sure to remain in Mossglow for life.

"The thing is." The dean looked up from the file. "You're not a bad student. You're not a bad student, but you're not a good one either. You just...flutter. Or that's what I like to call it. Flutter like a moth tied to a man's finger by a string." He stuck out his own pointer finger and aimed it at me for demonstration. "You fly a little bit, up or down, but all that someone need do is tug the line, and back you come. Do you catch my meaning?"

"I think so." There was a coldness in the room. I wondered if he kept it air-conditioned, which would have been bizarre for Mossglow, particularly at the beginning of what was always a frigid winter. But the temperature had to be degrees lower than in the rest of the school. I was dressed in one of the green wool sweaters Mother had knitted years ago, yet gooseflesh pimpled my arms. A small window to my left was filled with sea mist.

"Well, of course you do," he chuckled. "You think you know a lot of things. The truth, however..." He took his letter opener and held it forward. "Is that a flutterer will say anything to keep his wings a-flapping." He then took the letter opener and, without looking down, used it to unlock one of the desk drawers. He opened it and put the knife back on the table, along with his hands, which he laid flat upon the surface like strips of gray meat. "And that brings us to today. Why is it that you think you're here?"

I looked down at my lap. I didn't know how to answer, still holding out on the possibility that maybe I'd be accused of something I could easily brush off with a fabricated note from Father.

"Silence is a smart answer. But again, it's a natural tendency people like you have. Flutterers possess unintentional avoidance mechanisms."

My mouth was dry. I was close to freezing now even if I could feel no direct breeze on my skin. Most distressing of all, the cut on my arm from the previous night, while healing up quietly to the point of being forgotten until now, began to crackle with an evil kind of pain. I put my hand to it and began to rub.

"Chilly?" he asked thoughtfully. "The weather here grows frosty sometimes, but I don't notice. People think I'm strange, but I'm only from a very cold place. Before I moved to Mossglow, I lived in a land of snow. Have you ever been in a blizzard?"

I shook my head.

"No, no. You don't look like you have. You were reared in the rain." He kneaded his fingers together. "Anyhow, the reason why you're here is quite simple, Mr. Eberstark. It seems as if yesterday, you were absent from quite a few of your classes. Is that correct?"

He closed my file and exhaled through his nostrils.

"I wasn't feeling well. I had a stomach virus, I think. I spent the entire day in the bathroom."

"Well, that's understandable." He regarded me with a thoughtful deliberation. "Although you should have gone to the nurse."

"Yes." I wanted to rub my shoulders for warmth but refrained. "I won't cut out like that again. I promise."

"A promise is all I can ask for, Mr. Eberstark. A guarantee that as long as you're the responsibility of Myers High that you'll respect its rules."

"I won't."

"You won't?"

"I mean, I will. I will respect its rules."

The dean smiled. He then gestured with one mighty arm as if I should get up. I did so, easing up out of the chair and toward the door.

"Just one second, Mr. Eberstark."

I turned around.

In his hand was the sheet of paper the Hat had dropped by the hedgerow yesterday. The same message, though dirty and water damaged, still clearly read:

Mr. Blue can see you in the mirror.

Dean Veltry's face had gone blank. Or maybe that's just how I saw it. My gaze fixed on the paper in his hand. The Hat's red penmanship seeping into it like blood. I was so cold now I thought I'd exhale steam.

"I forgot to ask you about what I found yesterday." He shook the paper. "Out near the hedgerow."

He didn't wait for me to respond.

"It almost escaped my mind. Can you imagine that?"

"Dean Veltry?"

"I don't believe I asked you to speak yet, Mr. Eberstark."

"I'm sorry."

The dean frowned.

"What are you sorry for? Are you sorry because you wrote this note? Or because you spoke out of turn?"

"I've never seen that note before, sir." I tried to keep as calm as I could.

"You haven't?" The dean appeared coy. "If that isn't a funny thing. Well then, perhaps you can aid me in translating it then. Because I can't seem to figure it out on my own, and you are a student here after all, familiar with the local customs. As you might not know, I've only been here for two years. And I'm still adjusting." He shrugged.

THE SILENT END

"Mr. Blue can see you in the mirror." He put an emphasis on "mirror." "Now, what do you think that means?"

"I don't know, sir." I was somewhere between standing and sitting. "I swear, I don't."

"You seem so nervous. And all I'm asking you for is an opinion. But then again, sometimes it's good to be nervous. Especially when there's good reason. Do you have good reason to be nervous, Mr. Eberstark?"

"No, sir. And I don't."

"You know...I thought I saw someone that looked like you yesterday. Outside by the hedgerow. You and someone else. A man, perhaps. An adult in a suit. All while you were supposed to be expelling your innards in the bathroom."

He looked at me with a huntsman's gaze.

"You can sit down again." I did.

"I don't know who you saw." I thought I might have even said that confidently. "But it wasn't me. I was so sick I could barely walk."

The dean's lips curled.

"Well, of course there's always a margin for error. Why in the world would you, Mr. Eberstark, average student and infrequent diarrheic, be involved in any variation of malfeasance? I suppose it's possible that I'm just growing old. My eyes aren't what they used to be. And well, haven't you found it true that we're subject to seeing things that aren't there at all when it gets cold here in the winter? Things like you, standing in the rain. Am I correct in this assertion?"

"Yes, sir." I nodded. "You are."

"Good boy. Because I can tell you. Words like these..." He crumpled the Hat's paper into his hand. "Are nothing if not dangerous. Sometimes, what a person writes can have more of an effect than what he intended. A person's words can hurt people, Eberstark. A person's words can lead to blood. I would thus recommend…" His tongue went across the top of his teeth. "That you stay away from them. For your own good. A flutterer doesn't know that it can't get away, you see. It doesn't know that anytime the finger wants, it can drag the poor, disgusting insect into its hand and." He tightened his fist around the crumpled paper and smiled.

My vision felt blurry. Behind Dean Veltry, his shadow seemed to stretch long, growing into some creature of barbaric proportions that, a second later, receded. Then remained just the man, the massive man in his tiny chair behind his desk. The room even seemed to grow warmer, and my cut ceased to burn.

"That will be enough for now, Mr. Eberstark." The dean seemed farther away, concentrating on paperwork on his desk. "You can go now."

My legs wobbled. I edged out of the chair and felt like stumbling. I took slow, solid strides toward the dean's door and opened it as quickly as I could.

TWELVE

"WHAT THE HELL HAPPENED TO you?" asked Gus.

He'd caught me in the hallway on the way to Mr. Kraft's class. I must have looked awful because he went on to say, "You look fucking awful."

I stared at him and scratched my head. It was as if the dean had reached inside my body and disarranged a piece or three. For the first time in a long while, I actually thought about running straight home and telling Father everything that had happened. The impulse was so strong that I came a beat away from bursting into a sprint. Then I looked at Gus and decided I wasn't ready yet. "The dean…he just wanted to know why I was absent yesterday. When I was sick. It's no big deal."

"No big deal?" Gus, now that I had a chance to take him in, looked awful himself. His eyes, typically electrified with thought, were quiet. Though he had begun to go preemptively gray to a very small degree near his sideburns for a year now, since last night, I could have sworn the silver had snaked up the sides of his head. They'd frayed a bit, giving him the appearance of a mad professor.

"Good," he then said, looking left and right over his shoulders. "So you won't have any problems doing it again, right?"

"Doing what again?"

"Skipping class."

"Are you kidding me?"

"I know, I know, I never do this sort of thing. But there's something I've got to show you."

"I just got reamed for puking my guts out."

"Eberstark." Gus grabbed my shoulders and gripped. His nails dug into my skin. "I *need* to show you this. I don't want to. I don't like that I have to. But I must. I promise that I'll get you out of trouble with Dean Veltry. I'll take responsibility—I'll say I kidnapped you, for shit's sake. Please, just trust me on this one."

Gus Mustus didn't look like his normal self. The friend I knew smirked at superstition and made an art of naysaying. He wasn't against having a safe sort of fun. But ducking out of school? This I'd never seen before.

"Okay, Gus." I cringed, feeling like the two of us had for a minute switched brains. "But just one class."

Gus looked at me with the most genuine expressions of thankfulness I'd ever seen on him. It was almost ecstatic.

We headed to the club and student group offices in Myers West, a narrow hallway with five tiny rooms, some of which were shared depending on the size of the organizations occupying them. Since a few students were still trickling into their classrooms for second period, we didn't look out of place. Gus took out the key he'd been given to administrate the official Sword Star Society and scrambled open the door.

We met here every Friday, and tomorrow would be the last gathering before the tournament. Because of this, the tiny office space we'd been allotted, one small, yellow-walled room with a desk, file cabinet, and a bulletin board covered with Sword Star posters and tournament promotional materials, was now overrun with figurines and battle cover that would be used in the regional competition. Our room was also co-opted by Ronald Peterson's under-attended Manga Society, but since that only claimed two members for itself apart from the founder, Sword Star maintained majority rule.

Ajay's Night Lorque Squadron had already been assembled in epic formation upon a military bunker we'd built from paper mache and synthetic grass, flack, spray paint, and modeling sand. Designed to guard against enemy fire in style, we were proud of how it turned out. As of now, it sat on top of a box of printer paper in the corner as to stay out of harm's way. I was happy to admit Ajay's contributions to the project had rendered the scene worthy of snagging a Feral Dagger Prize. The amount of detail he'd put in was remarkable, and the fact that I'd be able to actually use it in play drew me away from my worries for a second. Each of the three squadrons he'd painted with an Aquadoom base and finished with highlights of Slimegrind Orange and Gunmetal. Since the Lorques themselves, as those who had envisioned the game wrote in the *Sword Star Origin's Handbook*, were disbanded from the Imperial Strand for their betrayal against the crown, Ajay had carefully applied stickers onto their field armor suits that featured anti-Imperium slogans he'd cooked up in Photoshop. One flag bearer even had a purposely distressed scroll that read *Storikhan's Bane* (a slogan mocking the Viceroy Paladin's illegitimate heir) in letters that looked like they had been painted with fire. Ajay was indeed the most creative of all of us. Though he talked about studying science or some shit when he got to college, he kept an impressive sketchbook filled with his Sword Star fan art. Gus was almost as good as him at figure painting and they'd become competitive. I, on the other hand, weighed in at about the same skill level as Ronald, who could be counted on to make his figurines look like animal scat.

Gus stuck his head into the hallway to see if anyone had followed us and, confirming no one had, closed the door and locked it. He was sweating to the point where dark patches soiled the armpits of his polo shirt. He took his backpack and delicately placed it on a chair.

"Okay," he said, taking a deep breath. "Are you ready?"

"For what?" I noted that Gus's fingers trembled as they gripped the sides of his backpack. In the quiet, as I waited, I thought I heard tiny noises. *Tck. Tchk. Thuk.*

"I'm not exactly sure," Gus said. "I can't understand it myself although I've been trying. All night. Thinking. Wondering. The whole thing—yesterday, now—it's all so absurd. Like someone is manipulating us, you know? Like something got dug up, and whoever's responsible put the shovel in our hands and walked away laughing. Do you know what I mean?"

"Show me," I said flatly.

Gus unzipped his backpack and took up the plastic Sword Star figurine case he'd been using to carry around his Demigods. All of the six spaces were empty save for one. The fourth from the end. Inside it, all I saw was Gus's Crow Seraph. The figure he'd spent weeks under a magnifying glass attempting to perfect. Its armor, two sets of bio-metallic wings attached to a triangular breast plate, rose up in triumphant arcs. The left hand held a flaming sword and the right a plasma pistol. The helmet was a series of plumes stemming from a small crown that cascaded behind its body and came together to resemble tail feathers at its back. Gus had painted it a dynamic combination of Tesla Blue, Blood Mahogany 2, and Slimegrind Orange, using the Bonecrusher White he'd gotten from Lexi for highlights.

At first, I just gazed at it with typical envy and admiration until I noticed something very wrong with my eyes. What they wanted to see was that the Crow Seraph was moving. And not only did they want to see that it was moving, they wanted to see that it was animated in every sense. That its tiny arms and legs were beating against the sides of the cage that held it. That its plumes swished and that its wings moved up and down with its shoulders, snapping against the plastic.

"Gus," I said as the little, scab-faced figure jabbed at its prison over and over again. *Tck. Tchk. Thuk*, like I'd heard earlier. "You've got three seconds to tell me what that is."

"Exactly."

"Did you find it?"

"Find it? I didn't *find* anything, Eberstark."

"But then, how?"

Gus sighed. "When I got home, my parents scolded me for an hour about how irresponsible I'd been."

"Where did you tell them you were?"

"I said that we got caught up preparing for the tournament at school. They weren't happy, but anything beats thinking you're son is involved in some sort of monster transport service."

"Anyway."

"So I went upstairs to my room, and the first thing I did—or maybe it was the second thing, I can't remember, my mind was batshit—was take the…whatever it was out of my backpack. The blue stuff. The stuff I took from…inside it." He quavered.

The Murje, I thought, thinking of what Father had referred to it as. But I chose not to say anything to Gus. I wanted to but couldn't imagine how to approach it without setting loose a host of other lies.

"Most of it had already gone gray by the time we got back. As if it had died or gone bad. There was a little bit of it that looked like it was still blue and healthy though, so I took my pen, scooped that bit out of the case, and put it under my magnifying glass."

"What did you see?" I remembered how Father had activated the mirror. How I heard what could have been little voices squeal and scream.

"What I saw." He laughed hoarsely. "What I saw…"

I noted that for the first time in our history as friends that Gus was genuinely at a loss for words, that he was coming apart. Seeing it frightened me. I knew the look. I'd had it on my face when I found Mother in the hallway. When blood swirled down the shower drain into the rusty pipes.

"It's okay." I tried to sound nonchalant. It seemed to calm him down. "You can tell me."

"Well." I could sense he didn't want to say what was on his mind. "It looked like…it was full of tiny people."

"Tiny people?"

"Or something like people. Each one of…whatever they were was less than a centimeter tall. Most were hairless, and they all had these eyes. All black. Like an insect's. And they were suffocating, Eberstark. They were dying right in front of me. Screaming. Holding their throats, gasping…like there wasn't any air. Then, they just kind of fell apart under the magnifying glass. Their bodies opened up, and their insides spilled out. Their organs…"

"Their organs?"

"Yes. That's what makes them go gray, I think. Their insides, they're like chunks of mud. And when the bodies fall apart, their skin turns gray. Or I think that's what happens. I can't be sure. It was the most horrible thing I've ever seen. To think that the monster is filled with thousands, even millions of them... What does it even mean? What are they? Aliens? I hope they aren't fucking aliens."

"I don't know what they are."

"Anyway. The next morning, I woke up and there it was. My Crow Seraph, hitting its sword against the case on my nightstand."

"But...how?"

"Does it look like I know how? I think, *think*, mind you, that some of the blue stuff might have gotten onto the figurine when I was putting it in the case. And that somehow, just coming into contact with it caused some sort of...reaction."

"So." I bent down to look at the Crow Seraph. For all intents and purposes, it appeared to have truly been brought to life. Its eyes didn't blink, and its mouth hung open in a silent cry, but its arms and legs moved with deliberation. Even the wings bent like wings. "Whatever this...stuff is, it brought your Demigod..."

"To life."

I let the words sink in.

"But your pen touched it too," I said. "Wouldn't that mean something would happen to it as well?"

"How am I supposed to know, man? Maybe it only works on certain things."

"But why?"

"You keep on asking that..." He chuckled. "I guess there was one more thing. Do you want to hear it?"

"What do you think?"

"I'm almost afraid to tell you." Gus closed his eyes a little. "When I fell asleep, I had this bizarre dream. It couldn't have been for more than an hour. I was up most of the night thinking, you see. Thinking, thinking, about the monster, about those things under the magnifying glass. Watching them turn inside out. I knew I needed to calm myself down, so I took a roll of toilet paper, wiped them up, and flushed them down the toilet."

"You just flushed them down the fucking toilet?" I was inexplicably angry.

"What the hell was I supposed to do? Let my parents find them? You know my mom *and* my dad inspect my room regularly for the drugs I never do?"

"I'm sorry."

"So after that, I went downstairs, got some cereal, and watched a couple episodes of Sword Star Prime."

"I still need to see that."

"It's got some issues, but all in all, it's pretty good. Anyway, I felt a little better afterwards. Felt like I might be able to get some sleep. So I ended up going back upstairs. I tried to pretend like nothing had happened. I fell asleep. But when I did, I had a dream."

His knees shook.

"There was this man in it. This man I'd never seen before. He looked like a movie star or something. Real good looking but in this weird, plastic way. His skin…it was so white. Almost albino white, but he had this black wig on. And perfect teeth. I remember it all so well. When he moved his mouth to talk, I kind of got the sensation that he wasn't even a man at all. But like he was wearing a man suit. And his eyes. They were filled with something dark…something I wanted to run away from."

I thought of the conversation I'd had the previous night with Father. "What did he say to you?"

"Nothing I can remember clearly." I could tell Gus was putting pressure on his brain. "I just know that I tried to get away from him, but wherever I went, there he was. Like he was attached to my back. I got so scared that he was going to open me up and take something out. Devour the rest. He started to reach for my stomach, and I must have called out for help because in my dream, there it was…"

"There what was?" I saw he'd gone quiet. "There what was, Gus?"

"The Crow Seraph." He went glassy-eyed, as if the memory were so vivid he were seeing it play out again in front of him. "It dropped down from the sky like some sort of god. It was just huge. And its sword was on fire."

I imagined the scene and my skin prickled.

"It and the man, they started fighting. I can't remember how they did it. Or with what. Maybe the man had a knife. Or a club. But whatever they were doing, the sound of it forced my eyes open. And that's when I saw it. The Crow Seraph, tapping against the plastic. At first, I thought I was crazy. To tell you the truth, I still think I'm crazy. There isn't anything in this world that can explain what's happening here. I feel so completely out of my mind."

"That makes two of us." I wondered why Mother's charm bracelet, which had been in the creature's mouth, hadn't taken on a similar affectation.

"I suppose that makes me feel better."

"Look at that thing go." The tireless Crow Seraph beat its blade against the plastic over and over again.

Gus rubbed his temples. "It's almost as if it's been growing stronger as the day goes on."

"We should show this to Lexi."

"I don't know, Eberstark. Lexi's tough, but I wonder if we should tell someone else about this. Someone who can really help. What if people start getting hurt? That thing is still sitting in a cave. What if it wakes up? What if it's dangerous?"

"No," I hissed, surprised at how vapid my reaction was. "We can't, Gus. Who would we tell? Your dad?"

"Maybe. Or yours."

"No. No dads. No moms. No siblings. Just friends. Just *us*. We don't know if this is anything to worry about. What if we're guarding a secret that *needs* to be kept?"

"Doesn't it seem like we'd be in deeper shit if we kept it a secret and it gets out?"

"I don't know, and I don't want to know. Far as I'm concerned, maybe we should just forget about this whole thing. Pretend it didn't happen? That sounds better than spreading the news around town and dragging everyone into our business. You know people here don't like to remember things. And they like to hear about them even less. They'll think we're loons."

"We are loons." Gus chuckled and pointed toward the Crow Seraph. "What am I going to do with this thing then? Put it in my closet and forget it exists?"

"Or destroy it. Let's ask Lexi what she thinks."

"Of course. Ask Lexi. Ask Lexi because we can't think for ourselves."

"I didn't mean it that way."

"Sure you did. You worship that girl whether you're willing to admit it or not."

"That's not true."

The next time Gus laughed, it sounded maniacal.

"Look, Eberstark. This is my last year at Myers High." He pointed at his chest. "If I can just get through it, I'll be able to leave this piss trough of a town and actually do something with my life. Not that you'd understand that. Being that you seem perfectly fine just ignoring your problems until they go away. Even if they never will. Maybe because you don't give a shit about your future."

"You're the one who asked me to skip class."

"You have no self-worth since your mother disappeared." He shook his head and closed his eyes. "You've been tragic. Everything is someone else's fault and, well, you're in a rut, man."

I felt pressure in my temples. I lived in a world where wrong had become the new normal. I kept secrets from everyone I knew. So many secrets, in fact, that there'd come to be more of them than truths. Was that way of life, built on trying to tilt untiltable scales, built on endangering those around me to save my own ass, sustainable?

"I'm sorry," said Gus, rubbing his forehead. "I didn't mean to unleash like that. Something's wrong with my head."

"No. It's my fault. I should tell you…" I felt like vomiting as I tried to force the truth out. "I haven't been…I haven't been completely hon—"

We turned as the Crow Seraph figurine, in a surge of strength, threw its body into the plastic, and the entire case clanged to the ground, the top flying off. Gus sucked in breath, and I shrieked.

"Get it!" Gus leaped after the tiny body as it scampered around the room, holding its sword over its head. I dove toward it and missed by a wide margin, smacking into the linoleum.

"Corner it," I yelled.

The Crow Seraph, no more than two inches tall, was backing against the wall with its sword drawn up in defense. It looked back and forth between the two of us with its empty eyes.

"One." Gus whispered as he crouched towards it.

"Two." I followed him.

"Three!"

We both dove. The figurine jumped away from Gus but, using its tiny sword, it stabbed my palm almost through to the other side. The pain was quick and awful, and there was an immediate flash of blood. I yelped.

"Okay." Gus was trying to think quick. "Get me that bucket." He pointed to a bucket filled halfway with modeling sand on the desk. I gripped it with my bloody hand.

The Crow Seraph had jumped onto the bunker holding Ajay's squadron and, in a bizarre display, began combatting the Night Lorques as if they were living foes. Scores of them plopped to the ground. Gatling guns and laser cannons came to pieces. Folding its wings into its back, it then scaled the bunker, reached the top, and carved a gash in the paper mache before disappearing inside.

"It's trapped," Gus said. "All we have to do is wait for it to come out the other side."

We crouched on the ground, Gus on one side and me on the other. My hand was now dripping blood and I wrapped the sweater sleeve over it. We heard a little rustling sound from inside the bunker and followed it to the best of our ability. All went silent for a second until the Crow Seraph burst through the bunker wall and sprinted toward the door.

"Get it!" Gus yelled.

But it was too late. The Crow Seraph slid underneath the tiny crack beneath the door and out into the hallway. Gus looked at me in sweaty alarm. His hair rose in curls.

"Come on," he growled.

We burst out the door of the Sword Star office and found that the Crow Seraph had already disappeared. There were only two ways it could have gone: down one end of the hallway or the other. Gus and I nodded at each other. We knew what to do. He took off down in one direction and I, taking a deep breath, found myself running toward Myers West. I rounded the bend and didn't see anything but paint-flacked old lockers. I squeezed my hand into my sweater, applying pressure as I ran. Thankfully, the hallway was empty, so I continued huffing around corner after corner, twisting aimlessly. I then found a set of stairs and flew down them, starting to lose hope. But as I got to the end of the stairs and looked up, I found a different kind of beast entirely than the Crow Seraph. Something that filled me with far more dread. Something with pigtails and a wide, protruding gut that grinned. "Well, what in the shit do we have here?"

THIRTEEN

CHARLENE POUGHKEEPSIE.
She stood like a living monument to all of my problems. Her expression was so placid it added a dimension of sadism to the deeds I already knew she was guilty of. Due to my avoidance tactics, I had never seen her this close before. From far away, I imagined her eyes as beady, downturned, and white-less and her mouth as filled with teeth so chipped they looked like tiny knives. But now that she was right in front of me, I found she wasn't as diabolical as I'd imagined. In fact, what I saw now was far, far worse. That she was a person, just like me.

She wasn't as tall as I'd assumed. She was just big. Round and solid. Her pigtails still stretched her hair back painfully in the way they had when I saw her boarding the bus. They pulled up the sides of her forehead, making her face look stretched and unhealthy; her cheeks had acne, and a long-healed scar twisted into her chin. It wasn't until she smiled that I saw why I and so many were truly frightened of Charlene Poughkeepsie. It wasn't that her teeth were serrated. It was that she felt delight when others squirm. Just seeing me cower in gape-eyed surprise brought her such unbridled glee that she nearly whinnied.

"I'm sorry," I huffed and tried to continue running. "I didn't mean to bother you."

"Too late for that." Charlene's rictus thinned as she caught me with her bear paw of a hand and gently pushed me back toward the stairs.

I heard snickering and noticed now that next to her, standing in a loose posture, was her cohort, Joe Ross, aka Mogadishu, and behind him, leaning against a locker, was Jesse Maroon, grinning ear to ear. It appeared as if the three of them were heading toward the double doors that led to the smokers' hill, and in my great luck, I'd happened to intercept them.

Jesse looked thrilled to have run into me. He was a sallow-eyed kid no taller than Lexi, and his body was a knobby, pinkish pole of flesh that finished in a crew cut. His jaw looked a little too simian. Unlike Charlene, there was no daylight between Jesse's physical appearance and his personality. He was one of those people who just looked like he had been built to make pain. He, Joe, and Charlene were dressed similarly; Jesse had just recently begun to hang out with the duo, and wore a cheap brown track suit with the zipper undone so that a white tank and silver chain were exposed. Joe wore a track suit too, but his was red like Charlene's, and he had a black tee shirt underneath.

"Hey?" Joe Ross, AKA Mogadishu, said. "Aren't you that kid... don't your dad own Stumart?"

His mouth was big and buck-toothed. Joe, like Charlene, also lived in Crowstone Heights, the son of a now defunct mining family that had lapsed into poverty in recent years, and his teeth were an offshoot of that: crooked, and unkempt.

"Y-yeah," I stuttered. "It's my dad's shop."

"Y-y-y-yeah," Jesse Maroon mimicked, standing between Charlene and Joe. "M-m-m-m-my name's Eberstark and I c-c-can't t-t-t-t-talk straight."

Charlene Poughkeepsie put her arm around Jesse's neck in a mock choke hold.

"All right, all right," she said with good humor. "Let's not frighten our friend here. This is Myers High, and he's got rights just like anyone else."

Joe looked at her bewildered, as if trying to understand the meaning of "rights."

"You know, Eberstark. Up in Crowstone, your dad's got a reputation for snobbery."

"He does?"

"Oh yes." Charlene cracked her knuckles. "Whenever one of ours comes down to the Main Drive to buy some fancy shit your dad imports, he treats us like we're stupid. Like we've never seen a fucking taco before."

"I've eaten tacos," said Joe, rubbing at his bald head. "Chinese noodles too."

Charlene sighed. "Anyway. I just thought I'd ask you about that. And some other things since we've run into each other."

"I...I don't know anything about that. My dad hasn't worked at the shop in a while. I'll make sure it doesn't happen again."

Charlene's eyes brightened. "Really? Well, problem solved I guess." She clapped me on the back. "Okay?"

"Okay." I tried to smile.

"No, not okay," said Jesse, his face flush with excitement.

"What, Jesse?" said Charlene in mock surprise. "Why not?"

"Oh, I don't know. That wasn't enough of an apology for me. And not just that, but you've been running up a record in the shithead department. Aren't you ditching class right now, E-E-E-Eberstark?" He came close to my face. I could see the painful-looking grind of his overbite and smell onions and nicotine on his breath.

"I wasn't feeling good."

"See, he's not feeling good," said Charlene. "Let's just get out of here, Jesse."

"Yeah, I would," said Jesse. "I really would. But unfortunately, I don't believe a word coming out of this toad-fucker's mouth."

"I'm kind of hungry," said Joe.

"Hold your fucking horses," said Charlene. "So wait, Jesse, you don't believe what Eberstark here is saying to you?"

"Fuck no, man. You know why? 'Cause I've seen this guy doing the sickest shit in the world."

"Oh, dear lord." Charlene threw her hands into the air. "Like what?"

"Like him 'n that black bitch, what's his name?" Jesse put his finger to his chin. "That's right. Gus Mustus."

"Oh, yep." Charlene nodded. "Yep. I think I've seen him before."

"Well, I've seen him too unfortunately. I've seen him real close up."

"How close up?"

"So close that I could see him slobber when he was sucking on Eberstark's rocket pop in the bathroom yesterday."

I gasped.

"You did?" said Charlene. "Holy shit, Jesse. Well, if that just isn't disgusting." She turned to me and put her hands on her hips, mimicking a worried mother if that mother had been dispatched from a sect of devil worshipers. "Now, just who do you think you are, Eberstark? Going all faggot on us like that?"

"But that's not true." My body went rigid. "I was sick, and Gus… Gus is just my friend."

"And you say you're sick now too, huh?" Jesse Maroon's face was enraged. "But you're here now, aren't you? Looking healthy as can be."

"He does have a point, Eberstark." Charlene's smile grew larger and larger until it truly did look monstrous.

"But when? How? I swear, Charlene, he's lying."

"Don't you dare accuse me of lying, faggot."

Joe was whooping hysterically, and Charlene, with dark satisfaction, had to stop herself from joining him.

"Thing is," she said. "Is that I don't know you, Eberstark. But I do know Jesse. And if Jesse said that black faggot was sucking your dick in the bathroom, then I'm inclined to believe him. I mean, we're not talking science here."

"But I swear." I was struggling to breathe. It was if I could already feel their fists and feet on me. "We're just friends. Please."

"Oh man." Now Charlene truly laughed. It was a rich and boastful sound. "If only I could make my problems go away by asking nice." She stepped closer so that I could almost see inside that dark mouth of hers. Breath redolent of cigarettes and fast food, maybe bacon cheeseburgers, filled my nostrils. "But here's the thing. If you are a faggot, then something's got to be done. You've got to bleed for what you believe. And if what you believe in is sucking cock, then you're going to have to bleed a lot. Call it a homo tax."

"Yeah, bitch." Jesse yelled over her shoulder.

"Money money," said Joe.

"You're name is Eberstark—that's cause you're a Jew or something, right?" said Charlene.

"Must be," said Jesse. "Cocksucker's dad owns a store. And probably everything else in town."

"Now, now, Jesse, let's not stereotype." Charlene wagged a finger before she convulsed back into laughter. "Oh, man." She wiped tears from her eyes. "I can't believe I just said that."

"Jews always got money," said Jesse. "Even when they don't."

"He'll pay one way or another. Especially after this story makes its rounds." Charlene's face contorted all of a sudden as her tiny ear caught a sound approaching from the top of the stairs. The sound of clicking heels coming down the hall.

She began backing away.

"What's up, Charlene?" said Jesse.

"Not now." Charlene nodded toward the sound. Joe Ross caught on, uttering, "Wu oh."

"We'll catch up with you later, Eberstark." Charlene trotted off and pushed open the doors into a light rain.

As Jesse Maroon followed her, he turned his neck and smiled. "Oink, oink."

I heaved with relief, my back against the locker.

The sound of the footsteps neared and eventually turned into a pair of stout legs in green wool warmers, followed by a knee-length skirt, blouse, and yellow cardigan.

"Mr. Eberstark?" Mrs. Duncan said, coming to a halt at the top of the stairs. "Is that you?"

"…Hi, Mrs. Duncan."

"Aren't you supposed to be in Mr. Kraft's class?" She came down to the bottom step to face me. Her eyes, like periscopes underneath her thick-framed glasses, searched me up and down.

"I was just going to the bathroom." I tried to act calm.

Mrs. Duncan looked towards the double doors.

"Outside?"

"No. I mean, yeah. It's out of order in Myers East, so I went outside to come back in the western entrance to use the one over here."

"Oh?" She noted my sweater-covered hand, now wet with a dark brown stain. "I didn't know the bathroom was out of order. Did you…" she pointed toward my hand. "Have an accident?"

I shoved the hand in my pocket. "No, no accident. Just…I've got to go. Get back to class, you know. Trying to get those grades, like you said."

I ran past her and started up the stairs.

"Mr. Eberstark?" Mrs. Duncan called as I reached the top step. "Mr. Eberstark. Please don't go!"

But I didn't listen. I ran. Ran as tears burned my cheeks. Ran as my stomach swung before my waist. I ended up back at the club offices. Ours was now locked from the outside. Gus was nowhere to be seen, a lunatic figurine was loose in Myers High, and I felt utterly alone.

FOURTEEN

I SPENT THE REST OF THE day squirming through Myers High like an injured earthworm. My senses blared. Every corner I turned, my eyes tried to lurch ahead of me in search of Jesse, Charlene, Joe, Dean Veltry; the world was becoming small and claustrophobic. At one point, I decided to cross the courtyard from Myers East to Myers West so I could make it from the cafeteria to Mrs. Adams' European History class. The air was crisp, and only one other student, a short, lonely boy wearing a doubledown coat, walked apace in the opposite direction. He looked up at me with shaken eyes that seemed to immediately regret the contact.

The second I got back inside, I skulked out of sight, head low, back bent under the weight of a book-filled backpack. I wanted to be invisible, I decided. I didn't want anyone to see me, not Mrs. Duncan, not Lexi, not even Gus. My stomach hurt, and my hand was wrapped in a mess of bloody paper towels and scotch tape I'd patched together in the computer lab in Myers East. I kept it in my pocket at all times so no one would think things amiss, but I knew I looked funny when I walked.

Myers High just didn't seem safe anymore. I didn't know what I'd done to incur the wrath of Jesse Maroon. I still held on to the hope that someone would expose the rumor as false before it truly began. If something like that took hold, the consequences would be disastrous. Mossglow wasn't what you would call a forward-thinking city. If you were singled out here, particularly for same-sex romance—a major infraction as far as many in the backwards Myers High student body were concerned, from teachers to students—then you'd never be able to live it down. When it came to townies especially, a fear of "fags" was commonplace. The whole thing pissed me off—they were a bunch of repressed rage heads with faulty brains. But it didn't matter if I didn't like how things were. If Gus and I were implicated in such a thing, particularly since he was black and I was Jewish (both of which were also unwelcome in Crowstone) we'd be doomed. *I should have just laughed the rumor off,* I thought now. I shouldn't have gotten so defensive. A deeper part of me suspected now that I'd have to start learning new ways to survive.

After 8th period, I decided to avoid Gus and the busses, hoisting my backpack over my shoulder and taking the long way home. I cut through the hedgerow to the faculty parking lots and moved along the chain-link fence that ran along its edge. On the way to the Thicks, I'd stop by Stumart for groceries, knowing that my rumbling stomach would come home to an empty refrigerator. As I made for downtown, I kept off Lectern Road, the main street leading into the business district, by treading a path few people knew about off the side through the trees.

Though walking briskly, I was still frightened that at any moment,

I'd be blown from the street by a nasty wind and never heard from again. My heart sank deeper into my chest, and my surroundings dimmed. Some trees kept their leaves, but others winter had shaken off. The gray sky turned a darker, bluer gray, and the mist thickened into slug-like shapes. I thought about Gus, Lexi, and Charlene Poughkeepsie. I thought about how escape was impossible when you had nowhere to go. I thought about Mother and how she'd tried to flee the ghoul in the mirror. I thought about where she was right now and how I'd probably end up just like her, lost and, for all I knew, lifeless. I'd put the bracelet in my pocket on my way out that morning, and now, my fingers traced a starfish charm. I missed her more than anything. All I wanted to do was wrap myself in her arms, cold and sad as they were, and feel my worries dissolve.

It was about 4:50 when I arrived at Stumart. Our store was open from 7 a.m. to 11 p.m. yearlong, and our perennial checkout employee and two-person team manager, Cory Bladenbelt, had his elbow on the register counter. He looked calm and a little bit bored as he flipped through a magazine filled with pictures of barbarians, spaceships, dinosaurs, robots, and mostly naked women.

"Yup," he said without turning his head as I hurried through the sliding doors. It was the same curt greeting he gave all Stumart customers.

"Hey, Cory."

"Shiiyiit." He snapped from his slouch as he saw who I was.

He looked almost impossibly thin, stoned of course, and his voice carried an unintentional petulance. Golden brown Jesus hair matched his goatee, and he lined his eyes with purple mascara. He liked to get high in the storage cooler, I knew, and tended to sit at the cash register most days, doling out orders to the other employee, a middle-aged woman named Cherry who had been working for us since before we changed names and corporate sponsorship. He did this without moving an inch so that he could play Cryocrabs on his cellphone. He wore his Stumart uniform with the top four buttons undone to expose a t-shirt with a faded Danzig insignia beneath and didn't seem overly thrilled with his life. But since I was the owner's son (and the owner himself hadn't been seen in months), he was nice to me.

"I didn't know you were coming by." He hid his magazine beside the register, which I didn't understand being that I probably would have liked it. "Grocery run?"

I snuffled something like a yes, not in the mood for talking. I walked past him toward the pharmacy, grabbed a box of extra-large Band-Aids and Neosporin, and drove my way toward the produce room where the employee toilets were.

"Well, don't let me stop you," he said as I threw open the doors.

In the bathroom, I washed my hand over and over again; the wound was a few centimeters deep and a little jagged, but the bleeding had stopped. I applied Neosporin and covered that with a large, purple Band-Aid. I then rolled up the cuff of my sweater to conceal the stain and groomed myself before the mirror, attempting to remove the glaze of self-pity from my face. A few minutes later, I went back into the store to load up groceries for the night.

Tortilla chips, bean dip, a half-gallon of skim milk, string cheese, jumbo-sized Kit Kats, a microwave turkey dinner, three cans of chili, one of chicken soup, and one of stewed peaches because I didn't like how unhealthy my cart looked without it. Two boxes of instant mac and cheese and four sticks of beef jerky.

I took everything to Cory to ring up.

"You got yourself some stoner rations," he quipped lazily. He bobbed his head and shoulders to a song playing in the background, some super hit from the eighties.

I tried to force a few words past my frown. "You know how it is."

"Wish I didn't though." He swished his hair out of his eyes. "This damn Mossglow weather—I swear to God, can you name the last time you saw sun around here? And not just sun, you know, but real sun. Blue sky sun. Like what most people see in most parts of the world." He rang up my stewed peaches. "Sometimes, I feel like we're living in Hades and forgot we're dead."

"I think I know what you mean."

"All I want to do is get out of here, you know? Turn tail, load up the Geo Storm, and scoot on down the coast until I find the most global-warming-scorched, ozone-fucking-free part of America where I'll get skin cancer and die happy."

"Would you leave the kid alone," said Cherry. She came to stand beside Cory from her previous post, restocking cans of coconut milk in the International Foods aisle. She had an everyday kindness to her. Her curly, jet-black hair was still as buoyant now as ever. Her strong, sinewy arms clamored with a combination of wrinkles, moles, and freckles; faded rose and skull tattoos trailed up her right and left biceps and disappeared beneath the uniform. She wore three rings with dark, inset stones that looked heavy on her fingers. She began the familiar process of bagging by using long, red fingernails to snap the paper bottoms flat.

"What? I can't talk about the weather?" said Cory.

"Not like that you can't." Cherry puffed out a paper bag. "With your filthy mouth—you're the last things these kids need. And besides, it isn't that bad out here. Mossglow has its positives and negatives."

"Name one."

"Name one what?"

"A positive," said Cory. "Name one."

"All right. It's quiet."

"Quiet? More like silent."

"Some people like silence."

"Yeah. Corpses."

"You're just a crybaby. A dirty-bearded study in scared. Sitting here telling the son of your *boss* about how crappy the town they set up shop in is. You should be so lucky."

"Come on, Cherry." Cory looked genuinely contrite. "I'm just saying that the weather's shit around here, that's all. And that no one seems to notice it but me. It's not like I'm showing him how to cook meth."

"I wouldn't put it past you if you were."

"Oh, please."

"Well, don't you listen to this future welfare case," Cherry said, winking at me with a wrinkled eye. "He talks and talks, but does he go? Nope. He stays right here with his foot up his ass and his face in a bucket of ice cream."

"What the fuck?" yelled Cory, attracting gazes from customers.

"Keep it down."

"Whatever, man." Cory finished ringing up the rest of the groceries. "Like I don't get paid to be here."

I smelled the fresh scent of water on produce as a misting spray blew from nozzles along the vegetable aisle. The walls had been repainted before Mother disappeared and still retained a burnt umber hue the Stumart décor consultant explained tested well with consumers. The parking lot in front was visible through the sliding glass doors and storefront windows, and a few cars were beginning to slip into spots. Customers came through in the after work rush;

you could tell by their vehicles which part of town they were from. Each time someone entered, a pleasant doorbell ding was followed by an automated voice recording made by a soft-voiced male that said, "*Welcome to* Stumart. *Your right start.*" I barely noticed it anymore. Since we'd transferred ownership to the corporation, they'd streamlined everything from our décor and security system to our payroll and accounting. I was thankful for all of it being that Father couldn't be trusted to handle such things anymore.

"Get home quick." Cherry handed me the groceries.

Cory sucked his teeth. "'Cause it's going to get shittier than it already is."

I hauled a bag into each hand and went through the sliding doors. The second I got outside again, anxiety took hold.

I made for the edge of the parking lot toward Bedford Ave as fast my legs could manage without running. I could follow it on through the Lower Thicks and be home in twenty minutes. But as I walked, I heard voices shouting. I tried to ignore them and picked up speed. I got to the rear of the lot, and a roar filled my ears as in a flood of light, I came face to face with the Shepherd.

"Eberstark," Lexi said from the window as she screeched to a stop. Half of her body was hanging out of the truck, and exhaust engulfed her. She was dressed all in black like some sort of assassin. "Get in. We're going to the cave."

I shook my head. "I've got to get home."

I saw Gus throw open the passenger door. He hopped off the bedside rail onto the pavement. I was surprised to see him out and about town on another school night. But more than that, I was surprised at how much I wanted to be left alone.

"Where did you go?" He was limping a little.

THE SILENT END

I held up the grocery bags.

"Did you catch it?" he asked of the Crow Seraph.

"Didn't even see it."

"Me neither."

"I wish you guys would have waited for me," said Lexi.

"I ended up telling her." Gus pointed his thumb at Lexi.

"You're all set then." I began to walk away.

Gus stepped in front me.

"I need to get a little more of that stuff. The blue creatures. That's why we're going to the cave."

"We're going to study it," said Lexi calmly from the window.

"And try to find out what it wants."

"What it wants?" I reared to face them. "Are you crazy? How do you know it *wants* anything? No. I'm done with all of this. I'm heading home to stop being a shithead and finish reading that stupid book for Mrs. Duncan. Good luck."

Gus curled his fists and confronted me face to face.

"You of all people are going to abandon us now for…for fucking homework? Just a few hours ago, you were telling me we had to handle all of this ourselves. Stop and think about it for a second."

"We'll only be there for a few minutes," said Lexi. "An hour tops and we're home."

I dropped the groceries. A couple of cars drove past; I was sure at least one of them slowed down to eavesdrop. But I didn't care. I'd had enough.

"I'm done with this. I'm done with everything. I hate it here. I hate this store. I hate our school. I hate Sword Star. I hate fucking everything. And yet I know no matter what I do, I can't get away. So… I'm avoiding everyone. And there's nothing you can say to convince me otherwise."

Lexi frowned. "Why don't you give that another try?"

"You hate Sword Star?" Gus said, agog, seeming to have missed everything else.

"Good God, Gus," I sighed. "You know what I mean."

"But what if this is the key?"

"The key to what?"

"To what's happening in Mossglow?" he said. "I mean, what if everything's connected? The monster? The Crow Seraph?"

He paused.

"Your mother?"

"Don't talk about her."

Lexi looked at her lap.

"Since when do you care about this piss trough?" I yelled. "Because that's what it is, right? That's where I'm going to be for the rest of my life. If I even make it out of high school without two broken legs."

Lexi jumped out of the car, leaving the door swinging open. She came up to me, gave me a thoughtful, even pleasant smile. This before she wound up her left fist and punched me square in the nose.

"What the hell, Lexi?" said Gus.

"What happened to you today?" She stood over me. My nose throbbed, and blood splashed out. But she didn't care. Her eye was crystal clear. "I know you think you're going to have to face this alone. What's happening to us? But you're wrong. We're…We're…" She strained. "We're…friends now, Eberstark. And that means one thing." She bent down to my level and offered up her hand. The Shepherd's headlights drew a mustard yellow halo around her form, and her face went dark.

"When I ask you a question, you tell the truth."

FIFTEEN

ON THE WAY TO GOON'S Cove, I rehashed my encounter with Charlene Poughkeepsie and her crew to Gus and Lexi from the front seat, pausing occasionally to stuff tissues into my bloody nose. They were quiet the entire time. When I brought up the part about bathroom blowjobs, Lexi shook her head, and Gus began to brood. I felt as if I'd conjured a storm cloud inside the truck. When I finished, however, I realized I felt better. It felt good to have one less secret.

"That evil cow." Lexi gritted her teeth as she punched the Shepherd's accelerator with a chuffed, red Chuck Taylor. The tires kicked up grit from the road. "Like she isn't just a big dyke in disguise herself."

"You think she's a...she's a..." I said.

"Lesbian, Eberstark?" said Gus.

I nodded.

"It's not a dirty word, man," said Lexi. "But yeah, girl's in denial.

It's that family she comes from. Both her and Joe. Old Crowstone townie shit. Their families helped found this rust town, and they don't want anyone to forget it. Lay of the land around here. Sometimes, I wish my parents would have ditched this dung heap and gone to Portland instead, but no, they wanted something 'idyllic.'"

"Townies." Gus simmered. "I hate that word. As if the place you live in decides who you are."

"It goes further than that with them," said Lexi. "They don't call themselves townies because they feel defined by the town but because they feel like they own it. And they don't like other people trying to own it with them. Scary folk."

"Scary, homophobic folk," said Gus. "I hate how closed-minded people are around here."

"They can't stand anyone who can't trace their ancestry back to some fucking wagon-toting gold and silver prospector in the eighteen hundreds."

"Seems like you know a lot about Mossglow," I said.

"I guess I do." Lexi's tone was more forlorn than usual. "Since last night anyway."

"What do you mean?" Gus's interest piqued.

"I couldn't sleep. I was up real late. That monster…the cave…I guess I didn't really think about how crazy it all was until I got home. Then I took a shower, tried to go to bed. But I couldn't stop thinking about it."

Gus tossed me a furtive glance in the rearview from the back seat, where he was laying out a few things. A stainless steel metal container, a ladle, and a pair of gardening gloves.

"So what did you do?" He started putting the gloves on.

"I went online, like everyone does." She turned off the Shepherd's floodlights as we headed closer to Goon's Cove. She looked in her rearview to make sure no one was behind us, comforted by seeing nothing but pouring rain. "And I didn't stop until, God, it must have been five a.m. I'm surprised I made it to class."

"But you said you read about Mossglow?"

"Yes. And no. To be real, there's not a lot out there on the town's history. But after I exhausted half of YouTube's poisonous snakebite videos, I fished around. Read about Mossglow's founding—what I could find of it anyway. And that's when I started noticing coincidences in the names. Like Poughkeepsie, for instance, and Ross. Maroon wasn't there, but there might have been some inbreeding; who knows? Guy looks like the spawn of a couple of cousins. But Poughkeepsie and Ross, they come from mining families. Mining families whose wells ran dry a long time ago. Their great-great grandparents, though, they were richer than shit. They worked with Thomas Hellwidth Myers back after he founded the town."

"I thought he just founded the school?" I said. I thought of the statue of Mickey the Bullfrog and its dedication plaque.

"Along with other things," Lexi said. "I remember Mr. Kraft saying something about how you can trace most everything here back to him in some way or another. He was a New England entrepreneurs who went west in search of wealth. Pretty all around Renaissance man. Amateur scientist. Expert botanist."

"Botanist?" Gus said.

"Anyway. He named the town after an unusual type of moss, I guess, that glowed in the winter. Or so that's the story being that no one's seen anything like it in the last two hundred years. And that could be because of Myers himself. He was kind of a recluse, kept lids on things. Didn't like to answer questions. I guess he spent most of his time out of the public eye after he built the school and then just disappeared one day. After his wife committed suicide."

I blew a tissue wad out of my nose.

"I guess she took a boat out on Goon's Cove, tied a stone to her ankle, and drowned herself," Lexi said. "She suffered from mental illness, depression or schizophrenia. But again, there's not a lot of information available, so most of what you'll find online is guesswork. The town has a website, but it seems like it hasn't been maintained in years. It's like someone started working on it and then just forgot about it."

"Did you read about the disappearances?" asked Gus.

Lexi chuckled. "Come on, Gus," I said. "You say it like it's something people actually talk about."

"You're saying they don't?"

"No. Well, okay, people might 'disappear' sometimes, but that doesn't mean you'll read about it in the *Mossglow Sentry*."

"I hate to burst your bubble," said Lexi. "But if there's one thing that you can read about in terms of Mossglow, it's the disappearances. It seems like this shit's been happening for a while. No one around here talks about it in a serious way, and I'd be surprised if you didn't get blank stares if you brought it up, but if you look at local news reports over the last decade alone, it's there in plain sight."

"Maybe people are scared of what they'll notice once they start paying attention," grumbled Gus.

"I read a lot of articles where the reporter talked about repeated incidences of 'skipping town.' As if Mossglow was just a crappy little place and sometimes people picked up and left. But if we could get an exact number on the missing people in the last five years from the Lower Thicks alone, I'm thinking it would blow our minds."

"So...what?" I said. "You're saying my mother vanishing is part of some conspiracy?"

I couldn't actually believe that I'd mentioned Mother so brazenly. I rarely did so around Gus, and this was perhaps the second time ever in Lexi's presence.

"Maybe I am." Lexi popped another cigarette in her mouth. "But I don't know anything apart from what I've read. One thing you might find interesting though..." She cracked the window, blew smoke, and put the Shepherd into third gear. "Is that everyone I've read about thus far? All the people that went missing. They all had one thing in common."

"They were all from the Lowers?" I said.

"Nope. But all of them were women."

"Women?" said Gus.

"Every article I read. Sometimes a young one. Sometimes an old one. Sometimes a little girl. But a full-on female each. From what I can see, whatever's happening around here, is happening to women."

"That's insane," said Gus.. "Isn't it?"

Lexi smiled. "You're not afraid of losing your mind a little, are you?"

"More than anything else in the world, actually."

"And you really think all of this is connected?" I said. "Connected somehow to that thing in the cave?"

"I'm not saying I think anything's connected. What I am saying is that we need to stop willfully ignoring the truth. Accept that things are not normal around here. That something in Mossglow is deeply fucked. And that we're involved in figuring out why that is now whether we want to or not."

"I don't see why we can't just stay out of it," I said. "It's not our business, monsters and missing women. My mom, she..."

"Skipped town?" Lexi grinned.

"I was going to say that we don't have to come to Mossglow's rescue. If we just back off and stop panicking, it'll all…go away. And we can just finish up the school year in peace."

"Just like Charlene Poughkeepsie, Joe Ross, and Jesse Maroon will go away?"

"That's different."

"Like it or not, we're in this now. And not only are we in this, but whatever happens to one happens to all. And that's why I promise you right now that if that closeted bitch comes near you—and I'll *be* watching, I promise." She put her knife on the dash. "I will cut off her ear and make her eat it."

"Jesus, Lexi," said Gus. "A little much?"

She took a deep drag, sucking the tobacco down to the filter. She threw the stick shift into low gear as she went down a small incline leading to the grottos off Goon's Cove.

We drove into the cave where we'd stashed the beast as a hard rain came. Water pounded the windshield as we entered. The ground grew slick and muddy, and the Shepherd struggled through it. At one point, the engine stuttered, and Lexi warned that it could stall if she turned it off. We decided we should thus keep it running as we sloshed to a stop and turned on the floodlights. They spit out into the back of the cave as if we were miners ourselves.

Once safely inside, Lexi opened her door first and climbed down into a chilling wet. Because of the rain, what had before been a few inches of still water had now risen up to her knees. Her jeans were immediately soaked, and she winced from how cold it was. The downpour raged outside and ran over the mouth of the cave in a curtain of silver-brown. I looked through the windshield for the creature and realized it was no longer where we'd left it face-down on the cave floor. I heard what sounded like a heartbeat ...*Fump... Fump... Fump...* and looked for its source. Was there something on the walls? I thought I saw worm-like shapes in the dark.

It was as Gus prepared to get out of the truck that Lexi screamed.

"What happened?" He practically fell out of the old Bronco on the passenger side, picked himself up and crept around front, dripping with muddy water. I exited through the driver's side.

"What is it?" Lexi said. She was looking down at her feet. The water, as a result of the rain, had risen up to about halfway up the Shepherd's tires. At first, I thought that's what Lexi was looking at but soon noticed she was referring to something else entirely. Sloshing through the wet, I came to stand next to her. I felt something rubbery and hose-like catch my ankle. I would have tripped had Gus not appeared as if out of nowhere to steady me with a hand on my shoulder. Something was in the water. Or multiple somethings. Long, slippery strands of red that could have been confused for rotting rope if they hadn't been glowing. There were quite a few of them, running along the cavern floor, obscured by the black water. They looked almost intestinal and swished slowly around Lexi's feet. Gus bent down to examine them and saw that they rose out of the water and onto the shallow embankment toward the back of the cave.

"Come on." He took a Maglite out of his pea coat and held it over his head in a gloved hand. He shone it along the length of the organisms. Lexi lifted her legs delicately out of the water and began to follow.

"Eberstark," she ordered.

"That smell," said Gus. "Like bad fish."

"Just ignore it," said Lexi.

THE SILENT END

Gus's flashlight skittered about until it flashed upon sharp, oily teeth. The monster was slumped up against the very back of the cave, near the corridor I'd once tried to enter years ago. Had it moved itself here? The glowing, intestine-like organs, I soon realized, had actually erupted out of its wound, pushing aside the heavy blanket we'd shoved in there the other night. The pulse-like *fump* I'd heard earlier had originated from there. Between each beat the glow of the organs grew pinker before returning to bloody red. *Fump...Fump...Fump.* The creature's body had deflated from the feet to the upper abdomen as if it were losing air. Its eyes had flipped open, and two crazed pupils aimed toward the ceiling. The bony snout was slack, and the tongue drooped. Some of the metal shards were starting to sag from the flesh of its body and the light bulb, once flickering under the chin, had gone dark. Now, there seemed to be other subjects emerging from its skin. Pieces of what looked to be glass and...was it plastic? Collectively, it appeared even more malevolent now, like some half-starved demon that had been unable to crawl back to hell.

Gus's body quaked with fear. "What...what's happening to it?"

"I don't know," squeaked Lexi.

"Let's get out of here," I said. "Fuck the sample."

"Maybe you're right," said Gus.

"No." Lexi balled her hands into fists. "We should at least try."

Gus fumbled toward his back pocket. "Goddamnit."

Gripping a ladle in his gardening glove, he edged toward the creature. He licked his lips and averted his nose. Nearing the wound, he touched at it with the ladle. The creature seemed to be barely breathing. If you listened close enough, you could hear wheezing like wind through a keyhole.

"Wait," Lexi said just as Gus was about to slip the ladle in.

We heard a car door smack shut before the mouth of the cave. We couldn't see well with the Shepherd's lights in our eyes, and I panicked, running away from the monster to crouch behind the Bronco's front fender. A figure ambled through the mouth of the cave with its arms shielding its face against the rain. The vehicle it had gotten out of, a shadowy mound with its high beams on, sat outside in the mud.

"There's no way out," I rasped.

I saw that Lexi had taken out her knife and was edging toward the front of the cave.

The figure ambled toward us. It was wearing a hood. Gus was about to say something, but Lexi put a finger to her mouth. She then flourished the knife in front of the mystery vehicle's headlights so that the blade shone.

"Who are you?" she yelled. Her voice echoed back to her. "I've got a knife, and I'm not afraid to get blood on it."

But the figure didn't seem to care about Lexi's warning. Or perhaps it didn't hear over the rain and the rumble of the Shepherd's engine. Stumbling once or twice, it eventually found its footing and pulled back the hood. The face beneath huffed with exhaustion. Gus sucked in breath and shone the flashlight. "Mr. Mustus," we heard. "Would you please remove that damned light from my eyes?"

"Mrs…Duncan?" I said.

"Yes, Mrs. Duncan," our teacher said ruefully. She came to stand beside the Shepherd's taillights and looked around the cave. She was dressed in a long rain slicker buttoned up to her neck and wore a wool beanie to protect her heavy ringlets. Her giant eyes gave her away, alert like a barn owl's. "And I'd ask you to put that knife away as well, Ms. Navarro."

Lexi slipped the knife back into her pocket.

"Mrs. Duncan," Gus said. "Did you…"

"Follow you?" She caught her breath. "Of course I did. I've been tracking the lot of you since seventh period. One grows stupid if she refuses to recognize when it's necessary to disregard professional constraints. And you three convinced me today," she looked at me, "that something is disturbing your lives. Also, my Prius can virtually drive undetected. Unlike your smog-spewing Bronco, Ms. Navarro."

She looked around again, covering her mouth and coughing. The monster was still enshrouded in the darkness of the back of the cave. Mrs. Duncan didn't seem to have noticed the growths in the water.

"So what is it you're doing here?" she said before sneezing. "And don't tell me nothing. I heard your conversation in class today. Teenagers think they're so devious."

"We were exploring." Lexi turned toward me. "It was Eberstark's idea."

I bristled but didn't argue. "I dared Gus and Lexi to come out here with me because I'd heard there's a path at the back of the cave that goes deep under the city."

"A path that leads deep under the city, hmm? Sounds interesting. Always been a secret passage enthusiast myself. Shall we see if the rumor proves true?"

Mrs. Duncan began walking around the Shepherd.

"Your flashlight, Mr. Mustus?"

Gus warily handed her his Maglite. She started toward the back of the cave. Gus, Lexi, and I followed, knowing what was in store. We stepped out of Shepherd's protective fog lights and into darkness.

When Mrs. Duncan saw the beast, she dropped the flashlight to the ground and stood frozen in the dark. She didn't scream. She didn't even cry out. Instead, she slowly leaned down to pick up the Maglite and, with a deep breath, shone it back into the creature's direction, studying it in silence.

"So this is your secret," she whimpered after a long pause. The flashlight trembled in her hands. She leaned against the cave wall and, shining the flashlight over us one by one, quavered, "Okay, I'm listening."

With Mrs. Duncan standing before us, all bets were off. Together, the three of us were able to piece together the story of how we'd found the beast. I of course left out anything that could be drawn back to Father, including seeing him at the hedgerow before we were ambushed by Dean Veltry.

Mrs. Duncan, maintaining her composure, listened quietly, pausing to ask an occasional question. At one point, a piece of metal embedded in the beast's body slipped loose and clanged to the ground, and we all scampered away before reconvening to finish the tale, ending with the Crow Seraph and Gus's fevered dream.

When we finished, Mrs. Duncan was chewing her lip. She took the flashlight and went back to the beast. She touched its skin. She drew one of her fingers carefully along the edge of one of the metal shards. She took in its scent and frowned in revulsion. She then turned back to us.

"There's something I didn't tell you all in class yesterday." She handed Gus the flashlight back and folded her arms across her chest. "About the previous night. About the previous month. About the open door I found flung wide this morning when I woke up, surrounded in cold."

Lexi took out a cigarette and lit up.

"Mind giving me one of those, kiddo? Off the record?"

Lexi handed our teacher a cigarette and lit it for her.

THE SILENT END

"This morning," Mrs. Duncan began. "It was like I woke up inside an icebox. Every breath I took was death, and my toes and fingers had gone numb. Like you hear about happening to people after a plane crash in the arctic before they start eating each other. I thought maybe we'd been hit by a blizzard and my thermostat had gone out. But when I looked out the window, I saw a normal gray Mossglow morning. I also remembered that Mossglow rarely, if ever, sees snow. I found the door open downstairs and surmised that maybe I'd been the victim of a rare a.m. cold snap. But when I closed the door and turned on the heat, blasted it as high as it could go for a good hour, I found that it was still freezing. Inside my own house! I decided I needed to get out and go for coffee to warm up."

She took a small drag off her cigarette. The rain drummed outside.

"Can we walk over towards the cars?" She looked back in the direction of the beast. "I feel like it can hear me." We made our way back to the Shepherd, trudging again through the water, whose depth was still climbing. "The second I stepped outside, I realized it wasn't nearly as cold as it was in my house. I went back in, determined to find out what could turn a well-insulated, four-walled structure into a refrigerator while the outside world remained relatively warm. I'd bundled myself up in layers of clothing and was prepared to turn the entire place upside down until I discovered the reason."

"Reason?" I asked, recalling the freakish cold of Dean Veltry's office.

"The heater, it was just fine. And I'd discouraged myself from believing that my house was slowly sinking into a polar ocean. So I went upstairs to the bathroom to try and get the hot water working, thinking that if I could resolve that problem, I'd emerge victorious."

She put the hood back over her head and rubbed at her shoulders.

"But then I saw him."

"Him?" said Lexi.

She blew smoke. "In my hallway mirror. Him. A man. He was watching me. In a terrible way. There was something in his gaze that conveyed want. Sick want. He didn't open his mouth. He didn't want to talk. He just wanted to watch. Watch the way I moved. Watch the way I moved so he could decide whether or not he wanted to carve my body into pieces…before taking the parts of it he liked. He was a monster, you see. Like those that once lurked in dark oceans when the world was young. And it wasn't the first time I'd seen him either. I think it was the first time I realized what he looked like. But he'd been watching me for a while. I know that now."

"And what *did* he look like?" asked Gus, thinking, I was sure, about his dream.

"Yes," Lexi whispered. "Can you remember?"

"It's hard to say." Her voice shrunk in its confidence. "His face… it was like a mask. As if he could be one man for a moment and the next someone else entirely. Like a shape shifter. In my presence, he resembled my ex-husband Paul…but only partially. As if he were a copy of Paul. Or something wearing Paul's skin and smoking Paul's cigarettes. But without being Paul."

"Both like him and unlike him," Gus said.

"The eyes, they gave it away. They were…" She coughed. "Cruel."

"Cruel," I said to myself, thinking of what Mother had said about the man she saw in the bathroom.

"And there was one more thing." Mrs. Duncan chewed on her lip. "This man, it was as if the world he existed in, it was underwater."

"Underwater?" said Lexi.

"Like in a tank of some sort. Filled with blue water."

THE SILENT END

Mr. Blue, I thought, recounting Father's words. Is that why he called him that? Things were beginning to circle back, and I wished they would stop.

"I thought that despite the fact that I tend to keep my mind sharp and stay clear of intoxicants that I'd lost it. I wouldn't have been surprised. This town can chip away at happiness until you've got nothing left. But you three..." She smiled and took a final drag off her cigarette before putting the tip to the cave wall and putting the extinguished butt in her pocket. "Your investigative prowess has given me hope. I'm thinking there may be a method to Mossglow's madness. That we can solve the riddle."

"What riddle?" Gus said.

"Well, Mr. Mustus. If I knew the answer to that, it wouldn't need to be solved, would it?"

We all nodded.

"This is what we're going to do. You'll leave this place right now and go back to your homes. Keep your phones on. Check your emails by the hour. I have someone I think who can help us. Someone who will know what to do."

"Who is it?" I asked.

"A friend," said Mrs. Duncan. "A friend we can trust."

"You're not going to alert the police?" said Gus. "The Sheriff?"

"Perhaps. Although I tend to find that when you're dealing with something beyond a normal person's understanding, that most normal people aren't going to want to see it to begin with. Police are normal in the worst sort of way. So, the secret is to foster a coalition of the willing before we head into the dark."

The dark, I thought. Where Mother floated.

We climbed into the car, and Lexi put the Shepherd in reverse.

The wheels began to grind. We were caught on something. Lexi looked out the window.

"Fuck," she said, pushing the accelerator. The intestinal organisms. They'd wrapped their way through the Bronco's undercarriage, curling through its metal anatomy. Lexi hammered the pedal again and again, rocked back and forth.

"Should we push?" Gus asked. But as he spoke, the Shepherd ripped free with a sickly squishing sound, pulling shreds of red biotic tissue away with it into the night.

Mrs. Duncan's aquamarine Prius waited at the bottom of the incline that led back to the road. We followed her up as the rain poured down, heading back to the Thicks in dead quiet. I felt my stomach rumble, craving sugar. There was nothing in the Shepherd that could help me, however; Gus was out of Kit Kats, and I was hesitant to make a mess of rummaging through my groceries stowed in the back. That's when I remembered the tin of mints the Hat had given me, still rattling around in my pocket, unopened.

Removing them, I examined the Hat's engraved likeness. I noticed that the pose he struck seemed different from before. Instead of standing with his hands on his hips, he turned to the side and crouched in some sort of action stance. I must have been confused.

I flipped the lid and popped one of the thick, yellow circles onto my tongue. I closed my mouth and chewed. The taste, it was exquisite, like nothing I could describe. Like spices I'd always loved but never tasted. Like a beautiful day I'd never seen. Not being able to sate myself with just one, I ate almost all the rest, letting them practically tumble down my throat. A moment later, a mild euphoria came over me, and I was able, for the rest of the ride home, to breathe easy.

SIXTEEN

I ENDED UP SLEEPING WELL. IT was the first time since the night in the forest that I awoke with renewed authority over my brain. I'd had a dream, but it was a watery thing. In it, I wandered through Stumart but one that existed as if in a different universe, one dislocated from the town of Mossglow, one that reached beyond its murky borders. In the dream, a voice called to me, quiet, high-pitched. One that rose sometimes to shrill heights but most of the time, whispered.

"Since you're here," it said. I thought it was female, but it also could have belonged to a young boy. "I'm here too."

It was almost like a song.

"Find the frog, and open the vault. Inside I am. Inside I am."

The differences between this Stumart and the one I worked at on the weekends were both varied and specific; its walls, for instance, were scorched as if by fire. They crawled with peeling, corpse-gray paint, and ashes floated through the air. It seemed like the ceiling itself was still slowly burning, and embers drifted from it. My feet swept char with each step.

While traversing the aisles toward the back office of the store, the voice kept calling, louder and louder, high-pitched and something else…frightened maybe. Each shelf, tall and well-stocked, featured food products of some sort, but all of them were rotten. The boxes festered with spoiled innards, the cans were bloated, and the fruits and vegetables in the produce aisle crawled with maggots. Moving itself was hard, like walking in a vat of jelly.

"Since you're here, I'm here too," the voice continued uneasily.

I arrived in the back office and found that it also had been burned by fire. Everything, from the account books to the desk where Father would kick up his feet in the early days, was ash. The voice was coming not from that room, however, but from the janitor's closet. Carefully, I opened the door to it and stepped inside. The closet itself had been burned as well. Trash littered the ground, and embers floated in the pallor.

"Since you're here, I'm here too." The voice had gotten louder. Its melody was accompanied by a glittering light, brightening beyond a dislodged wall panel at the end of the room. I knew I'd seen the panel before in the real world but never paid attention to it.

"Find the frog, and open the vault. Inside I am. Inside I am."

I came toward the panel, toward the light.

"Find the frog, and open the vault. Inside I am. Inside I am."

As my fingers touched the wood, it buckled. I began to fall inward and that's when I awoke.

Mrs. Duncan hadn't texted any of us last night, but at a later hour, she had sent an email. One message shortly after 11 p.m. I checked it bleary-eyed from bed, which I managed to clear of Sword Star figurines and restore its original function before I nodded off. The email read as follows:

> Subject: Moving Forward
> Young ones,
>
> As promised, I've informed my friend of your discovery, and now, a plan of action is being hatched. Said friend is well-reasoned on the subject of Mossglow's mysteries, and I trust him to carry the secret well. Considering sensitivities, however, I shall delete all records of this email and suggest you do the same. I've told my friend that he should meet you in person before revealing your names as to protect your anonymity prior to consent. I think you will be very surprised to learn of his identity, however. Sometimes, answers to distant questions lie within a finger's reach.
>
> Please arrive 30 minutes before first period tomorrow (8:30 a.m.), and meet me in front of that horrid bullfrog mascot so that we can find a quieter place to plot out our path to truth.
>
> Respectfully yours,
> I. Duncan
>
> PS: And please do complete *The Trial of Xerxes* as we will discuss its cultural implications during class.

Since I'd awoken early, I spent a few minutes attempting to correct the sorry state of my room. Clutter had started to accumulate in layers worthy of archeological survey. I organized my paints and Sword Star figurines on an end table near my bedroom window. As I did so, I noticed that the indoor screen was loose. It looked like it had blown slightly ajar, and the metal frame was bent on one end. I reset it and made my bed, sequestering role-playing and video game magazines into shoeboxes to store beneath it. In the rusty dark of predawn, my life felt somewhat reconciled again. My room was a refuge of order in our empty home, and mine was the only window emitting light.

By 7 a.m., I had made my way downstairs. Lexi, Gus, and I texted each other to organize an early rendezvous at the octopus fountain in the Lower Thicks at 7:45. I expected we'd be driven to school from there in the Shepherd.

Fearing the state of the kitchen as I set my mind to breakfast, I expected it to have been ransacked by my ravenous father in the dead of night. But when I got there, it was as pristine as I'd left it, shined up and clean, and not a shelf had been disturbed. Had he not come home the night before? Was he still out in the bunker?

I scarfed down a quick bowl of cereal that almost fully consisted of neon marshmallows and ran out the front door in the first clean pair of clothing I'd worn since Wednesday: a pair of dark blue jeans with an elastic waist, yellow t-shirt, and red flannel coat. I didn't want to meet Mrs. Duncan. I didn't like that she'd gotten involved in our little mess. What power did she or her "friend" possess that could possibly set things right? As I made my way to the octopus fountain, unease swimming over me, the calm I'd awoken with dissipated.

The sun withered behind green clouds as I approached the octopus fountain. Gus and Lexi were already there, discussing something in a harried tone. Gus, typically fussy about his clothes, was dressed haphazardly; he seemed to be wearing two different pairs of shoes. Each was a loafer but one was black and one was brown. His shirt was as upended as his hair, and he hugged his pea coat.

Lexi didn't look much better in a dirty pink hoodie with a cartoon rhinoceros and the words TRAMPLE DAT. She also wore a distressed black skirt, and her ponytail stuck out sideways. She was sporting a different eye patch than usual—yellow as my shirt and rubbery in texture. At her and Gus's back stood the once-spouting fountain, rising from a hunk of grass a few yards behind the bus stop. Each tentacle was a spout, but none had worked in years. The base of the fountain—modeled to resemble an octopus rising out of a well—had now grown over with ivy and graffiti. Standing water from the previous night's rain pooled up to the rim. Someone had spray painted NEVER SLEEP across the base in red, and it looked livid in the light of morning.

"You're not going to believe this," Gus said as I approached. He gestured to Lexi.

"The Shepherd," she said. "I woke up this morning and…it was gone."

"What?" I yelled. "Was it stolen?"

"I don't know." Her typically steady fingers fumbled her cigarette to her mouth. She broke down with a spat of smoker's cough after taking a deep drag.

"Did you sleep well last night?" she asked me.

"Me?" I watched a couple of other students walk towards the bus stop. "Yeah, actually.

"What about you?" she turned to Gus.

He shifted from foot to foot with nervous energy and shrugged.

"Me, I barely slept an hour. Worse than the night before. Not that it matters. But then…" she wavered. "I had this dream. This screwed up dream about the Shepherd and something…I can't even remember what. All I know is that when I woke up and went downstairs, Mom was on a tear. The fucking truck was gone. Like whoever took it didn't even make a sound."

"A dream?" Gus was suddenly attentive. It seemed to be the only thing he'd heard. He scratched his face, head, and then face again. I didn't know why he hadn't told Lexi about the dream he'd had yet, but from looking at him, I got the feeling it might have been out of forgetfulness or even confusion rather than secrecy. "Can you...tell us about it?"

"Later. We've got to meet Mrs. Duncan and..." She pointed toward the end of Cranberry Street, where we heard the shifting of heavy gears. "There comes our bus."

Anxiety ate away at me as we rode. The three of us were forced to sit in different seats due to crowding. After we settled in, we refrained from looking at each other. Strangely, after a few minutes, I'd forgotten Gus and Lexi's presence completely, only vaguely aware of them like muscles I rarely used.

I'd plopped myself next to a freshman I vaguely recognized and opened my backpack to take out *The Trial of Xerxes,* still pathetically unread. I decided I was at least going to start the damn thing during the 20-minute ride, so I opened to chapter one.

Though the first few pages were difficult to get through, I quickly started to fall into the story. Not insomuch as I embraced what it was about as I fell in tune with the language, how it gripped me, almost without mercy. The author was like someone leading you through a dusty museum where you looked at characters and their troubles through exhibition glass. Ripples of pain followed each finished sentence. The words themselves could have been barbed with needles. As I continued, I became angry. Mostly with Father. I hated how he treated life like conspiracy and how he didn't put enough stake in books. I hated how he had me associate literature with stagnant nights and suicide, with pretentious college types and upturned noses. Was this what Mrs. Duncan had intended for me to understand from her after-class pep talk?

When we arrived at Myers High, there was traffic unlike any I'd seen before. Not just the usual bus frenzy that crowded the entry lanes from the front gate to the quad but other cars too. Sirens, we heard. I saw the flashing of police lights as two local MGPD squad cars squeezed past us; one drove right onto the sidewalk. Our bus driver, a middle-aged woman with a cleft lip named Louise, ordered us all to stay quiet as we pressed our hands and faces to the windows to make out the source of the commotion. When we stayed stalled in traffic for another few minutes, however, amongst the flurry of horns and people yelling, other busses in the row started letting their students off by the main gate to the school. Louise then gave in and shuttered open the door.

"Exit in an orderly fashion," she yelled. But none of us listened, piling over each other toward the main lot.

A parking attendant screamed at Louise, "Are you crazy? Don't let them off!"

"Something's wrong," I said, jumping onto the sidewalk.

Students ran between us. A backpack slapped me in the shoulder, and Lexi pushed its wearer aside. People were screaming. A mob had amassed on the front steps and courtyard leading up to Myers High. Students, teachers. Shrieks of terror. Police meandering and shouting orders. Sheriff Earl Nichols was there, I saw. I hadn't seen him in a long while, and now he waved his chubby arms to calm the crowd while simultaneously pushing them away from the area around

THE SILENT END

Mickey the Bullfrog.

"Everyone stay back!" he yelled.

Mrs. Sherwood, Mr. Schmidt, and Mr. Kraft echoed this phrase. They formed a little battalion to force the students back from the steps into the parking lot. It was as if Myers High had vomited out every last member of its student body onto the front lawn. "Stay back!" "Return to the busses!" "Don't come any closer!"

Behind the teachers at the top of the steps, I saw Dean Veltry standing with his arms crossed, glowering. His tie flipped in the wind, and his mood seemed darker than the throng of black clouds now coming in from the west.

"What happened?" Lexi said, standing at the outer rim of the crowd.

Gus squirmed his way through, waddling in his mismatched shoes. I went alongside him, pushing students with the bulk of my body left and right. I saw the police unrolling yellow tape. Each strand flickered in the wind. Flashes of skin and blood. So much blood.

We pushed to the front of the crowd, meeting a barrier of Mossglow Police and caution tape. A somewhat pleasant breeze blew my hair out of my eyes, and that's when I saw her: Mrs. Duncan.

She'd been ripped apart as if by a mob of hungry animals.

Her legs were stuffed inside Mickey the Bullfrog's mouth and protruded from its bottom lip like tusks while her torso and head sat at the statue's foot. Her eyes were callow and mystified. Her mouth contorted in what looked like curiosity. Seagulls circled in the sky above, and there was blood on the steps. Smeared around the bullfrog's mouth. I didn't see what had happened to her arms. They were nowhere to be found.

I had to avert my eyes. Vomit threatened to surge, but I swallowed it down. She'd been so alive. So alert and clear-headed

A revolting compulsion came over me that made me look up again. Blood had been used to write a message above the main doors to Myers High in jagged screed. A sentence derived from Mrs. Duncan's mangled remains.

STAY CLEAR OF THE SILENT END

Gus Mustus, in feeble shock for a few seconds, opened his mouth as if his jaw had unhinged and gave off a long, horrifying wail.

PART TWO

THE ATTACK

ONE

School was dismissed for the rest of the day. The majority of the students were carted out to their allotted neighborhoods with grim determination. Gus, Lexi, and I managed to get off back at the octopus fountain, and we headed over to Gus's house, sobbing hysterics. None of us could manage to formulate so much as a cohesive thought, our words running right past each other.

"But it's not really her, right?" One of us said.

"Last night—last night she was…she was…" said another.

"Did you see the blood? So much blood."

"Of course I saw it!"

"That's not what I meant."

"Who did it?"

"How can you be thinking about who did it at a time like this?"

"Because I'm scared."

"I'm scared too."

"Poor Mrs. Duncan. Poor Mrs. Duncan."

The second we got to the front door, Gus's mother, Denise Mustus, snatched her son off his feet and hugged the living hell out of him. She was a slight woman with short-cropped hair that looked a lot like Gus's, a smartly casual pair of thick-legged tan slacks, white blouse, and, as of this moment, tear-smeared mascara.

Her sobs were monumental as she felt his body for wounds he didn't have. Lexi and I, not accustomed to such acts of affection, stood by the doorway. Denise, wiping at her eyes, looked warily upon Lexi in particular, invited us in, and told us she'd already ordered pizza from Tinos, three fully baked meat pies. We were shivering with a harrowed sort of cold and could barely talk as she led us through their warm-hued, academic home, adorned with abstract paintings, overcrowded bookshelves, and wares that Marshall had collected abroad.

She sat us down on their leather, L-shaped couch in the living room. A dim but warm fire burned in the fireplace, and she asked us to take off our shoes to keep dirt off the area rugs. I did so, and she relieved me of them, pinching the heels in her fingers as she brought them to the front foyer. Numbly, I rubbed my socks on the rug. Liquid murder slushed through my brain. I almost heard Mrs. Duncan's soothing, fractious voice. "What happened to me, Eberstark? Why is it so cold?" I envisioned screaming freshmen and the great Dean Veltry presiding over the scene like a haughty lord of pestilence.

Marshall, cranky and tired-looking as he walked into the living room, sat down in his armchair, a comfortable-looking leather recliner. He listened as we tried to explain what had happened without giving away anything that would hint at our recent activities. He nodded every once in a while. In the middle of one of one of my sentences, he got up and took the remote control off the coffee table and turned on the television. With a couple of taps, he flipped to Channel 5 News. On the screen, from a bird's eye view, came the front steps and face of Myers High, expanding into a surreal panorama. Police swarmed Mrs. Duncan's dismembered body, her blood slathered about the stairs and statue. The camera then cut to a reporter with yellowish, short-cropped hair in a dark blue suit. He stood by the front gate in the backdrop of police vehicles, commenting gloomily on the scene.

"…We're not sure who's responsible. But I'm hearing now that state police are sending an investigative team."

A pundit in an adjacent news' box with the name *R. Norton, ALCPU* stamped below the border then popped up beside him on the screen.

"But in these early stages, what can we attribute this to? Terrorism? Surely, this was not an arbitrary act?"

"Like I said before, Richard," said the yellow-haired reporter, "we don't know what happened here. But a very disturbing scene has been painted in Mossglow. A town so small and quiet many in the region never even knew it existed. We had a hard time finding it ourselves."

"But wouldn't you agree that our nation's schools aren't safe anymore?" said the pundit. "If it's not a group of students being shot, then it's the teacher. What's next? The parents? Isn't it about time we insert regular armed guards in the halls?"

"So this is what school is now?" Marshall said, turning down the volume and setting the controller on the arm of his chair. He was wearing his spectacles, and his mustache had grown bushier as of late. His eyes were crossed with veins. He looked positively wrecked with sleeplessness. "You kids say you knew this teacher?"

"She taught us first period English," said Lexi.

"For the last two years," I added.

"I've told you about her a bunch of times," said Gus.

Denise chewed her lip when she heard that. I could tell she'd been weeping. It was a look I was familiar with. When she noticed me watching her, she turned away.

"Who'd want to kill an English teacher?" Marshall said.

The three of us remained silent, thinking about "the friend" Mrs. Duncan had mentioned.

Denise began to say something as well but then trailed off. She didn't look well. She looked pale. Scared. Much like Mrs. Duncan herself had.

She went into the adjoined kitchen and, after clinking around a bit, came back into the living room with a tray topped with cups of hot tea.

"I can't say I understand what we're doing in a place like this anymore," she said.

"And just what is a place 'like this?'" said Marshall.

"Oh, I don't know. Redneck suburbia? Rustbelt shadow's-ville? Present company excluded, of course." She gestured toward Lexi and myself.

"That sort of thing is everywhere," said Marshall.

"Yes and no." She set each cup on a coaster before us. "You have a PhD. From Yale. You edit one of the leading archeological journals in the country—or at least you used to. And yet you *elect* to stay in this nowhere place. Sometimes I wonder…"

"Give it a rest in front of the kids." Marshall threw one hand in dismissal without looking at her. It wasn't an aggressive gesture as it was removed. Like Denise had been an insect he flicked away. "Especially after what just happened."

"Don't throw that on me."

"I couldn't work in the city," Marshall whispered as if we weren't just a few feet away. Gus looked a little embarrassed. "I needed to get out. And Mossglow...it's quiet. I like how quiet it is."

"That's what you say."

That's what everyone says, I thought.

"Me? I call it cold," she continued. "I've supported you through every decision you've made. You know that. Mostly because your decisions typically tend to make sense. But Mossglow...something wrong is happening here. And not just with the school. With me, Marshall. With..." She looked at us, and and trailed off.

"Oh, stop it, will you." Marshall got up from his chair and walked toward the back porch. "After what these kids have just been through, we shouldn't be discussing this at all."

"We shouldn't?" Denise looked hurt, even a little betrayed. "How's your book coming along, honey?" Marshall stopped walking. "Oh yes. I nearly forget. You haven't finished a chapter since your son turned sixteen."

"Guys," said Gus. "Please stop."

Marshall looked at Denise with what almost became anger, but he then blustered his lips and went toward the back porch. He seemed achy and uncomfortable.

"Something's wrong, Marshall," said Denise. "I'm not being difficult. It really is. And I'm getting...scared. I'm...I'm seeing...I don't know how much longer..." she looked at Gus and curtailed the end of her sentence. I think she also must have thought she was making me and Lexi uncomfortable even if, compared to Father, Gus's parents at their worst were a model of poise.

"I'm going outside," Marshall announced as if to convince himself he still could. He then opened the sliding glass door, stepped onto the raised wood porch, closed it behind him, and sat in his Adirondack chair with his tobacco pipe in his mouth. The mist entangled him as he smoked.

"Damn it." Denise hissed quietly, her hands digging into the back of Marshall's armchair. She then turned to us with tears in her eyes and smiled. "Sorry, guys." She stood beside a wall-mounted mirror that reflected her body in profile, and I thought I saw a figure in it for a moment, a pair of eyes and blue, dark blue, and my heart zipped to life. But when I did a double take, nothing was there. Just Denise in her slacks and blouse. Gus watched the television and stretched his feet out on the rug. He looked childlike. Even happy.

TWO

I WAS SIGNED UP TO WORK on Saturday morning at Stumart. Though I didn't have to do it, I liked to come in on the weekends and work the registers. Besides, it would distract me from what had happened to Mrs. Duncan, the details of which I was trying, and mostly failing, to put out of mind. Manning the store reminded me of the days when our family first came to town. Though murky now, I remembered us being happy when we exited Cleveland, driving a UHAUL cross-country to arrive in a place none of us could believe was actually called Mossglow. Father had recently experienced the failure of his small textiles business. He negotiated the buyout of the new store through an acquaintance who'd been sniffing out opportunity for small-town growth throughout the western United States. He financed the acquisition by selling his company and hawked our townhouse in two weeks flat. The increase in both space and land became an incentive. But there still remained too many unknowns for comfort.

Moving cross-country was the biggest risk my parents had ever taken. They weren't daring people by nature. Working-class Jews from big, New England families, they valued opportunity but huddled close to home, rarely staking out new territory if they could avoid it.

Mother's sacrifices for the move were far greater than Father was willing to give credit for. He seemed to have expected her to follow lockstep even if she had to leave friends, family, and opportunity behind. I'd known her as Father's secretary for so long I'd almost forgotten she'd once been a real estate agent who, at one point, actually surpassed her husband in income, slinging property in Cleveland like she she'd been born into the trade. Maybe I shouldn't have been surprised that Father hadn't liked that. The man had been open in certain ways but closed in others. Even though it jeopardized our economic status, he demanded Mother stop working to take care of me. I remember that even as a child, I found it unfair. He was a step away from being so scared of his wife's success that he'd lock her in a cage.

When I got to Stumart, Cory had just stepped out of the cooler. His eyes were red, and his cheeks were rosy, and I knew he'd just sucked down a spliff. Cherry had the day off, and I was going to take over her shift. I'd just put on my uniform with the Stumart logo stitched on the left chest pocket and eaten a couple more of the Hat's mints. I was trying to conserve them now as I only had a few left, and they tasted so good that I believed they were affecting the chemical makeup of my brain.

"Eberstark," Cory said, scratching his ass. One of the ends of his Stumart uniform was untucked, and he shoved it back in. His weed was skunky, and the smell pissed off Cherry, but he seemed not to know or care. Groups of morning costumers rolled their carts through the aisles to the backdrop of yet another set of popular eighties standards.

"Aren't you going to say hi?" said Cory.

"Hi," I said and even managed a nod

"I'm gonna check inventory." He sidled up next to me at the register where he uncapped a two-liter of soft drink and began to chug. When he finished, he said, "On second thought, we're all good."

"You sure?"

He pointed his thumbs at his chest. "They don't call me manager for nothing."

Cory was an apt cashier, but the only thing he was really capable of beyond that was torpedoing a business like a set of tomahawk missiles. I thus disappeared into the back office and performed a thorough inventory check, filing a request with Stumart Corporate to replenish what amounted to multiple depleted products. The truth was that although Father hadn't set foot in the store in months, profit margins had actually been maintained due to me picking up the slack. I didn't love the job, but I might have had a knack for it. I could account for what people wanted and use that information to give them more. We had state and national correspondents to handle our accounting, but it was necessary to have someone answering emails and maintaining the books. If the store collapsed, I knew everything else would follow. Our lives would not be wrecked by monsters or mirror men but by lawyers with court orders to freeze our bank accounts.

Mr. Kraft came into the store around two o'clock.

As the glass door slid open, he stepped in, glowing as if he'd absorbed every last bit of the scant sun Mossglow had to offer. His face was perfectly symmetrical, almost to the point of being unreal. Although he was dressed in unassuming, teacher-appropriate clothing, he could have been a high-profile fashion model. He imparted beauty to everything he touched. Watching him smile was something to regard with wonder, and I seriously contemplated whether he were a handsome alter ego concealing a secret identity.

He looked around for a moment at the signs for discounted strawberries and the box display of chocolate marshmallow snack cakes. His eyes finally found me, and he exclaimed, "Eberstark."

I made sure my Stumart uniform's buttons were all fastened as I greeted him, crawling from behind the second of our three registers. What was I supposed to say?

"We're offering two for one special on Chilean strawberries."

The teacher scratched his well-groomed golden head of hair and regarded the display, topped with an old cardboard picture of smiling cartoon strawberries holding hands. "They do look delicious."

He put his hands in the pocket of his overcoat and looked at his shoes.

"I know that what happened at school yesterday must be absolutely devastating for you. I'm not an expert on what effects these sorts of things have on the mind, but I'm sure they can't be good."

"I'm actually trying not to think about it."

"One could hardly blame you. I wish I could keep myself from thinking about it as well, but since Mrs. Duncan and I were friends, it's hard for me not to. Will you be attending the funeral?" He was referring to the service that would be held at the Mossglow Civic Center's non-denominational church on Sunday.

"It depends on how far I get on my homework."

"I suppose that's diligent of you. Well, if it's any consolation, you're more than welcome to put off the assignments from my class until Tuesday. Although I believe we missed you on Thursday already."

I hesitated, looking in every direction but his. "I...well..."

"It's quite all right. No need to provide explanations. We've all been through a lot this week, and I'm willing to forgive an absence or two. I have a feeling you'll be back on track before you know it."

"Thank you, Mr. Kraft." I genuinely meant that. The tone of his voice was soft enough to unspool every knot in my body.

"Oh, Eberstark. We're not in school right now. You can call me Dennis."

"Okay. Thank you, Dennis."

"You're welcome." He then looked around the store for a moment as if searching for something. "So the real reason I came in was to talk to your father. Is he around?"

A lump formed in my throat.

"My father?"

"Yes. If he's available, of course. I had some questions for him about his…property. If he's not around, I can take his phone number instead."

"Phone number?"

"Yes. I'd leave mine as well, but I know how busy he must be."

I took a pen and piece of blank receipt from the roll and jotted down the number for our home line, which nobody ever answered.

I handed it to him.

"Splendid. And do you know the best time to call?"

"Afternoon is best."

"The thing is, your property—your father's property—what you have right here, is of intriguing historical significance."

"Really?"

"Oh yes, I believe so. I've been looking into some of the old town plans. There was a big fire here in 1926. No one really knows how it started, but it has something to do with a spate of violence that took place in what is now the downtown district. This structure in particular was built upon the foundation of another that burned down."

"I didn't know that."

Mr. Kraft licked his lips in an odd, off-putting manner. "It's a fairly small thing in the grand scheme when you think about it. Mostly, I'm just interested for archival purposes. The library and I…we have a bit of an arrangement should I unearth anything of use. Do you know if this property contains a cellar?"

I hesitated. I knew there was a cellar—or that there used to be one beneath where the janitor's closet now was—but I'd never been down there. Honestly, I wasn't sure if it was possible to do so. A great deal of restructuring had taken place prior to Father buying the property.

"I don't know."

"That's okay," said Mr. Kraft in departure from his normal voice. He sounded cranky. "Not like you'd have had any use for it. In any case, would you mind if I had a look around?"

"I don't know…"

Mr. Kraft held his hands together in front of his abdomen. "I'm interested in seeing what might be left over from the previous residents. You don't think that would be a problem, do you? I assure I won't touch or take anything without your permission."

I noticed an unusual shift in Mr. Kraft's tone. He was becoming more insistent.

"I'd better wait for my dad to give me the go ahead. I'm sure he wouldn't mind but, you know, he's the boss."

"But you're the boss's son. Surely, that means you can use your own judgment."

"He's warned me not to let non-employees into the back office. I'll have to get the go ahead from him first."

Mr. Kraft stared at me. His smile had turned into an odd, lipless frown that, for a brief, almost indeterminable moment, diminished his handsomeness. The perfect symmetry of his face, it was as if it worked against him, made him look plastic, like a clothing store mannequin. He then curled his lips into a smile, bared his healthy teeth, and returned to sterling normalcy as he shook my hand.

"Thank you, Eberstark. I hope you can manage to enjoy your weekend following the tragic end of our dear Mrs. Duncan. And tell your father I'll be calling him very soon. I wish I could say I was a patient man, but the truth is, I'm anything but."

"Thank you, Mr.—I mean, Dennis. Have a great day."

Mr. Kraft left without buying strawberries. Cory approached me with both his fist and mouth full of some cheese ball snack.

"I think that is the most attractive man I've ever seen," he chomped.

"Like a movie star," I said.

"No," said Cory with a nasally trill. "Not like a movie star. Movie stars have their good and bad days. That guy…it's like he was just born or something. He's got skin like an infant. There's not one man or woman in this city that comes near that much sexy."

"You think so?"

"Know so. A man like that can't live in a place like this. He's breaking some sort of rule."

"Oh, come on."

"I don't trust his kind."

"His kind? Like handsome people?"

Cory smiled as he prepared to impart what I'm sure he thought was wisdom.

"Handsome people get doors opened for them by ugly people. It's part of human nature. Most of us, you know," he indicated his own body as a specimen, "are a bunch of out of shape animals. Anneroxic rabbits. Sloths with beer guts. A guy like that, though?"

Cody shoved another handful of cheese snacks into this face. Some of them crumbled into his goatee.

"…He's a lean, mean wolf. And he knows it."

The day wound on. Cory left at nine o'clock in his ancient VW bug, and I spent the last two hours before closing organizing shelves and readying Sunday promotions, which included a sale on cooking chardonnay. I hadn't heard anything all day. From anyone. Not from Father. Not from Gus and Lexi. Even our customers seemed low for a Saturday. It was as if Mrs. Duncan's death was now a gaseous haze causing us to forget what should have been eulogized for months to come.

Not one customer showed up between ten and eleven, and I ended up shutting the music off early. I heard the spray mechanism occasionally wet the vegetables in the produce section, and I was conscious of my every footstep. I couldn't stop thinking about Mr. Kraft's interest in the cellar. Not to mention how he'd looked when I refused him access.

At eleven p.m. sharp, I removed the cash from the drawers and shut off all the lights. I locked the doors, set the alarm, and headed into the back office. No matter how often I tried to keep that place clean, papers piled up. It also didn't help that Cory sometimes took his breaks at Father's desk and left crumpled fast food bags in secret caches around the room. One stuck to my ass as I got up from the chair, and I had to peel it off.

As I squared things, I popped one more of the Hat's mints, and my mind jolted awake. What the hell was in those things? As I cleaned up, feeling energetic, my eyes were drawn to the rear end of the back office. The janitor's closet. Had our store really been built atop the remains of a fire? I knew Father had said something about the downtown district being the oldest in Mossglow, and there was that dream I'd had a couple of days back. But old in the Northwest United States wasn't the same thing as old elsewhere, particularly where we'd come from, so it hadn't seemed important. It was only my curiosity that was eating away at me now. Enthusiasm freaked me out in general, and I wasn't the courageous type. But now, for some reason, it seemed like it would actually be fun to get the jump on Mr. Kraft even if I didn't know what exactly he was jumping on.

The janitor's closet was more of a hallway than a cramped storage space. I flipped a light switch, and halogen tubes buzzed on. I looked over the various cleaners, mops, buckets, and brooms—all of which, I knew, lazy Cory left Cherry to handle. But what I really couldn't stop looking at was the end of the corridor, where lay a wood panel in the wall. It was designed to cover up something once but was now sealed. I remembered the dream I had again, the high-pitched, worried voice calling from this very place, but decided I should probably ignore it. I could barely even remember what she'd said. Until, that is, I neared the panel. Within feet of it, I began to hear, "Since you're here, I'm here too." I could even envision that light I'd seen glittering beyond it.

I got hold of a broom handle and prodded the wood from a few feet away. To my surprise, just touching the surface revealed that it had already been pried loose. I went back into the office to lock the door and grabbed a flashlight. Moving a box of bleach canisters aside, I put my hands to the panel and pried it from the wall, setting it aside.

I shone my flashlight into the dark. Right inside the door on a ledge that stuck out a couple feet was a modest pile of porno magazines. Cory's, I presumed. I avoided them as I stuck half of my body through the door. Right past the ledge was a drop off. I couldn't see how far down it went. And though I wasn't feeling especially scared, I didn't think I should try and find out. I turned back and decided to head to the office, close up, and call it a night. But then...

"Since you're here, I'm here too."

The voice again. But now outside my head. So close it could have been coming from right inside the room.

"Since you're here, I'm here too."

"Hello," I whispered.

"Since you're here, I'm here too..."

"Hello?"

The voice quieted as I found myself moving toward the hole in the wall.

After I stepped through it, I almost slipped forward and fell off the ledge. Thankfully, I was able to steady myself by leaning back against the wall. The ceiling within was tall enough for me to stand without bumping my head. I aimed my flashlight down into what I realized were the contours of a damp, brick-lined pit. I discerned a bottom below lined with dirt and a ladder a few feet to my left that led down. Relaxed or not, I swallowed deep. Was I really going to do this?

The smell of damp and something worse than damp, something rotten, entered my nostrils as I descended. With each step, I felt lonelier, stupider. Nobody knew I was down here. But again, that voice...I felt it right at the threshold of my mind's eye, threatening to resume with a vengeance if I didn't keep going.

I reached the bottom and looked back up. The light from the janitor's closet shone meekly at the entrance. The ground at my feet was littered with shreds of insulation. Leftovers from what must have been the reconstruction preceding Stumart.

I took a few steps and came into a capacious entryway leading to a separate room and aimed my flashlight. In the dark, I discerned great, white mounds. I halted, almost afraid of shining the light again, wanting to remain unseen. But realizing that I'd have to turn my back if I wanted to climb back out, I did it anyway. Boxes, mirrors, pieces of furniture—that's what they really were, not spider eggs or sheeted ghosts but old wares draped in dusty, white cloth.

I moved among them, wary of touching anything. I passed what I thought could have been a baby piano from the shape. Stacks of old portraits and paintings lay uncovered against an armoire. I rubbed at the charm bracelet in my pocket and hoped it would bring me courage as I lifted one of the pictures to the flashlight.

The portrait in my hand was of a couple. A man and a woman from a different time. The man had a Hungarian-style moustache, and his eyes were filled with something somber and angry. The woman, the wife presumably, looked to be holding herself back from the brink of an even greater despair. It was almost as if something painful were happening below her waist. They stood before the gate to Myers High, when it was still called Myers Academy.

I set the portrait back down quietly, listening for movement. The walls of the cellar were comprised of cold brick, and I felt, for a second, a faint draft coming from the end of the room. I walked toward it and found myself before a heavy, iron door. It was large, and well made. Sturdy to the point of impressiveness.

As I neared it, my sneaker accidentally kicked something across the room, and I heard it clink against the wall. My eyes followed it. It was a key. An iron key. The head of it fashioned to resemble…was it a frog? A frog remarkably similar to our school mascot statue where Mrs. Duncan had been found with her body in pieces? I felt like I'd seen the effigy somewhere else, in Dean Veltry's office perhaps, at the

THE SILENT END

end of his letter opener.

I picked it up and held it before my chin. Odd things happened to my vision as I studied it. The key itself, it looked as if for a second it blurred out of sight. Just briefly. Whenever it happened, though, it was as if its weight went away as well. As if I was holding nothing at all. I almost dropped it a couple times because of this, until I decided that the darkness was playing tricks on me and concentrated on the door instead.

That was when the dream voice hit me again.

Find the frog, and open the vault. Inside I am. Inside I am.

This time, I felt as if I could definitely identify it as female. Shrill and trembling, afraid and demanding. It repeated the phrase over and over again. It was so invasive I'd have done anything to make it to stop.

Find the frog, and open the vault. Inside I am. Inside I am... Find the frog and open the vault. Inside I am. Inside I am.

I'd begun to sweat. It was hot down here, and a moist, warm wind licked at my heels as I turned toward the door. The slab of metal had no handle. No knob or latch either. Only a keyhole in its immense middle. There was also some sort of design above it, I noticed. I tried to make out what it was with my flashlight and found that I had to step back. As I did so, I discovered it wasn't actually an image but a series of letters. They read:

NON ENTITIES ONLY

I shivered. The calm I'd been feeling before was beginning to fade. Was I really going to open this door? If Lexi and Gus were here, surely they'd have told me to do so without question. But then again, they weren't here. Nobody was. And besides, it's not like they would have known what the hell a Non Entity was either. *If an entity is a thing,* I thought, *then is a Non Entity a…not thing?* The whole idea was confusing. If beyond this door was a place for nothings, I assumed I should have been offered VIP access. I had to wonder what Mr. Kraft was intending to do down here. Never mind the fact that he'd just recently moved to Mossglow a year ago, but how many of the city's longtime residents had knowledge of its underground passageways?

The voice returned as I stood before the door, reminding me I had a job to do. Its feminine trill was getting louder and louder.

Find the frog, and open the vault. Inside I am. Inside I am.

"Fine," I finally said out loud. I could taste the Hat's mints on my lips. For just another second, my body was filled with warmth.

THREE

Nonentities, I thought as the door swung open. Someone had fashioned quite an elaborate system to protect them, whatever they were. As the hinges groaned, I noticed the entrance was reinforced with metal plating that could have walled off the Federal Reserve. The hallway within comprised of dark blue stone. It rose in an arc and looked cool and damp, as if at one point this had been the part of the cellar where element-sensitive items were stored. A faint wind blew stronger here, and it commingled with a carcass stench lurking in its molecules.

I took a step forward, and something below me clicked. I gasped and jumped back, expecting some Hollywood trap to drop me into a pit filled with cobras and poisonous dung beetles. But instead, I heard a low buzzing sound. A dim, white light began to ebb from around a bend in the corridor, accompanied by a swift ticking. I followed the sound and came to the end of the hall. There, as if waiting for me, was an alcove with a small, wooden desk. It was an ordinary desk. Four legs. A surface swollen in some parts from the moisture of the cavern. In front of it sat a rickety, wooden chair, and upon it sat three objects, each positioned equal distances apart. The first was an electric lamp from where the light had been emanating, the second was a book, and the third was what appeared to be, I realized, some sort of weapon.

Behind the table lay another passageway: a simple, lockless wood door with a latch and handle. The weapon itself looked like a pistol, but there was something strange about it. It had a scaly, alien texture, and was lemon-colored. I'd have thought it for a toy if its mechanics didn't seem so intricate. The oddest thing of all about it was that where there seemed to be a piece missing. A gap where perhaps the ammunition would go, right above the grip. I leaned in closer and, sucking in breath, picked it up. This pistol, it was almost weightless. So much so that I wondered if it were hollow. Along the grip I also noticed were carved three letters in perfect cursive: E.H.M.

Attempting to be delicate, I set the pistol down. When my fingers slipped off it, I picked up the book, which, although wide and tall, was very thin. On the cover—it was hardbound dark leather—were written the same words as on the door: *NON ENTITIES ONLY.*

I opened it cautiously to the first page. Blank. Along with every other subsequent page after that, I quickly found. I turned through from beginning to end and vice versa. The paper was old and sturdy, but there wasn't so much as an inkblot. Or at least at first glance. The more I looked, the more I swore I saw something there, but my eyes began to hurt eventually, and I had to stop concentrating.

The ticking came to an end, and the lamp on the desk, an antique-looking brass thing with a dusty shade, began to fade. I found myself again in silence and dark, clicking my flashlight back on and returning the book to where I'd retrieved it.

I heard a noise. A crash. Then something else…

BEEEEEEEEZZZZZOOOOOO BEEEEZZZOOOOOOOO. The drone rose louder and louder. I held my breath and listened. The store alarm. Either it had been tripped accidentally or someone, somehow, had broken into Stumart.

I ran toward the door and wondered what in the hell I would be able to do to stop a burglar. I took out my phone and searched for reception. Nothing. Only the time: 12:16 a.m. But even if I could have, did I really want to call the police and alert them to this hidden cellar? Especially since the alarm would bring a squad car by anyway.

But then came another sound. A sound that loosened my bowels.

ALLLLLLLOoOOOOoooOOOOOOOOOOOOooOOo

Loud. And close. Someone—something—was coming into the cellar. Something whose howl was similar to the beast we'd stowed in the cave off Goon's Cove. But rougher, stronger. I heard the porno mags come fluttering down, followed by a mighty crash. Whatever it was must have slammed through the panel in the janitor's closet and guttered to the earth below. My body shook from the impact. Something was coming. Something that moved with thunderous strength. And no matter how euphoric I'd felt from the mints, all my pleasant feelings had transformed into one mass of craven horror.

I shut off my flashlight and slipped toward the iron door. It was still open.

ALLLLOOOOOOOOoooOOOOOOooOOOOOOOOOO

I had to cover my ears. A shadow grew toward me. A shadow blacker than the dim blue dark of the cellar. The door had opened inward, and I was standing right up against it. I froze, my hand upon the key, still fixed in the lock.

THE SILENT END

Whatever the creature was, it stayed still, snorting at the air outside the room. With a growl, I heard it take a step forward. Frozen as I was, I tried to take a look. Near the baby grand piano at the edge of the cellar, I saw a foot emerge. It was human-like but mixed with something else. Something bestial, maybe amphibian. I tried to hold my breath. Only my fingers stayed steady on the key. Which, I noticed, seemed to be blipping from view yet again. When it faded completely, my fingers just slipped past it into the metal, catching it again as it reappeared.

The creature took another step closer and stopped.

A lone slippery thing, a tentacle not so different from what I'd glimpsed in Father's bunker, wallowed into the cellar. It slurped from somewhere near the creature's foot and slowly, wetly, traveled along the ground. There was something at the end of it, I saw. Some sort of growth. A few seconds later, when it rose like a cobra and slithered in my direction, I realized the growth was a small recording device. An old, frayed, carbon microphone embedded in the skin.

The appendage snaked its way through the cellar, prodding at various objects. At one point it accidentally banged a few keys on the baby grand piano and then continued on until it felt up the creases of the open door. A second later, it was at the key hole, missing my hand by little more than an inch.

It came toward my mouth, swaying hypnotically, and I felt my grip on reality slip. I now understood what it was like to never want to be anywhere deep and dark again. There was something familiar about this beast. Something I almost recognized as human, and knowing that filled me with dread. I sensed what I perceived was its desire to murder me and realized my death could be so quick and stupid the universe would snicker. This instant horror shattered my paralysis and removed the key from the lock so I could run behind the door.

The second I did, the monster honed in on my location. Crash, crash, crash—it barreled toward me. The tentacle tried to wrap around my arm, and I dodged to the side even as black slime slathered my cheeks. I heaved into the iron door, and as it shut, the thing's head, a large, bony thing, met it with a resounding slam.

The creature continued to ram its body over and over again into the door. *SLAM. SLAM. SLAM.* It made dents in the alloy, and a couple of them showed through on my side until, with a desperate howl, the physicality ceased, and a scream of mad frustration ensued.

A few seconds later, I heard a high-pitched voice squeal, "Whoooooooo is it behind the door…"

Breath heaved from the crack at my feet, and I saw tentacles, several tentacles with endings varying from microphones to old telephone receivers and fungal looking cords, trying to squiggle through it. I backed away quietly.

"Does it think I'll tear its body to bits? That I'll swaaaaaaaaaaaallow its parts?"

I remained silent.

"Is it a Non Entity? Yes. Of course it is. A dream beast. Murje made. Or something new? Something delectable? A boy, perhaps? Or a girl? Yes. A girl would be bessssssssst. A girl would be useful."

The tentacles retracted from under the door.

"Whatever it issssssssssss…you'll keep your brain if you let me in. If you open the door, I'll not dissemble you. Or drink your blood or snap your bones. If you let me in, I will only ask for what is not yours. The maker rewards. Even dream-things like yooooouuuuuu…."

The creature sniffed.

"It doesn't answer?"

I remained quiet, and a second later came a baritone chuckle in great contrast to its high voice.

"Silence is the end." Its high pitch returned. "Silence is always the end. Your mind wants life, but death is where you head. I have your sound in my insidesssssssssssssss. It is like no other. You will be found, and I will rrrrrrrrrip your skeleton from your skin. The maker will enjoy what I ccccrrrrrreeeeate from your ribs."

The creature then went silent. I assumed it had something to do with the sirens, which I could now hear blaring from Stumart with increasing severity. I then heard a strange sound. It was like sucking. Like a deep, phlegmy inhale. I anticipated the creature to stomp off but instead heard the sound of what could have been dress shoes clicking fast against the ground. A moment later, they faded. I was almost confident enough then to open the door, but something held me back. I threw the flashlight against the ground in a fit of stupidity and shattered it beyond repair and slid to the floor in a useless heap.

After a few moments I collected myself and came to my feet. I was covered in sweat, and my head pounded. There was no way I was going back upstairs. Not even if that thing was gone. I turned and tapped through the darkness for the stone that had set the desk lamp alight. Finally, I heard the click again and followed the glow to the end of the corridor. I was relieved to see the small, wooden door standing there. From behind it, a warm wind blew. I felt abandoned and began to cry, sinking to the ground again in self-pity. I sniveled and slobbered until I felt Mother's charm bracelet press hard against my thigh. Wiping my nose, I grabbed the pistol, shoved it in the front of my jeans, took the book under my arm and, breathing in what I hoped would be the last breath I'd know as a coward, disappeared into a fuming blackness that went on for who knows how long.

FOUR

THE CORRIDOR DISTENDED AND SHORTENED, sometimes to the point where I had a hard time breathing. My thoughts screamed out with such insistence I began speaking them aloud. I recited Sword Star oaths—*We crack Xeno skulls. We drink Doral wine. When we sleep, we dream only of war*—and lapsed into fragments of popular songs I'd heard at Stumart. This worked for a little while as a distraction. Until it didn't. The longer I stumbled through the dark, the more crowded my brain got. I heard voices that weren't mine. Voices that belonged to Charlene Poughkeepsie, Jesse Maroon, and even Gus and Lexi. "Fat." "Faggot." "Liar." "Coward." "Waste of space." "You might as well have killed your mother." I tried to argue with them, but it was like arguing with a storm. I felt embarrassed. repeating "I will go somewhere someday, okay? I will go somewhere someday, okay?" until the words themselves began to run together, and I shook them from my mind. I misplaced my sense of direction, not sure whether

THE SILENT END

I was moving forward, down, or back the way I'd come. I started to hyperventilate and took out my phone, using the its scant bit of green light to reassure me I was still alive. The battery was running out, it was just after 2 a.m., and there was no reception to be had. Craggy rock surrounded me on all sides. It was wet, and sometimes, there was enough water present that as I hugged the walls to slide by, water it trickled onto my hands and clothes. If I listened close, I thought I could hear the sound of swishing tides.

My battery died shortly after 3:30 a.m., when, after getting reception for less than ten seconds, I received a text message. The screen went black as I tried to open it. After that, I plodded forward for what could have been hours. At one point, I beat my hands against the rock. I wondered if anyone could hear me. I wondered if I'd succeeded in becoming one of Mossglow's disappeared. It would certainly show that not only women were being plucked from the population. That boys could be lost too. Mossglow, for all its quaintness, all its allure as an ocean side city with supposedly scenic views, was a poisoned place. People vanished into nothing here.

I kept going. Finally I caught a glimpse of dim light. When I saw it, I leapt forward at a frantic pace, tripping multiple times before lurching onward again.

The foul smell grew stronger. It was particularly horrible because I needed the air, but with every gasping breath, decay filled my lungs. I hunched over and dry heaved and stumbled on. A few minutes later, I emerged out of the passage, pushing—and then painfully squeezing—myself through a narrow interstice. I actually fell from it, sliding into murky water and mud, somehow managing to hold the book above my head. The pistol, stuck into the front of my waistband, pinched against my stomach.

I clambered to my feet, tried to wipe my face clean, and shrieked. A monster loomed before me. The very same creature I'd tried to escape, lurking on the other side of the tunnel. I prepared to cry out and accept my fate. Fall to my knees and surrender to the merciless judgment of beings greater than myself. But then my eyes adjusted to the light. This wasn't the beast I'd run from in the cellar of Stumart. The creature before me, sad, diminished, was the same one Gus, Lexi, and I had hidden. I knew where I was now: the cave on Goon's Cove. Despite the fetid odor, I jumped up and down, holding the book above my head like a trophy.

What remained of the monster between today, Saturday, and last Thursday wasn't nearly as frightening as I'd feared. It was disgusting, but no longer did it look like it could tear a man apart. The lower half of its body had almost completely unspooled, skin, organs, and all. The only part of it that remained recognizable was the head. Or part of the head. The bony snout was now drooping from the creature's face as if melting. The light bulb hanging from the edge of it had cracked, and its eyes had popped loose from their sockets, trailing down its cheeks.

Through the water floated bits and pieces of what had once been its body. For a few seconds, however, I had no idea what those pieces were. Something bizarre had taken place. The creature's body had begun to come apart, perhaps signaling the final stages of its death. I wondered if the organs we'd seen emerging from the wound previously had marked the beginning of the process. For now, its flesh didn't really resemble flesh at all but rather an accumulation of disheveled objects. I saw what looked like stitched-together shreds of lampshades mixed in with broken light bulbs and ceiling fan blades. Some objects had detached themselves completely from the body and swam through the water like debris from a flooded warehouse. Even the parts of the body that were marginally intact—the upper abdomen and shoulders—were starting to exhibit the same symptoms. The creature was turning into a mountain of mop heads, porcelain lamp bases, mucky, pink muscle strands, and pieces of plastic tubing. I saw a plush stuffed cat and a shredded car tire. Scissors, kitchen knives, broken medical syringes. It was as if the beast's true nature was being exposed. And that nature was nothing more than an accumulation of garbage.

There was one notable exception, however. Inside the creature's ribcage, in a pile of decomposing flesh and the last of the glimmering substance Father—and now the creature in the cellar—called Murje, was a human being. Or parts of a human being. I saw eyelashes, lips, dark hair, and half-open eyes. Although all of them were misplaced like a figure from one of the Picasso paintings Mrs. Duncan had shown us last year. One of the eyes, which was lodged between a pair of lips and what might have been an ear, flickered open. A dim, wet orb shone through the dark. The lips above then twisted into a frown and began to speak.

"B-b-boy," it sobbed. Its voice was wet and sad. I also couldn't shake the fact that it was vaguely recognizable. "M-m-m-m-make me whooooooole again?"

I couldn't speak.

"K-k-k-k-illllll it. Preeeeeefer to e-e-expire."

Its teeth were bleeding.

"K-k-killl it. K-k-k-killlll me. K-k-k-k-k-k..."

The lips spit up a red, glowing bile that flew in my direction. I jumped out of the way and ran out of the cave.

Stumbling stupid into what was the beginning of dawn, a hint of sun brought the sky from purple to gray. I was freezing in my soaked clothes, I was frightened, and my lips flaked from thirst. I began hiking up the small atoll toward a road that could lead me back to town. Behind me, the ocean at Goon's Cove raged. The metal of the pistol stuck to my back flesh, and my fingers cramped around the spine of the book.

I heard a roar and, for a second, thought I'd fallen into yet another livid thing's clutches. I almost started laughing at the notion. But no, I realized a moment later. It wasn't a monster. It was the Shepherd. Hurtling toward me.

I put up my hand and signaled, but it didn't slow down.

"Hey!" I was beyond thankful. But that truck was coming at me fast. "Hey, slow down!"

I dove for cover as, with a dovetailing screech, the tires whooshed to a halt.

"Lexi?" I yelled, coming to my feet. "Goddamnit! You could have killed me."

There was no response.

I came to the side of the truck. The windshield and windows were dirty beyond belief. They almost looked to be covered in a mustard-like substance. Arcing my neck, I peered through it into the cabin.

The engine rumbled and sputtered. I scratched my head.

With a click, the passenger door flipped open.

I walked around to the passenger side and looked into the cabin. Empty. The wheel fidgeted a little on its own, and occasionally, the engine rumbled. I looked at the gas meter and noticed it had fallen past E. There were no keys in the ignition. On the outside of the vehicle, a veiny sludge crept from the undercarriage and into the engine under the hood, continuing up the windshield. I bent down to get a better look and saw a bubbling, orange-yellow mass pulsing out in all directions.

"No, thank you," I said to myself, sidestepping the Bronco and trudging up the surf toward the main road.

The Shepherd's tires whirred and bounded after me. I tried to run, but it was no use.

When it came to a stop, the passenger door opened again.

"You've got to be kidding me," I said.

The Shepherd revved its engine as if in response.

I gave up and hopped in. The door slammed shut, and the radio turned to static mixed with occasional flurries of Lexi's treasured Black Metal compilation skipping in the CD player.

FIVE

I DIDN'T KNOW WHERE WE WERE going or if I cared. The previous night, along with everything else over the week, had led me to believe that no matter where I went, something bad would follow. I wasn't any safer at Myers High than I was at work or home. If not running from a nightmarish monster, then I was running from the human kind. Of the two, I honestly didn't know which was worse. Those lips that had spoken in the cave moments earlier, they'd been human lips. Human lips and human eyes at the core of a biology otherwise alien. What were those lips really trying to tell me? If not with words than by their presence alone? It was too much for me think about with my body lacking rest. Inside the Shepherd, I surrendered to thoughtlessness, emptying myself of reason in this living machine raging around Mossglow in the early morning that had, for some reason or another, insisted I climb inside.

That rest was disturbed, however, as I found myself being launched

THE SILENT END

from the passenger side door of the alien vehicle into the morning air. It was as if the seat sprang sideways and flung me from the cab. I thumped onto the ground like a sack of stupid, barely awake until I focused my eyes and found myself looking up at the Mustus family's geode mailbox. It sparkled with an uncommon luster.

I shook my head and propped myself on my elbows and saw that the Shepherd was already screeching around the corner of Ashton Avenue in a fury of yellow smog. I checked my belongings. I still had the pistol I'd taken from the desk, but the empty book reading *NON ENTITIES ONLY* on its cover was gone. I'd left it inside the truck, resting against the driver's seat. I wanted to smack my head against the sidewalk. Thankfully, I at least had the pistol, which I made sure was hidden well beneath my shirt as I gathered my body and walked up the Mustus driveway.

It was a little after seven a.m. on Sunday, and I was sure the family would be asleep. I went around the side of the house to Gus's window. Thankfully, his room was in the basement now. Denise and Marshall had finished it three years back. Gus had asked to relocate there from his cramped room on the second floor in order to better spread out Sword Star battle terrains. We'd labored over them intensely in our newb days. Denise had given Gus two folding tables as each terrain could measure up to six feet in length, and he set them up on the far side of his large, beige-carpeted room, filled with empty Sword Star kit boxes, books, model Japanese robots, and a DVD tower stacked mostly with Hayao Miyazaki films.

I crept around the side of the Mustus yard, ducking through a gap between two haggard pine trees and reaching over their gate to unlock it from the inside. I tiptoed through and crouched past the raised patio where Marshall often sat, smoking his pipe and staring into the mist. The Mustus family had a fence up between themselves and their neighbors on both sides, but the back end opened into a sprawl of leafless trees that continued on an incline toward what, a half a mile down, would eventually become Graywood Forest. A hammock had been detached from the two that lay closest to the patio, and one side hung limply from a knot.

I rapped on Gus's window and waited. No answer. I rapped again and wondered if he'd already gone upstairs early to sit at his father's desk and do homework as he was wont to do on weekends. But when I rapped a third time, I saw movement in the tiny space between the drawn curtains. A moment later, Gus's face was shoved up against the glass.

"Eberstark?"

With a finger to his lips, he slid open the window and I climbed inside.

"What are you doing here?" He looked even worse than the last time I'd seen him. One of his eyes bulged out more than the other although that could have been because he'd just woken up. "And what...what happened to you?"

I told Gus everything. Well, almost everything. About Mr. Kraft. About the cellar. About the book and the pistol, the Shepherd and the monster, and the piteous mutant waiting on the other side. I told him about the Non Entities; I mentioned the key. Filled with newfound urgency, I almost even told him about Father, but thought again before unfurling that lengthy scroll.

As Gus listened, he seemed less concerned than usual. His room was also unusually messy for someone so obsessed with order. What looked to be all of his clothing had been flung into one mountainous pile on the floor, and echoing Friday's fashion missteps, he wore different colored socks and donned a cream-colored chiffon scarf that might have belonged to his mother—but without a shirt beneath it—to bed.

"Well," said Gus, watching the pistol as I removed it from my waistband and placed it on his bedside table. His eyes grew small as he studied it.

"May I?" He reached for it.

I nodded. He took it by the muzzle and grip and weighed it in his hands.

"It's heavy. Doesn't look like it should be, but it is. I wonder what it's made out of..."

"Really?" I said as he handed it back. Though I'd remembered it being so light the previous night, I had to admit that it was indeed heavier now.

"What did you say the book had written on the cover again?" he asked.

"The same thing that was written on the door. Non Entities Only."

"Curious." Gus walked in a slow circle around the mound of clothes in his room. "Non Entities Only..."

I nodded.

"The idea itself is a paradox, don't you think?"

"Yea?"

"Try and keep up with me now," said Gus with unintentional arrogance as I sat down in his rolling chair. "If something is an entity, then that means what?"

He looked at me for an answer I didn't have.

"It means that it exists. As in it is a thing with a precedent that justifies its existence."

"But isn't that something that, well, everything does?"

"An entity is a something, Eberstark. A creature, a conglomerate. An idea. An entity need not be visible to the human eye like the chair you're sitting in is, for instance, but it must be self-contained to its own definition, philosophically speaking. As in it must have a set of parameters that grounds it in reality. So to call something a *Non Entity* is basically to call it a Non Thing. A lack of formulation. Do you understand now?"

"Are you saying the book I left in…whatever the Shepherd is now, is something meant for…a nothing?"

"How the hell am I supposed to know? If I had the book, I might be able to provide an educated opinion. But as of now, what you're telling me makes no sense. From the Shepherd to Mr. Kraft to this pistol—if it is indeed a pistol and not something else entirely—leads me to doubt your ability to maintain perspective. You're talking about light bulbs and ceiling fans… I'm wondering if you've lost your grip. And then there's this matter of the creature you ran into in the cellar, perhaps trying to get its hands—or tentacles, I guess—on the things you took. Which I'm thinking you should have left untouched, by the way."

I found that my eyes were closing as his words spun circles around me.

"Maybe you're right," I said. "Fuck, I'm sure you are. But can you tell me what we should do now? As opposed to what I should have done yesterday?"

"You want to know what *I* think we should do?"

"Why do you think I came here?"

Gus looked down at his open-toed, orange slippers.

"I guess I thought you didn't have anywhere else to go."

His words stung, and I could tell he immediately regretted them, but I tried not to let him see that. Mostly because he was right. Where else could I have gone? I could have tried to track down Father, but seeking him out was as difficult as it would be fruitless. The thought of returning home after last night filled me with dread.

"Do you think we should try and track down that Shepherd... thing?" I asked.

"Not yet." Gus sat down on his bed with his head in his hands. On the ceiling above was a poster of a middle-aged, mustached man wearing a tie decorated with cosmic bodies. Between his hands grew a menacing-looking galactic black hole. "First thing's first; we call Lexi and tell her what happened to her vehicle. Although, I have a feeling she knows about it already. In her own way."

"What do you mean?"

"You know how I had the dream about the Crow Seraph, and then the next morning, it came to life?"

"The day after it touched the Murje?"

"The what?"

"The—the blue stuff."

Gus groggily shook off the suspicion he'd heard something different. "Exactly. Well, I've been thinking that maybe the same thing happened to the Shepherd. After the tires got stuck Thursday night on that stuff in the cave, you know? Those red intestine things? She did say she had a dream, a bad one. And who says that the blue stuff can't be red as well? Or green?"

I nodded as Gus walked over to the remaining Demigod figurines. He'd arranged them on a specially installed wall shelf he'd installed for the purpose of displaying his prized work. Five of them were lined up next each other. Only the Crow Seraph, typically occupying the spot two from the right in the presentation, was missing now.

"You know," Gus frowned. "The tournament's coming up."

"Next week, I know. Are we…"

"Still going?" He took his Minoczar off the shelf and held it on his palm. The circular disk it was situated upon had been decorated with bracelet beads he'd fashioned to look like skulls crunching beneath the warrior's steel-booted feet. It was an appropriately bleak design regarding Sword Star's dim outlook on the future, in which aliens and humans were engaged in endless war over dying planets. "After all that's happened? I don't know if I'd even be able to remember the rules."

"Don't say that."

"Why shouldn't I say it? Our teacher just got murdered, Eberstark. Torn to pieces. And now, we're being chased by fucking monsters through the streets."

"Beneath them, technically."

"Look…that's not all. I'm…I'm starting to…"

"Starting to what?"

"I'm starting to forget things, okay? I don't know why, but…I have these dreams now. Waking dreams. Which I guess makes them hallucinations. I'll just flash to another place. Like I'm traveling through a hole between minds. Flash, boom, and there I am. Inside something that's…not me."

"That doesn't make sense."

"No, it doesn't. But that's what happens. I go inside something that's definitely not me. It gets angry. Confused. I can't control its actions. I'm just along for the ride. Not that it's fun in the slightest manner. Right after it occurs, I can barely remember it. And right before it occurs, these little light worms start swimming around the edges of my eyes."

"What the hell is a light worm?"

THE SILENT END

"I hear a whispering sound, and then they come. They come, and they dig as if burrowing, burrowing into my pupils or something. I don't know—I must be crazy. Or sick. But after they come…I'm in a different place. Perhaps only for a few seconds."

"How often does it happen?"

"It's getting worse. Yesterday, they came while I was on the couch watching Sword Star Prime, and when I snapped out of it, I was standing over the kitchen sink, pouring a bottle of milk down the drain. Thankfully, my parents didn't see me."

He scratched nervously at his chest. "With my mind in this state, I don't know if I play in the tournament. I'll…I'll just bring us all down."

I put my grubby hand on Gus's bare shoulder. It felt cold.

"Look," I said. "We've still got one week until we have to get down to Ozark. And as far as I can tell, that means we've got seven days to fix this mess."

"Five days. Not counting today. Remember that set-up starts the night before."

"Fine. Five days. That's still enough time to get to the bottom of what's going down in Mossglow. And after we do, I swear to shit, we're going to take home every Feral Dagger Prize the tournament has to offer."

Gus smiled. It felt like finding a lighthouse in a storm.

I wanted to lay everything on the table. All of my deceits. All of my fears. All of my foul and stupid thoughts. Fuck, Gus still was under the impression that I lost my virginity when I was thirteen to my old babysitter when in fact she'd only caught me masturbating with an old electric back massager I found in my parent's closet. He thought Father was a recluse and that I'd earned better grades in all of my classes than I actually did. He thought I read books I'd never opened and traveled places I'd never been. This year, since I'd turned seventeen, though it became easier to lie to others, it had become harder and harder to hide things from myself. Overall, I wanted to tell Gus so much that I couldn't tell him anything at all.

"What's the next step after we call Lexi?" I managed to say.

He paced back and forth. "If what you've relayed to me is at least partially accurate, we head down to Stumart."

"You want to go back to the store?"

"I want to see what happened, so yes. And besides, technically, you've been the victim of a burglary. I'd be surprised if the police haven't already sent a squad car by your house."

"Really?" I hadn't even thought about that. The fact that the police might have had a chance to search Stumart aside, what would Sheriff Nichols think if he found Father skulking out of his bunker in our front yard with a ray gun?

"Do you think the police will be there now?"

"Might be. There's a good chance they've already arrived, waiting for you to open shop."

"But what if they ask about the cellar? Or what time I got home?"

"I never thought I'd be saying this myself. But you'll lie, Eberstark. You'll say you don't know anything about the cellar. And that you left right after work to sleep over at my house."

We heard the sound of footsteps upstairs. The slow, purposeful thumping of Marshall's bare feet entering the kitchen.

"Okay," I said. "So after we talk to the cops, what then?"

Gus took off his scarf and threw on a checkered shirt backwards and inside out. I didn't have the heart to tell him he'd done so. "Surely, you've heard of surveillance cameras?"

I thought about it for a second and remembered. We did

THE SILENT END

have surveillance cameras. Genius. Save for a few minor instances of shoplifting, we rarely found the need for them, but Stumart Corporate had sprung for a state-of-the-art installation to protect themselves legally. The good thing was that I had access to the wall locker containing the DVD, which I could obtain and conceal quietly. Following that, I'd be able to claim the system had broken down, and with hope, no one would know the better.

"And your father's traveling for work, right?" said Gus.

"What?" I said before remembering I'd told him that on Friday. "He'll be back in town next week."

"Seems like that's always the case."

I nodded warily.

"Well anyway, that's good. Because I think we may be able to see exactly who, or what, broke into your family's store last night. And we don't need anyone getting in the way while we gather information."

"No, we don't," I said, thinking about Father and the fact that I still had a message on my dead phone. Gus was putting on deodorant. "Hey, do you have a cell charger?"

He took the phone from me. "Let me check my dad's office."

A few minutes later, he came downstairs with a cord that awoke my Motorola. The display flickered on, and I quietly read the message in the inbox. It was from Father.

And it was blank.

SIX

SHERIFF EARL NICHOLS WAS WAITING in front of Stumart when Gus, Lexi, and I arrived. We'd hopped on the Mossglow Main, one of eight rundown minibuses with cracked windows and rotting interiors. On the way, I'd tried to bring Lexi up to speed on yesterday's events from the creature in the cellar to the creature in the cave, but she seemed just as dazed as Gus had been when I'd come through his window. When I told her about the Shepherd, her eye grew big and teary. Her skin, typically soft, was cracked and dry.

She was the last to get off the bus when it stopped a block away from Stumart. Stiffly stepping onto the concrete, she lit the cigarette that had hung off her bottom lip the entire ride over, closed her eyes, and exhaled.

"You're saying my truck's running around with no gas? Like a zombie or some shit?"

"I don't know what it's running around on," I said. "But no. Not gas."

"It's so hot out here." She pulled off her hoodie to reveal a tank top with shoulder strings. She'd sweated through it, and I could see the outline of her bra. She wiped sweat from her forehead before staring at two squad cars sitting in the parking lot.

"Really?" I pulled my flannel coat around my shoulders. I thought it was one of the coldest mornings we'd had in months.

The second Sheriff Earl Nichols saw me approach, he took his cup of gas station coffee from its holder and stepped out of his squad vehicle, a white Chevy Suburban with blue trim. Before he shut the door, he grabbed his campaign hat from the passenger seat and fit it over his bald head. Folding his arms right below his badge, he waited for us as another member of Mossglow PD, a tall, long-chinned deputy with a red handlebar moustache named Ted Stapleton, climbed out of his own squad car, a squat sedan, a few feet away.

When I saw the front of the store, I was able to muster enough shock for my surprise to seem convincing. The face of Stumart had been outfitted with six bay windows, through which you could see the actual insides of the store. Each had been reinforced with a modern security film (another of Stumart Corporate's legal team's suggestions) that was supposed to protect against break-ins with some new technology called "blast mitigation." But whatever had smashed through last night had bypassed that mechanism, obliterating one of the window frames as if it had been sugar glass. Inside, aisles were toppled, and the tower display I'd set up for Cohagen's Cooking Wine had been destroyed. A sour, stale liquor smell wafted into the parking lot, and something had been ripped out of the ceiling.

"The store," I yelled as I ran up to the sheriff.

"You've been robbed." Sheriff Earl Nichols put his hands on his prodigious stomach as I came to a stop. "Or broke into anyway."

"More like bombed," said Lexi with a drunk-sounding snigger.

"It's not good to joke about things like that, young lady," said Deputy Stapleton, straightening his back.

"Who said I was joking?"

Deputy Stapleton narrowed his eyes. "You watch your step. I'm not in the mood for lip this morning. Considering all."

"Oh, calm the hell down, Ted," said the sheriff, taking a deep breath. He put one of his hands in his pockets, took a small square of gum, and put it in his mouth. "It's Sunday. And Miss Navarro might have a point. It looks like whomever did this came loaded with some sizeable munitions. You know how much force it requires to take out one of these Duratech windows?"

He turned to the lanky officer, who was rocking back and forth on his feet.

"Not exactly, sir. But I'm thinking you wouldn't be able to knock it in with a Louisville Slugger."

"Hell no, you wouldn't. Unless that slugger had a stick of dynamite at the end of it."

"You think that's what might have happened, Sheriff?"

The sheriff looked at Deputy Stapleton cockeyed. "No, Ted. I do not think someone took a baseball bat attached to a stick of dynamite on it and swung it at the window. What kind of nonsense…"

"Well, damn. Sorry for trying."

"Sorry is right. Now, Eberstark, I've been trying to get in touch with your dad since late last night but couldn't get through. I even took a quick drive by your house this morning to try and catch up with him."

"You did?" I asked.

"Damn place is harder than all hell to find, but yeah. Rang the doorbell, but no one answered. Including yourself. Come to think of it, I haven't seen your father at the store for a long time now. Not that I've been looking. I know I'm an early riser."

I shrugged. "Well, he hasn't been around too much."

"Oh, yeah?" The sheriff raised an eyebrow. "Where's he gone off to then?"

"Florida right now. For a corporate conference."

The sheriff eyed me.

"And you've just been at home? All by yourself?"

"He's been staying at my house for the past few nights, Sheriff," said Gus politely. "Always does when his dad's gone."

"That's fine." The Sherriff scratched his shoulder. "I'll be damned if my daughter isn't at one of her friend's houses every day of the week doing God knows what. By the way, Mustus, did you know your shirt's on inside out and backwards? You look like a goddamned dyslexic."

"What?" Gus looked at himself and then to me with an expression of betrayal. "No, I guess I didn't."

"Thank God for that. And Eberstark." He looked over my filthy clothes. "Have you been sleeping in a swamp?"

"No, sir."

"And Miss Navarro, I know your mother. I think she's a fine lady, so I'm not going to comment on your sorry appearance. Although it should be noted that I could have."

She blew out smoke. "You're a generous man."

"I know I am. But I'm telling you right now if she's giving you cigarettes, I will have her prosecuted to the fullest extent of the law."

"I found this on the street." Lexi stubbed the cigarette out and put the butt in the pocket of her jeans.

"Lucky I don't fine you right now. Anyhow. With your permission, Eberstark, we'd like to search the premises. Gather any evidence we can so that your dad can make his claim to the insurance company. Lotta money in damage over here."

"Lotta money," echoed Deputy Stapleton.

"Would you mind?" said the sheriff.

"No, sir," I said.

"You sound more polite than you should for your age. Someone should give you a million dollars."

"After that Duncan murder, all the kids are all running scared," said Deputy Stapleton. "It's giving them a healthy respect for authority is what it's doing."

"How the hell do you know anything about how the kids are running?" said the sheriff. "Aren't you twenty-three?"

"Twenty-three and a half."

"Well, I'm forty-five, and I'm scared shitless. So what's that say about me? I look at you and see a pair of pampers."

"Oh, come on, Earl."

"That's Sheriff to you, Ted."

Bitterness formed at the edges of Deputy Stapleton's mouth.

"Can we look around too?" I said a little louder than I meant to. Both the officers glanced at me curiously.

"Sure," said the sheriff. "Since I know where you live and all. Just be careful not to touch anything. I know this is your family's store. But it's also technically a crime scene."

Since the entire window had been blown out, Gus, Lexi, and I walked through the gaping hole, cringing as we stepped over broken glass. Deputy Ted Stapleton clicked on his flashlight.

He shined it over a mess of thrashed open cereal boxes and cake mix. "Maybe someone had a midnight craving."

"They definitely were looking to take out the security cameras." The sheriff pointed up to two sections of the ceiling that had been practically disemboweled. The cameras installed there were now a mess of wires, circuit boards, and shattered glass. Gus looked at me and Lexi with disappointment. "And in a big way too. Damn." He shone his flashlight up into the damage and then stepped outside the shattered window to point up at the ledge above the Stumart Sign. "Like a bear tore through here."

Deputy Stapleton eyed the gash. "What in the world?"

"Good news is, though, that he, they, whatever didn't catch the security camera above the sign." He smiled cautiously and stepped back inside the store. "Those are always the trickiest ones to find. There a light around here, Eberstark?"

"Yes, sir" I walked toward the back office.

"Good boy."

Gus and Lexi both gave me an "I'll cover you" look as I hurried toward the rear of the store. The light switches were right outside of the back office, not inside it, but I was sure the sheriff didn't know that.

The door was already open, so I could see the damage before I walked in. The back office had been laid to waste. The desk had bashed to pieces, and papers, from bills and statements to receipts and order forms, littered the floor. I walked into the janitor's closet and gasped. The creature had not only gone through the panel at the end of the room but had taken a little bit of the wall with it. Insulation spilled out.

I tried to think quickly, looking around for a way to conceal the damage. The last thing I wanted was to try and give Sheriff Earl Nichols a new set of suspicions. I saw two large boxes containing bleach. As quietly as I could, I heaved each one off the ground and stacked them against the hole in the wall. Stepping back and making a couple of adjustments, kicking the debris under a shelf, the scene looked relatively untouched in comparison to the rest of the store. I picked up a couple of buckets and toppled-over boxes to complete the picture, shut out the light, and closed the door behind me with barely a click. Now, all I had to do was turn on the light and retrieve the disc from the surveillance deck.

I flipped the switches in the hallway and yelled out, "Okay?" as the lights hummed on.

"Okay," said the sheriff.

I then returned to the back office, creeping up to the small wall locker where I knew the surveillance gear was kept. Taking my key ring out of my pocket, I jingled to a small key and unlocked the mini padlock. Swinging open the panel, I looked upon a simple DVD recorder hooked up to a series of monitors. Three in the aisles, one in produce, one above the registers, and one looking over the storefront onto the parking lot. All the feeds had been cut off but the last. Pressing the eject button on the player, I took the disc and hurriedly stuck it into my pocket, hoping not to damage it. Directly after I did so, Gus and Lexi hurried into the room, followed a few steps behind, I knew, by Sheriff Nichols and Deputy Stapleton.

"Must have been looking for something back here," said Deputy Stapleton as he turned the corner and looked upon the mess of the back office.

"Yep," said the sheriff, as I refastened the tiny padlock. "Probably thought they'd find some money. Well, let's see if they got it. Where do you usually keep the day's earnings, Eberstark?"

I referred to a heavy safe, half buried beneath the broken desk on the floor. The deputy leaned toward the ground and pushed aside some scattered papers. "Looks like they didn't even try and open it."

"Not that they could have anyway," said the sheriff. "But still, doesn't smell right. First, this grizzly murder over at the school, and now, your store gets terrorized by what could have been a fleet of Bengal tigers and for no reason at all."

Sheriff Earl Nichols, with his finger on his fleshy chin, bobbed toward the janitor's closet and stopped in front of it, pondering. He reached out and opened the door before turning on the light. He squinted into the room from the doorway, his eyes beading on the stacked boxes of bleach at the end. He seemed transfixed for a moment. He then shut the light off, closed the door, and walked back toward us, sticking out his upper lip.

He took his hat off to wipe a little sweat off his forehead. "Is that over there the surveillance deck?" He put the hat back on and pointing toward the locker.

I felt the DVD, rigid in my pocket. "I think so...but my dad's got the keys to it."

"Then that means he's got the keys to perpetrators too," said the sheriff. "Your father...he is a funny man, isn't he?"

"I don't know, Sheriff."

"Did I tell you I saw him?"

"I thought you said you hadn't."

"I said I hadn't seen him at the store. But outside's a different story. Because I did. About three weeks ago. Down by the school actually. At least I think it was him. I tend not to forget a face, and hell, I used to say hello to him near every morning since four years last July before he put Cory in charge. But at the school, well, he was dressed all crazy. In army fatigues or something. Like he was on his way to war. Involved in one of those redneck militias or something."

He jabbered in Deputy Stapleton's direction, and the deputy joined in. "I didn't know what to think."

"Army fatigues?" Gus tried to restrain a guffaw. "I can't imagine your dad in anything but a three-piece suit."

"I thought it was funny too," giggled the Sherriff. "Even tried to call out to him, say hi, you know. Ask him how his life's happening. He and I used to be pretty friendly. But he was gone before I could do so. Him and some other crazy-dressed weirdo with a hat. Hand on my heart. It was the strangest thing."

"Are you sure it was him?" I was attempting to steady my voice. "He was traveling three weeks ago."

"Travelling again, huh? Man certainly does have a lot of places he needs to go. Well, it was late. And I was on patrol. It might have been a case of mistaken identity. Mossglow is small, but once in a while, I'll still see a face I don't know. But anyway, when you see him, tell him to come by the station. I can't really set things straight here without him involved. Especially since he's got the key to the surveillance video. Hell if I don't suspect it's a group of delinquents from Crowstone Heights that's responsible. I'd just love to cart a whole truckload of those shitheads out to Ozark County for a few years in the cage."

I knew who the sheriff was referring to: adolescents like Charlene Poughkeepsie, Jesse Maroon, and Joe Ross. Truth be told, if I hadn't seen the monster with my own eyes last night, I'd have made the same connection.

"I wouldn't put it beyond their capacity, anyway. Did you know that I confiscated a RPG cannon from one of those assholes last month? A goddamned loaded one. Can you believe it? Enough firepower to blow down a house. They said they found it in a dump outside the city. Though when I ran the tags, it came up stolen...I'm still looking into it."

Lexi's eye lit up. "A bazooka? Really?"

"All right, that's enough," said the sheriff. "The three of you get out of here. We're going to look around for a little while longer. Then, we're going to go ahead and file our report so we can get things in order with your insurance and board up the window so no one else gets any bright ideas. You tell your dad to call whomever your representative is immediately before he comes to the station, by the way, so you open back up for business as soon as possible. I don't want to miss out on my breakfast this Monday. Yours are the only microwave burritos worth a bite in thirty miles."

"Thank you, Sheriff," I said.

"You don't need to thank me." He nodded at Deputy Ted Stapleton, giving him a look that implied he should continue surveying the property. "That would be your father's job."

SEVEN

AFTER I CALLED CHERRY TO alert her to the news and received her promise that she'd oversee the clean-up, we headed over to Lexi's to watch the video. As we came upon her home, I noticed how empty the garage looked without the Shepherd. It was almost as if a vital organ had been removed from someone's body.

Lexi propped up the garage, and we went in through the back door, squeezing by a washer and dryer with two litter boxes on top. I realized as I stepped by them into a hallway adorned with family photos that this was the first time I'd actually been inside the Navarro household. I wasn't sure what to expect, but was pretty sure whatever I would have expected would have been proven wrong. The first thing I noticed was how clean it was. And comfy. Gus's house was also clean but dusty in parts as a result of the decor. The Navarro house, on the other hand, while not as elegant in its piecing together of comfort-driven furniture and department store art, looked lived-in. To the point where you could imagine the owner suspected she would die here as well. Each ashtray, of which there were many, had been emptied and shined clean. Lexi took one with a map of the Philippines embossed in the ceramic and carried it with her into the living room.

"Cool vaulted ceilings," said Gus.

Lexi looked up toward the open peak of the house that rose above the front foyer as if she hadn't noticed it before. It declined as the foyer led into the living room, where it rose once again. It was halved in the center by what appeared to be a loft reachable by ladder. "The cats like to go up there. You guys want anything to drink?"

She took a cigarette from one of her mother's packs. Gus nodded, and Lexi told him he could take whatever he wanted out of the refrigerator. He fished out a cherry coke and snapped the can open with a satisfying fizzle. The second he did so, one of Lexi's cats, a muscly tuxedo with intense eyes, came chirping from the dining room and rubbed against Gus's leg.

"Heya, girl," he said.

"It's a he," said Lexi. "His name's Ignatius. And careful. He'll pet you, but if you pet him, he'll put a hole in your hand."

We went into the living room, and Lexi, with a tired wave, indicated we should take a seat in one of two lazy boys before a 42-inch-screen television. I could smell tobacco wafting up from every pore of fabric. A glass candy dish filled with York Peppermint Patties sat upon a glass coffee table. Lexi unwrapped one and swallowed it down with a sound that was vaguely reptilian. I couldn't help but notice that something had changed about her in the last couple of days. In a way, she reminded me of Mother after she returned from the hospital, just before she began to slip back into depression. When loading up the DVD player, the girl's movements had an uncoordinated, careless quality to them.

She picked up a couple of remotes and toggled the DVD to its menu stage. "My mom's staying with my aunt in Ozark; won't be back until tomorrow night. So you can kick your feet up."

"Lexi," I said as she practically fell back onto a loveseat in exhaustion. "Is everything okay with you?"

"Is everything okay with me?" Her one eye dilated, so dark it looked bruised. "You're the one whose store looks like it was raided by paramilitaries."

"We know you had a dream," said Gus, watching Lexi as she chomped down another peppermint patty. "A dream a lot like the one I had before my Crow Seraph came to life."

Lexi coughed. "Look, guys. All this 'we' talk, and whatever, like Musketeers or ninja turtles. Great. Fine. But with everything that's going on lately, how am I supposed to know when something's important or not? Mrs. Duncan got fucking killed..." she paused. "Because she chose to trust someone with what we'd found. Someone who thank shit doesn't have access to our names. At least I don't think. Now, I'm wondering whether I should get on my bike and go running around town trying to catch my Bronco or if that will just lead to someone else being torn to pieces." She began to tremble, bundling herself up in a felt blanket up her neck and rocking back and forth. Ignatius the tuxedo cat jumped on her lap and nuzzled her chin. "Jesus, it's cold. You guys can't feel that?"

Gus rubbed at his arms and gave me a look of concern. "It feels fine."

"Same for me," I said and couldn't help but think of Mrs. Duncan. How she'd woken in inexplicable subzero conditions. "And you were hot earlier. Outside, right?"

"What's this?" Gus said.

"She said she was hot earlier. In front of Stumart."

"But it was cold."

"Hey," she growled, tossing me the controller. "Stop talking about me like I'm not in the room. God, I hate boys. Like every girl you know is made of glass."

"I was just asking a question," I said.

"And I don't have to answer it. Let's watch the video."

Ignatius mewed. Lexi's words stung a little, but I'd seen Father treat Mother as a delicate creature that only he could protect. Protect to the point where protection meant safeguarding her from herself in every way imaginable. Lexi's teeth-chattering shivers worried me in a way I hadn't felt since I saw Mother bleeding on the bathroom floor. Behind the girl was a small wall mirror, hanging above the couch, and I imagined a man's face peering through, surveying her body with hateful eyes, pondering how to dismember it. Lexi's face, Mother's and Mrs. Duncan's, all began to meld together in my mind, painting a picture of women who'd searched for their own reflections and stumbled instead into something far more terrifying.

I quieted down and turned on the video. The DVD menu featured an interface that allowed me to browse through feeds over the last ninety days on each different camera. Those from within the store were interesting. Around 11:32, following what looked like an explosion from just outside the store, they cut to static one by one. We couldn't see who was responsible. Whatever the creature had been, it had been smart, slinking about the store's perimeter and decommissioning the cameras before it got to work.

After we discovered the internal camera feeds would reveal nothing, we turned to the storefront one and set it to the time of the break-in. Around 11:31, we witnessed a blot of movement. I rewound. Paused. Gus and I leaned in close, and when that wasn't enough, we got out of the lazy boys and moved within a foot of the screen. Lexi, wrapping her blanket around her and shooing Ignatius off her lap, did the same, shivering as she came to stand between the two of us. I rewound the segment again, hit play, and paused after a couple of seconds.

A figure walked across the empty parking lot. Without fear or hesitation, it made a slow, deliberate line for Stumart. Its body was sturdy, and the clothes it wore, though rendered black and white by the display, were familiar. A long coat, khaki pants, and oxford shoes. Clothing I was sure I'd seen before along with the body wearing them. But the face...I truly couldn't understand what I was looking at. I twisted my head left to right and paused the reel.

Gus squinted at the screen. "Eberstark, can you zoom in?"

"I don't know how,"

"Let me see that." Lexi's clammy hand swiped the controller. She pushed a couple of buttons, and the screen faded and reappeared again a few frames closer.

Gus leaned in. "What is that?"

Lexi refreshed the frame again so that a blurred but identifiable image came up on screen.

Before us was a head. But a head splitting in two. Two petals of flesh, parting so that something else inside could bloom. An oleaginous tar was erupting from the neck. An oily slick that, when you looked at it closely, was made up of tendrils. I honed in on the split head itself, noting the wavy blond hair and sharp, handsome chin.

"Mr. Kraft," I whispered. "That's Mr. Kraft. I'm sure of it."

Or something like Mr. Kraft. A different person observing this video, like Sheriff Earl Nichols, for instance, if not drawn into instant doubt of everything he'd ever known, likely wouldn't even have recognized our Myers High US Politics teacher. The only reason I had was because of the halves of the head. They looked just as plastic as they had when I didn't allow him to look around our store.

Gus's eyes registered the same recognition. "It is Mr. Kraft. I can tell by his walk."

"No one else walks like that," said Lexi, still twitching with cold. "No one else in town."

"Play the rest of the tape," said Gus. "Slowly."

Lexi pressed the play button and made an adjustment so that the reel would slow. We then stared in horror as what we'd known as Mr. Kraft, the handsomest man in Mossglow, was fully and grotesquely inverted. Folded into himself like a bloody water skin. The creature that emerged from the interchange unfurled like a caterpillar with a multitude of misplaced limbs while Mr. Kraft himself, it appeared, was tucked somewhere inside. The camera was so fuzzy and the creature's movement so quick it was hard to make out anatomical details. All we understood was that whatever we were dealing with was quicker and stronger than I'd previously imagined. Its head was a web of tentacles that could have been hair on an inhuman scalp. The body itself was stark white, just like the other creature's had been, but this one was uncloaked, nude, and absent of metal shards. It was gaunt but muscular, sinewy and swift. Its buttocks faced the sky and throbbed as the appendages crawled along.

"We're all going to die," said Lexi softly.

"What?" I almost laughed.

"You heard me." Her eye fixated on the screen. "We're not going to make it out of this city alive."

Gus stood up. "Will you stop it, Lexi? That's nonsense."

"It's not. I just saw it, Gus. Like how you can see when the sun's about to set. That thing…it's too big. I'm talking size, man. Take a good look in the mirror. If we keep going, we'll end up neck-high in each other's blood."

Gus was fuming. "Enough with the histrionics. We're not going to be killed by anything, okay?"

"You're right. What's going to kill us is hardly an anything at all." She looked toward the loft, where we heard a little movement. A slight scratching sound. "Petey? Are you there, kitty?"

She heard a mew, and her second cat, a smaller-built calico with a slim torso, skipped down the rungs and came to brush against her legs.

She picked him up. "Good boy."

Gus held out his hands. "Have you ever thought about the fact that the reason that we're calling this thing a monster in the first place is because we don't know what it really is? It's like Picasso said. 'Everything you can imagine is real.' Which means that, if this monster does exist, it exists because someone figured out how to make it exist."

"I don't think that's what Picasso meant, Gus," said Lexi, petting Petey.

"Maybe not. But I've got another point. About perception. You're letting your fear control you, and you're not even aware of it."

"Give it a rest."

"It's unbecoming of you. You're supposed to be the brave one here. Or have you forgotten that?"

"You're confusing bravery with the fact that I'm just really good at dealing when things go to shit. It's all about appearances, don't you know." She put tiny Petey down. "My father left one day without a fucking word. I woke up, went downstairs, and my mom was crying into a bowl of cornflakes. She hadn't eaten a bite. It took her three days to tell me what had happened. That my good old dad had 'elected' to live with his other family. It took her five more days after that just to put on a new pair of clothes. I'm not an idiot, Gus. It's just hard to fight when you only give half a shit."

She stuffed another peppermint patty into her mouth.

Gus watched her chew. "Sounds like you're giving up."

Lexi chuckled. "We're three kids with a DVD. You like those odds?"

"You're sitting here looking at me like you never gave a shit about anyone. When you—you, Lexi—led us into this quagmire to begin with. Tell me; where would you be now if we hadn't come along that night when you discovered a monster in the woods? Where would I be? Huh? Where would Eberstark be? You're acting like *we* let *you* down. I hope you can grasp the irony."

Lexi looked at Gus and me, and for a rare, strange moment, it seemed as if she was pleased. That brief satiation faded, however, as she returned to shivering under her blanket.

"Look…I've been…there's something…" She looked toward the wall mirror and took a deep breath. "Never mind."

"Never mind what?" I said.

She rewound the reel and paused again upon the creature, its mass in full stride as it smashed through the store front.

"All I want to know is how you, skinny Gus Mustus, and you, Eberstark flab abs, are planning to get the jump on Cthulhu over here?"

"Easy." Gus turned away from the television and walked toward Ignatius. Lexi protested as he picked the cat up and pet him under the chin, eliciting a happy purr while I looked down at my stomach in shame. "Tomorrow, after school…" Ignatius gave him his belly. "We break into Mr. Kraft's house."

EIGHT

AT FIRST, I'D THOUGHT GUS was crazy. But the more he talked about how the plan would play out, the more sense it made. Citing the need to transport some Sword Star terrain to his house to be worked on, Gus would borrow his parent's Dodge Caravan to take to school. We'd then follow Mr. Kraft after 8th period to his house, stake him out, wait for him to leave after a phone call he'd receive from Lexi posing as a member of the Mossglow PD, and break in to search for clues. It all seemed like a good idea when discussing it from the safety of Lexi's living room. But as the hour drew closer, my courage tank sprung a leak.

I stayed at Gus's house, feeling unsure of what would be waiting for me at home. When we arrived, Marshall was already on the back porch, smoking his pipe. It looked like he wasn't wearing pants, but I couldn't tell from where I was standing.

Denise proceeded to make us dinner. As we watched Sword Star

THE SILENT END

Prime and ate chicken salad sandwiches, I found that I could barely pay attention. It wasn't because the show wasn't good—it was—but because I'd begun to think about Father, about the sheriff, about the fact that it was possible the break-in had left me exposed. I took my phone out of my pocket and, after deliberating for a good fifteen minutes, sent Father a message.

Dad? U okay? Someone/thing broke into the store.

After hitting send, I immediately regretted it. The sheriff had seen him, anyway, running around Mossglow dressed in camouflage with the Hat. This unnerved me in particular because no one, to my knowledge, had seen the Hat yet but me. Everything was getting very messy very quickly. A couple of minutes later, however, when I received a reply text, I was strangely gratified.

Out of a-penumbrics. Demons in the dark. Trust no one.

This message was followed quickly by a second one.

Not even yourself.

I then closed the phone and looked over to Gus, whose face was glazed over and puppet-like. His eyes were fixed on the television, but he didn't seem to be registering the images. When we went to sleep that night, me lying down on a cot on the floor beside his bed, he started murmuring to himself. I couldn't understand what he was saying, but the words seemed foreign. Something Germanic maybe? Middle Eastern? All I knew for sure was that he wasn't speaking

English and that it made it difficult for me to sleep.

Myers High the next day was more rambunctious than I thought it would be following the death of Mrs. Duncan. Apart from the presence of a few additional armed police officers pacing the corridors, the main atrium roared with the usual chatter. Students zipped about in a sticky, pubescent fog, smelling of freshly smoked cigarettes and over-applied cologne, mixed with the tang of underarm sweat. Masked by the lazy initiative of Monday morning, a collective attempt was being made to ignore what had happened last Friday. As we entered, teachers were handing out fliers that set out the schedule for the day. It didn't even make sense that we were back at school at all not only because of the murder's resultant trauma but because of the fact that Mrs. Duncan would have to be replaced. Dean Veltry would be addressing the entire student body in Myers Gymnasium at nine a.m., after which classes would resume according to their original schedules.

Ajay Kapur and Ronald Peterson were waiting by our lockers as Gus and I approached. They were ready for class already, saddled with backpacks and books, and looked perturbed, particularly Ronald. His mouth was so large that when he frowned, he appeared to suck his chin into his upper lip.

"Everything okay, gentleman?" I said. I saw Lexi walking toward her locker across the aisle and shot her a nod, which she cursorily returned. She was wearing a heavy, plaid hat and puffy winter jacket that caused her to move with uncharacteristic bulk.

"What do you think?" Ajay snapped. I noticed the collar of his navy blue dress shirt was buttoned up to his neck.

Gus turned to Ajay. "Sounds like you're going to tell us."

"My bunker." Ajay's arms crossed his chest. "It's been damaged. Along with my Lorques."

"Seriously?" Gus put on a concerned face. "That's awful."

"It is awful, isn't it? You know what's also awful? That as far as I know, the only people with keys to the club office are Ronald here. And you."

"And I haven't been up there since last Tuesday," said Ronald.

"When I went with him," Ajay added.

Gus narrowed his eyes. "What are you trying to imply?"

"I think you know perfectly well what I'm trying to imply."

I felt the mental equivalent of my hand slapping my forehead as I remembered the Crow Seraph and the damage it had wreaked. I was sure Gus was feeling something similar although he seemed more apt at concealing it.

"Don't be ridiculous." I know Gus didn't like to lie, but he didn't have a choice.

"Why would we do something like that?" I said.

"Come on, guys," said Ajay. "We're not idiots."

"Him least of all," said Ronald, nodding toward Ajay with his taffy strand of a neck.

Melinda Valdez passed by Ronald in conversation, brushing into him accidentally with her shoulder. She then went to her locker a couple of spots down from mine. She was talking to her sister, Nadia, who, while sharing Melinda's age and last name, exuded a confidence that distinguished the two considerably. She was also more adult-looking, with a body accentuated by curves that contributed to her dating older townies. One of which, a thirty two-year-old from Crowstone Heights, had actually gone to jail last year when discovered atop Nadia in the backseat of a station wagon.

Melinda had a wisp of a voice. "The entire lab? That's crazy."

Nadia concurred with a bored look on her face. "And most of the second floor. They've closed it down for repairs or whatever."

I tapped Melinda on the shoulder. She shrank away. "What... what are you guys talking about?"

Nadia turned to me, scowled at what I assumed was my inborn ugliness, and canted her chin toward her backpack to search through it.

"Someone trashed the second floor." She brushed her chestnut brown hair out of her eyes. "The entire chemistry lab is busted up."

"Are you serious?"

She looked at Nadia. "They closed the whole floor off."

"Who did?"

"The administration, I guess. They're not letting anyone upstairs."

"Do they know who did it?" Gus said, opening his locker. I saw as he did so a copy of *The Trial of Xerxes*. He almost put it in his bag before he remembered why he didn't need it anymore. I saw his fist clench.

Melinda turned to Nadia, who rolled her eyes for more of an explanation.

"No," the older sister scoffed. "But apparently, there's, like, this big hole up there, or something? Like someone tried to break down a wall?" Nadia talked as if every one of her sentences was a question. "I really don't care as long as the cafeteria's open. This school is such a shithole; it's the only thing worthwhile. God, I can't wait for ASU." She turned to Melinda, and they gave each other a high five, chiming in sync, "Early enrollment!"

Gus turned to Ronald and Ajay as Melinda and Nadia walked away.

"Well, it seems like you've found your culprit," said Gus.

"What do you mean?" said Ronald.

"I mean that whoever vandalized the second floor probably found a way into the Sword Star office."

Ajay glared at Gus. "Bullocks. None of the other clubs were touched. Why would someone single us out?"

"Yeah," said Ronald. "Seems fishy."

"Either way, we'll help you fix everything up," Gus said.

"My dad says that the government's putting something in the water here," said Ronald with plenty of saliva. "That when you drink out of the tap, there's these micro-organisms that get into your brain and make you want to masturbate."

"What does that have to do with anything?" said Ajay.

Ronald shrugged. "Just thought you'd want to know."

I reached toward my locker and put in the combination, which was almost second nature now. I hadn't changed it since freshman year, and my fingers knew the numbers instinctually. I heard the click and pulled it open. When I did so, Ronald screeched and jumped away. "What the fuck?"

A horrible smell surged into our nostrils.

In the locker was a stick man made of rotting pork. Skewers had been used for the arms and legs. And on each were bunched together chunks of stringy, pink flesh that had probably been festering over the weekend. The head was a round chop with two nails to represent the eyes and a hole for the mouth. And in that hole, a red sausage had been stuck. Juice from the meat had leaked all over my books and papers. Notebooks were stained with melted, rotten fat.

"Oh, Eberstark," said Gus. "This is...man."

"What type of sick shit?" Ronald was covering his mouth with his shirt as he ran away. "That's it; I'm outta here. You freaks are on your own."

I shut the locker. "Will someone just get a trash bag?"

"Aren't you going to report this?" said Ajay, mouth agape.

I snickered darkly at the possibility.

Gus returned a moment later with a plastic grocery bag—from Stumart no less. I put my shirt over my nose, opened the locker, and, using a ruler, pried the rotting pork man from my locker. I noticed as I did so that "Oink oink!" had been written in red marker on the forehead. A small group of students slowed their pace as I carried out the exercise, and my stomach began to turn.

I walked over to the nearest trashcan and threw it in. I leaned my head against the wall and couldn't help but cry.

"Come on, Eberstark," I heard Lexi say as she tugged on my sleeve. Her eye was filled with sympathy. "I'll walk with you to the assembly."

Face to face with her, I noticed that beneath her hat were the stippled marks of an electric razor. She caught me looking and turned away.

"Lexi, did you?"

Sighing, she took off the hat and revealed a buzzed down head. It made her head look large, her body look small, and the eyepatch more medicinal than menacing. Seeing her like this was almost painful. An attempt either to alter her personality or reveal it a little clearer.

"Damn, Lexi," said Gus. "I mean, I like it, I think. But…"

She rubbed her head with one hand. "It felt too heavy, so I took it off. Stop looking at me like that. We've got a big day."

She put her hat back on, put her hand on my shoulder, and began to escort me out of the atrium. The three of us left Ajay at his locker, gazing at our backs like someone assessing the aftermath of a car crash.

Myers Gymnasium clamored with noise. Students filled the unfurled bleachers on the basketball court. Gus, Lexi, and I looked around for seats together. But since we hadn't arrived early enough, we were forced to sit in the mostly abandoned front row with uneasy underclassmen and seniors like Danny Feld, who'd had his ribs broken by Charlene Poughkeepsie last year. He in particular still looked just as emotionally injured as his body had appeared the day he returned to school from the hospital. Though we'd all known who'd been responsible for his bludgeoning, something had kept him from pressing charges. A something that remained with him even now, that turned his droopy, green eyes downward beneath a military burr cut. For a raw moment, I saw myself in his place. I saw my shoulders hunched and my gaze at my shoes, just trying to pretend I wasn't alive.

As we approached the bleachers from the side door to the gymnasium, I couldn't help but notice Charlene Poughkeepsie, Joe Ross, and Jesse Maroon perched like vultures on the very top row. Everyone else had cleared out around them, giving them full reign over the shadows cast by team pennants billowing lightly from the rafters. Jesse was making a jack-off gesture with his hands, squeezing his facial features into a constipated grimace as his wrist shook vigorously. The second he noticed me, I tried to look away, but the damage had already been done. He stopped his juddering and whispered to Charlene and Joe. Charlene then turned her lupine gaze on me, grinned, and put her thumb to her nose in mimic of a pig's snout.

Lexi flashed Charlene a rage-filled eye. "Don't pay attention to them, Eberstark." Charlene then looked back at Lexi with what could only be described as unbridled violence. It was look I never wanted to see again. Not on anybody, anywhere.

Mr. Kraft, looking prim and handsome as usual, crossed the gymnasium court from the east doors and came to sit in a row of folding chairs before the bleachers between Mr. Schmidt and Mrs. Sherwood. As he did so, whispers and coos came from many of the girls in the crowd though they were the kind only audible to student ears. Noticing me, Mr. Kraft stood up, turning around to give me a friendly wave.

"Eberstark!" He angled his neck to make sure Dean Veltry hadn't arrived yet and stopped short of approaching me. He looked nervous. Did Dean Veltry have as much of a paralyzing effect on the teachers of Myers High as he did on the student body? "I heard about the break-in. And just wanted to say how very sorry I am. I hope they catch whoever did it soon."

"Thank you, Mr. Kraft," I said, noticing how umblemished he looked. It was almost as if he'd been renewed, dipped in some fountain of regeneration. I wondered if he really thought he'd been careful enough for me not suspect a thing about the secret within him.

"No need to thank me. It's I who should be thanking you for putting up with all my questions. I'll try and get in touch with your father next week, after the drama dies down. Until then, you just take care of yourself." He turned to Lexi. "As for you, Ms. Navarro…"

"What?" she snapped.

"I'd like you to take off your hat."

He smiled and pointed to his own head.

Lexi put her hand to her wool hat, rubbing it for a second before returning it to her lap.

"I…I don't want to."

"It's not whether you want to or not, young lady. This is school policy we're talking about. No hats in classrooms or assemblies."

"But." Her voice was actually pleading.

"Do it now, Ms. Navarro," said Mr. Kraft in a low, authoritative voice. "I'm not going to ask you again."

Lexi, cursing to herself, dragged the hat away. Without her hair, her eye seem smaller and her cheekbones more angular.

"Hey, Lexi," yelled Jesse Maroon from the top of the bleachers. "You got leukemia?"

Charlene and Mogadishu exploded with laughter.

Mr. Kraft hissed in their direction before turning back to Lexi.

"Don't be so embarrassed." He could have had honey on his tongue. "It's not a bad look for you. There's even something, might I say, daring about it."

The handsome man then shot me a wink and rejoined in conversation with Mr. Schmidt, the balding biology teacher. Gus leaned toward us and whispered as a reminder, "Eye on the prize."

"You have no idea," Lexi whispered through gritted teeth.

At the precise moment the clock hit 9, Dean Veltry entered the gymnasium from Myers East. His head, turned sideways, still almost swiped the top of the doorframe. The entire student body went silent. In the center of the gymnasium, right over the Myers High Mickey the Bullfrog-themed basketball team logo, was a standing microphone. He walked right to it, his smoldering features cloaked in woe. His nose looked down the center of the receiver. Silence ensued. All I could think of was the shadow I'd seen grow and shrink over him in his office. That and the sharpness of his letter opener, whose frog head was similar to that on the key I'd obtained from the cellar.

"Myers High has been dealt a devastating blow," he bellowed.

He paused, and the bleachers creaked.

"Sometime between last Thursday night and Friday morning, our dear Mrs. Ilana Duncan was murdered. All of you know about this. Some of you saw the aftermath with your own eyes. Some of you might know more than you're letting on. And even more of you might be afraid of what this means for us at Myers High."

His steely eyes passed over the crowd.

"Truth be told, I can't tell you how you should feel. There is no emotion more complex or frightening than loss. I can't say with certainty that you will grow from what you've seen. Nor can I say that you'll gain perspective. What I can say is that what happened to Mrs. Duncan is a lesson if you choose to accept it. For from death comes wisdom. This is something all of you should understand."

Someone giggled, and Dean Veltry's gaze honed onto the source of it like a hawk. A whoosh of terror came over me as he did so even though he hadn't directed his eyes toward me. He went back to his microphone as what could have been a mighty vacuum sucked up all our breath.

"I'm not sure if all of you grasp the gravity of death. So let me explain it to you better. Death is a war the body fights against itself. The brain shuts down each of your internal organs. One by one. The lungs rattle out the last of their breath. The bowels evacuate the remainder of their feces. Click. Click. Click. Switches on your brain stem. Important, since it is the brain that outlives the rest of the body. Even when the heart ceases to pump, millions of terrified cells scramble for oxygen until they suffocate. Millions of parts of you choking under a sealed dome. Trapped in a cage of your own useless biology, moments pass as you await the no longer. And then, once you fade, your muscles continue to spasm. The flesh dries and shrinks and crumples."

My knees wobbled. Gus's did too.

"Mrs. Duncan's body was ripped to pieces. Her death was vicious. And painful. As opposed to being reassembled for a coffin, she elected in her will the graceful path. Fire and ash. Ash that, if you were within three miles of the Mossglow Mortuary this weekend, you inhaled deep into your lungs." He looked over the crowd with an amused sort of anticipation. "You breathed in Mrs. Duncan. You consumed her. She is part of you now."

As the dean spoke, I saw Mr. Schmidt and Mrs. Sherwood exchange quizzical looks. Mr. Schmidt then cleared his throat as if to voice his discomfort, and the dean went quiet. He gave Mr. Schmidt such a stare that the man practically wilted.

"I'm not here today to make you feel better. Every fiber of your being should embrace the eventuality of your decline. Mrs. Duncan should inhabit every inch of you. For death shows us we are small. It shows us that selfishness is the human way. If I were a smarter man, I'd say a new species was needed in our place. Something stronger, more capable of understanding what it's been given. Something that can't be so easily dissembled. This is why I admired Ilana in particular. She didn't just look at you as a reflection of herself, but she tried to see you as you were. Her mind was keen and her emotions in tune. She understood the constraints of our species and was better for it. Some may even say that she was too smart for her own good. That intelligence may have killed her."

He took a deep breath, and so did we.

"This is why, after having a conversation with the regional board, I've made it my personal mission to honor her legacy here at Myers High. When we expand the library next year to include a new section on American and European history, we will rename it in its entirety. What was once known as Myers Library will hereby be known as the Duncan Library. We will do this to remember that knowledge can be expensed by blood and that while we're on this planet for a short while, we must be diligently, obsessively attuned to its great dysfunction."

He stepped away from the microphone and walked back toward the door heading to Myers East. Jesse Maroon, Charlene Poughkeepsie, and Joe Ross began clapping and whooping. I shut my eyes as Mrs.

Anderson went up to the microphone and shakily informed us on how we were to return to our regularly scheduled courses. I couldn't believe that no one had mentioned the vandalism on the second floor, where apparently there was a gaping crater in the wall. My body rumbled with the feet of students hopping off the bleachers. In my mind, I saw them as small, furry creatures with button-like eyes. Squirrels or rabbits. Tiny, fearful animals searching for a corral in the panic. I saw them spilling out the doors of the gymnasium into the halls of Myers High, dropping pellets and nibbling at the walls.

NINE

WE SKIPPED EIGHTH PERIOD TO stake out Mr. Kraft. Gus had done the diligence of parking in the same lot where the teacher kept his red 1999 Toyota MR2. Gus's idea of a disguise involved wearing identical gray rain ponchos. He gave us each a sealed package, and we removed the rubbery fabric from inside. Fitting the slickers over our heads, we climbed into his parent's Dodge with Lexi in the passenger seat and me peeking through from the back. We were parked near the exit from the lot, the last in a queue of cars lined along a grassy knoll. I wondered, as Gus finished his disguise with a pair of almost comically large sunglasses that would look out of place on any normal Mossglow afternoon, if our cover rendered us more conspicuous. Thankfully, the mist had drifted in heavy today and darkened all the windows and faces it passed.

About twenty minutes before the last bell rang, we saw a large figure walk to the edge of the parking lot. We ducked down so that we could peer just above the window pane.

"Dean Veltry," said Lexi almost at a whisper.

The great man's presence was unmistakable. He walked with long, controlled steps, arriving at a garbage bin at the edge of the parking lot. Looking left and right, he put his hands into his pockets. He then removed his right hand and raised it to his lips.

"What's he doing?" Gus said.

Lexi squinted. "Talking, I think."

He was indeed speaking into what could have been his fingertips. He then returned whatever it had been to his pocket and checked his watch.

"Who's he waiting for?" I said.

"There's something about that man…" Lexi watched the dean stand, stone-eyed as as he surveyed the parking lot. The van's angle made it difficult for him to spot us, but we remained still. "I wouldn't be surprised if he was operated by remote control."

"Talk quieter," Gus said.

"Why?"

"I'm worried he'll hear us."

We saw two more figures step out of the south entrance to Myers High and approach the dean's location. Charlene Poughkeepsie and Joe Ross, walking side by side. Charlene's fists twisted in front of her wrecking ball of a stomach with every step. She almost looked like a cartoon villain. Something from an old, black-and-white animation with bad guy belly laughs.

Gus chuckled with a glint of satisfaction. "Looks like a classic Veltry ambush in the works."

"Can't wait to see this go down," said Lexi.

"I hope they get suspended for the rest of the year. Actually, I hope they get expelled. No, let me correct that. I hope he finds hard drugs on them and they go to prison for twenty years. And then I hope they get murdered in prison."

"Wait." I focused in. At first, I'd thought the same thing: that Dean Veltry would pounce on the unsuspecting Crowstone teens and drag them down to his office. But when Charlene came around the side of the dumpster, her face wasn't fearful. It was expectant. The three greeted each other, shaking hands. A few seconds later, they were engaged in quiet conversation before the dumpster.

"This is...unholy," said Gus.

Charlene was smiling, and Joe chuckled a couple of times. The three seemed to have a rapport that went beyond what any of us knew. Dean Veltry, with his hand on Charlene's upper back, directed her and Joe toward the parking lot. They stepped off the sidewalk that led back to the school and began walking in our direction.

"Holy shit," Gus said. "Get down."

We ducked out of view. I was afraid if he saw me, he'd just rip my heart from my chest and take a bite out of it like a bloody apple. Every part of me screamed out in avoidance, and I put my fingers on the charm bracelet in my pocket, feeling it for safety. But then I saw Gus peeking back outside.

"Now, I'm truly confused."

Lexi and I looked up to find that Charlene and Joe had climbed into the dean's car, a shiny black Buick Regal sitting in faculty parking. The dean himself got into the driver's seat and started the engine.

"I don't like this," I said.

"Me neither," said Lexi.

"Where are they going?"

The car pulled out, revealing the words RESERVED FOR F.

THE SILENT END

VELTRY on the concrete.

"Duck," I said as the Buick turned toward us to exit. We hit the floor, and heard the motor purr by. When we came back up, they were already speeding off down Nigh'Sow Road.

"I'm not sure what I'm more afraid of," said Lexi. "'A Mr. Kraft monster or whatever the hell those three are up to."

"Maybe we should keep from comparing," I said.

About twenty minutes later, as the eighth period bell rang, Mr. Kraft hurried out of the southern exit with a book under his arm. We were thinking he'd get out later being that he, like all of our teachers, often had after-school commitments. But there he was, looking jaunty as usual even as a gust of wind slipped inside his jacket and set it alight. Around him, students and a peppering of police officers sprayed out in a fan into the lot, creating a post-school confusion. The mist swirled, and a thundercloud coughed overhead. It appeared as if Mr. Kraft were whistling as he got into his car.

"Okay, Gus," said Lexi. "Nice and easy."

Gus waited until Mr. Kraft pulled out of the parking lot and followed him at a safe distance. He kept his low beams on so that the fog would conceal us better. As we continued on through Mossglow, he maintained a steady tail, straining to concentrate so that an adequate distance was maintained. We heard an increase in rain patter on the van's hood as we headed toward downtown, joining a sparse arrangement of cars as we passed the main rural stretch of chicken farms and grain silos. Last night, Denise had told us we were in for a big storm due to begin this afternoon. This drizzle was only the beginning, and already, Mossglow had taken on a deep tone of green.

Lexi fidgeted with her hat on the floor. "I need to smoke."

"Not in the van," said Gus.

Lexi rolled her eyes and mimicked him. "Not in the van."

Inspired, I did an impression as well, folding my arms across my chest and shaking my head with disapproval.

"I know you guys are making fun of me," Gus said.

"How?" giggled Lexi.

"Because I'm smarter than you." He sped up a little. "You reprobates."

"My name's Gus, and I use words like 'reprobate,'" said Lexi in a robotic voice.

"I am the Mustus 9000," I continued. "I come from the future to reevaluate your vocabulary."

"All right, all right," said Gus. "Just remember that I'm driving us to break into a man's house right now—hey! What are you doing?"

"What?" Lexi took a puff off a cigarette.

"I said no smoking!"

"What about drinking?" Lexi pulled a flask out of the pocket of her jacket and took a slug.

Gus opened the passenger window; Lexi shrieked as she was sprayed with cold rain.

"I'm sorry, okay! I'll put it out."

Gus looked heroic with satisfaction as Lexi pitched the cigarette out the window. We all then struggled to keep from being seized with laughter. Following Mr. Kraft had been the most fun we'd had in weeks; quite possibly the most fun the three of us had ever had together period. For a moment, Lexi seemed unworried, unburdened. Gus was unserious, and I was able to forget about where we were actually going. Into a house inhabited, in all likelihood, by a nightmare.

Our teacher ended up living on the edge of downtown in more of a cottage than a house. It didn't have a garage, so he parked his MR2 on the street. Gus hung back about one hundred feet, pulled over, and shut off the engine in front of a blue Victorian. Mr. Kraft climbed out of his car, stretched his long, muscular arms into the air, and jogged up the path to his front steps to the door. His was a quaint neighborhood, what could be considered one of the scant acculturated populations of Mossglow. A few local artists lived in the area alongside middle-class townies that kept businesses on the Main Drive.

"Now what?" said Lexi.

Gus checked his Casio. "We wait for about an hour. Then, you'll call posing as a representative of the Mossglow Police Department."

"Noted."

"You'll ask him to come down to the station in reference to the recent break-in at Stumart. That'll get him stirred up."

"Damn," I said. "Will you be able to pull that off?"

"Of course I will," said Lexi. "Do you have any idea how many times I've posed as my mom over the phone?"

"If all goes according to plan, it'll buy us at least thirty-five minutes, granted Mr. Kraft spends at least eight inside the station," said Gus. "Though in all likelihood, we may have closer to an hour. Once he starts talking to Sheriff Nichols, they'll all get so confused there's a chance they won't work it out until midnight."

"Where did you get his number?" I asked.

"I looked it up in the registrar's office."

"One of the side-effects of being an exemplary kiss-ass," said Lexi.

"I can't believe we're actually doing this." My entire body was on edge. "Lexi, can I have a swig off whatever it is you're drinking?"

"Come on, Eberstark." Gus rolled his eyes. "Don't indulge your reptile brain."

"Are you trying to say I'm simple, Mustus?" said Lexi, handing me the flask. I took a deep swallow. My throat burned, but no more than a few seconds later, I felt less anxious.

"Not intrinsically. You're just weak."

"Am I really?"

"I'm not saying I'm above such urges. Only that I'm choosing to ignore them until the time is right."

"And when will that be?"

"College."

"Come on, Gus." She offered him the flask. "Considering what we're about to do, I think you can afford to indulge at least some of your 'urges.' Before they end up running away without you."

Gus chewed at his lip and, with a groan, reached for the flask. Unscrewing it violently, he took a small sip and gagged. "Get this poison away from me…"

"Gladly." Lexi took another slug, after which she handed it to me. It truly did taste like poison. A few minutes later, we'd emptied it to the bottom.

An hour passed. Lexi, taking a deep breath, had her smartphone in her hand with Mr. Kraft's number on the display. "All right. Here we go."

As she made to press the call button, however, Gus whispered, "Stop."

We saw Mr. Kraft come out of his front door. He was dressed in track pants and a sweatshirt. He seemed to be going on a jog. Stretching a bit and kicking his long legs out side to side, he began his workout.

"Shit." Gus slammed his hand against the dashboard as our teacher, running in the opposite direction of the van, disappeared into the mizzle. "Wasn't expecting that."

"What are we going to do?" I looked from Gus to Lexi.

"We're going to do exactly what we came here to do." Lexi was loose-limbed with liquor as she made sure the poncho was fixed over her shoulders.

"But how do we know how long he'll be gone for?" I asked.

"We don't," said Gus, starting the van and pulling up closer, about thirty feet away. He put it in park and took out the keys. From the glove compartment, he then snagged three ski masks.

"Put these on. One of us will keep watch by the front window while the other two look around."

Lexi nodded as she tugged one over her newly shaved head. I reluctantly did the same.

"All right." Gus opened the door. He looked nervous, and that nervousness made his body wiry and taut. His eyes burned behind the ski mask. "We've only get one chance here. So be quick, be careful, and most importantly, be quiet."

TEN

WE FOUND OUR WAY INTO Mr. Kraft's cottage through a mullioned window in the backyard. He'd left it open a small crack, and the heavy, brown curtains that lined the inside fluttered from the wind. He didn't have much of a backyard to speak of, two chairs, a pinewood table and a patch of grass. But it was fenced off, which made me feel comfortable pulling up my ski mask.

"Put that back on," whispered Gus.

"But nobody can see us."

"How do you know that?" His eyes were bloodshot.

Sighing, I put the hat back on, and we shoved the pane up as high as it could go. Gus, noting how grass-stained his penny loafers were, took them off and handed them to me before Lexi helped hoist him through. We waited nervously until, with a slow creak, he opened the back door. I had a hard time swallowing as I wiped my feet on the coir mat and prepared to step inside. Lexi handed Gus back his

THE SILENT END

shoes, and a rumble rolled down from the clouds.

Mr. Kraft's home was soothing and earth-toned. Finished with lacquered, hardwood floors; walled with expansive, black mahogany bookshelves; and sparsely, yet elegantly furnished with two leather reading chairs, a coffee table, and chaise lounge, it was largely what I'd have expected out of a place inhabited by a man of such implausible symmetry. A cello with antique varnish stood on a stand in the corner of the living room beside a wicker bin filled with music books. Beyond that lay a spotless, white-tiled kitchen with granite counters and a butcher board island. A single house plant, a cultivated money tree, sat in one corner in an earthenware pot, and I smelled something... something fertile and mushy I couldn't quite place.

Gus tried to keep his lower lip from twitching. "I'll keep watch. You and Lexi check around. Remember, leave nothing out of place."

The taste of liquor lingered on my breath. Exchanging a committed look with Lexi, we began to search the house. I'd never done something this illegal before. I'd burned things I shouldn't have burned; I'd shoplifted. I'd done drugs. But casing a house, looking through another person's things? Even if I knew it all needed to be done, it felt wrong.

"Faster, Eberstark," whispered Lexi, noticing my hesitation as I hovered between the living room and kitchen.

I began rummaging through anything I could—which wasn't much. I lifted furniture, rifled through a small entryway table near the front door. Under the couches, I found nothing, not even dust tumbleweeds, but in the table were receipts—some of which were from Stumart, no less—along with take-out menus and stamp strips. I skimmed over them quickly. Items bought were bags of ice. Pine Sol. Bleach. Antifreeze. More chemical cleaners than food. Overall, Mr. Kraft could have been one of the sparest people I'd ever encountered.

Even his refrigerator seemed to be for show. I'm not sure if there had ever been food there to begin with being that the only consumable product was an unopened box of baking soda on the top shelf. A row of electronic kitchen aid items—a blender, a mixer, a juicer—still had their tags, and the butcher block wasn't so much as scratched.

I peeked my head from the kitchen into the living room, where Lexi was flipping carefully through the spines of books on one of the library shelves. "Nothing here."

"I'm not finding anything either," she said.

"Guys," whispered Gus, pointing opposite the kitchen. We both turned our heads. There was a door, I hadn't even noticed it previously, sitting at the far end of the room.

Lexi, as if expecting to be shocked by it, fingered the knob. "Locked."

I turned to Gus and mouthed the news.

"Hold on." Lexi reached into the pocket of her jeans and pulled out a paper clip. Unfolding it with trembling fingers, she wiggled it into the lock. She put her ear to the door and listened closely, sticking her tongue out as her fingers shifted in tiny, purposeful vectors. A moment later, *we heard a satisfying click.*

The door swung silently, and we peered inside. A haze of light from the rest of the cottage cast gray-blue shade on the entrance, but beyond that was a pitch so dark it was as if the dark itself were a hungry, living thing.

"Flashlight," whispered Lexi.

Gus tossed her his Maglite, and she shined it into the room. The beam appeared to travel a yard or two, but then, as opposed to hitting an end, was swallowed as if into nothingness. The room appeared to go further back than the house itself should have allowed.

"Hurry up…" Gus was whispering though his voice felt far off. A steely cold cut away at my nose and cheeks. I heard a soft sucking sound.

My sneaker toe tested the ground at each step to make sure I didn't fall forward. A few feet in, something stringy and web-like brushed across my face. I would have panicked had it not been for Lexi. She put her hand on my shoulder and shushed me before reaching out to tug what turned out to be a string. She pulled it and—*click*—a hot, yellow light flooded the room.

A gigantic spread of black sludge was eating away at the wall. A sprawling fungus that traveled across almost the entire width of the room from floor to ceiling. Off to the left, near the door, was a simple, well-made twin bed, and to the right, in almost exactly the same position, were two metal filing cabinets and a small, wooden table. One of the cabinets had been left ajar, and upon the desk lay an open file. But the tapestry of murk kept our full attention.

Lexi made a chittering sound, and when I looked at her, I saw her breath was steaming.

"Are you okay?" As I spoke, I realized mine was doing the same.

"W-w-what i-i-is it?" She was almost incomprehensible.

I stepped toward the wall, conscious of the fact that my clothes, already wet from the rain, were hardening up so quickly with frost I could barely walk. *Is this how Mrs. Duncan had felt?* I wondered. Had she woken up to an unworldly temperature that turned her blood to ice? And how the hell did Mr. Kraft sleep in a place like this?

Staring into the mass on the wall was like staring into a cavern. A hole that had been dug to an evil dimension. I discerned some sort of movement inside. Or at least I thought I did. A liquid-like compound sloshing around like water in an underground well. I almost wanted to drive my hand into it, into that cold, rippling dark, but kept a careful distance. This was when I noticed an event occurring. Something at its edges. The mold, it was shriveling. Peeling from the wall. Stepping back, I understood this was because it had begun to shrink. Slurp toward its center as it receded. Squiggling spores puckered from the drywall, leaving it wet but unblemished beneath.

"It's shhhhh-shhhh-shhhh," I stuttered. "It's g-g-getting smaller."

Lexi, beyond words at this point, hobbled up to it. Her body looked injured, her hands in claws, but she didn't let that stop her.

"C-come." She flipped back her hood, turned her ear, and motioned me closer. "L-l-l-listen."

I lifted my hood and at first I heard what could have been the same sleepy rush I'd heard inside conch shells. Ocean and surf. But then, it got more complicated… I couldn't quite understand what I was hearing until it was obvious that someone was crying. A woman's voice, husky and low, grew in volume. Sobbing, struggling for breath between her tears, it was as if she'd been trapped behind a glass wall. I listened harder. Came closer. Another woman with a higher voice, she was also crying. Hers was a suffering, dungeon captive's song, and when the sound of hers rose with the others, a torturous chorus emerged. If that weren't enough, soon, there came the tears of a little girl. She couldn't have been older than ten. As I continued to listen, it only got worse. There were two little girls now. Or three? Five? As I tried to parse out each, they grew more numerous until there were too many to count, joining together in a demonic fugue. I found myself leaning. Falling forward. This until a hand on my neck yanked me back, and I found myself on my ass. I then looked up and saw Lexi, her chest heaving as she stood above me.

"C-c-careful," she said.

The mass was receding rapidly now. First, it shrank to the size of a trampoline. A few seconds after that, a car tire. Soon enough, a dinner plate. And, in its final stage, it became nearly indistinguishable from a pushpin on the wall, which is how it remained. The cold was gone now. Or at least lessened. Lexi shook out her hands and feet.

"The file," she said, not wasting a second. She ran toward the small, wooden table next to the cabinet.

I was still dazed from what I'd seen and heard, but I tried to keep my mind sharp as we set our eyes upon what Mr. Kraft had been looking at before he went out on his jog.

"Hurry up, you guys," we heard Gus say as he neared the doorway.

Lexi put her finger to the file to track the words. She read better that way, I knew. Sometimes, I'd see her in class whispering words to herself as she tracked them, and she was doing the same thing now. After she'd reached a certain point, however, she stopped, in her eye in a look of confusion. I leaned in and began to read, skimming over the contents to see why. When I finally did, I almost didn't believe it.

LEXI NAVARRO

Her name glared up at me like it had been written in fire. Printed a quarter of the way down the page, it was positioned in a sort of information ledger, similar to the sheet you'd see in a doctor's office or with someone collecting stats for the national census. Strewn throughout were preliminary facts about Lexi that spanned from her physical attributes, weight, height, eye color, and health history, to family members, sexual orientation, and academic performance.

"Lexi..."

"Turn the page," she said.

I nodded. The next section contained an entire write-up on what could only be defined as Lexi's personality. It was written in a formal and antique script. Almost out of a different era. The language was bizarre. I saw words I didn't understand in the context in which they were being used. Sentences like, "Given her acute disdain for hysteria, I reason she'll adjudicate subject 72's hyper-frensitivity." Another read, "Her partial blindness, as it is and will be, has resulted in emotional solemnity, making L.V. a plenary antidote to subject 13's moral vacancy."

Lexi maintained a severe sort of calm. "Keep going."

The next page was the most disturbing of all, for it featured pictures of Lexi. Pictures of Lexi at school. Pictures of Lexi at home. Pictures, I noticed before turning my head, of Lexi nude and half-nude, changing in her bedroom. Lexi with her eyepatch on. Lexi with her eyepatch off. Lexi walking to school and Lexi climbing into the Shepherd. Lexi at dinner with her mother and Lexi crying on her bed. There were so many photos I began to feel sick looking at them. Some in particular, those taken in her bed and bathroom, were invasive. Menacing.

Unable to look any longer, I turned to the next section, which consisted of endless, maddeningly meticulous notes on Lexi's lifestyle and habits. These were observations only someone watching her on a near-constant basis could know. How she ate. What cigarettes she smoked. What made her laugh or drove her into anger or brought her to tears. There was something about her ability to solve complex problems. And another section about her empathy toward animals, and yet another about her absent father. This entire document was a work of harrowing obsession. Whoever had compiled it viewed Lexi as more of a taxonomical species than an individual. Lexi was being picked apart, and pieces of her were being pinned to corkboard like insects in an entomologist's lab.

As we continued to look, her face grew paler and paler. By the time we got to the last page, I felt so piteous I couldn't carry on. Lexi closed her mouth and retracted her hand as I closed the file. On the front of the folder, we then noticed, was a stamp of red ink.

FIT FOR COLLECTION

Gus hissed at us from the entryway. His eyes were large and furious. "We've got to get out of here. Now."

The urgency in his voice made us scramble. We flipped the folder back to page one, shut off the light, and closed the door softly on our way out. Rushing through the back, we emerged into the yard; rain slammed into our ponchos until they clung to our bodies. We ran toward the van without looking back. Without knowing what was behind us.

ELEVEN

I DON'T REMEMBER QUITE WHAT HAPPENED after that. All I knew was that we were moving. And fast.

First, there was rain. Then, there wasn't. Then, there was a throttling engine and speed, and without warning, I soared, and my skull smacked against some rubber structure. Light shuttered, and the world went grey. When I came to, Lexi and Gus were peeling me off the floor of his van. While lurching out of the Main Drive district, we ran a stop sign and were nearly plowed by a pickup. We swerved into a ditch, and while collision was avoided, I'd not been wearing my seatbelt.

"Eberstark," Gus yelled. His voice sounded remote.

I heard Lexi saying something as well, but it drifted off. What appeared before me in a stretch of dream was the mold in Mr. Kraft's room. The screams of women: nearby yet out of reach. I saw the creature from the cellar again. It lumbered through an underground passage, carrying someone in its arms. A woman who appeared to be Mother.

THE SILENT END

She was unconscious and covered in an emerald-green membrane from head to toe. Her eyes were shut. The creature cradled her head in one of its many limbs. Its hand, a grotesque stump whose end was a mess of flesh feelers and plastic knobs, stroked her filthy hair. The tentacles from its head slithered behind her ears, across her eyelids, nose, and lips. She shook her head and moaned, imprisoned in sleep. I tried to call out to her, but not a sound came, and the harder I screamed, the weaker the words. Around me swam a watery haze. On an altar at the end of a staircase loomed an entity. It was blue, and it bubbled and thrashed. A pair of eyes like a reptile's brimmed with fire.

When I awoke in Lexi's house, she and Gus shrieked with joy.

"Thank God!" He gave me a rib-crushing hug. "I thought you'd gone full coma."

Lexi, unable to set aside her concern, ran over to the kitchen and brought me a glass of water after shaking a couple of pills into her hand. I'd been wrapped in a fleece blanket. I groaned as I tried to sit up.

"Don't move." Gus pushed me back into the lazy boy.

I felt my head. A bandage had been tied around it. A dull ache throbbed from my scalp to my neck.

"Take." Lexi handed me two pink pills. I popped them in my mouth and let them sit on my tongue.

"Drink," she said.

I drained the entire glass. I was hungry. A hearty aroma wafted from the kitchen, and I wanted to be absorbed into it.

"What's that smell?" I said.

Gus was checking the oven timer. "Pizzas. Three Tino's prebaked Lexi's mom had in the freezer."

My friends protested, but I felt strong enough to stand up and go to the bathroom. I tried to avoid looking in the mirror when I got there but couldn't. I marveled at how shitty I looked. Like someone who tried hard not to care.

The bandage around my head had been applied haphazardly. Blood and sweat seeped through, and my hair stuck up in all directions. I washed my hands with warm water, and they pinkened. I then splashed my face and let it drip. My eyes were glistening, just like Mother's had, even without moisture. Father had told me that while I had his body, his thick-set shoulders and blockish waist, my face belonged to her. We shared a soft, almost invisible chin. Even my emotions, my moodiness and tendency to give up, were growing to resemble hers.

I checked my pocket and realized the charm bracelet was still with me. Feeling it was comfort and reminded me of whatever home we'd had. Regardless of who I became one day, the bracelet would be clear proof I survived.

When I rejoined Lexi and Gus, they were cutting the pizzas into uneven slices on the dining room table. For some reason I was still freezing, despite the blanket over my shoulders.

Gus explained that he'd told us to leave the cottage when he thought he glimpsed Mr. Kraft jogging back toward it. Upon reflection, he admitted he couldn't have been sure if the runner had been our US Politics teacher or not. But he hadn't been willing to take any chances.

"It all went fast. We got in the van, started driving. The next thing I noticed, you were on the floor with blood in your hair."

The rain worsened as we sat down for dinner. When big thunder came, I waited for a pit to open beneath our feet.

"So what happened in there?" Gus took his first bite. We continued to smack away at the pizzas until we were practically inhaling whole slices. I hadn't been this hungry in a long while, and eating helped me forget about the gash in my head. I folded greased bundles of bread and cheese and pepperoni into my mouth, almost taking down half of the first pizza in under two minutes. Lexi looked embarrassed for me. I decided to reduce my pace.

We tried to explain to Gus what we'd seen in Mr. Kraft's bedroom. When we spoke of the mass on the wall, I could barely do so without recalling those screams. When we got to the file, she went quiet, and Gus stopped eating. As the recount came to an end, it appeared as if he'd lost his appetite completely. Wiping his hands on a paper napkin, he nudged his plate aside.

"Fit for collection? What could that mean?"

"Nothing good," I said.

Gus shook his head. "Certainly not. But it is funny, don't you think?"

"Hilarious." Lexi bitterly dragged her fourth piece to the plate. For a girl of her size, she processed food like a trash compactor.

"Not funny like ha, ha. God. Who do you think I am? I mean funny as in strange. Why would someone maintain a thorough filing system like that for a high school student? And for such a long period of time? Your physical attributes. Your 'personality'—whatever that means. And that mold on the wall…you said there were other files in the cabinet too, right?"

"Uh huh."

"But we didn't have a chance to look at them," I said.

Lexi took a loud sip of her cherry coke and set it down.

"You were saying that women have been disappearing from Mossglow for a long time now, right?" I said to Lexi. "According to the town's history?"

"Yep."

"So what if…What if one of those things…what if Mr. Kraft

marked you? For abduction, I mean. Like my…"

"Mother," Gus finished my sentence.

"Maybe."

"I don't want to talk about it." Lexi's hand tightened around her napkin.

"He might actually have a point," said Gus. "I know I wouldn't listen before, but what if it's all true? What if Mr. Kraft is just serving someone? Like a henchman."

"I don't want to talk about it. Okay?"

"Exactly," I said, ignoring her. "Like…what if these monsters… what if they're taking orders from someone else? What if they're just servants? Or…or…Collectors."

The words sent my arm hairs on end.

"Where did you get that name?" Gus folded his arms on the tabletop and looked down at his plate. "Collectors…"

Lexi coughed and drained the rest of her coke.

"And these Collectors, they're swiping up women all over Mossglow. Enough of them put our town on the weird side of normal but not enough to attract outside attention," said Gus. "Very smart. Very quiet."

"But then why did Mrs. Duncan get killed?" I said. "As opposed to taken?"

"Maybe she got too close to the wolf's mouth. I wonder if there's a file with her name on it in Mr. Kraft's cabinet."

"I don't want to think about that."

"Either way, if this is true." Gus looked at Lexi, whose face had grown stormier than the torrent outside. She was staring down at her slice in silence, chewing her lip. "Then that means… Lexi, we've got to get you out of here."

Lexi picked up her plate and, in a fit of rage, let it fly across the kitchen. It smashed to the floor, and the pizza landed beside it in a wet clump.

"So, I'm just a problem that needs solving. Might as well be a set of integers."

"Whoa, what?" Gus threw his hands out in supplication. "I just meant that we might want to think about this. Why are you so angry?"

"Why the hell do you think? If all this shit's true, then that means you fuckers get off the hook while I—and every human with mammary glands around here—doesn't. It's so typical it's not."

"But what if he's coming for you right now?"

"You know what we saw in there," I said.

"Why are you still talking about this?" said Lexi.

"Come on," said Gus.

"SHUT YOUR MOUTH!"

She got out of the chair, sank to the floor on her knees and as if she'd been holding hurt in for a long while, and began sobbing. Her cries were throaty and vicious. I tried to put my hand on her shoulder, but she swiped it away.

"Lexi," Gus said. "I'm not—we're not like those other kids at school. We only want to—"

"I've seen him!" Lexi sobbed. "The man in the mirror, okay? The man that Mrs. Duncan saw. That fucking thing…"

"Who?"

"The man. In. The mirror. I've been seeing him. It. Whatever. Sometimes, it looks like my dad. But other times, it's just…it's just this red-eyed thing. All surrounded in blue."

Mr. Blue, I thought.

"For how long?" Gus said.

"I don't know. Maybe a month now. It's hard to remember when it actually started. I think…I think it was a couple of weeks before we found the creature out in Graywood. I was brushing my teeth before bed…then, it got cold… Not as cold as it gets when he comes now but chilly. In a strange way. Like the cold was coming out of me." She put her hands to her collar and coughed. "I was looking at myself, you know, brushing my teeth. Then…" she stopped crying and swallowed hard. "I just noticed I wasn't there anymore. That someone else was instead. I thought I was crazy, so I shook my head real hard. But still, there he was, smiling…and looking a lot like…my dad. He was wearing this NAVY bomber jacket he used to have, and nodding and winking at me. But I knew it wasn't him. There was a wrongness in the eyes, you know, like Mrs. Duncan said. Like the man in the mirror could borrow every part of someone but that."

I recalled what Mother and Mrs. Duncan had said about the eyes as well. I could almost picture them.

"A moment later, it was only me again. The man. He was gone…"

"Until he came back?" Gus was picking the pizza off the floor.

"Until he came back," she agreed. "I started seeing him more and more around my house. It happened gradually at first. But in the days before the monster, it felt like I was seeing him everywhere. The kitchen, my bedroom, even in the TV screen. Sometimes, I think he tried to talk to me. But it was like his words were coming from underwater. And that blue…the more he came around, the more it worked its way in. Blue in everything. It got murkier as time went on until I could barely stand the color at all. Used to be my favorite…" she sniffled.

She looked around.

"Where are my cats?"

"I, uh." Gus barely registered the question as he grabbed a rag to wipe the tomato sauce from the floor.

"Anyway...the cold got worse. It was almost like he was trying to freeze my body from the inside so that I could be...preserved. That's one of the reasons I was so ready to go into the forest on Halloween. Yeah, maybe I thought it had something to do with what was going on with me, but more than anything, I wanted to get out of the house. It was either that or break all our mirrors and make Mom believe in the devil again."

She'd practically melted into the floor as she finished. I couldn't speak for Gus, but the expression on his face suggested he felt as horrible as I did. Yes, it sucked, being lied to by Lexi. It might have even put us in danger. But what I'd done to the two of them, to everyone, was far worse, and if Lexi's lies tasted sour, mine were pure rotten. If I were only a little less of a coward, I could have told her and Gus about Father, and maybe, just maybe, we'd all be hiding a lot less from each other. Maybe even Mrs. Duncan would still have been alive. But instead, we were helpless. What did these creatures want? To terrorize women? There were plenty of horrible men in the world. They outnumbered horrible women by the hundreds of millions, smashing and consuming like hungry ogres. Women suffered most. In real life as well as movies, books, and games. In Mossglow, however, this tiny speck of a city that could fade in a whisper, the monsters were more than just men.

"We can go to my house," Gus said wearily. He was done cleaning the floor. "At least until we figure out a plan."

"No," said Lexi. She wiped her eye and took a cigarette to her lips, blowing out an unsteady stream. "I'm tired of trying to escape myself. It obviously hasn't worked so far. I know you guys mean well.

I really do. But I'm staying here. Alone."

"You can't be serious," I said.

"Why not? What's wrong with fighting my own battles?"

"Nothing. But what if it's one you can't win?"

"Then I'll lose." She shrugged.

"Impossible." Gus grabbed his slice of pizza back and took a bite.

"What's impossible? That I'm making my own decisions?"

"No. I've just decided that if you're going to lose, we might as well lose with you. By the law of averages, we're better together than apart."

"What are you saying?"

"I'm saying we're staying."

"We are?" I said.

"I can't ask you to do that."

"But you're not asking us. We're offering. Aren't we, Eberstark?"

"I…I guess we are."

"Well then." Gus took a deep breath. He didn't seem nearly as squeamish as he had even five days ago, when he was dragged into the forest to confront the insane. A recklessness lurked in his gaze. He had been thinking of his death.

"I have a feeling we'll be receiving a visit tonight." He surveyed Lexi's house. "Your file was open on the table for a reason. Call it a hunch, but we need to get ready."

TWELVE

WE BARRICADED THE FRONT AND back doors with the lazy boys, turning them on their sides, and angled the couches upward to block out the windows. We took whatever we could that was made of heavy wood or plastic, being careful not to break anything. Thankfully, Lexi's mother wouldn't be back until tomorrow. If something happened, the goal was not to damage the house but to keep whatever wanted in, out. As I thought about our situation, I realized how much Lexi and I had in common. I knew what it was like to come home to an empty house. I knew what it was like to take care of myself and not want to. What it was like to be tired and hungry and have no one around but yourself.

As a last-minute precaution, we took every mirror we could off the wall and put them in the broom closet. Regardless of how these creatures behaved, we knew that reflective surfaces were somehow involved. We sealed the garage, double locked it with a chain, and spread mattresses against the windows of each bedroom, supporting them with desks and bureaus.

"Where are my fucking cats?" Lexi reiterated with increased annoyance as she finished helping Gus push a set of drawers to her mother's bedroom window. She cupped her hands to her lips and belted out, "Ignatius! Petey!" She checked corners and opened closets. "You guys sure you haven't seen them anywhere?"

Gus and I shook our heads.

"They couldn't have gotten out," said Lexi. "I would have noticed."

"Maybe they're hiding somewhere," said Gus. "Cats do that, right?"

"Not mine."

"They could have gotten scared by all the furniture moving," I said.

"Yeah," said Lexi, still looking around the room. "Yeah."

After a good hour, we withdrew to the living room, under the loft that spread halfway across the vaulted ceiling. With the majority of the furniture pushed to the edges of the house, we felt safer. We couldn't see outside. Rain hammered down the shingles, and thunder bellowed.

Lexi had her knife, which she flipped freely in front of her, stabbing and swiping to regain confidence in the blade. I'd chosen one of her father's old golf clubs, a 7 iron from a set in the garage, and Gus took a pair of long steak knives. We then huddled together with backs facing on the beige carpet, each of us keeping a lookout. I thought about Sword Star of all things. I don't know why. This was no fantasy. There were no space suits and highly mechanized weapons. No flaming swords. No plasma rockets. No hit points and armor class and best-two-out-of-threes. Only some teenagers in a house sealed off with furniture. All I could picture was that high-pitched voice. Those oily feelers and gangly limbs. What would we do when it finally got here? I could see it happening, and my stomach acids boiled.

The rain occasionally slapped the house so hard that it could have been something trying to break through. We'd run over and peek through a slot in the furniture only to find nothing but tree branches thrashing. About an hour in, we heard a loud clang in the garage and looked at each other.

"Come on." Lexi took her knife in hand. "It could be the cats."

"I don't know," I said. "Seems like bad stuff can happen to people when they 'check' things 'out,' in garages."

Gus crossed his steak knives in an ex before him. "Grab your club."

We nudged the door to the garage open. It was musty, and water was trickling through holes in the roof. Grime, oil, rust, and something earthy and fertile. Lexi, putting her finger to her mouth, flipped on the light. Gus and I jumped back, and I started flailing the club around my head.

"Eberstark," yelled Lexi as I swung and swung. "Stop. You're going to hit me; there's nothing here!"

I let the club hit the ground and opened my eyes. Gus was holding a paint can that had fallen off one of the utility shelves lining the wall. It had brought down some thinner with it along with a tin of nails. "This place is leaking like crazy."

"Petey?" Lexi searched around the garage for her cats. "Ignatius? God damn it. Where are you guys?"

We headed back inside to the living room to resume our watch. I thought of the encounter I'd had with creature in the cellar of Stumart and how, when I emerged through the other side, I'd promised myself I'd no longer be a coward.

"Okay," said Lexi in a sharp voice. "I'm getting really worried now."

"I think we're all worried," said Gus.

"I mean about my cats. What if they got outside?"

THE SILENT END

"Then they'll probably just hide somewhere until the rain passes."

"I don't know." Lexi drew her finger up and down the length of her blade. "I don't like this. I don't like this at all."

It was only a few seconds later that we heard the sound.

Mewwwwwwwwwwwww

It was small, unmistakable.

Lexi shot to her feet.

"Petey? That you, sweetie?"

Mewwwwwwwwwwwww

We heard it again, a little louder but muffled. It was coming from the loft.

"They must be stuck," Lexi said. "That's why they didn't come down earlier. They're trapped in a crawl space. Here, help me with the ladder."

Gus and I quickly hoisted the ladder from where we'd set it as a barricade across the back door and set it carefully up against the loft.

"I'm coming, kitties." She began to ascend.

Mewwwww…Mewwwwww…Mrrrrrrrrrrrrrrrrrrr…

"I'm coming." She climbed faster. "Mama's on the way."

She reached the top of the ladder and went silent. She looked like she was about to fall. Her body teetered backward. And then, she was screaming.

Dead.

Both of her cats. Torn to pieces just as Mrs. Duncan had been. I understood this before she rushed down the ladder, and parts of Ignatius and Petey began flying off after her, landing around us with meaty thumps. Lexi fell from halfway down the ladder and, landing on her back, crab-walked across the room. The parts kept being flicked off, piece by calico and tuxedo piece.

I was rubbing my arms for warmth. The air had turned glacial. After a moment, a hairy orb rolled off the ledge. Ignatius' confused, contorted head.

Lexi wailed. It was a horrible sound.

Meoooooooooowwwwwww...

The sound came again.

Meooowwww...rrrrrrrrrr...

I then saw poor Petey's head peek out over the balcony, its feline mouth gawping in confused terror, blood matted in its fur.

Mewwwwww...meeewwww—hee hee...hee hee...hahahaha...

I saw a hand. A hand holding Petey's head. It was making it dance playfully from side to side.

"*Were you looking for meeeeeee—ow?*" a familiar voice said. "*I wish you would have found me sooner... Now, it appears you've lost my head. Don't you want it back?*"

Lexi screamed as Petey's head was pitched down toward us and rolled to a bloody stop on the rug. A dark figure was crouched on the loft, leaning over the edge. Its eyes glinted silver.

"Hello, children," Mr. Kraft grinned.

He shimmied herky jerky down the ladder. His movements were erratic and stilted. He hopped off at the bottom rung and walked toward us casually.

"I hope I didn't catch you off guard." He grinned. There was something insect-like about his eyes. "It's just that, well, it never bores me. Watching you." He looked at Lexi, and his tongue came out of his mouth. "It never bores any of us, really. Hearing you breath. Watching you sleep."

"What do you want with us?" said Gus.

"What do I want?" Our US Politics teacher sounded like he'd

been touched by the question. "Oh, my dear Gus, it's not what I want. It never really has been, to be honest. In my line of work…you're required to make sacrifices. Do you understand what that means? To do questionable things in service of…a greater good?"

Gus was speechless. I could see him trying to keep from looking at the cat parts around the room. Even though we'd seen the Stumart surveillance tape, it was still difficult to associate handsome, pleasant Mr. Kraft with the beefy smell of death filling up our nostrils.

"How silly of me; of course you don't know what I mean." He threw a hand out in dismissal. "Not that you'd understand should I explain. How could you think of anything at all with this…angel in your midst?"

He looked to Lexi with wet lips.

"I'll fucking…kill you." She held out her knife.

"Oh, will you now?" He gibbered. "Truth to be told, I would continue laughing if I wasn't so convinced of the possibility. There are evil forces at work in Mossglow; haven't you noticed? Dark winds blowing. Take poor Reed Granger." He went quiet and frowned. He looked childish as he did so. "I believe his existence was brought to an end sometime last week when that strange earthquake struck. Though I doubt you children had anything to do with that. The sort of power required to stand in our way is one not easily grasped by gray minds."

"Reed Granger?" Lexi's eyes were red. "The…the mechanic?"

"You knew him, then?" said Mr. Kraft jollily.

"He was… He knew the Shepherd inside and out."

"He knew you inside and out as well, Lexi. Or at least he was beginning to before he disappeared last week. Poor creature."

It was all starting to became clear. I understood what Lexi had meant the night she first brought us to the forest when she said she felt like the creature recognized her. It was because that creature had. Granger was a local mechanic who owned a shop on the edge of the Main Drive.

"But no." Mr. Kraft wagged his finger. "You aren't going to kill me. Don't you wish you could, though? I certainly do. I've spent so much time learning about you, Lexi. Watching you. Smelling you." He looked her up and down and salivated. "I'd be happy to bleed out for someone like you. But the truth is, you want to hurt me more than I want to hurt you. See. I want to help you. And so does He, believe it or not. He…wants to help everyone."

"He?" She drove the knife forward, toward Kraft's throat, coming shy of actually stabbing him.

Kraft smiled at the knife. "He. It. Such distinctions are arbitrary when it comes to us. The only thing you need to know is that you are destined for greater things. Haven't you ever thought before of what it would be like to really make a difference on this mindless rock? To commune with the future?"

"You're not taking her anywhere." Gus held the knives tight in his fists.

I lifted the 7 iron. "You leave us the hell alone."

"What is this now?" Mr. Kraft turned to look at us, cocking his head like a deranged rooster. His eyes didn't have pupils now. "What is this that speaks to me? What are these little bugs?"

"I don't need them to speak for me," said Lexi. "I'm not going anywhere with you."

Mr. Kraft began to laugh again. It was a hoarse, bestial sound that I immediately recognized. From the cellar. On other side of the door.

"Get away from her," yelled Gus as Mr. Kraft took a step forward. He then took one of the kitchen knives, grit his teeth, and sliced out wildly. A gash appeared across Mr. Kraft's forearm, right below the cuff of his sleeve.

Mr. Kraft stopped in his tracks. He didn't scream or curse. He just looked startled. He then turned to Gus as blood welled up in the gash.

"How did it feel?" he said.

Gus froze.

"It's okay." Blood gushed over Mr. Kraft's arm, dripping down his fingers to the carpet. "You don't have to answer." His body hunched. His shoulders began to bulge and swell. "I'll answer for you…" His voice became high and tinny. "I'll answer for you…"

ALLLLLoooOOOOOoOOOOOOooOOOOOO

With a sickly squelch, Mr. Kraft's head split in two, and from his neck erupted a mass of darkness. It was as if he exploded at first until all the muscle and skin that came from within him began to retract. I heard the sound of radio feedback. Clinking metal and labored breath. Something about the thing was human. Something about it was not. The back muscles, buttocks, and the limbs—there were at least ten—could have been modeled after a man. Some had five or six-fingered hands. Some—like legs—had feet. Others had bits of electronic equipment spiking from the flesh—an mp3 player, a wifi hub, earphones, dials and stereo speakers. Some were so small, so stunted and wrinkled, they looked barely formed. The skin itself could have belonged to a shark. It was naked but didn't have genitals, just a sharp tongue of flesh that rose up between and behind its legs.

Roughly the size of a tractor, the living room was almost too small to hold it. Its head was covered in tentacles that writhed over its face. They began to rise, and a white, mask-like face appeared. It had a toothless mouth. Three hallow eye-holes expanded and contracted. The tentacle with the carbon microphone squiggled toward my face.

"…It *was* youuuuuuu behind the door…" Its shrill voice cut into me deeper this time. I no longer had a wall of iron to protect me. The beast stomped forward, and the house trembled. "Yooooooooooou… the fat Eberstark boy. I recorded your breath. I know your sound." It gave off a disgusting chuckle, like mucus through a fan. "For a moment, I thought you were non-life. A dream creature. You surprise me, fleshboy…you and the Mustus…all to help the one-eyed girl."

"What the fuck are you?" My head quaked as I looked into its eye hollows.

It reached out with its tentacles and felt along my face and chin. They ran behind my ears, my back, and between my legs, caressing and tightening, gentle and deadly. I felt myself being lifted off the ground.

"Meeeeee?" It barked with laughter. "I am…two. I am…three. I am the maaaaster's…favorite…"

I tried to scream but couldn't.

"Did he smile his work to seeeee…" Its fingers were at my feet, neck, and shoulders. "Did he who make the lamb make thee…"

I was choking. It squeezed harder.

"And what shoulder…and what aaaart." Its mouth contorted. "Could twist the sssssinews of thy heart…"

My feet weren't touching the ground anymore. Each of its eyes were like the void on Mr. Kraft's wall. Brimming with hungry darkness. I felt my arms stretching. My legs parting. My body being torn in five directions. Fingers on my ankles. Fingers on my neck. Ripping. Pulling. I couldn't breathe. The cold had moved into me, and pain swerved in a route dull and evil. The thing's face contorted with rage, and the carbon microphone, the very one I'd seen in the cellar, entered my mouth.

ALLLLLLOOOOOoooooOOOOOOoOOooooO!

THE SILENT END

Lexi, springing from her haunches like some vengeful creature, chopped off one of the beast's tentacles with her knife. A knobby bunch of metal, plastic, and flesh fell to the ground, and from the wound spewed the blue stuff. The Murje.

Howling, the beast flung me to the side, and my shoulder shocked the ground with a crack. Pain devoured me. My bandage fell over my eye, and I scratched it off just in time to see one of the beast's massive limbs shunt into Lexi's cheek. She went spinning to the ground and hit it hard.

The creature trampled toward her, its body low and predatory. But as it picked her up, Gus yawped and leaped onto its neck, his steak knives dissevering flesh. He sliced and screamed, shredding and shredding until, with a snake-like hiss, the beast wound up and kicked him square in the chest with one of its feet. An *oomph* preceded Gus sailing then tumbling to the ground. He squeaked out for help but was silenced as a horror grew in his eyes, one limb grabbing his waist and the other, his head. With a roar, they began pulling in opposite directions. I dragged myself from the ground as Gus gurgled with pain, picked up the 7 iron, and sloughed toward the scene, knowing what would come next if I didn't. As the beast began the process of trying to detach Gus's skull from his body, I began beating it with all of my might. Slamming the club over and over again into its ribcage and face. Gnarring. Spitting. The club made contact with something like bone, and Gus fell to the ground. One of the beast's hands, however, then almost automatically snatched me up by the neck and slammed me down with so much force I'd be dead and buried had there not been concrete instead of earth.

"Stupid flesh-boy," it snarled, squeezing my throat. I could feel my eyes bulging from their sockets. "You are filth," it spat. "You are waste. Your bones are for teeth-picking."

I tried to cry out, but my mouth filled with blood.

"Lllllisten as life leaves you…" it groaned. "As you spillllllllll into oblivion… Let your voice die inside me. Let me be your keeperrrrrrr…"

As everything blurred, I heard a crash. Colors exploded and swirled in a display that reminded me of a science video I'd watched in the seventh grade of erupting volcanoes. Strombolian was the word I remembered, where bursting gas bubbles were seared skyward by magma. I wondered if what I was sensing was my brain toppling from its spine, collapsing my senses like Dean Veltry had warned. I smelled ash and dust. Something like ammonia. And then something sweet as my breath—it returned. Yes, I was breathing. Then, I was falling, and I heard a new sound. The sound of an engine.

The Shepherd rammed through the western wall of the Navarro house and *thunked* the beast through brick, wood, and glass into the backyard.

I struggled to my knees. The Shepherd, alive and savage, revved its engine. Yellow smoke spewed from beneath the undercarriage, mixed with soot and a raging downpour. Both the passenger and driver doors snapped open, and two figures took on fighting poses before the headlights.

"Ready yourself for death, you perversion of the shadow," I heard Father growl.

He stood tall in his infrared goggles and army fatigues. His yellow teeth were arranged in a crooked smile. In each of his hands, he carried silver guns with long, cylindrical barrels stretching four feet each. Their hilts had tubes running to hip canisters attached to a holster belt, one of which was filled with a green liquid and the other, blue. The Hat, in his Ray Bans and unblemished seersucker suit with matching derby hat, carried a bow and a quiver filled with oddly shaped arrows strapped over his back.

"Mr...Mr. Eberstark?" Gus was lifting himself from the ground. He was limping. "What happened to you?"

"Let me see your face," said Father, marching over to him. Letting his right gun hang from a shoulder strap, he pulled Gus's face towards his and stared deep into his eyes. "You've got the shadow in you, son." He angled his gaze left and right. "You're infected as a germ."

The Hat scribbled something on a piece of notebook paper and held it up.

Have you yet to meet your dreams?

Father then looked over at Lexi, who was also dragging herself from the ground. A streak of red sliced down her neck, and her eyepatch was partly shredded, revealing her gray, blind eye.

He took her chin in his hand.

"By shit, you've been taken by it too. Spending time with bedwetter here has turned your brains to pudding."

The Hat tapped Father on the shoulder and pointed to the backyard, where we heard an inhuman thrashing from the trees where the creature had been launched. The Navarro house had been smashed open on both the north and western side.

"Right you are, Hat! Can't go on vacation if you don't have a job. Teenage parasites, get off your ass sacs, and take these."

He reached into the Shepherd and withdrew a Kevlar duffle bag like the one I'd seen next to the hedgerow, throwing it to the ground. It was already unzipped, and inside was a gleaming panoply of guns, clubs, and other objects of destruction.

"Mustus," he yelled. "You diseased idiot, catch!"

He threw Gus a pair of pistols. He only caught one of them but picked up the other quickly. Each was forged of a dark green alloy and had yellow, spore-like bulbs at the muzzle. They pulsed like the bodies of jellyfish.

"Bedwetter." He tossed me what was no less than a fucking cannon, metallic and marked with grooves that traversed its entire top. A magazine of delicate-looking glass capsules containing a black, jelly-like substance cut a belt vertically along its base. I barely kept on my feet as I caught it.

"How do I use it?" I slurred through a swollen tongue.

The Hat shoved a note into my face.

Defy your mediocrity.

"You, female," Father said, turning to Lexi. "You stay out of harm's way."

"Fuck that," Lexi said, walking up to Father and kicking him in the shin. "Give me a gun."

"Take whatever you want, you one-eyed monster."

Lexi reached for the bag, but as she did so, the beast crashed back into the house, throwing its entire bulk into the Shepherd after a running leap. The vehicle spun sideways through the back hallway into the garage. We ducked in all directions, and Father screamed, "CLAIM ITS HEAD!"

We opened fire or tried to. I began squeezing one of three triggers on Father's weapon, under a handle on its rear, but nothing came out.

"Give me that," Lexi said, snatching the cannon away from me and heaving it onto her tiny body.

THE SILENT END

The house was a maelstrom of rain and fire. I wondered if someone in the neighborhood had called the police. Father, standing bowlegged like a cowboy, toggled his guns; the fluids from his hip canisters burbled through the tubes.

"Hat!" he yelled. "Take out its limbs while I charge the antipenumbrics."

The Hat nodded and, with the agility of a panther, skittered beneath the beast as it tried to squash him and came out the other side near its pointed tail. He reached into the insides of his suit and removed a black cube studded with pink ball bearings. It was attached to a stretch of metal cord. He compressed a button on the object, and it whirred and beeped. The beast noticed his location when he did so, turning about face. The Hat then ran and slid on his knees beneath the creature's granitic belly, whipping the cord above his head like a lancet and letting it fly. The weapon wrapped around one of the creature's two rear limbs, a heavy trunk of flesh with an eight-toed foot. The monster grunted and looked back, whirling its body into a skyward kick. The cube was launched into the rain. A blood-red explosion thwacked far above us.

"Be damned," muttered Father. As the fluids stopped sluicing through the tubes, his guns began to make a gurgling sound, as if something inside them was about to vomit. He smiled and prepared to fire. As he put his finger to the trigger, however, the beast threw out a long, heavy arm and knocked him across the living room into the kitchen, where he smashed into the stove, denting the oven door. Gus, still limping, then concentrated, aimed, and, gritting his teeth, fired a solid shot. The jelly-like spore at the end of his gun inflated like a piece of rotten bubble gum. It made a flatulent sound and popped forward a gob of sticky, green fluorescence that sizzled into the beast's face. Some of its tentacles began to melt away, and an alloy smell singed the air.

ALLLLOOOOOOooooOOOOOOOooOOOO

The creature looked like a wax monster under a blowtorch. Hollow-eyed and half-mad, it launched itself toward Gus. Lexi, meanwhile, knelt and braced the cannon between her arms. With her one eye down what I hadn't noticed before was a sighting mechanism, she flicked as if instinctually a series of toggles and switches. The black jelly in the munition pods began to animate, spreading into star-like anemones. Thunder crackled. Lexi straightened her shoulders and took a deep breath. All of her was ignited with a predator's fire that had burned out the core of her fear. Surrounded by the wreckage of her broken home, pieces of her cats strewn about the rug, boys, men, and monsters, she became raw purpose. It almost brought her a smile, but her misery snuffed it. She aimed the cannon at one of the beast's appendages as the six-fingered fist attached to it hammered down towards Gus's face. In the muzzle grew a hot, red glow. The pod clunked into the barrel and discharged the glass capsule. What came forth was black and twisted with life. It grew broader, flatter, becoming a discus of hurt as it zinged toward the beast. It slicked right through the top end of the limb, making for Gus's head and went flying away into the rain. The beast lowed and stumbled backward.

Lexi rose from her knee and wiped her brow.

"Thanks," Gus gasped.

We doubled back as the beast thrashed, preparing to engage it again. But instead, it began to run.

"No time for gratitude." Father lifted himself from the stove and ran out into the rain. "It's high time to rip out this devil's oily heart."

I heard the scream of an engine, and the Shepherd busted back into what had once been the living room. The Hat hung off the open front door with a look of mute rage on his face.

"Get in," yelled Father.

Lexi helped Gus off the ground. They hopped to the passenger door, and Lexi shoved Gus into the backseat. Lexi and I piled in afterward, pulling the weapons with us. There were so many of them in our laps I was afraid one would accidentally fire and we'd all be incinerated. The Hat took the wheel, and Father jumped into the passenger seat, angling his guns out the window.

"Hold on for your dear, stupid lives," he said.

The Shepherd charged into the night. The Hat was only half steering as the truck screeched around corners.

"Where did it go?" I said trying to see through the filthy, slime-drenched windshield. My head spattered with blood, sweat, and who knew what else.

"Eberstark." Gus was still gripping his jelly pistols tight. "Your dad…I thought you said…I thought you said…"

"There he blows," screamed Father, throwing his head out the passenger side window. He was soaked with rain, but he didn't care.

We were driving out of the Lowers toward the Uppers. We trampled yards, busted mailboxes, destroyed pergolas, and screeched madly around one panicked city service vehicle. The beast, wounded but still running at a steady clip as we rushed past Gus's house, was fast enough to keep a small lead on the Shepherd but not outrun it. The rain poured, and I could barely see the white body, hemorrhaging blue as it galloped.

"It's banking west!" Father said. "Towards Graywood." He looked over his back at the three of us, his infrared eyes needles of red. "We're not done yet, bedwetters!"

The Hat scribbled a note and held it up to all three of us.

Shoot like stars.

Gus gave me one of his two pistols, and I went to the right side of the car with him, squeezing our upper bodies out the front side windows. It was a tight fit, but Gus was able to get his torso through. Lexi went to the other side with the cannon and hung most of her body out the side window, bracing her legs against the rear bench. We met the forest line with a whisper, and the Shepherd swerved through trees and slammed down hills. I almost fell out a couple of times, but Gus pulled me back in by my jacket collar. The beast was doing nearly the same, loping horse-like on its wounded appendages, leaving the ground occasionally and dodging trees.

The second we got into a sparser clearing, Father yelled, "Fire." Green and yellow, red and purple popped and burped and crunched into the night. The beast continued running—at one point, it ran into a tree and splintered it in two. Streaks, blobs, and bullets zipped and zoomed. Some glanced its hide. Most missed. One shot I fired latched to its loin, and it screeched in pain. I could tell it was scared now. Scared and trying to escape. If he kept on going this way, he'd end up in the hills beyond Graywood, in the wet and cold where it could lick its wounds and hope to survive. But Father and the Hat weren't going to let that happen.

The Hat snapped his fingers, and Father came in from the window with a stupefied look on his face.

"Swift thinking, Hat," Father then said before leering at him like a lunatic. He then hopped over and took the wheel as the Hat, putting his left hand outside on the hood, swung himself on top of the car.

THE SILENT END

When he landed, his feet dented the roof. He wobbled intuitively with the Shepherd as it swerved and dove, pulling the bow from his back. He notched an arrow from his quiver, a long, maroon shaft with a tip shaped like a sea urchin. Drawing back the feathers to the lip of his derby hat, he clucked his tongue. His Ray Banned eyes reflected the beast, and with a soft *phew* of breath, he let the arrow fly, zooming through the air with a brisk squiggle before burrowing deep into the beast's rump.

ALOOOOOOOOOOOoooOOOOoOOoOoOOOOOOOOoOoOoooooo

It roared made distressed, pig-like squeals. A moment later, it tumbled to the ground, seizing. Black veins ran through its body, spreading into his limbs like instant gangrene. It shook and wiggled until, with a *WABOOM,* every one of its appendages exploded; a shower of Murje sparkled into the sky, and the Shepherd halted. The Hat leaped off the hood and slid yards away to a stop, returning the bow to his back.

We ambled dizzily out of the Bronco toward the smoldering creature. The rain stayed even. I felt like throwing up and then did. Father, however, no matter how sick he was from all the swerving, stomped toward his enemy, rolling up the sleeves of his fatigues.

"Not so big now, huh?" he yelled as he came upon it. "Nope. Just a spider without legs. Pathetic. Bleeding to death on the earth you so loathe. Come here." He bent down to its face: its half-seared, half-blind face, the tentacles grizzled and bleeding. "Let me look at you, you thief. You perversion."

The creature opened its eye hollows.

Father laughed, taking one hand to wipe some rain from his brow. The monster seemed to be swallowing some of it to hold onto life. "Yeah…drink up, pal. Drink deep."

Father than wound up and punched its face with a stony crack. The monster moaned.

"Hurts, huh?" Father punched again. And again. He punched and mashed, brought down knuckle and elbow and blood upon the mask-like contortion of mouth and eyes until he was tearing his own skin along with that of the beast's.

"Where are you?" he growled. His hands clawed beyond the face into glutinous zones within the skull and neck. He began pulling out great handfuls of Murje along with diodes, wires, speakers, and various other bits of electrical wiring.

"Where are you, you fucking crony? You excuse for life?"

Father was covered in bright, glowing blue like some sort of phosphorescent insect as he finally reached a point of importance within the beast. His hands scratched something hard and heavy, like coming upon a chest beneath layers of mud.

"There you are," he said with mock cheerfulness.

It was Mr. Kraft. Or Mr. Kraft turned inside out, anyway. Inverted, mismatched, like the creature I'd seen in the cave. His body was twisted, recognizable, but mangled into a ball of parts. With his lips turned sideways and his eyes near his nostrils, he sputtered Murje and wept.

"I'm only going to ask you once." Father sat on the ground and flung Murje from his hands. "Where is she?"

"Wh....where....where...where...where...where..." Mr. Kraft seemed to be stuck on the word.

Father, shrugging casually, then hammered the mushed-up half-man in the nose with his fist.

"That help?"

"No!"

"No?" Father held up his fist again.

"No, yes—I mean. I know. I know… She…she…she is…your…your wife." He gasped for air. "Your wife. Who…you are looking for, yes? I remember now. I do. I don't remember things well but that."

Whatever Mr. Kraft was now, he no longer wanted to die. I almost felt bad for him and could see how, if realigned, his features could once again take on that beautiful symmetry.

Father leaned in close to the face. I noticed that the Hat was standing behind him, waiting patiently.

"Tell me where she is," Father said.

But by that point, Mr. Kraft was looking over his shoulder at the Hat.

"A Non Entity?" His sleek eyes flickered. "I thought…I didn't know they were real."

"That's not important. Tell me where she is."

Hot, red mucus erupted from Mr. Kraft's mouth, and he began choking. His eyes burned as they looked death in the face.

"I…I…" He was slipping.

"No!" Father grabbed the sides of his head. "No! Not yet! You have to tell me where she is. You have to…"

But it was too late. Mr. Kraft's croaked for air and found none. His twisted lungs spit up fluid, and with a rattle, he expired.

"No," Father heaved. "No, please…please no."

We stood above as the rain came down. As the Hat bowed his head and turned away. Father's back tightened, and I thought he was going to yowl and tear the carcass to pieces. But instead, from his throat came a dejected moan. He put his head between his knees, dropped into the mud, and started sobbing.

ONE

WE TURNED UP A FRONTAGE road we all recognized but never went down. Nobody but occasional Mossglow youths—usually Crowstone types—came up here anymore. It was dark, but in the near distance arose the jagged shadow of Hinterlord, burned out, dilapidated. Wild grass grew along the roadside. I thought I saw something scamper out of it and dart in front of the truck. Something small with gleaming eyes. My head was spinning, and I was still thinking about Mr. Kraft's mangled face. About Lexi's cats and the fact that Gus, sitting on the opposite side of Lexi next to the window, wouldn't look at me.

The mood in the car was somber. Father was at the wheel. His eyes were cowlike, teary, and his skin was encrusted in filth. After the Murje had splattered all over him, it gradually turned the color of silt. It was just as Gus had observed under his magnifying glass.

"We're going to Hinterlord?" Lexi said.

The Hat turned to look at her, before scribbling on his notepad and held it up for her to see.

A safe place.

Lexi threw her back against her seat. "I don't believe in safe places."

"Good girl," came Father's grim whisper.

When we moved to Mossglow, Hinterlord was only just beginning to fail. According to Gus's father, who'd been approached with a consultant position from them early on, a pair of Swedish businessmen had founded the company. They claimed that our local steel reserves were especially unique. Extremely durable yet easy to meld. Combined with some worthwhile tax incentives, the two set up a manufacturing facility with the aim of producing a new breed of snowmobile tracts for snowy climates the world over. The majority of our region's inhabitants had no need or care for hard terrain vehicles, but knowing that new industry meant new jobs, the addition was welcomed with open arms. On the day Father sat down to break the news that we'd be leaving Cleveland, he'd explained that the town we were heading didn't have an economy of its own. Mossglow had been funneling money into nearby cities like Ozark for years, and industry always seemed to travel elsewhere. He'd been hoping to change that and, in a way, would end up succeeding when he opened up our store. But Hinterlord had carried the promise of a new life for much of the city, which is why it had been so hard to watch it burn when a mysterious chemical fire ignited within.

The Shepherd drove us to the foot of the factory. We hopped out, and as if the truck was in need of rest, the engine quit. Half of the factory had been burned and since then decayed to the point where it looked like it could crumble any moment. Graffiti was sprayed on the lower brick walls at ground level. Phrases like *BETRAYERS SCREW* and *GO WHERE THERE'S SNOW* abounded in now-fading spray paint alongside pictures of dicks. Few came up here anymore, not even to hurt people or have sex. Only one man claimed this outpost—or so I would find out in just a couple moments as we made our ascent.

Father's weary hand pointed to a staircase. Since half of the building had been burned out, much of it was now exposed to the elements. Broken in spots and only half-covered by the remains of the structure, the staircase didn't look safe.

"Come on." Father started up it without a care. "It would take another fire to knock it down for good."

Each step was slippery from rain. I kept a firm grip on the railing. As we climbed, the clouds began to clear, and murky Mossglow came into rare view. The rain cut the fog. Looking out over the railing, I could see from Hinterlord to Goon's Cove. I could even see the rough edges of the Horn at its end, encircling the raging, black-green waters of the bay just beyond Crowstone Heights. Much was happening in the Lowers as well though I was too far away to see exactly what. Smoke plumes rose from the part of the neighborhood that contained Lexi's house. I didn't know what had caught fire, but it had attracted the fire department and a host of police cars.

We kept on climbing until I was almost wheezing. Gus was even worse off with his injured ankle, dragging it step by step. When he nearly collapsed, the Hat turned back and, silently, hoisted the boy over his shoulder.

"Almost there…" Father paused for a second, placed his hand on his lower back, and groaned.

We finally emerged onto the roof. Heavy winds had carried the rain away, but being so far atop this brittle structure made me feel like I was in a rickety treehouse. When I looked down over the ledge and began fidgeting, Father took my arm and said, "It's got strong foundations."

He directed us toward a ladder leading up to a watchtower. It was at the northern end of the partially caved-in roof.

"The crow's nest," he said as the last of us climbed up and in.

Here, Father seemed to have established a secondary reserve for his armaments and operations. Maybe it was even where he'd been hiding out for the last few days. The crow's nest housed a more mobile version of what I'd seen in his underground laboratory: a stockpile of curious armaments and contraptions I didn't recognize, some of which looked to be in the process of being either built or taken apart. Monitors were hooked up to various rotating satellites and portrayed graphs, radars, and weather maps. A smaller version of the motorized mirror, or the supernatural copy machine, as Father had referred to it, leaned against one of the walls, and on the ceiling was a tangle of gear work.

The Hat slumped Gus against one of the walls, and Lexi kneeled to him, checking his ankle. She didn't look well either; she'd lost her hat, and her head was scratched up and bleeding. Now that my adrenaline had slowed, I began to feel just how badly my right shoulder had been injured. I looked at Gus, and he was glaring at me.

"Business trips, huh?" He sounded cruel. In a way, he was looking at me in the same way I often looked at myself, with that expression that asked: "what, exactly, are you worth?"

"I tried, okay. I wanted to…but I couldn't."

"Why not?"

"Because I…" I looked at Father as he and the Hat loaded

something into a centrifuge atop a table. Father voiced an annoyance with the machine before pressing a button and watching it spin round. It made a whirring sound, and I whispered beneath it. "I didn't want you to know that *this*," I nodded toward Father, "was what happened to my family, okay? I thought you'd stop talking to me. I thought…I thought you'd…"

"Look down on you?" He winced as Lexi took off his penny loafer. His ankle had puffed up beneath his sock like a cotton balloon. "Why? Because you'd look down on me if I was in your position?"

Lexi regarded Gus's ankle. "Looks like it's just a sprain. But a bad one."

Gus *oofe*d as he set it out in front of him. Lexi brought a small step stool over and lifted his leg onto it.

I hung my head. The centrifuge stopped spinning, and Father, removing something from it, turned around and stomped toward Gus and Lexi. He was holding two metal canisters in his hands. Much like the same ones I'd seen him inject into his neck the day I caught him out by the hedgerow.

He bent down to Gus and took the lid off one, revealing a needle. Gus regarded it with interest, as if Father only wanted him to be impressed by its sharpness. But then Father jabbed it fiercely into Gus's neck and depressurized the fluids into his bloodstream. He yelped.

"Yeah, yeah." Father turned toward Lexi.

"Get that away from me."

Father then nodded with a tired look toward the Hat, who came over and gripped her arms.

"Hey," she said. "Stop it. Stop it, I said!"

The needle pricked her neck. When it was done, she leaped back.

"Teenagers these days." Father was sour. His face could have aged five years since I'd seen him five nights ago. "All of you are so frightened of everything you touch. I would say that it's good to be scared out of your mind at least once a day. But what you have…it's a soul disease. It makes you all think that for some reason, the world cares about your feelings."

He laughed bitterly and took four sticks of Krigly's Cheddar-Infused Beef Jerky, tossing one in each of our laps (save for the Hat) and keeping the last for himself.

"I'll tell you, though, from firsthand experience. You can scream and throw a fit all you want, but when it comes down to it, the world doesn't care about what you want. You and your feelings run up against a little something called 'what happens.' And that's where the bullshit ends."

He bit off a chunk of his jerky and chewed it maniacally.

"God, this shit is good." He seemed surprised at that fact himself. "Probably made of cow skull and dextrose, but the taste is sublime."

"Mr. Eberstark?" Gus's eyes began to glow with something like health.

"Father crouched down and sat on the floor. "You're feeling better, aren't you?"

"I think so. Not my ankle, but—"

"Your head." Father tapped Gus on the skull.

"It's almost like I'm…quieter again. Like before I stopped losing track of myself."

"Well, that'd make sense." Father took another bite of his jerky as Lexi and I opened ours. "Mostly because your brain's been swimming in Murje since whenever you found something for it bond with."

"Murje?" Gus tried to sit up straight. "What's Murje?"

"Why don't you ask bedwetter over there?" Father said, grinning in my direction. "Didn't mention it, did he? I wouldn't have thought he would. Courage isn't his default." He eyed me closely. "Son of a bitch hasn't even been contaminated. How in the hell is that possible with all the slinking around you've been doing?"

Lexi looked at me with a little bit of pity and, seeming to feel better herself, said, "All right, that's enough. Just tell us what it is."

"What? The Murje? Hell, if I knew what it was, do you think I'd be up here in a goddamned watchtower with enough weaponry to get noticed by Homeland Security?" He laughed crazily, and jerky bits sprayed off his teeth. "Thanks to the Hat here, the only thing I know about Murje is what it's called. That and that from it, things…they grow. Once you touch it to something important, that is, and dream on it hard enough… Anyway, what I just gave you is the antidote. An anti-penumbric, we call it, made from the Murje itself but containing the opposite of it. Oh, don't look at me like I should know the science. The Hat's in charge of that area. Brilliant bastard"

The Hat, chewing a piece of bubblegum, smiled.

"Don't get too comfortable though. It won't last that long. The Murje always wins in the end. No matter how many times you prick yourself with this little concoction."

Lexi took a bite of her jerky and reached into her pocket. "My cigarettes…"

The Hat, regarding her behind his Ray Bans, walked across the room and sat down next to her. He reached his hand into his coat pocket and pulled from it a fresh pack. He tapped it against his palm, tore off the top foil, and flashed it toward Lexi with bravado. Its logo stood out immediately. It was a drawing of the Hat himself, holding a ray gun, and illustrated in an antique style, like something you'd see advertising a movie poster from the 1940s.

THE SILENT END

"Careful," Father said as the Hat allowed Lexi to withdraw one from the pack. It had a red filter and was extra-long. "That'll probably be the best cigarette you've ever had…and will have as long as you live."

Lexi looked at Father like he was crazy as she took one to her lips. The Hat lit it with a silver zippo and rocked on his haunches in anticipation of her response.

"It tastes like…like…" Lexi inhaled. A second later, she was glowing with happiness. Every part of her, from her ears to her fingers, radiated.

"You can't describe it, can you?" said Father.

Lexi stared at the Hat in awe. "I want…I want a million more."

"Well, that's impossible. Not unless yours learns how to produce them itself. Though I doubt it. There's no assurances when it comes to these creatures. Not that I've encountered many."

"What do you mean, these creatures? And what do you mean by 'yours?'"

"On second thought, it's actually a good thing you took one of those cigarettes." Father ignored her. "You won't like smoking regular ones that much after tasting some of the Hat's. Which is good thing being that you've got one disgusting habit going for you already."

"Fuck you."

"Mr. Eberstark." Gus took his beef jerky and aimed it at the Hat. My heart sank as he did so; he was now avoiding eye contact with me, looking everywhere but in my direction. "What is he?"

"He?" Father looked around with genuine confusion. "Oh. You mean the Hat. It's all right. I've made the same mistake."

At this, the Hat looked up from the ground and opened his mouth in silent laughter.

"Are you kids ready for a story? I'm thinking it'll answer some questions you've been having. And then, when I'm done, you can help me answer some myself."

Gus and Lexi nodded.

"What about you, bedwetter?" When Father looked at me, I felt my body crumple. I didn't even feel like I was part of this group anymore. Like I'd been kidnapped and hoisted into a van. "Are you finally ready to stop pretending you don't know where you came from?"

TWO

"THE NIGHT YOUR MOTHER WAS taken," began Father before trailing off. He'd burrowed into a cabinet and turned around, hugging a stash of Stumart-bought items: Kit Kats, Chicken Squares, Corn Scoops and Coca Cola; I didn't know when or how he got them. I thought about asking him if he even cared about the fact that his store had been trashed but didn't, afraid of what the answer might be. He scattered the snacks at our feet and plucked a bag of Chicken Squares for himself. Lexi smoked another one of the Hat's cigarettes, and Father shut off the ceiling lights and clicked on a small camping lamp, which he set on the floor.

"I haven't really talked to you about it before." He looked at me. "At first because I didn't want to frighten you. But later because I saw the way you looked at me and the whole damned world in general after your mother was taken. Like all of it was too bizarre to be believed. I didn't think you could handle what had come through the window.

THE SILENT END

What I chased into the forest that night. When I was a kid, I faced hell early on. Stuff you kids don't want know about. You, though, bedwetter, you…I knew that you couldn't hold your hands before the flame no matter how low it was.

"I remember it was right around after things got real bad with your mother. You know, with the shower? That was your final straw, right? When you checked out and crawled into your hidey hole? Anyway, I was racking up the hours at Stumart, and meanwhile, I'd come home, and she'd be spouting all this shit about men in mirrors. About someone trying to freeze her to death that looked like an old boyfriend of hers. I tell you, I thought she was one of two things: either crazy or full of it. No good option either way, am I right? Who the hell talked like that? Who, apart from a certified mental case, isolated herself in a room without windows and rattled on about people coming to get her? I convinced myself I was the only rational one in our family. And no offense, bedwetter, but I didn't see you as much different from her. You were always your mother's child no matter how much I tried to change that. Everything I did to recognize you as mine ended in failure. You were just so damn delicate, you know? Like some insect you killed accidentally by stretching your arms. You were scared of the dark. You were scared of the light. After your mother went south, I just had this feeling that I'd sealed my fate by marrying into mental illness and would have to take care of the both of you for the rest of my life once you ended up walking off the same ledge she had. Your mother, even before this crap started, she had a dark streak, you know. She could look at her life like it was worthless, and I had to accept that standing up or else she'd shut down. Maybe you can't understand what that's like, but I was just trying to wake up on the right side of the bed each morning."

Lexi wilted. I couldn't say why, but it was the first time she'd truly encountered Father. Even though he was infected with the same stuff as she and Gus, it was possible she sensed his callousness ran deeper than what the Murje could explain.

"The night it all happened, your mother came to bed. This wasn't normal, you know. You might not have noticed at the time, being that you were consumed in your figurines and masturbation, but we'd been sleeping separately for months. She in the den and me in the place I'd always wanted to sleep: the king-sized bed with memory foam I'd paid too much for, thinking it would help sort our bad backs when we moved out of that Cleveland shoebox we'd been suffering in. But nope, instead, she tried to throw away every mirror in the house like a lunatic."

He stuffed a handful of Chicken Squares into his mouth, took five savage chews, and swallowed. His teeth were slick with snack chemicals. Before he resumed speaking, I almost jumped to my feet and yelled that I did indeed remember how bad things had gotten. That I'd been there to keep Mother from bleeding out while he'd been off at work, ignoring the family he felt didn't deserve him. But I decided to keep quiet. With Gus still angry at me and Lexi trying to decide whether she could trust anyone after her cats had been killed and her house destroyed, I thought it better not to say anything at all.

"So yeah, she came to bed. But not to talk. Not even on her own will, I don't think. With her eyes open, she seemed to be sleepwalking. She was looking straight ahead toward the window, waiting for something. That's when things got real cold… You know the kind of cold I'm talking about now, right?"

We nodded.

"That's when I first felt it. It didn't make sense, the way it came from inside my body, but I didn't have a damn clue about what that was at the time. Instead, I just tried to talk to her and, with a little force, managed to get her to sit on the bed. She looked possessed with her head turned out the window, waiting. Like something out of a horror movie—which would've been great if she were on a screen and not barely breathing right beside me. I kept on getting colder though, so I went downstairs to turn up the thermostat. I put on my overcoat and my hat, Father's hat. I'd had that thing re-stitched a hundred times so I could keep on wearing it without looking like I should be hopping freight trains.

"That's about around when I heard something. Not what you'd typically think—a crash or the sound of windows breaking. But footsteps…the floorboards started creaking, and there was a thump outside. I'm sure you know by now, bedwetter, but when someone moves in that house, everyone hears it. So anyway, I grabbed the first thing I saw, the poker from the fireplace, and ran up the stairs in my coat, hat, bicycle shorts, and flip-flops. I think I half-expected your mother to have jumped out the window and couldn't believe I'd left her alone. I'd always been the type to not give a damn about where she was. And I don't mean anything having to do with jealousy, thinking she was messing around behind my back. I mean to the point of forgetting she was in my life at all. Sometimes, when I was working, well, I'd pretend I didn't have a family. I'd treat our house like a hotel I crashed in for a few hours a night. And if I caused you guys suffering from that, well, that's because I reasoned it was your fault. If you weren't doing big things, you weren't doing anything. That's how I saw it for a long while, especially after I came to Mossglow and ran into money for the first time. You don't grow up with toys, you end up wanting them more than a needy child when you grow up.

"But the second I heard that sound… my entire life changed. I think I saw past myself. Into the future, or something a lot like it, where I was standing over a casket with you, bedwetter, at my side. I saw that everything I'd worked for, everything I'd thought was right, was just me trying to convince myself I wasn't miserable. Looking back, what I'd really wanted was your mother, but I couldn't understand how to want her good enough. Or how to make her want me. I was a failure, doomed for the rest of my life to have been unable to care enough about anyone to know when they wanted to stop living."

He ran his tongue across his teeth. The Hat watched him with a somber expression, and for a moment, I felt pity for the man. Sure, I still feared and loathed him—how could I do anything but remember his neglect, his way of making me think he'd just get up and leave one day? But now, I could also see he knew how much wrong lurked inside him.

"When I came upstairs, I was already on my way to losing my mind. But what I saw up there finished the job. The creature…no one had seen anything like it before. I didn't get a full look, mind you, and wondered for a second if I just hadn't been sleeping enough and my brain was out for revenge. It had already taken your mother from the window and was galloping like some great albino hog into the night, making this grunting sound. I didn't know what to do, so I just jumped out the window, I shit you not. Jumped three fucking stories and snapped something when I landed. It hurt like nothing else, but do you think that stopped me? I've been in a lot of fights in my life—I grew up in Boston—and one thing I can say for myself is that I never stop slugging. Maybe that's why I'd never lost a brawl… until that night anyway.

"I sprinted after the creature. It was so big…the biggest thing

I'd ever seen. To be honest, I haven't seen one that big since; I have a feeling it's their version of a Capo or something. I ran after it, barely able to keep up, and then I just called out to the fucker, something stupid and desperate like, 'Give me back my wife!' By that point, though, I couldn't ignore that I'd been screwed up from that fall.

"Me and the creature, this hog beast, we were by the edge of Graywood Forest by the time it turned to look at me. Must have thought I was persistent enough to grace me with its presence. I almost ran away right there. Size aside, I'd never seen such anger before in something. Except maybe myself. There was a rage in that creature I thought would blow up my heart if I stared at it a second longer. It had these short legs that looked like they could have been made of out mesh; a big, fat, white belly; tentacles for hair; and gigantic, metal tusks. And there it was, holding my wife in those tusks like it was bringing her home to be its bride. Well, yeah, I almost booked it back to the house and probably would have too had the signature Eberstark crazy not taken over. The same crazy that had allowed your grandfather to paratroop into Germany like a demented flying squirrel with a backpack full of dynamite. Before I knew what was happening, I was charging the damn thing. Me and a fireplace poker against a five-ton goliath with tentacles spewing out of its head.

"As I ran at it, I saw it was laughing at me, like he'd find my death funny. But then I leaped on it anyway—right on its face—and stabbed the hell out of it over and over again! I don't even remember feeling anything when it tossed me. But I know I pissed it off. Pierced it right in one of its squiddy eyes. In response, it launched me good, right into a tree. I must have snapped another thing when I hit it because there was bombloads of pain. The sort of hurt you'll feel forever. Pain like that sticks with you. Every morning even to this day, when I wake up, I can count on, for a split second, truly believing that I'm back in the bushes in Graywood, my spine pulverized to dust."

Father slugged down half of the two-liter of Coca Cola, the black liquid funneling like oil, greasing the engine within. He could have been drunk for his loose-limbed gestures and drowsy eyes, but I knew now that it wasn't the case. Father was affected by the Murje alone. What had attached itself to him had been building up for months now. He was developing a substance abuser's sense of shuttered movement, and I could tell he recognized that himself.

"That's where I woke up, anyway. In Graywood Forest. In a bush. Only a few hours later and only for a few minutes. It was still nighttime, and I could barely move. Something horrible had happened to my back, and my face had blood all over it. I felt my ribs, and it was like my fingers were blowtorches. I didn't cry—I swear I didn't cry—but I just lay there, thinking about how broken I was. Broken just like my dad had been. He'd tripped, you know, over a telephone wire at work. He was a service clerk after the war at a computer chip manufacturer. The fall ruptured his spine, and he couldn't do so much as sit at a desk for the rest of his life. That's why he died so young. Not sure if you knew that. And not because of the injury either. But because of the near-constant shame of it. He was a hard person who in his heyday could haul a refrigerator on his back up a set of stairs. He didn't have much of a head for anything else. After years of screaming at his wife, trying to blame her for what had happened, he just ended up wasting away and was gone before you were born.

So anyway, when I woke up in the forest, lying there, I felt as if I was just like him. Broken. Pitiful. Useless. I'd been unable to notice the tripwires around me and instead made a show of stumbling over each one. At least Father had had a wife to yell at afterwards. I didn't even have that anymore. I'd spent all this time building up a business and bench pressed the equivalent of a sedan in the basement three times a week to keep my body strong. All for nothing. All for a hat. That fucking fedora was the only thing I had left of him—a reminder of how family's a circular thing, I guess. It seemed right for me to have been wearing it when that behemoth shattered my bones. My dad, he hadn't treasured much in life, but that hat he'd kept from the War until the grave. I don't know why; it held significance to him.

In the forest, in the bush, I held that hat in one hand. And in the other, I found the fireplace poker, right at my side, bringing it to my chest as well, just to feel something solid. It was covered in these oozy blue-gray chunks that got all over Father's fedora. But before I could care enough to wonder what they were, or whether or not I'd be breathing by morning, I drifted off again and went somewhere very, very far away.

"That's when I had the dream...if you really want to call it that. Gus, Lexi, I'm sure you know what I'm talking about by now. Because it wasn't a dream as much as it was some tripped-out nightmare where the world around you is melting. It reminded me of some shit I took in college that made the walls turn to jelly; not my kind of thing. But there I was, tripping balls in the middle of the forest, stuck between living and dying.

"In that dream, I saw a man. A horrible man with horrible eyes. I remember it vividly to this day. He was on a throne, a throne made out of groceries from Stumart, I think, some weird, spaced-out thing built out of snack cakes and soup cans, and I'd been brought before him to kneel like an unworthy subject. It was so humiliating. He'd stripped me naked. I was in chains. I think he was getting ready to execute me—execute me, Morrison Eberstark, can you believe it, like

I was Louis the fucking XIV? And it was so strange; I almost thought that if he succeeded, then I wouldn't ever wake up again. That my head would roll in the dream, and that would be the end. There was this ax at his side... And he probably would have gotten down to business had it not been for my dad. He strode into this royal chamber we were in with this John Wayne swagger, and he was wearing his favorite hat. His favorite hat and this seersucker suit he'd been sporting at my high school graduation, just a few weeks before he got put in a wheelchair. He looked good. Tough. He was full of confidence, just like I remembered him when I was a kid. The only thing I noticed was that he couldn't talk. It was like his mouth had been sewed shut, and when I tried to shout out to him, he made this tight-lipped smile as if to intimate that everything would be okay. I still don't know why. All I wanted to do was hear his voice; it had always soothed me in the past. One of those voices that spoke only when it needed to.

"So my dad, he pissed off the man in the throne. I could tell instantly since I don't think he was suspecting any visitors. That man, whose identity I've been chasing from mirror to mirror around this town, wanted me dead and gone. But for some reason, my dad wouldn't stand for it. He and the man in the throne, they started fighting—Olympian style, you know? Wrestling and punching and whatnot. I couldn't tell who was winning, but as that was becoming clearer, I woke up. It was mid-morning by that point, and to my genuine surprise, I was still alive. I was still alive, and my body, I could move it a little. Not perfectly, mind you, but I could tell I wouldn't be in a wheelchair for the rest of my life like my old man. I was able to scoot around onto my shoulder, and I think that's when I first saw him, it—whatever. I don't really care what you call the Hat, and I don't think he does either."

As if to make sure, he gestured toward the creature in the seersucker suit, who turned to us and bowed.

"The fucker was holding me in its arms…spooning me, actually. Freaked me out! This thing with my dad's hat, my dad's suit, and in some ways my dad's face, had his arm around me and was stroking my chest. I didn't know what the hell to think of it. He looked like my dad to a certain degree, but to a more certain degree, he didn't look like him at all. It was like the Murje, whatever it was, had tried to make a copy of what I saw in my mind when I thought of him, and this," he gestured to the Hat, "was what came out. I didn't know whether I should have been more afraid of it than I was, but for some reason, my mind was at ease. Maybe because from the get-go, right when I opened my eyes, I could hear its voice. Or no, not hear it, but understand it, kind of like how you don't have to actually tell your legs to walk. Something told me that *it* had come from *me*.

"Soon after that, though, the troubles began. The Hat, he used strange remedies to nurse my wounds in the forest. He had this way of manipulating things, technology in particular that was preposterous. He's sentient in his own way, you see. He has autonomy. He knows how to think about things, and what he thinks about is far beyond what we think about things. It's the stuff he's made of—it's just more complete. In certain ways, it makes us seem inferior.

"Anyway, that's how the laboratory would be established. Yes, he required me to obtain certain pieces of hardware that no one outside of a biochemistry or particle physics laboratory would have use for. But what he used those things to culture was simply incomprehensible; a mixture of science and dream logic. I'd started losing my grasp of reality by that point, you see. We both noticed that I couldn't concentrate. That I started blanking out and forgetting where I was.

Things were getting increasingly worse to the point where I started misplacing whole days only to wake up with my hands covered in mud, digging in some cave off Goon's Cove. That's around the time when I disappeared, bedwetter. Thankfully, no one found me in that state. I'd have been committed faster than you can say straightjacket, and you'd have been sent to Massachusetts to live with your uncle.

"The Hat, he devised a way to help me out. He took the Murje, the very last bit of it still living on the end of the fireplace poker, and while I was careening around Goon's Cove like a lunatic, was somehow able to create a living culture. To grow the stuff. From that, we would eventually be able to fashion weapons. But first, he created the anti-penumbric, which is the closest we've come so far to inhibiting the dementia brought on by interacting with the Murje. It doesn't cure the disease, not by a longshot, but it makes it more manageable.

"The aim, of course, of all of these months of hard labor was to rectify my greatest regret: losing your mother. But in the process, I'd be driven just as mad as the man in the mirror himself. Creatures like the Hat are made of a substance that latches onto intention. I don't know exactly how it works. I don't know where it comes from. I just know that the man in the mirror, Mr. Blue, has control over what's producing it. That he's right here in Mossglow, and for some twisted reason, he wanted your mother enough to ruin our lives. That's why I went out on the prowl. Why I started chasing shadows. Why I set off a damned bomb in the woods to bring that first beast to its knees. Damn, if only that had worked out right. Did you know that bomb actually ended up wounding the Hat? It was a calibration error that didn't account for the photospheric resistance being generated by the creature at that particular moment, so we had to get out of there quick before things got hairy. That was a little one too. What a botched opportunity. Could have gotten all the information we needed."

We sat in silence as we heard described the circumstances behind Lexi discovering the monster in the forest. Father, taking a deep, anxious breath, then made a gesture to the entity currently supplying the girl with her sixth consecutive cigarette.

"So…then…" Gus said, shimmying his back up the wall a little for comfort. "This man is not a man at all. But…a hat?"

Father sighed.

"Mustus, for a brilliant boy, you sure are stupid. Hat, show them what I mean."

The Hat stood up, seeming a little bored, and stepped to the side of our little circle. He put his right hand on the top of his head, on the bone-white derby hat my grandfather had worn, and pulled. It took effort to take it off, like unscrewing a cork from a bottle. With a soft *tick*, however, it detached, and I saw that his head was flat on top, as if the upper portion had been removed by a machete. But then, he kneeled down and dipped his scalp forward. We all peered inside. Within the Hat's head was, in fact, nothing. Only a thick, endless black. An emptiness like the one I'd seen on Mr. Kraft's bedroom wall.

Presumably not concerned with putting himself up for spectacle any longer, he stood up again and put the hat back on, crackling his knuckles in front of him in sign of a job well done.

Lexi smoked the rest of her cigarette to its filter.

"Don't even try to ask him to take the glasses off," Father said. "You couldn't do that with the jaws of life."

The Hat sat back down and resumed his lazy posture.

"Does he sleep?" Gus asked.

The Hat scribbled down a note on a piece of paper and held it up.

Not like you.

"Amazing," Lexi said.

"You get used to it." Father drained the last of his two-liter. "Not that any of that matters anymore. We lost our last lead tonight in Graywood Forest. That monster…I'd been stalking it for months. Almost had it too—multiple times. And there's no way we'll be able to take out the big one."

"The big one?" said Gus.

"The one that took bedwetter's mother away. You don't understand what that sort of thing is made of. Hell, I don't. And look at us. Look at what we've got. Me. The Hat. Three teenagers, a bunch of weird jelly guns, and a truck that thinks it's alive." He laughed bitterly. "And now that Lexi's house got destroyed—sorry about that, by the way, you must be very upset."

Lexi glared at him.

"Now that her house is destroyed, you can bet it'll be looking for us. And that, I can tell you now, is worse than not having a lead."

The electric lamp buzzed, and Gus pulled his arms into his sleeves and began shuffling in his shirt.

"Don't put any weight on it," said Lexi as he removed his foot from the stool and reached around to his back. With a sound of relief, he pulled something out from underneath his shirt. It was a book. The same book I'd found in the cellar at Stumart. The title shone in bright gold lettering. *NON ENTITIES ONLY.*

"What have you got there, Gus?" Father was fidgeting.

"Proof." Gus held the book out before the camping lamp. "That we might not be so screwed after all."

THREE

WE SPENT A GOOD LONG while after that filling Father in on everything that happened since Lexi discovered the monster in the forest. We talked about Gus's dream creature, the Crow Seraph. We talked about Mrs. Duncan, the Shepherd, and the mold on the wall. As we did so, Father jumped in with questions and comments, his eyes building with renewed confidence and then brooding with something darker, like envy.

"How is it you figured out so much?" He tightened his fists and marched back and forth. "I've been running circles around Mossglow for months—months! Staking out suspects. Breaking into homes and hiding in attics. Watching. Searching. Watching. Searching. It doesn't make any sense that in less than a week, you've been able to dig up so much. You're a bunch of fucking kids."

The Hat wrote on a piece of paper and held it up to Father.

THE SILENT END

It's possible we got lost.

Father bit his knuckles and crouched. He was sweating pretty profusely despite the fact that it was cool in the crow's nest. "...I guess it is. Sometimes, when you're not around humans enough, you stop behaving like one. Damn you, Hat, and your alien wisdom."

Lexi tried to get me to tell the story of what happened in the cellar. But sensing Gus's anger, I couldn't bring myself to speak. Lexi sighed and pieced together the encounter based on what I'd told her. She revealed where I'd found the book. She told Father about the gun with the missing piece, which currently sat in a sock drawer in Gus's room. As she finished, Father leered at me.

"Wow, bedwetter. If I didn't know better, I'd have said you went and did something brave by going down there. Not that an empty book and broken pistol are going to help worth a shit, but still."

"Mr. Eberstark," Gus said. "Stop."

"Stop?" Father looked as if Gus had used a word outside of his vocabulary. "Stop what?"

"Bedwetter. Stop calling him that."

"Where do you get off telling me what to say, Mustus?" Father growled. He came up from his crouch and stood taller even than before, uncurling his shoulders so that he rose to an intimidating 6 foot 2. His brow creased, and his mouth opened to reveal crooked teeth. "You're walking on shaky ground."

"I get off telling you what to say because it's harmful. And not only harmful." Gus puffed out his chest and tried to ascend to Father's height; at five foot nine, and with a body type the pole opposite of beefy, he didn't stand much of a chance, but that didn't stop him from trying. "But stupid. That's what a person who doesn't care about anyone says. And I want to think you care about people, Mr. Eberstark. I want to think you're not a self-centered asshole who treats family like the garbage he forgot to put out."

Father looked like he'd been punched in the face. And he might have punched Gus back for the infraction had the Hat not accidentally intervened. Taking the long, thin, hardbound cover reading *NON ENTITIES ONLY* in his hands, the creature in Ray Bans sat down on the ground and began flipping through the pages. Father's wrathful gaze turned toward the book and, like a child with limited attention span, forgot what he'd been angry about, sitting down on the floor as if preparing to be read a story.

I looked at Gus, feeling overwhelmed with gratitude, and knew that ours was the sort of friendship so strong that it could only be broken by an act of murder. Thankfully, neither of had plunged to such levels yet, and I hoped we never would. He didn't look back at me though—he wasn't ready.

After running throughout the expanse of the book, the Hat returned to page one. As he touched the paper with his fingers, images began to form upon it. Serpentine shapes that became lines of penmanship. The light from the camping lamp flickered. With each subsequent page the Hat turned, the more words and pictures began to swirl to life, filling out the book like blood into a circulatory system. As he finished, I realized that the man in the seersucker suit was exactly as the cover had described. A Non Entity. Something that was, in fact, created from someone else's consciousness. I didn't know how it worked, but I knew it had astonished Mr. Kraft before he suffocated and died. From the look in our US Politics teacher's fading, mismatched gaze, the Hat could have been an angel, someone sent to escort the foul creature into realms beyond. This also signified that the Shepherd and Crow Seraph (wherever it had gone) were also Non Entities. Creatures born from dreams. Gus told me he'd seen the book wedged beneath the back seat and, without a thought, had it out of the Shepherd before we ascended the stairs to the crow's nest.

When the Hat was finished bringing the pages to life, he closed the cover and held it to his chest. The process seemed to have tired him.

"Non Entity, huh?" said Father grumpily. I could tell that he'd gone a bit too long without taking his anti-penumbric. "Sounds like nonsense squared to me."

"May I?" Lexi motioned for the book.

The Hat cautiously placed it in her arms and backed against the wall, where he dipped his head to listen.

"Thank you." She opened to page one. Taking a deep breath, she began to read.

8th July, 1837.
Dear Non Entity,

I am not long for this world and will be gone before he knows it. Though before I depart, it must be resolved, even if posthumously, this issue of the Living Artifact.

My husband has gone mad with arcane science. The device he discovered in the quarries beneath Goon's Cove six years and eight months ago has now claimed his judgment and good name. I don't know if I can blame the events on him in entirety. This technology is not of our world. I don't know whether it was forged in Heaven, Hell, or some realm beyond the immortal stars where orbs of darkness dwell. But it wasn't meant for us. Of that I am certain.

When Thomas first alerted me to the nature of his experiments, it was more by incident than not. He'd tried to keep his happenings a secret to those who'd not enlisted in his peculiar cabal and hoped I'd be content inhabiting my ignorance in the house he'd built off silver money in the Crowstone Heights. But since curiosity is a nasty trait my own father couldn't get me to abandon, and Thomas himself stopped returning home for reasons that were as bold as they were suspicious, even to a new wife as myself, I spied upon his dwellings beneath the Academy, where he'd been busy constructing something of a monster. I do not speak in exaggeration; nor do I attempt to belittle the imagination I've been gifted with talk of creatures meant to frighten children. But this was my experience, and I will not abandon it, even against my better judgment.

When Thomas discovered me in the caverns beneath the Academy, I won't say he didn't harm me. Fury had attached itself to him like a parasite, and he'd been taken by what I can only describe as affliction. But thankfully for my health, he retracted his hand eventually and tried, like a man who only dabbled in unreasonableness, to explain the philosophy behind his experimentation. "I've discovered a way to combine elements," he said. "Using this machine, this Living Artifact, I can create not only new minerals but new forms of life. The possibilities are endless, Edwina, and I shan't share the knowledge with others. Please see this blessing for what it is."

Upon challenging his ideals, however, he blamed my sex for its moral and intellectual insufficiencies. A woman this and a woman that. The path he'd gone down had already collapsed upon him. In the man I married, a devil did alight, and like all creatures who think themselves capable of greatness, he was given to greed in the end.

Chances are that, Non Entity, you are not conscious of the contours of my husband's mysterious machine, which he unearthed during a mining exhibition just less than seven years ago. Finding it began by happenstance alone, in search of a bountiful silver quarry in the northwest. After weeks of surveying, the men of my husband's expedition stumbled upon an odd breed of glowing moss that grew upon the ground where the current Academy stands. Its effects were nothing short of mesmerizing.

Thomas in particular was driven to astonishment. Some within the party thought the substance for a sprinkling of divinity that should be handed over to a clergyman while others saw only how it might lead them to wealth or posterity. Thomas, as chief financier of the expedition, chose something in between the two, coveting the discovery as a secret all the same. When they began digging, the spores released from that soil were said to have driven those around them mad. The affected began to forget their names and left pools of blood throughout the mining camp from resultant brawls. The deaths came early on, brutal murders that rendered men less than beasts.

Thomas claims it was not his fault that the entire party, save for himself, eventually disappeared. Since I've grown to know my husband, however, and understand the lust in his soul, it seems possible that he convinced himself survival relied upon the torment of others. Of the thirty-one who embarked, only one lived. This was the man who sent for me in Massachusetts to come join him as his bride in the west.

As of now, Thomas has found a way to sever his own self from the world above. He believes he is capable of living the equivalent of a dozen human lives, perhaps more, though he cannot articulate his aims in all of this. Recently, he has begun to insist that I, too, must engage in this plan of life elongation, a prospect that terrifies me for its conflict against God and nature. It is refusing his wants that contributes to my reasoning in writing this letter. If I do not act soon, I will be taken against my will. Of this I am sure. And before I can resist, I will become the wicked queen of his underground kingdom, indulging his spawn in eternal tribute.

As a word of warning, let me assure you now that words cannot describe the Living Artifact's manufacture. It looks like nothing created on or for Earth. And it is far too crude for God to have a hand in.

The machine does indeed create. But the manner in which it does is so often demonic. I tried to explain this to Thomas, to appeal to his pragmatism as a Harvard-educated businessman of known repute, but his mood had already been too far diminished. Unsatisfied in his drawing together of fallow elements, he began trying his experiment on animals. His most successful of which involved bullfrogs and a local iron alloy. The result, as I'm sure you might appreciate as the inadvertent offspring of this process, was hideous. But not to dwell on such unpleasantness. Thomas always did cherish discovery to a fault. Perhaps this is why he behaved so abhorrently. From speaking to him in the lighted halls of the Academy, you wouldn't know he harbored such a madness within him now. But when he began engineering creations beyond his capacity, I knew the power he'd been given would drive him to fanaticism.

I won't describe in detail what precipitated my own infection with the substance known as Murje, but I hope it will suffice to say that, as I write this letter, my mind swims with waking nightmares. I forget my place on Earth and often wake in obscure locales, with townsmen staring at me like a silly woman at the edge of her sanity. I can't even say if it was Thomas' intention to infect me. I believe it was not being that, even as madness consumed him, he wished for me to remain apart from his lesser trials. All I do know is that my Non Entity (a term I've created for your kind) came into being on the night of June 21, 1837, after the substance contaminated a pistol my brother had taken to the Barbary Wars; he left it to me before he died in the winter of last year. The Murje infused the weapon with magnificent power capable of blowing down an entire home with one discharge. I was astounded by its capabilities. Especially as, with time, I began to hear its thoughts. Hear its thoughts as, Non Entity, I am sure you hear the thoughts of your creator.

It is also the truth that I would have used that pistol to try and dismantle the machine and put an end to the evil below Mossglow, had I been able. But even creatures such as yourself are unable to effect its constitution; this has been proven time and again by Thomas' reckless trials in combination.

I write this letter, however, only because I did come along a scant bit of hope. For a long while, Thomas had been attempting to conduct a dangerous experiment. One which involved combining an inorganic substance with a piece of the machine itself. During one particularly disastrous trial, a small splinter of a shard jostled loose from the Artifact. When Thomas glimpsed it, his brain leaped to the only possible conclusion. It was a mad idea but not an unreasonable one. Why not attempt to introduce into a machine that combines entities a piece of its own self and discover the outcome?

The result of his experiment, however, was near cataclysmic. Introducing a piece of the device into itself created something that almost turned Mossglow into a crater in the Earth. It also came close to terminating the Living Artifact itself. Thomas was horrified by the threat he'd unwillingly unleashed against what had become his life's greatest passion. If he had succeeded, I wouldn't be writing this letter today. But instead, he only came close to sealing his demise, interpreting his misstep as a valuable lesson. What the experiment had produced in place of total destruction was a new and entirely volatile mineral. An "unstable element" is what Thomas termed it. Apparently, it was so dangerous that, if you were to insert it into the Living Artifact in the manner done before, it was almost certain the device would swallow half of the city whole.

Afraid to leave this mineral unattended, Thomas secured it in his quarters, in a place where no one from the outside world would ever find it. He was intelligent to do this but made one grave error: he hadn't reasoned I would have mind or will capable of devising a plan of my own. A man's biggest fault is his inability to understand the brilliance of woman. Discounting female ingenuity is responsible for the majority of Earth's woes. Though I must admit that my eyes

THE SILENT END

see only clouds these days and thus are incapable of entirely lucid thought, the scheme I have concocted I hope will right this wrong. Even to bring myself to scribble these words has required the utmost concentration. Thomas does love me, and I suppose I do love him as well. It is for that reason I hope to bring his world crumbling down around him.

My plan will begin with sequestering my Non Entity, my brother's pistol, in the vault in which you have discovered it. I knew it should be protected there being that I had a trusted metalsmith with an aptitude for secrecy erect the door securing it. The key itself will only be visible to you, Non Entity. I have had it crafted as such. You will come for it when we find you in a dream. And when you take this book from its pediment, it will be visible only by your kind alone. You may have to learn how to unlock its contents, but it takes only a moment to understand the method as it is a matter of internal comprehension.

"Wait, what was that last part?" I thought I had misunderstood.

"Let me finish first," said Lexi. "The letters…they make my head hurt."

The Hat, as if reading Lexi's mind, lit her another cigarette and gave it to her. She took a puff and relaxed.

"Keep going," Gus said. "I want to hear the end of this."

Please do take the armament with you, and note its craft. I knew that if I were going to attempt to steal the unstable element, I'd not take my pistol with me and risk losing it to the hands of Thomas' henchmen. I will infiltrate my husband's laboratory and retrieve it from there. I will then run for my life and end in death. With the piece I've removed from the pistol, the piece meant for holding ammunition, I have fashioned a receptacle for containing the weapon. I will tie this receptacle around my neck and jump into the Horn, where you, God willing, will discover my skeleton after it has long been picked clean. After you retrieve the unstable element, I can say with certainty that you will know what to do. Sometimes, in order to end a nightmare, you have to refashion the logic of dreams.

A Non Entity can understand better than most the need to end this vicious cycle. If I have succeeded in obtaining the unstable element by the time you have read this, I will be long dead. In the note left to Thomas detailing my suicide, I will plead to him to abandon his enterprise. Though I doubt it will do much good. Thus, as not to alert him to my body's location, I will write him a note. In it, I will profess that I plan to take a boat off Goon's Cove, travel miles from shore, and tie a stone around my ankle. Thomas has always been afraid of water and will not think in a million years to search the cove, not to mention the bay itself. When I disappear, he will believe me dead, and the matter, in his head, as to the whereabouts of the unstable element will be forgotten.

I do all this because I hope, at some point in the future, before this diseased machine spreads beyond the constraints of our town, that someone like yourself will be able to finish what I could not. The one thing I regret in taking my own life is that, in a fitful night a few months ago, Thomas had managed to impregnate me. I would have been glad to bear him a child when we lived in Massachusetts, but here, with the evil that intercedes in those ugly catacombs beneath

THE SILENT END

the village, I cannot abide such a measure.

Herein, you shall find maps and diagrams of everything I could manage to record, including those detailing my body's location and how to enter the realm of the machine. When you see me next, it'll be in the dark. And I'll be wearing light around my neck.

Sincerely,
Edwina Hailee Myers

"What in the fuck?" Father said after a long pause.

"Do you still have that key?" Gus wasn't yet comfortable making eye contact with me. The Hat was currently bandaging up his ankle. Before he applied the wrap, he took a vial filled with silver salve and spread it around the swelling.

I drove my hand into my left pocket, the one opposite the charm bracelet, and fished around. Though I couldn't find it at first, after a moment, I gripped and pulled out the iron key with the frog imprint at the head. I realized as I did so that I hadn't shown it to anyone until now. Not Gus, not Lexi, surely not Father. Fearfully, I then held it up for the room to view. I could barely see it now. It was light and transparent. No one else could see even so much as that. Save for the Hat, they squinted at my fingers, unable to bend their eyes around the object they held.

"There's nothing there," said Lexi.

"There is. I swear on my life."

The Hat, after rapidly finishing wrapping Gus's ankle, walked up to me. I offered him the key. He plucked it from my fingers and bent down, holding it before the camping lamp. I saw what he was doing, but the rest of the room thought he was poring over a handful of nothing.

After a moment of examination, the Non Entity stood up and scribbled on his notepad, holding it up for everyone to see.

He doesn't lie. A key is here.

The Hat then motioned Lexi, Gus, and Father to come forward. He held the key out to each of them so that they could feel the object with their fingers. Each of their faces paled as they found their fingers prodding, tapping, and slipping through the contours of an invisible suchness.

"It's almost like the air around it is weak," said Gus.

"Fine, I'll buy it," said Lexi. "Invisible key. Great. What I want to know, though, is why the hell you can see it, Eberstark? You're not a Non Entity, whatever that means. At least I don't think you are."

"Of course I'm not a Non Entity! How would that—I can barely see it compared to before. And look at that *thing* over there. It can't even take its glasses off."

I pointed to the Hat, who sunk its head. He scrawled a message on his notebook.

Things (and non-things) have feelings (and non-feelings) too.

"Take it easy, bedwe—"Gus shot Father a glance and he caught himself. I could see he hated the fact that he'd done so. Men like him didn't take advice from teenagers. Or adults. Or the elderly. "Son," he corrected. "If there's anything I learned from working with the Murje, it's that nothing is what it seems to be until it becomes something different."

Gus refused to abandon his fascination with the key.

"I can attest that Eberstark doesn't have any superpowers like the Hat here," said Lexi. "And he certainly can bleed."

"Still am, actually." I pointed to the glistening gash on my forehead.

"And if he were a 'Non Entity,'" said Lexi, "wouldn't that mean he had to be created from someone else's possession?"

"Maybe it's something else." Gus tapped at the key, breathless every time he touched its surface. "Maybe it's not only Non Entities that can see things humans cannot but that Non Entities view reality in a peculiar way."

"Great theory," said Father. "What's it mean?"

"Shouldn't we be concentrating on the important thing at hand here?" I said. "Like this journal, for instance, of Thomas Hellwidth Myers' wife?"

"Who's Thomas Hellwidth Myers?" Father was looking dimmer by the second, as if wires within him were being snipped and re-soldered.

"He's the man who founded this town?" said Lexi. "The man she was talking about? And, I'm willing to bet, the man I've been seeing in mirrors."

"Mr. Blue," Father said.

"Why do you call him that?" Gus said.

"Why do you think? Might as well be in a fish tank all the times I've seen him. Granted, those times have been few and far between. The most recent was in the house of that teacher woman who got murdered. What was her name?"

"Mrs. Duncan," we all said.

He snapped his fingers. "That's it. Poor woman didn't even know what she was up against. The shadic trackers picked up a threat level

2 right from underneath her house, so the Hat and I broke in while she was sleeping. Mr. Blue wanted her real bad. So bad he almost froze the house off its foundations."

"I don't want to talk about Mrs. Duncan anymore," Gus said.

"Let's get back to the map," said Lexi.

"Right, the map…" Father laughed. "Let's just take the advice of a two-hundred-year-old woman who jumped off a cliff. Think for a second, kids. Who the hell knows if we can trust any of this? What if she and Mr. Blue are one in the same? What if she is Mrs. Blue, for instance? It's okay if you admit I blew your mind."

I looked at Father. He looked uncomfortable in his body. I wanted to help him, wanted to say something, but was afraid of provoking the worst.

"Dad," I chanced. "Do you need another anti-penumbric?"

"I know what I need when I need it."

The Hat put a hand on Father's shoulder, and I could visibly see the man calm.

"Okay." He nodded his head. "I know. I will."

"This book," said Lexi, "is our key to cleaning up this mess. The only thing we don't know now is why this man, Thomas Hellwidth Myers, whatever he is now, is only targeting women…women like your mom, Eberstark."

"And women like you, Lexi," said Gus.

"Thanks for reminding me. Here, look at this." Lexi turned a few pages and held up one for us to observe. The sketches Edwina had left behind were often crude, not the work of a great artistic talent, but they were meticulous and accurate enough to act as guides. Lexi found a map of Mossglow and studied it. It was, we soon discovered, meant to direct us to the "unstable element" Edwina had described.

THE SILENT END

The city was laid out differently since the time she'd drawn it out. I could see that there was a small foundry in place of where Stumart now stood and that the Lower Thicks had not been named as such; a scant row of houses called the Pennybrook occupied the space, and a little north, where Gus lived, was another stretch called Upper Pennybrook. I also noticed that Myers High was called Myers Academy. I'd known that before but never thought anything about it until now. Right below Myers Academy, at its foot on the map, was a scribbling of words and a jagged, red X. They were messy but seemed to read *home of the device.* The X, drawn right over the front drive of the Academy, drew our attention.

"He's under Myers High?" said Gus. "I never would have thought…"

"Of course you wouldn't have thought," said Lexi. "Nobody would. That's probably why he built the school there in the first place. To draw attention away."

"You're right. What better a place to carry out evil work than beneath the halls of learning?"

"Someone famous said that, right?" I asked.

"If someone famous is me, than yes," he said, annoyed.

Father jumped to his feet and grabbed what appeared to be a harpoon whose tip was run through with yellow circuitry. His eyes bulged. "What the hell are we waiting for? Let's go to Myers High and beat the fucker senseless."

"Hold on now, Morrison," said Gus. "The letter said we need the 'unstable element' first."

"Exactly," said Lexi. "Even if it ends up not being important, I'd rather know first before we go in guns blazing."

Father pondered Lexi's reasonableness, and then consulted the map. He drew his finger to the Horn, where, right off the coast, was a small drawing of a woman in a white dress, floating dead with chains around her foot and torso tied to a block stone. It seemed overly macabre, but looking at the schematics of the map in general, her location was accurately placed, right below one of the western cliffs that overshadowed the bay and turned into a deep trench off shore. I imagined now what she must have seen: the rushing black waters, the foamy surf, impact before disappearing below, drowning, gasping, heart exploding, wondering if she'd hung salvation around her neck or condemned the town to ruin.

"Lexi's right. We need to go to the Horn first." That voice in the dream, it had come back to me quietly. I could hear it singing in the back of my brain. Something inside me just knew that we needed to retrieve whatever hung around Edwina's neck and bring that with us. Into the dark world inhabited by a man who may have once been Thomas Hellwidth Myers, a silver prospector perverted by a machine. The very same machine that had produced the creatures that tormented our lives, that had stolen Mother—that had stolen many mothers—and sealed off our town in a wall of forgetfulness.

Father looked at me, eyes still hard and unforgiving. But then, as if awakening from a trance, they softened. Maybe it was because I'd spoken up for myself. Or maybe because he was afraid of incurring the mistrust of Gus Mustus, a boy whose words could truly shave ribbons of muscle off your heart. Either way, I wasn't going to complain when he turned to everyone and said, "He's right. It's time to stop letting our minds stray like lost sheep. You kids lead the way to this…this 'unstable element.' And then." He looked out the window of the crow's nest. "I'll go in and get it."

FOUR

ONE OF THE BIGGEST HURDLES to accessing the Horn (apart from the multitude of reasons why no one liked to go there to begin with), was the fact that entering required crossing the old townie neighborhood named after a giant, crow-shaped rock. The rock was roughly twenty-five feet tall and composed of the same black stone that made up the rest of the bay. An ominous thing to behold in the rain especially, it truly did look as if a gigantic crow encased there could, at any moment, break free and surge into the sky.

To the rear of the rock was the bay, and to its front stretched a collection of beaten down Victorian homes, all of which were large and looked capable of capturing a modest sum had the rules of desired real estate not applied. This neighborhood was what was formally known as Crowstone Heights. Since the residents of the area were proudly unprofessional, and anyone who did have money carried it over from shares in a silver mining industry that had collapsed generations ago, there existed a limbo where wealth looked like poverty and vice versa. There was no real telling as to whether anyone had more than anyone else did; a fierce denial of privilege ran through the living room of every home and manifested itself quietly on the streets. I'd only been inside a couple of the houses themselves back when I first moved to Mossglow and, for a couple of months, took up with a group of older Crowstone kids I met behind the Lucky Start. I couldn't remember whose homes I visited or, due to the fact that I'd been stinking drunk as a fourteen-year-old, why I was there at all. All I could recall was how the insides were both grand and bare, with peeling wallpaper and exposed wiring. The windows were cracked, and what little furniture there was had a look of disrepair. The bathroom I'd used, I remembered, though featuring a large, ornate mirror, was filthy and filled with mold.

We were wary as we made our way up there by turning onto Crowstone Road. Or at least most of us were. I don't think Father had ever given a damn about offending townies. If anything, he'd taken wry enjoyment in seeing the occasional Crowstone resident sneak off to Stumart to examine items he or she could never hope to get a hold of in his own neighborhood. To Father's credit, he shunned any sort of local pride, no matter what city or state, with a sneering, "Everywhere is just as bad as anywhere," mentality and seemed to despise anyone who felt differently. But Lexi, Gus, and I didn't have that sort of luxury. As we rolled onto Crowstone Road, the entryway to the neighborhood, in the Shepherd (which was doing its best to not seem like it had a mind of its own), I wanted to sink to the floor and drip out through a hole in the undercarriage.

"It seems pretty calm tonight," Gus observed of something from the front seat. Father, the Hat, and I remained in back, packed in with an arsenal of weapons. "The Shepherd, I mean. Before, it was shooting off steam like a mechanical dragon. Now, I don't know if I could tell it apart from a normal truck."

Lexi had a placid look on her face. She put on the left blinker and turned the wheel to steer the vehicle. "I think it's actually letting me drive."

"Really?" said Gus. "As in drive, drive?"

Lexi nodded. "This is going to sound strange, but it's almost like I'm beginning to be able to hear it talk. Or no. Not talk. But transfer thoughts. I don't know if I can explain it right now."

"You'll never be able to," grunted Father, whose elbow he'd shoved into my eye to free up arm space. "It's just the way they are. The longer you live with them, the more you realize they're a part of you. A part of you that, somehow, has a life of its own."

"A part of you?" Gus looked worried.

"Yes and no. Think of it as a reflection of a reflection that forgot it was a reflection and thought it was reflecting itself instead."

"Can we please stop talking about reflections?" said Lexi.

"I second that," muttered Gus.

It was late now, after 2 a.m., I saw as I fished my phone out of my pants. It vibrated, and a little black shape of an envelope popped up on the display almost as soon as I did so.

1 new message —Unknown

Pressing the button, I read the following. It was from the same anonymous number that threatened to stick me like a pig. I quivered.

We need to talk.

THE SILENT END

I thought about the message for second and, feeling brave, typed back, "*who is this?*" But after waiting a few minutes, no response came. We'd been making our way through the Heights without incident, rolling past Victorian homes larger than three of our own combined but ugly and corroded, with twisting, iron-wrought fences winding through cratered lawns. The streets were empty, and trash tumbled into ditches with passing wind.

"There." Father pointed. Through the mucked up windshield, which had cleared a bit since last night's rain, the stone of Crowstone Heights jutted into the murky, post-rain sky. It truly did resemble the scavenger bird. Clouds had gathered above it, silent masses rolling in from the Horn. I shivered knowing what lurked below it and tried to understand how we were going to dive into those dark, deep waters.

As we reached the stone, a figure jumped out in front of our car. Lexi slammed on the breaks, and the Shepherd for a second betrayed its character with something between a whinny and a roar.

"Easy." She patted the dash. "Easy."

We piled out quickly, ready for confrontation. Nothing could have been worse than last night, and we had the wounds to prove it. Father held a harpoon at his side, and the Hat kept one of the pistols with a jellyfish-like muzzle at the ready in his coat pocket. The figure, I saw, was hiding behind the crow rock, right around the corner of its expansive base, and seemed to be trembling there. Only the top of his head stuck out.

"Come out where we can see you," Lexi yelled, her hand on her knife. "We'll give you to the count of three before we drag you out. One. Two."

"All right, all right," said a boy's voice. He crept from the shadows, hands held out before him. In the Shepherd's headlights, I recognized the sunken cheeks, the wiry frame, the sallow, angry eyes and rounded shoulders.

"Just don't hurt me, okay?"

It was Jesse Maroon.

Trained to fear him now, I flinched away the second he'd appeared. This before realizing that he was alone and I had more firepower behind me than a squadron of Techno-Lorques.

"What do you want?" said Lexi.

Father came and stood beside her with the harpoon. He had no idea who Jesse was, but he could tell that we did and appeared happy to intimidate the boy.

"Look, man. I don't want no trouble, okay? I'm just as confused as you are." He then looked at Father's harpoon. "What sort of fish you hunting with that?"

"What do you mean, confused?" I said. "About the fact that you put a bunch of rotten meat in my locker?"

"He did what?" Father was disgusted. I think for a moment, I caught a trace of guilt in his expression. Acknowledging the fact that while he'd been running amok, my life had disintegrated.

"No, man." Jesse pulled at his hair. "Or okay, yeah, I had a part in that. But that was a different me, you know…I even texted you! Didn't you get it?"

"I also got the one where you said you wanted to stick me like a pig."

"Aw, man, I was just fucking around. And you know, that was the other two. Charlene and Mogadishu. They used my phone; I had nothing to do with that."

"Didn't look like that the other day in school."

"And I have a feeling you didn't protest," said Gus.

"Look, man, please." As he approached, I could see that Jesse had been hurt. Bad. His face looked like a popped corn kernel, and some of his flesh had been peeled off. Someone must have scraped him against something rough, a slab of street or a brick wall. His injuries actually made ours pale in comparison; he'd been brutalized.

Lexi took her hand off her knife, knowing she couldn't do much worse than what had already been done. Jesse was limping, and he was hiding his hands in his sleeves. "What happened to you?"

"That's what I've been trying to tell you." Jesse came to an uneasy stop a few feet before us. His lip was swollen, and he blanched as he tried to cross his arms. "I'm all fucked up."

"I can see that," Gus said. "But who did it to you?"

"Charlene and Mogadishu. Who do you think?"

"I think," I said, "that the three of you are good pals."

"I know, man. I thought so too! I thought we were all set to take over Myers High. That we were gonna gang up and teach all the weaklings a lesson." He eyed me up and down. "No offense."

"Fuck you."

"Okay, okay, I deserve that. But listen, what I heard today changed all that. Shit got weird. Real weird. I thought the three of us were cool: Charlene, Mogadishu, and me. I guess I should have known better. My family tried to fit in here, but these townies, man…they're fucking crazy. My family's Italian, but someone got it into their head that I was Latino. I think that's why they wouldn't let me in on their secret, right? 'Cause they thought I was some sort of bean-eater."

"Are you trying to make us feel sorry for you?" Lexi motioned the Hat for a cigarette, and he tossed her one.

"No, man. I don't want no pity or nothing. I just want someone to know what happened. I fucked up, okay? I know I did. But what

Charlene and Mogadishu were talking about, that shit was straight up evil."

I looked around at Lexi, Gus, Father, and the Hat. I could tell they were all leaving Jesse's fate up to me.

"All right," I said. "Out with it."

"Thanks, man," said Jesse. "I promise it'll be worth your while. And I'll leave right afterwards."

"You've got five minutes."

"I won't even need three. Look, so here's what happened. I came back from school and saw Charlene and Mogadishu. You know, my crew. They were getting out of some dude's car. I thought I recognized whose it was but thought again; that would have been crazy. But when the driver opened the door and they all said goodbye, I realized I was right. Dean Veltry, you know. The fucking Dean of Myers High."

"I know Dean Veltry."

"Guy's like the goddamned Terminator," said Jesse. "He could have steel testicles or some shit." He wiped bloody snot from his nose. "Anyway, so I see Charlene and Mogadishu get out of Dean Veltry's car, and since they didn't tell me about this little meeting earlier, I get suspicious. I thought we were crew, you know. So…I kind of follow them for a while, all cautious-like. I can hear them talking as they go to the Circle D for some Slushees. And they're talking about all this fucked up shit. Tradition, family, some underground place where they can get all beefed up. I'd never heard them talk about stuff like that before, so I keep on following. I can't hear exactly, but I know Charlene says something about being put into this machine that'll give her super powers or something fucked up like that. I thought they were just talking crazy, right? But no, they was serious. It gave me the creeps. 'Specially when they started talking about you three."

"What do you mean, us three?" said Gus.

"I'm trying to tell you, man. Don't you understand? I'm trying to help."

"Forgive me if I don't give a damn."

"I'm just gonna keep talking, okay?"

"Now there's an idea," said Lexi.

"Right. So there I am, listening to them as they roll up on Skippy's, that shitty burger place on Hovel. They're talking about how the dean told them they need to fuck you guys up. But not just fuck you up, you know. But put you out. Of commission. You know what I mean, right?"

"Just finish your story, Jesse," I said.

"They were talking about killing you, man. All three of you. And about doing something fucked up with your bodies, too, to send a warning. It…it got too sick for me, man. I mean, I'm into kicking the shit out of a fat ass or three, and I hate cocksuckers as much as the next guy, but what they were talking about? Hell no. That's not me. Not Jesse Maroon."

"What an upstanding citizen," Gus said.

"Jesse." I had to keep from wanting to hit him. In his state, I certainly could have done some damage even with my awkward fists. But I couldn't manage more than the thought. He was just too pitiful. He reminded me of a scrawny rodent that had gotten flushed down a ditch. "How did you end up like this?"

"Well, that's just the thing, man. When I heard about that killing shit, I decided to take off. Murder? Hell no, that's where I draw the line. But when I snuck away, Charlene, she comes after me. It's like she's got a sixth sense or some shit. There's something wrong with her insides. I mean like the way she's built. I wouldn't say that about anyone normally, but the second she found me, I knew I was dealing with a genuine psychopath. She started saying things like, 'What did you hear?' And I was like, 'Nothing, I promise.' She didn't believe me though. Thought I was going to squeal, which, hell if I know, I might have even if she didn't tear my shit up. I tried to run away, but Mogadishu caught me, and after that, it was all blood. They threw my head into the concrete and rubbed my face all raw. And that wasn't the end, you know. They dragged me into an alley and started… started…" He was crying now as he held up his sleeves and let them drop, revealing his hands; his fingers were bent in wayward directions like twisted, blood-covered roots.

"My God," said Gus.

"That's what I said too, man. And I would be stopping right there, but the thing is that wasn't the worst of it. They was going to cut me. My throat. They had this knife out and were talking about where they'd put my body when they were done. Mogadishu had his hand over my mouth, and when I heard that shit, I just bit as hard as I could and went running. I didn't look back, not for an hour, man. And when I did, they were gone—Mogadishu can't run too fast, and Charlene can barely even walk. I didn't know what to do, so I sent you a text. I've been hiding around up here; I don't have money and can't go home because my dad, he just might finish the job Charlene and Mogi started. Then I see Lexi's truck, and I'm like, 'thank Yahweh.' Thought I'd try to cut you off at the Horn. And here I am. I just…I just thought I should tell someone. Someone…"

"Trustworthy?" Gus finished.

"Yeah, man. You guys, you know. You're just all fucking perfect."

Lexi started laughing.

"It's true! And you don't even care about townie pride or any of that shit. You're lucky."

"I might as well have won the lottery," said Lexi.

"Look, I'm sorry for the way I acted. I know I'm not right in the head. But I do know I'm righter than those two are. That I can say for fucking certain."

"Thanks, Jesse," I said. As I did so, Gus and Lexi looked at me like I'd turned coat. "And…it's okay."

"It…it is?"

"Yeah," said Lexi. "It is?"

I took some money out of my pocket. I didn't have much, but thirteen damp dollars were crumpled into my wallet. "Take this."

Jesse's broken hand clawed at it carefully. "Are you…sure?"

"Use a little to take the five a.m. bus to the Main Drive. Go to Stumart, and tell Cory that I said you could stay in the back office for a while, and help yourself to some food. I'll let him know you're coming."

"Son." Father eyed me with concern. "Are you sure about this?"

"I am. With one condition, of course."

"Anything, man," said Jesse.

"You keep your eyes open wide. And if you hear or see anything having to do with Charlene or Mogadishu, I want to know immediately."

Jesse looked like he'd been handed a sack of gold coins and, for a moment, stopped sniffling. He had been badly hurt, I could see. This wasn't an act. He might have required serious medical attention.

"You know what, man?" Jesse said. "It if it weren't for people like you, people like me would never stop fucking up."

He took the money and, nodding to all of us, sunk back into the shadows of Crowstone Heights.

"Bad move," said Lexi. "This could have been a trap. Some sort of plan Charlene and Joe came up with to catch you off guard."

"I wouldn't trust Jesse Maroon with a pencil sharpener. That kid's a psycho," Gus muttered. He'd addressed me directly for the first time since yesterday but didn't seem happy about it.

"People can change." The words, as I said them, felt personal. "If I'm wrong, then fine. I'll live with it."

Father stepped up beside me, his harpoon at the ready. "I think it's about time we go for a little swim." The Hat stepped beside him, a wetsuit hanging from his hand like a floppy piece of rubber. "I've been practicing my breast stroke."

FIVE

THE SHEPHERD TOOK US DOWN the only road that led to the shore, a craggy snake of a thing whose curves narrowed as we drove. Rumbling over potholes and fallen rock, I looked out the window and tried to find the ocean. But below was only black, a sinkhole of darkness. I couldn't see water or the roll of foam against the shores like I could on even the murkiest night at Goon's Cove. Moonlight on the Horn was almost nonexistent, and the clouds were hardened like stone. Without rails to guard the Shepherd from falling off the road, we were nosing right up against what felt like the edge of nothing. The only reason I knew we were close to water was that the air grew brisk and salty.

After a few minutes of descent, the truck halted.

"We're here," Lexi said.

We stepped out onto the surf. The sand and rock beneath our feet was almost lunar in its whiteness. We knew where the water began only by where the paleness ended, and the more my eyes adjusted, the more I could see a syrupy tide slurping in and out.

Without warning, Father dropped his pants, the army fatigues falling away to reveal pelts of leg fur and orange, cotton underwear. He then took off his shirt to put on the wetsuit, and we whirled about face as he did so.

A few moments later, after he'd stretched the neoprene fabric over his bulk, he fastened his cap and said, "Done." We turned around carefully. The Hat then handed him a regulator for his breathing whose valve was covered with a slick, yellow membrane.

"Don't you need an oxygen tank?" Gus was eyeing Father's suit with a dubious expression. "I'm assuming it's a long way down."

Father rolled his eyes and fit the regulator over his mouth, holding his arms to his side and turning in his fingers as if to indicate demonstration. As he breathed, the membrane on the valve expanded, growing to the size of a cantaloupe, and then shrunk back to its initial position.

"This'll give me plenty of time." He removed it from his mouth. "The Hat developed it from silicone, sugarcane, Murje, and ingenuity. All of which work better than a can of compressed wind."

The Hat scribbled on a piece of paper and held it up for us to see.

4 hours Oxygen plus blood oxidization aid.

Father grunted in approval, took his harpoon in one hand, and in the other reached for the *NON ENTITIES ONLY* book in Lexi's, which she'd opened to the page with the map. A pair of goggles hugged the fabric above his eyes, both of which were filled with sleepless fixation, and atop those goggles was a specialized water lamp.

"Looks like the right place." He regarded the map as he flopped toward the tide. "If I go five meters that way, it'll drop off a good bit; maybe a lot bit. Should be back in no time, though, or if not no time then some time…"

The Hat stepped up beside him and, putting its hand on Father's shoulder, nodded toward the water.

"No, Hat. I need to do this." He shook his head as if to keep the Non Entity from running around inside it. "I know…I just do."

The Hat sulked, but eventually stepped away.

"Just be careful, okay?" I said.

I watched him fit the regulator over his mouth. He snapped the book closed, handed it to Lexi, and gave a thumbs up. He stretched his arms, preparing to make the plunge. But before he could wade past his knees, Lexi yelled for him to stop.

The membrane on his regulator puffed up like a yellow balloon.

"We can take the Shepherd."

Father ripped off the regulator. "Don't be ridiculous. Otters don't fly south for the winter, and you've got a truck, not a boat."

"No." Lexi scratched her shaved head. "But I can make one."

"What the hell're you talking about?" said Gus.

"How about I show you."

Father sputtered his lips as Lexi took a deep breath and, straightening her shoulders, marched toward the Shepherd. It sat purring on the beach, its headlights bright. She hopped on the bedside step into the driver's seat, buckled her seatbelt, and put her hands on the wheel. With a rumble, the truck rolled into the surf.

"You sure about this?" I yelled.

Either she couldn't hear me or chose not to as she drove deeper and deeper. The undercarriage disappeared into the waves, followed gradually by the rest of the vehicle, headlights, hood, and roof. A moment later, it had been swallowed up entirely, a surge of yellow bubbles rising from where it sank.

We watched the water for a few seconds. Father made a humming sound. The bubbles stilled, and the waves rushed over. A little wind came and went. Then it became too quiet. Gus's nerves took over. "She's sinking! Mr. Eberstark—you've got to go in there."

"She'll die!" I shrieked.

"Goddamnit." Father fit the regulator over his mouth and charged into the water. Just as he was about to dive in, a cavernous *SPLOOSH* erupted twenty feet offshore.

From the sea rose a vehicle that was the Shepherd and yet not quite the Shepherd. The Bronco had transformed, folding its wheels beneath it, and growing a thick, orange sealant over the doors and windows. Its body had been stretched and narrowed to give the truck a missile-like shape with a sharp fin rising off the back. It chugged with some sort of flotation thrust, and in place of the bumper now stood a crude propulsion motor, propeller, and rudders.

Lexi opened the passenger door as the craft rotated in our direction, buoyant on the waves. "You guys ready?" If it was possible, she looked even more commanding than ever before. She could have been a one-eyed lady Nemo with a shaved head and a mouth full of cigarettes. "It's okay," she reassured us. "I can hear it now."

The Hat beamed, and with a running leap, skipped through the water to the rear passenger door. She puttered closer, and we filed in after him, shaking the wet from our clothes. Father was the least enthusiastic since for some reason, he'd been set on doing this himself. Keeping his gear on, he shuffled into the front seat and angled his harpoon toward the windshield, shutting the door behind him. "This better work," he grumbled.

"It's stable," said Lexi. "It knows what it's capable of. You of all people should get that."

"But, Lexi?" Gus tapped at the walls, examining the craft's solidity. The various dents in the roof had been ironed out by the transformation though the craft couldn't keep from looking beat up. "How can you be confident in this craft's engineering?"

"Sureness is what cowards eat for breakfast." She threw the stick shift into first gear. "Now, zip your mouths, and buckle up."

SIX

AFTER WE SUNK INTO THE trench, it was as if we'd been sucked into something's belly. It was blind, muddy, and filled with decapod ghost forms slipping past the headlights. They never stayed long. Though at first it appeared as if we were diving through a void, I began to sense thousands of eyes upon us in the dark. As Lexi drove, she seemed to maintain instinctual command over the controls, applying a steady amount of acceleration to push further and further down. She clung as close to the trench wall as she could, descending at medium speed. Some pressure knocked at the sides of the hull, but the Shepherd seemed to knock back, snapping its skeleton taught. Oxygen flowed easy, and every so often, I heard the faintest sound of breathing—the gusty exhales of the Non Entity itself, maintaining circulation.

The darkness was too much for me. I stared into my lap. "I don't like it down here."

THE SILENT END

"Close your eyes and pretend you're someplace else." Though I could hear the rancor in Gus's voice, I took his advice.

Closing my eyes, I transported myself to a different place. Or tried to. There was nowhere good to go. My imagination rumbled with one bombed-out landscape after another. Shattered mirrors. Blood and beasts. Mrs. Duncan in pieces under the gaze of Myers High and Mother being dragged through an underground hell. I put my hand in my pocket to feel for the charm bracelet. Safety came as my fingers found it. I remembered a nice day, years ago. A nice day before I'd come to Mossglow. Dawn came through the windows of our Cleveland apartment, where outside the skyline glimmered auburn and gold. It was a good morning. A Saturday. Father was home from work after a lucrative week, and he and Mother were huddled together on the couch. Deep, restful breaths, coffee sips and page turns. Mother was reading the newspaper and reflexively handed Father the crossword and funnies. Smells of breakfast still hung in the air, and a stereo played something quiet and instrumental. As I soaked in the landscape, I didn't even know if I was visiting somewhere real or whether I'd compiled it from stray memories and wishful thinking. If I had never been there, however, I wanted to go one day.

"There." Father's voice brought me out of my trance. He was pointing out the windshield. "Two o' clock."

"I see it," said Lexi.

"Come in easy."

The Shepherd bucked, the propeller slowing to a low chug as we settled against the bottom of the bay. Before the windshield, about ten feet out, was a winsome glow. Though difficult to make out, I took in the limning of a skeleton attached to a great, gray stone, just as Edwina had specified in her letter. Something hung around the neck that gave off yellow light. Her bones were draped in rags, and the skull flowered with gray strands of hair.

"That's her," I said.

"Some creepy shit" said Father.

"So…now what?" Gus looked toward Lexi.

"I hadn't thought about that part." She closed her eyes. "Let me see if the Shepherd can help us out. Maybe it can change its shape or, I don't know, grow a set of arms. Hold on…"

"How about I go get it?" Father said as her brow creased in concentration.

"Because water will get in," Gus said.

"You could use a bath."

We allowed Lexi a moment of silence so that she could try and reinitiate whatever process had transformed the Shepherd to begin with. But after a moment, she sank into her seat and groaned. "I don't think I can get it to change. It's doing too much already."

"See." Father pulled his goggles down. "It's settled then. I'll handle it."

I gulped. "That sounds risky."

The man then looked at me with an expression I'd never seen before. It wasn't filled with shame at the fact that I'd let him down. No. It was soft. I could see that in me, he saw Mother. And that in Mother, he saw his own failure. The only thing in his life he could have nurtured and supported he'd treated with neglect. His expression might have even said that he was trying to apologize.

Lexi rubbed at an ache in her forehead. "I think we can make that work—but go quick."

"Yeah, yeah." Father put on the goggles. He handed me his harpoon. "Hat, make sure you shut this door after me before too much water gets in."

The Hat returned his request with a reticent thumbs up. Even though the Non Entity's eyes were never visible, I could tell it felt unsure.

"I'll be back in a second." Father winked at me as he put the regulator on.

The membrane expanded, and he held up one finger. Then two. Then three. On what would have been four, water flooded into the Shepherd. I screamed but felt silly for it as the Hat had yanked the door closed with colossal strength. Water splashed up to our knees. My feet and shins went cold, the bay water soaking into my skin. But a moment later, something remarkable happened. I heard what sounded like a deep set of lungs inhaling somewhere in the truck's body. With a sound like slurping through a straw, the water was sucked out through a fleshy hole in the floor. A hole that puckered itself off as soon as it was dry.

"Incredible." Gus was shaking his head in awe as he removed his loafers. He peeled his wet socks off and set them on the floor.

We squinted through the windshield at Father. With bulky prowess, he swam toward the skeleton. He kicked his flippered feet, and bubbles trailed behind them. His normal bigness was insignificant inside this great dark. The Shepherd's headlights only went so far. A small thread of light also came off the lamp attached to his goggles.

When he neared Edwina Myers' skeleton, he back-kicked to an upward position. He paused for a second to appraise this woman who'd sacrificed herself for this moment. She was alone, with an unlatched jaw and silver gown of hair. It was possible she'd been beautiful once. The chain tied to a large stone around her leg made me imagine her death. How sick and determined she must have been.

Taking his time, Father used his fingers to identify the receptacle. It was made of a soft, ruddy metal, and it gave off a sickly light. Carefully, he tried to lift it from the skeleton's neck but soon realized that it had been tied in a knot; a precaution likely taken by Edwina to make sure it wouldn't be carried away from her body by more than a hundred years of tide. Father pulled at it harder and harder. He then withdrew, inhaled his regulator until the membrane shriveled inward, and with brute exertion yanked the receptacle so hard that the neck popped off with it. Flipping backward with the relic in his hands, Edwina's skull thumped to the ground.

"Poor woman," said Lexi.

"Now, we can finally get out of here," said Gus, watching Father make his way back to us. "I guess that wasn't so bad after all."

With unexpected force, the Shepherd rumbled a little. It was an odd sensation, as if a small wave had rolled into us.

"What was that?" Gus asked.

"Probably just the tide," said Lexi.

"Seems a little strong for 'just the tide.'"

"Excuse me for not knowing the rules of maritime travel. This is only my second time piloting a submarine."

Lexi anxiously tapped the dashboard. She hadn't had a cigarette for a torturous hour. She watched Father intently, as if staring at him would make him arrive faster. Though he drifted along, as if savoring his heroic moment, a little light glowing in his fist. Another wave came over us, this time stronger. It might have moved the Shepherd back a full yard.

Gus repositioned himself. "I'm now officially concerned."

My eyes stayed on Father.

"Guys." Lexi's hand trembled as she pointed out the windshield.

"Do you see that?"

"Do I see what?" A familiar fright returned to Gus's voice.

Lexi put her back against in the driver's seat and paled. It was not long after that that I saw her breath turn to steam, and my body felt the danger before my brain did.

She pointed toward a shape moving behind Father, a great mound of white, necrotic flesh creeping on him from the dark as he kicked toward the Shepherd. I saw tusks, tusks that glinted as if they were made of metal, and a shark-like mouth filled with rocky teeth. It was another Collector. But this one was big. At least twice the size of Mr. Kraft. Sweeping toward Father silently, mouth gaping, it wanted to shred his bones. Father's story came back to me, the tale he'd told of the hog-like beast that stole Mother away.

"Dad." I mouthed the word. I saw him in the dark, slow, oblivious. He was so small-looking, this man that, since I could remember, had seemed larger than life.

"DAD!" I finally found the voice to scream. "Behind you!"

"He can't hear you," yelled Lexi.

As we flailed about helplessly, the Hat jumped from the back seat and slapped his hand against the horn. A flatulent *WAAAAAAAAAAAAAAAAA* came from the Shepherd, and Father looked back. The second he did so, his body went into overdrive. As he got to the door, the Hat was already throwing it open. Water surged in harder than it had before, up to our waists; he yanked Father in and pulled the door closed with all his might.

"GO!" screamed Gus.

Lexi slammed on the accelerator and the Shepherd spun from the ocean floor, gaining speed as it lifted.

Father tore off his regulator and gasped, "It's the big one."

"How did it find us?" I said.

"I don't know…I don't know!"

"Oh my God, it's right behind us," Gus yelled.

I screamed.

"Put on the speed, Lexi," commanded Father.

Lexi honed in on the surface and ramped the acceleration, throwing the Shepherd into rocketing ascent. The rear lights illuminated a mottled, white snout like a pig's, a smiling mouth that itself was bigger than three Shepherds combined, and tusks that were made of something metallic, like sewer piping. It could gulp us into its Murje-filled belly only to later spit out parts of the Bronco like bones. It kept right at us, closing, closing, and even as Lexi pushed the Shepherd to its limit, we realized it wasn't enough.

"Son." Father put his hand on my chest and pushed me against the backseat. He glared into my eyes, and I could see them squirming with terminal fear. "I want you to listen to me. Are you listening?"

I nodded.

"Good. Because I'm going now."

"What do you mean?"

"I mean. That I'm going now."

"Dad," I began to cry. "No…"

"I'm going now," he croaked. "I'm going now. I did so much wrong and don't deserve good."

"But—"

"Take this." He reached into the neck of his wetsuit and yanked a chain from it. It was attached to a key—a long, metal key with numerous ridges. "Take this to the bunker. There's a door in back you'll need to open. Inside is everything—everything, son. You'll know what to do."

"Dad." I was sobbing. I couldn't hold it in any longer. If he left me, I'd truly be alone. Even if I hated him most of the time, I needed something to call home. I wanted Morrison Eberstark to be fucking immortal.

"If I can do one thing now." His eyes filled with tears. He was terrified, I could see. He didn't want to die either. Didn't want to throw himself into that sea of unknowing. His sanity was fading, but he still retained a gleam of what it meant to want to survive. "Then it's to give you the chance to be the man that I couldn't. You're not a bedwetter… I'm sorry the penumbra took my brain. I'm sorry I didn't believe your mother, and I'm sorry that avarice took my soul. That's why you need to take the key and use it to find her. Please, son… Become something great. And when you do, put me to shame. I'll die happier knowing I'll be bested, for that is the way of the warrior."

The Hat, shocked as he understood what Father was proposing, threw his hand out and slapped him in the face.

"No, Hat!" Father threw the Non Entity against the passenger window. I looked back and saw the great white Collector right at our tail, its teeth chomping at the Shepherd's rear. "No. You watch these kids and protect them with every fabric of your fucking absurd being. I don't care what you want. No—no!" He held his head as if it were exploding. "You listen to me. They'll need you when the time comes, and *you will be there*."

The Hat grabbed his head and was seized with such mournfulness it looked as if he'd shatter into pieces. Father then took him by the chin and drew his face into his.

"Know your purpose, and shut the door behind me, you damned figment of imagination. The chicken and the egg both came first, and nobody fucking cares."

I wailed as Father took Edwina Myers' glowing vial and shoved it into the Hat's breast pocket. He then took the harpoon in his hand and clicked a button on the shaft. The blade hummed, and a bright orange light sparkled from it. He reached out with one hand and put it on the handle.

"Son," he said before shoving the regulator in his mouth. "I'm sorry."

Water rushed in, and Father was gone, into the blackness of the Horn. The Hat shut the door, the Shepherd sucked itself dry. I threw myself against the back window along with Gus and the Hat, looking for signs of the miraculous, hoping Father could drive the creature back. But instead, hope died in the abyss that night. Through the windshield, I watched as a rapidly diminishing man unleashed tiny sparks against a titan in the deep. Flickers of orange faded into nothing, and I knew he was gone.

SEVEN

THE SHEPHERD LAUNCHED ITSELF OUT of the Horn like a frog fleeing the jaws of an alligator. Frightened and demoniac, it couldn't discern a way to land. We crashed into the surf, and our world flipped over, hurtling through darkness and sound. I'm not sure if I lost consciousness, but I wouldn't know where I was until later. The sound of Father's voice echoed in my ears. "I'm going now. I did so much wrong." Over and over. A gone man's loop. I saw the monster too, the cavern of its mouth and the flames from Father's harpoon dying in the black. My cord had been cut, and I was alone. Motherless, now fatherless Eberstark.

I was holding something tight with my hands, gripping fabric to the point where it crumpled. A hat. A bone-white fedora. The Non Entity was carrying me, along with Gus and Lexi, at a speed beyond what any human could. I was on his back; Gus was under his left arm and Lexi his right. He jumped from roof to roof to

THE SILENT END

escape Crowstone Heights, his feet snapping against shingles with barely a sound. Every time we jumped, it was as silent and stealthy as a bird of prey. In the distance, we heard a warlike sound, louder and more sinister than any of the other creatures had made. *KRRRRRRRRRRRAAAAAAAAAAAAAAALLLLLOOOOOOOOO*

The Hat skidded to a stop as the sound faded, trying to pinpoint its direction, and with a fearful squirm picked up speed again, trying to escape as fast as he could. I tried to say something, tried to call out for Father, thinking if I did, he'd crawl from the depths of the bay unharmed, but blood rushed to my brain, and then things did go black. Truly black. The last thing I remembered was soaring and skidding and the Hat's unidentifiable smell. It was like cookies, like perfume, like Sword Star paint. Like a million different strange and wonderful things.

EIGHT

I AWOKE LEANING AGAINST A TREE trunk in Graywood Forest. Fog was coiling around my arms and neck. A flicker of firelight blurred to being, and I saw a small circle of stones, in the center of which wood was burning. The Hat crouched beside them, stoking the flames with a stick. His Ray Bans reflected embers, and the mouth below them sank in remorse. Lexi and Gus were already awake. They sat silently by the fire, watching the light, their faces marred by scratches and dried blood. Gus saw me sit up and clucked his tongue toward Lexi, who regarded me like a stray dog, with pity and unease.

I stood up and limped toward them, sitting between her and Gus before the fire. I folded my arms over my knees and soaked in the warmth. The Hat continued to stir the wood. The fire crackled. There was nothing to be said.

After a few minutes, the Hat got up to add a few logs to the flames. The fire ate them right up.

THE SILENT END

Gus watched the smoke rise. "I'm going home."

"Now?" said Lexi.

"Yes, now." He stood up. His sweater, made of dyed blue sheep's wool, was torn through, revealing a yellow shirt stained in some parts with blood.

"But…what about the pistol? And the unstable element?" said Lexi.

"All of that can wait until tonight." By tonight, he meant the next time it got dark. Morning was coming, and Mossglow was turning a greasy shade of pink. I went to check my Motorola for the time, but it had been lost in the crash.

"My parents have no idea where I am. My mom's probably already in the ER, waiting for me to show up in the back of an ambulance. Your house got blown up, Lexi. I'm injured, I'm hungry, I'm filthy, oh, and I've been blacking out again." He pinched the bridge of his nose. "Just there by the fire, I went someplace else…it felt like Myers High."

Lexi looked down at her lap, her filthy hands and torn up tennis shoes. "I should go home too. What's left of it. My ma, though…she's not going to understand."

"Nobody's going to understand," said Gus. "You know that's how this stuff works," said Gus. "Three kids uncover an evil force infesting their backwater town. They confront it alone. Meanwhile, everyone else ignores the problem, and in the end, it's just them. Kids versus monsters. Talk about well-worn territory."

Lexi chuckled darkly. "It's true. I always thought I could avoid becoming a cliché by trying hard enough. But it's not that simple, is it?"

"Everyone's like someone in the end. That goes for me too. I'm just the same story with a different narrator."

"There's no way to escape how common we all are."

"Yes there is." Gus shoved his hands in his pockets and tried to walk on his hurt ankle. Straightening out seemed to help ease the pain. "You just try not to think about it."

He turned to leave.

"So you really are just going home?" said Lexi.

"I'll see you guys tonight."

"Where?"

"Where else? Myers fucking High."

"But what if something happens to you? Whoever they are, they know who *we* are."

"I'm going home. I'll bring the damned pistol and make sure to wear my finest dying shoes when I meet you at 10 p.m. By the frog."

He turned away and hobbled into the forest. The fire continued to roil. The Hat hadn't moved since I'd awoken, staring into the flames with eerie placidity.

"He's right, you know?" said Lexi, after a long pause. "About us? It's the same story, just told different."

The Hat prodded the fire, and I stayed quiet.

"What? You're not talking now?"

I wanted to tell her that it wasn't that I didn't want to talk about what happened. I just didn't have anything to say. My family had been canceled, like a bad TV show.

Lexi eased up with a grunt. "Well, I'm going to go too. Find a phone, call my mom, make sure she knows I'm not dead. Try and explain what happened to my poor truck."

"Lexi," I said as she turned to leave.

"Yeah?"

I dug at the ground with a finger. Father's face kept returning to my vision. He'd looked so terrified.

"Why are you friends with me?"

"What?"

I kept my eyes on the fire. "You say it's all the same story. That we're stuck in this endless cycle. Why not just walk away from it and never come back? Find your mom…go down to Ozark to live with your aunt…get out of this cesspool of a town? Your house is gone; you'll have the money to move." I chucked a shred of wood into the fire. "It doesn't make sense that Gus would stay. So why the hell would someone like you?"

"Someone like me?" Lexi scratched the skin under hey eye patch. "What does that even mean?"

"I don't know." I looked up at her. In the firelight, head shaved and body hurt, she had a strong sort of beauty. A mature, woman-like command of herself that made me ashamed of how small I viewed the world. Through Lexi's one eye, life was bigger than what I perceived with two. "I guess what I'm saying is that people like me belong in places like Mossglow. Narrow-minded backwaters where no one dares ask to have it better. People like you though…it's like you stay here because you think you have to. Because you think you have something to prove."

Lexi gave me a thoughtful look and bent down to my level. She placed her hand on mine, and I felt her fingers; they were calloused but warm and nonthreatening. I couldn't help but stare at her.

"Don't get the wrong idea, big guy," she said, observing my facial expression. Embarrassed, I quickly adjusted it. "You don't have the right equipment."

"Wait. Does that mean you're a…you're a…?"

"I'm a lot of things, Eberstark. And you are too. That's why you have to be responsible for yourself. As far as I see it, no one deserves anything in this world. No one deserves love or happiness or success. Think about me for a second. I mean, really think about me. Think about what I have at the current moment. I *had* my cats. I *had* my father. I *had* a house and a truck and a long head of hair. But now? I don't have any of those things. Only you, Gus, and my mom. And yet, sometimes, I think I could live without you three too. So really, I should be asking you that question."

"Which question?"

"Why are you *my* friend?" she said, leaning in close so that I could smell her breath. It was warm and sweet with rot from all the cigarettes she'd smoked, but I could have inhaled it all day. "What did I ever do to deserve your friendship?"

I went quiet. The Hat still stared into the flames, and Lexi removed her hand from mine.

"Take some time to think about it." She stood back up. She began to walk away into the forest. I watched her sway into the mist and started to cry.

NINE

THE FIRE EVENTUALLY FIZZLED, AND the Hat and I made our way back to my house. Between my shoulder and some hip pain from the crash, I couldn't walk that well, so the Hat propped me up. His strength was so endless that it practically carried me the rest of the way.

We approached the house from the rear, watching out for interlopers. Someone had known to alert that creature of our location, and whether or not the Hat could be injured in the way that humans could, I saw that he was growing despondent.

Thankfully, home looked just the same as it usually did: a looming mass of wood secluded by a ring of thick, leafy trees. It was encrusted in fog. We hurried past it into the front yard, keeping low to the ground, and neared the hatch. When we got there, however, I saw that the padlock Father used to lock it down had been busted and the door itself pried off its hinges. Crumpled, it lay yards away on the grass, and a hazy, green smoke wafted from inside the bunker.

I looked at the Hat for guidance, and without so much as a glance, he ducked into the lab, sidestepping the stairs with noiseless feet. He disappeared into the cloud of fumes, and I waited anxiously, looking over my shoulder at every shadow cast by the slowly swaying trees. A moment later, I saw the Hat's hand stretch out from the smoke. His fingers gestured that I should come inside.

The bunker was in a state of cataclysm. A huge crater in the center of it about three feet deep, right after the first doorway that led to the arsenal, suggested heavy impact. The weapons Father and the Hat had fashioned, the tank containing the tentacles, the multicolored fire extinguishers, and other intricate machines, had been mashed to bits. The floor was covered in a sticky soup of green, yellow, blue, black, and orange fluids. Occasional reactions took place, in which a bubble of sludge rose, twisted, and popped or two colliding elements caused smoke to hiss skyward.

I stood in the center of the gooey rubble, taking in the ruin of my deluded Father's life. Multicolored fluids crawled up the walls as if searching for a way out of this prison, and a horrible smell like urine mixed with candied sugar filled the air.

The Hat tapped me on the shoulder, and I turned around to find a piece of paper in my face.

Around your neck.

"Huh?" My brain was foggy from all the fumes.

He took a fed-up finger and shoved it right into my chest, where I felt metal beneath my shirt. The key. The key Father had given me before he was killed. I could barely even put my hand around it; just touching it reminded me of the final look in his eyes, hatred of both himself and others combined with the terror of knowing he'd never see the world again. But I could see that the Hat was not in a patient mood, so I grabbed it anyway. *What happened to a dream creature when the dreamer died?* I wondered. Perhaps something similar to what I was feeling. Perhaps the Hat, like me, had lost his parent, and we were mourning on different planes.

At the end of the bunker, belying a veritable mountain of half-exploded boxed macaroni and cheese, was a safe-like door. It looked as if whatever had broken in here had tried and failed to gain entry to it; there were multiple crenels in the surface, but nothing had broken through.

The Hat shoved me, and I found myself right in front of the door. Taking the key, I wondered if I was ready for whatever I'd find beyond it. Trying to clear my mind, the key entered the lock with ease. I turned it all the way to the right and the door swung open silently.

My eyes were filled with blue.

TEN

MURJE.

The crystalline material of which the Collectors were made. The organisms that spurred the creation of extraordinary beings and who turned to waste if detached from their brethren.

This was the culture Father had referred to; the cache the Hat incubated when they began their crusade. It was kept within a gigantic glass cube framed with steel. It was almost as tall as I was and four times as wide, filled to a foot below the brim with an undulating tide of alien matter. I stared at it in the dark of the back room. It was phosphorescent. I came to it and hung my head over the edge. Though you had to observe closely for a moment to discern it, a distinct rhythm of activity could be detected. Tiny columns of Murje would rise and fall by the hundreds, maybe thousands. They spiraled upward like towers and as they went higher grew branch-like appendages. Those appendages then joined with the appendages of neighboring towers and, violently, gripped each other. They then began tightening so that the columns were pulled apart, collapsing back into the whole. Forming, joining, collapsing. The more I watched, the more transfixed I became. There might have been a pattern to it all, a way in which these life forms attempted to express themselves to creatures like us. I thought that maybe if I looked long enough, I'd begin to get a sense of what they were trying to say. Maybe I could even understand their origin. But the more I watched, the more unpredictable the patterns became until I found there weren't any at all. This sea of Murje was like a complex ecosystem. It could have been a planet of its own, frustrating the efforts of astrophysicists trying to understand its behavior. Within this cube was infinite interpretation.

I turned around and saw the Hat looking at me. His head was cocked to the side, and his mouth was straight. He drew his notepad from his breast pocket and wrote, lifting the message toward me.

You know what to do.

I looked at the Hat quizzically. Then, I turned back toward the Murje. The same material that had brought Gus's Crow Seraph to life. That had sent vigor and transformation through the Shepherd before it crashed on the Horn. The same sea of dream-catalyst that created the creature standing behind me. I suddenly understood what Father had meant for me to do when he gave me the key. He couldn't have known about the charm bracelet in my pocket, but he did know it was time for me to discover what it was that my mind could create.

I took Mother's charm bracelet in my hand. I held it over the surface, afraid. I heard a distant chattering in my ears, something between shrieking and singing. I thought of Mother, I thought of her eyes, I thought of her bleeding on the bathroom floor, and drove my fist into the sparkling sea; it sealed itself over my hand like a glue that repaired wounded souls.

ELEVEN

AT FIRST, I FELT DRAINED. So fatigued it was as if the all of last week had finally caught up with me, dealing a vicious blow to my dome, opening up everything inside. I made my groggy way up to my bedroom, my hand steady on the bannister. Even though it was Tuesday and, for all I knew, Myers High was holding classes, I couldn't imagine making the trek down Nigh'Sow Road. When I made it to my room, my clean, ordered room that hadn't been touched by whatever wasted Father's laboratory, I put on Mother's bracelet and fell onto the bed face-first, noticing the Hat leaning over me as I drifted off.

At first, it was as if I'd just shut down. Stray reams of activity rattled through my brain. Until around midday that is. At some point, while there was still daylight, I was jolted awake by a nameless horror. I couldn't even remember what it had been. It was like the sensation of endless falling but far, far worse. Like plummeting through ice and flame. Bleary eyed, I lowered my head back to the pillow. I wanted to stay awake, but who was I kidding?

In my head was born a classroom. One of the very same I'd sat in for years at Myers High. The white walls were streaked with rubber burns, and the ceiling panels were perforated. A single clock ticked at the head of the class, and below that clock was Mrs. Duncan. She sat on top of her desk, right at the front of it as she always did, her legs plump and sheathed in knee-high red boots, crossed, and her large, cartoon eyes observed me.

The desks were arranged in a normal fashion, five rows of five, and I was in the very front center. I looked left and right; the rest of the row was empty. But I could feel eyes on my back. I tried to turn and toward them, but my head, it could have been in a vice. All I could see were formless bodies at my periphery; shadows twisting.

My eyes returned to the front of the class. My desk had moved closer to Mrs. Duncan. Closer so that my face was right in front of her legs. I saw the flesh of her kneecaps and thighs before they disappeared under a black skirt. They were spongy, like angel food cake. Carefully, she uncrossed them, and I didn't move, just stared, my jaw dropping. In the hollow between was the same sort of darkness I'd seen in the mold on Mr. Kraft's wall. I heard the sound of whimpering, beckoning from the pitch. Mrs. Duncan recrossed her legs, and I was consumed with want. I heard laughter and tried yet again to look behind me. The shadows were excited, bobbing, pointing, but this time, I could only barely see. I looked back to Mrs. Duncan and gasped; she was right in front of my face. Our lips almost touched, but I was too scared to kiss her. The shadows jeered, and I looked down at myself. I was naked save for a pair of cotton underwear. The very same white briefs I'd worn as a child with a green, elastic waist and itchy rear.

I tried to draw back from Mrs. Duncan, reclining in my chair.

But as I did so, her head grew bigger and bigger. It grew so big that it outsized my entire body, inflating like a parade balloon. When it was finished growing, it leaned over me. Each of the eyes was larger than my own head and flickered with curiosity. I tried to move away from them, tried to get out of my chair, but they followed me, bearing down upon my body with a force that pushed me into the ground. It was then that I realized that the eyes of Mrs. Duncan didn't belong to Mrs. Duncan at all. Her eyes had been smart and anxious, kind at times. These, however, were hateful. Inquisitive in a maniacal way. They were the type of eyes that looked past your own into the very makeup, exploring your organs and what made them work, assessing a few for ingestion.

The Mrs. Duncan creature reached behind her back and withdrew twin, shining objects. Two pairs of wicked-looking office scissors. Each was gigantic and sharp and red. *Snip, snip. Snip, snip SNAP.* She cut the air before my face. She gleamed with perverse pleasure as she did so, and when that happened, I saw she wasn't a she at all but a very haunting, very foreign he. A man with skin so white it was almost like Styrofoam. As the mask faded, I found myself glaring into the murderous eyes of a sadist with scraggly, jet-black hair; orange eyes; and a toothless mouth. The scissors seemed to grow larger as he brought them toward me. He opened one pair and slipped the bottom blade beneath my left knee. The other he enclosed around my right arm. With one squeeze, both would pop off, and the pain would be impossible. I felt the dread of death surround me and saw a blackness approaching, filled with the voices of sobbing women.

I screamed.

My voice echoed through the classroom. I thrashed but couldn't wake up. But then, I noticed that the man hadn't snapped the scissors.

And not only had he not done so, he was frowning. A distinct feeling of warmth came over me. My heart almost exploded when, for the first time in months, I heard Mother's voice.

"Nathaniel," she said as she stepped into the classroom. I could feel her before I saw her and was finally able to turn my head. The shadows she'd scattered like a prophet splitting seas. She was wearing slip-on aquamarine shoes with no socks and a simple V-neck black dress. She looked calm and composed. "It's okay now, honey. I'm here."

The creature lifted itself off me, and I looked at Mother head-on. I was frightened and half-naked on the cold classroom floor. The man slipped an oily tongue across his lips. Mother looked so small. Still a little less than five feet tall. But in her hands she carried a sledgehammer that was made of steel.

"Mom," I whimpered. "Mom, it's you."

"Run along and play, Nathaniel." Her eyes burned at the creature rising from the ground. It lifted the scissors and began snapping them. The snaps turned into cavernous booms, and he rose to the height of the classroom ceiling.

"Mom." I cowered to the side of the class. "Be careful. He's really, really mean."

"He's a man." Mother gripped the sledgehammer. She let her wire-rimmed glasses fall to the bridge of her nose and flipped her shoulder-length, black hair around her neck, revealing cool, assured eyes. "That's all he is, Nathaniel. And I'm much, much meaner when I need to be."

Mother ran toward the man, the sledgehammer trailing at her side. He looked at her and roared, his jaw unhinging like a snake's to the bottom of his neck. He charged Mother with the scissors snapping, his mammoth footsteps cracking the ground. Mother swung the sledgehammer around her back, put her foot on a desk, and soared into the air. Her eyes were filled with a determination so electric it might have overloaded all the circuitry for twenty miles. He tried to slice out at her, but in midair, she threw her head sideways and dodged. She brought up the hammer, and the force was so vigorous it cracked and then crushed the man's skull.

"Wake up," I heard.

His head broke apart. From it came tiny, wiggling organisms, like the ones I'd seen on the Collectors, surging toward the ceiling like a swarm of locusts.

"Wake up."

The sledgehammer rose again.

"Wake up!"

The world went white, and my eyes flashed open. I was sweating and heaving; the classroom was gone. "Wake up," I heard. "Wake up. Wake up!" Shaking me by the collar of my shirt was Gus. He had ripped me out of bed and looked delirious. As he saw me come to, he said, "It took her."

"What?" The world crawled with little slugs of light. Squirming organisms at the corners of my eyes that faded quickly, as if receding into my brain.

"It took her," he sobbed. "It fucking took her."

"Who?" Something was wrong with my body. My arm in particular. I could barely move it. "Who got taken? Lexi?"

"Yes," said Gus as if he'd almost forgotten. "I saw it happen—on the way to the Octopus fountain. I was..." Mucus covered his face from crying. "It was horrible. I was helpless. It would have killed me if I had been on time..."

"I thought we weren't meeting until ten?"

THE SILENT END

"No, no." Gus shook his head. "No. Ten. Yes. But I needed to get Lexi. I needed to get you. Because that's not all, Eberstark."

"Gus, calm down—what are you talking about?"

He turned to the ceiling, tears streaming down his cheeks.

"It took my mom!"

TWELVE

"DO YOU HAVE THE PISTOL?"

"The pistol?" Gus was looking at my arm. "Yes."

"Give it to me."

Gus couldn't keep his eyes off my arm as he reached into his backpack and removed Edwina's pistol. The Hat was standing in the hallway, arms across his chest as he kept lookout.

"It happened to you, didn't it?" Gus sniffled. "What did you use?"

"Hat." I was unable to answer the question at this time. I didn't think I even could have if I'd tried.

The second I said the Non Entity's name, the space around him seemed to fold. I shook my head, unsure of what was happening, and held up the pistol to him. It shimmered even brighter than before.

"Here."

The Hat walked back toward me. He looked the same as usual, but something was off. A dim light seemed to glow behind his Ray

THE SILENT END

Bans that made me dizzy.

The Hat took the pistol and held it to his nose, sniffing it.

"Where's the unstable element?" I said.

The Hat held up a finger, reached into his coat pocket, and removed the glowing, yellow receptacle. It was crude, rocky. Like gold ore. He held an object in each hand, weighing them.

"Can you put them together?"

The Hat scoffed and set both objects down on my bureau, removing his notepad.

Yes.

I watched him. "So go ahead."

The Hat shook his head and scribbled on another piece of paper.

It will take time.

"We don't have time!" Gus yelled, shaking his finger in the Hat's face.

The Hat scribbled on another piece of paper.

These things can't be hurried.

"What the fuck are you talking about? They have my mom, Hat. My fucking mom—and Lexi! They have her too."

I put my hand on Gus's shoulder and gently pushed him back.

"How long will it take?" I said.

The Hat scribbled.

Not long.

"Can you be any more exact?"

More scribbling.

No.

"Ah, screw this." Gus threw his backpack over his shoulder. "I don't care if we have that stupid pistol or not."

"Come on, Gus."

"No. You and your bullshit—after everything you've done, I still can't count on you? I'm going to get my mom back, that's what I'm going to do. I'm going to get my mom back, and that's it."

"How? We don't even know where the entrance is. Or if there even is an entrance at all."

"The map says it's below Myers High." Gus removed the *NON ENTITIES ONLY* book from his backpack. He opened up to the map of Mossglow and stabbed the red X with his finger, drawing a circle around it. "I'll figure out the rest when I get there."

The Hat was examining my arm. He flicked his fingers against it, making little metal dings. They felt almost ticklish, and a shocks of sickening electricity ran through me afterward. I was both energized and depleted.

The Hat finished looking at my arm and scribbled on a piece of paper.

Powerful.

I shucked my arm into my puffy, gray winter coat. Gus sped out of the room, running down the stairs. I saw that it was already dark outside. I looked at my desk clock. Just after eight thirty.

"Hat," I said, listening to Gus's steps as he reached the bottom of the stairs. "I need to go with him. Can you find us when it's ready? No matter where we are?"

The Hat scribbled on another piece of paper and handed it to me. I wasn't sure I'd read it right.

Don't forget. Fresh breath is important.

I studied the Hat, wondering if he could break down, develop glitches like broken software. So instead of asking him to elaborate, I ran out of my room and down the stairs, catching up with Gus, who was already in a full sprint across my front lawn.

THIRTEEN

Gus's ankle, though healing quickly from whatever the Hat applied to it in the crow's nest, was still swollen, and he pushed through the pain. He'd gone home, he explained in gusts, to find his parents gone, which was strange for a weekday morning. Though maybe it was good they wouldn't see how filthy and bloodstained he was, especially since he was planning to skip a full day of school for the first time in his life. He went upstairs, took a shower, nodded off for an hour or two, and came back down. There, he found his father on the back porch, smoking his pipe in nothing but his underwear.

"I'd never seen him that bad before. Babbling—all this stuff about how he'd known something like this was going to happen."

"Known something like what was going to happen?"

"Don't know." Gus was using snippets of sentences, unable to slow himself down. "He didn't recognize me—covered in sweat—saying something 'bout how a couple years back, he was curious about the history of the town. Found strange-looking minerals near a cave at Goon's Cove—went to see what else he could dig up." Running out of the Thicks, we saw a small huddle of police cars, *state police cars*, with their lights flashing. They were sitting at an intersection a couple of streets down, blocking the road. We hugged the sidewalk so they wouldn't see us and whirled the opposite way toward Myers High. "But he went too far. To a place where he found something."

"What kind of something?"

"I tried to ask him. But he was crying so much I couldn't get it. Started throwing his fists. Started screaming the word 'geode' until his voice went hoarse."

"Like the one you guys use as your mailbox?"

Gus nodded. "When I said I understood, he calmed down—not a lot but a little—and explained that he'd found it in a bad place. A place where skin grows on the walls."

"Skin?"

"Unnatural things down there, he said. Caverns of sick. He picked up the geode, took it home. Then, the dreams started. When he awoke the next day, he was obsessed with the damn thing. Was all he could think about. Where it had come from, how it evolved. He knew something was wrong with him, but it didn't matter."

When we got to Nigh'Sow Road, we took the path that ran through the woods alongside it. A siren howled in the distance.

"One night, he broke down. Attempted to get it out of the house. But the furthest he got was the edge of the lawn. That's when he put up the mailbox. I remember him telling us the idea came to him in a dream. It was weird. My dad's not the kind of guy that has visions. But we gave him the benefit of the doubt. We didn't know how bad things were already. Wasn't long before he started spending entire days on the porch, staring into that fucking mist."

I was surprised that, for the first time ever while running, I wasn't out of breath. "The geode? Is it a Non Entity too? Like the Shepherd?"

"Don't know. Don't care either. What I want is my mom back. The house…" he forced back his tears. "It was so cold. Yeah, that kind of cold."

He then explained that after he realized what happened to his parents, Lexi went to meet him at the Octopus Fountain. Gus commandeered his family van and sped to the Lowers. He found a parking spot down the street, jumped out running, and was just far enough away not to be noticed when he saw the creature. The same we'd encountered beneath the bay.

"It was hideous. Strong. It came from the bushes behind the fountain. Took Lexi in its arms and was gone a second later. I didn't know what the hell to do."

No one but him saw the girl get swept up, and Gus almost fell to pieces then and there.

"How are we going to stop something like that?" I said. "It…it killed my father, Gus. What chance do we have?"

As I said those words, I truly realized Father wasn't coming back. Before, I'd had this notion that when he swam to meet the beast that the worst hadn't happened. That he'd return strong and obscene as always when we least expected to save the day. But no. Father was gone, and I was alone. I'd known so just glimpsing the Hat; he had a broken look to him, like something now unsure of its use. In a way, I could relate to the sentiment. My future was dim. All I could see was death and disappointment, faces that faded or remained in the dark. And though Father apologized before his final plunge, I still considered myself a bedwetter.

My arm throbbed, pushing into the edges of my jacket. Although I felt like I'd had the worst sleep of my life, I wasn't in pain. If my mind was asleep, my body was awake and with endless energy. I could keep up with Gus for the first time in my life.

"Are we just going into this without a plan?"

"We'll figure it out as we go," Gus said.

"No offense. But that doesn't sound like you."

"My plan." Gus ran faster. "Is to get my mom out of the hellhole she's been dragged into. Does that sound good to you?" We reached Myers High soon enough, hurrying toward Mickey the Bullfrog. The slab of a school towered above us like a giant's sarcophagus, and beneath, we knew, lay its long-decayed bones. The lights were all out, but the darkness inside the top two floors seemed thicker. I thought I saw something new above the front entrance, a sculpture I'd never noticed. Its silhouette was that of an angel, and it stood directly in the middle of a pediment that bore the words UNUS MUNDUS.

Gus came to a stop before the statue and bent over, panting with his hands on his knees.

He removed the *NON ENTITIES ONLY* book from his backpack and flipped through the pages, settling on a sketch of Mickey the Bullfrog. On the top of page, a hurried, Murje-ridden Edwina had written the following:

Main Entrance

The drawing looked much the same as the statue. She understood that there was something hateful about it, something angry in the way its legs were positioned. If this were a real frog, it would be preparing to crush us under its fat, stone belly. But because it wasn't, we noticed the only difference between it and the picture. A tiny human hand, like that of a child's, was drawn inside the mouth, sticking out of the throat. It had slender fingers and was curled a little, as if waiting to be grabbed. A line was drawn from that hand to a scrawl of Edwina's. It read:

Pull for entry.

Gus climbed up on the pediment and stuck his head in the statue's mouth. "There's nothing here."

"Maybe she drew it by mistake?"

"Nah. This Murje stuff, it reshapes your brain. But it doesn't make you stupid."

"It does make you delusional though."

"This is all we have. Though maybe we could have known more by now if you'd have been honest with me to begin with."

"Gus, I—"

"Don't. It doesn't matter anymore. You're here now, and that's all I care about. Don't let me down again though. Okay? I have to be able to count on you."

He reached into the mouth and touched at the back of it.

"Eberstark. Come up here."

I obliged. My body, even with its sizeable gut, jumped gracefully to the pediment in one leap.

"Touch back here," he said, pointing to the back of the stone throat.

I reached out with my non-throbbing arm. My fingers felt around and at first found nothing. Just damp stone that was smooth and cold. My thumb, however, ended up brushing against what felt like a ball of static. I put my entire hand in; there was the slightest bit of resistance.

"It's just like with the key." Gus also tried to grasp the invisible material but couldn't. "You try."

I made to grab it, imagining a hand in my own as I did so. I could almost get a grip but each time slipped away, as if my fingers were covered in grease.

"You feel it, right?"

I nodded. "I just can't see it this time."

When I concentrated, I thought I glimpsed disturbance in the air.

"Eberstark. I need you to think. Why could you see that key before when we couldn't? There had to be a reason. A physical reason."

"I don't know. I really don't. I just saw it. That's all."

"That can't be all. Nothing works like that. Even if the reason is stupid, there has to be one. I want you." He sniffled. "I want you to tell me everything that happened leading up the day you found that key."

"But I already told you what happened."

"I need you to tell me again. And this time, I need to hear everything, Eberstark. I want you to wring your memory dry."

I sighed and gave in, going back to the day before we found the key. The day in the cave when we were ambushed by Mrs. Duncan. I recounted waking up, what I had for breakfast. I drew out the conversation with Dean Veltry unlike I had before, even describing the shadow over his body. I then remembered the Crow Seraph and how Gus and I parted ways. I squeamishly rehashed the encounter with Charlene Poughkeepsie, Joe Ross, and Jesse Maroon. I remembered that I stopped by Stumart for food afterwards, saw Cory, patched up my hand. I talked about how Gus and Lexi found me outside, and we went to the cave only to have the Shepherd get stuck on its way out. I remembered that I was craving sugar and almost downed the entire pack of the Hat's mints and that they made me feel loopy and euphoric.

"Stop there," Gus said. "What mints?"

I told Gus about the tin I'd received from the Hat the day I found him and Father in the hedgerow at Myers High, outside of Mr. Kraft's class. How I'd been hungry and eaten too many of them. How afterwards, I'd felt drugged and had a dream that night leading me to the janitor's closet. As I spoke, I began to understand myself what Gus had already realized.

"The mints."

Gus looked me up and down. "Do you still have them on you?"

I reached into the pocket of what happened to be the same jeans I'd been wearing on the night we'd visited the cave for the second time (I only had two pairs). They were torn up, and I was still filthy. But I rummaged through anyway, pulling out my wallet, house key, and a bundle of Stumart receipts. No tin.

"Wait." Gus pointed to the ground.

In my search, something tiny had popped from my pocket. I bent down to examine it.

The mint was soggy. But there it was. A yellow half-circle made of sugar, sorbitol, and something far stranger.

I bent down and picked it up carefully. It was filthy, covered in pocket lint and dirt.

"Do you want me to eat it?" Gus put his palm out.

Before he could finish, I'd swallowed it, dirt and lint and all. Gus watched me, waiting for a change. All I could do, meanwhile, was think of the last thing the Hat had written.

Don't forget. Fresh breath is important.

My body rushed with airy energy. The mint, despite its filthiness, was not just delicious. It was dangerous. Dangerous in that if I had an endless supply, I could see myself eating them until my mind wasted away.

I found it unlikely The Hat could have known about the hand inside Mickey the Bullfrog's mouth. That wasn't why he'd written that message. Perhaps he wanted me to consume a part of him so that he'd be able to locate me wherever I was. This especially seemed the case as our persons connected. Maybe the Murje had compounded the effect of the mint, but for some reason, my eyes entered his. For a brief moment, I witnessed the splendor of his vision. I saw colors that were impossible to describe. The world itself was coming apart before me, devolving into patterns that revealed how unique and unpredictable everything was, with parts detaching and rejoining, revealing newer patterns. In this vision, I saw that he now not only knew exactly where I was but who I was as a person inside and out. This act was invasive and made my stomach turn. Although I didn't know where he was, I could see what he was doing. Committing an act of creation. Initiating the unfathomable process of soldering the unstable element into the pistol. Even he was afraid as he did this, I sensed. Even he knew he was creating a weapon of mass destruction.

"Eberstark," Gus said. "Can you see it? Wake up."

He snapped his fingers before my face.

I opened my eyes, gazed about. Myers High looked to be covered in a glittering film of silver paint. Below, however, on the ground, emerged a rotting, green, mossy smoke that swept the front steps, statue, and grass. I could almost smell how putrid it was, and I knew Gus couldn't see it.

I peered into Mickey the Bullfrog's mouth. Hazily, at the back of the throat, formed a hand. A child's hand, made out of silver, as intricate as any real one I'd seen. I reached out toward it, grabbed the tiny fingers. The hand was not concrete as the key had been. The half of a mint I'd eaten hadn't been potent enough to render it completely solid. But still, I found a grip. Pulling as hard as I could, the hand clicked forward with a clunk. A cough of mud and water slipped out behind it. We jumped back before the statue split in half, rumbling to reveal our descent.

ONE

THE SIDES OF THE STATUE finished drifting away from each other on large, metal slabs. As they separated, I noticed that the statue was not only made of stone. Imbued in each half were actual bones. Mickey the Bullfrog, it seemed, had been sculpted over the skeleton of an oversized amphibian. Some of the bones, such as the spine, were set parallel, and some, such as the ribs, were only identifiable as knobby, white ingots, inset like jewels. The silver hand itself stood separately from it all. Fixed to the end of a long, iron pole that drove up from below, it stood still as the halves came apart. Right at the base of the former structure, began a staircase that journeyed down.

"Damn," Gus quavered. He took his Maglite from his bag and shined it down the stairs. We saw damp, muddy walls. A kind of yellow slime coating the steps. "We've got to go down there, you know."

"Yeah." I looked into the dark.

We heard what we thought was the sound of footsteps within. The tapping of shoes slowly approaching.

"Do you hear that?"

"Shit," Gus said.

I thought he was referring to the sound but then heard car doors slamming shut behind us. Spotlights hit our backs. Sheriff Earl Nichols and Deputy Stapleton. They came jogging toward us from their vehicles, which they'd parked near the front entrance. The lights on the sheriff's Chevy Suburban flickered, and I wondered if they'd followed us here.

We turned around and faced them, hands in the air. I found that upon lifting my right arm, it made a series of pressurized mechanical sounds beneath the jacket, and Gus gave me a reproachful glance.

"Eberstark! Mustus!" Sheriff Earl Nichols was nearly breathless from the short run. He took off his campaign hat and used his sleeve to wipe sweat from his forehead. "I have been running around town for the last thirty-eight hours looking for you two idiots. I don't what you're doing over here, but I know for shit sure it's not right."

Deputy Stapleton walked up to the edge of the stairway. He looked down, and his lower lip curled in disgust. "What in the hell is this?"

"I'll ask the questions here." The sheriff put his hat back on. "Like for instance." He pointed to the stairs. "What in the hell is that?" The sheriff shone his flashlight into the cavern below. "Wowee. Never seen anything like this before. And I've been here a long time."

"Sheriff Nichols." Gus was trying to approach him. "There's… something happening in Mossglow."

"Something really bad," I added.

"Something terrible."

"Well, of course there's something bad happening in Mossglow."

The sheriff blustered his lips. "You think we don't know that?"

"I don't think you know what kind of bad," Gus said shakily.

"He thinks I don't know what kind of bad is happening in Mossglow." The sheriff laughed and clapped Deputy Stapleton on the back. The deputy didn't look happy about it but grinned anyway. "Mustus, I've been working this town for thirty years. You don't think I've realized how shitty the air smells? Of course, you never put your finger on terrible until terrible has got your whole hand in its teeth, but you can get close enough to know when you're about to get bit. The Navarro house looks like it's been hit by napalm, and I heard about some sort of ruckus over on Crowstone last night involving her beat-up Bronco." He shrugged. "Honestly, I barely even care. I've been up all kinds of horrible for years. Something bad happens, someone disappears or gets killed. Everyone gets scared for a day, but a morning or two after, will you believe it, they don't give a damn anymore. Selective memory, you know? Like no one here sees the gun at their head until they aren't seeing anything at all. You should know about this kind of thing, Mustus, with your dad not leaving the house in a good year. And you, Eberstark. For you, it's the opposite, with your dad running around the forest like Vietcong. Don't talk to me about not knowing what kind of bad is happening around here. I'm practically swimming in a river of shit."

At mention of Father, I went quiet. I heard the footsteps in the tunnel growing louder.

"Someone's down there, Sheriff." Deputy Stapleton was shining his flashlight down the stairs.

"I hear it." The sheriff approached the edge of the stairs as well, putting his hands on his hips and bending halfway to shout. "Hey! Who's that down there? Come on out."

"You must respond." Deputy Stapleton yelled into pit. "I repeat, you must respond."

"What are you, Robocop? Stop talking like an idiot."

The footsteps became louder, and Deputy Stapleton started down the stairs, coming to a halt on the third from the top. Removing his gun, a .40 caliber, from its holster, he assumed a shooting stance. Gus and I watched, nearly petrified.

"Announce yourself," said the deputy.

"Careful now, Deputy," said the sheriff. "That is a gun you are holding there."

"I repeat." The deputy clicked the safety off his weapon. "Announce. Your. Self."

At first, there was a zipping sound and then no sound at all as Deputy Stapleton went rigid. His hands held the gun high for a second, but then, he dropped it to his side and tried to turn around. A hole had been put in the man's head, right between his bushy, red eyebrows. A gash so large it was like he'd been gored by a railroad spike. The wound began to gush, and the deputy looked confused, trying to speak but saying nothing. He then fell flat on his face on the top stair, blood and brain pooling around him.

"What in the shit?" The sheriff's face paled, and he stumbled backward. His gun came out before him, a Springfield XD, and getting back to his feet, he fired three shots down the stairs.

After they fired came a brief pause followed by a baritone voice. "Bam. Bam. Bam," it said before a chuckle. "Bam. Bam. Bam."

"Who…who's there?"

A man emerged from the darkness. His metallic blue eyes glowed bright, and the sheen of short-cropped, silver hair joined them as he came into the light. Dean Veltry was well-dressed as usual, in an unblemished, black suit with needle-thin red pinstripes and a red tie to match. He stood at the bottom of the stairs, simpering.

"Faustus?" The sheriff kept his gun level. "What are you doing down there?"

"Nothing good, Sheriff. Nothing good at all. Just thought I should answer the door when it rings."

"What that's supposed to mean? You give me a good reason you're down here and why my deputy's got a hole in his head, and I promise not to cuff you too hard."

The dean laughed. It was a low, hungry rumble of sound.

"But that's the problem, Sheriff. The reason I have for being down here isn't going to sound good to you. Tell you the truth, it's going to be sound so bad you'll probably want to unload the rest of those bullets here and now."

"I don't like the way you're talking, Faustus. Come on out of whatever the hell this pit is, and we'll talk like men?"

Here, the dean frowned. He looked offended.

"But I'm not a man." The dean removed his right hand from his slacks. It glinted as if made of steel.

The sheriff's breath went cold and he took one of his hands to his lips and hot steam came off them.

"Not an old, smelly, fat-bellied man. Not anymore."

"Hey, keep your hands where I can them," yelled the sheriff, but Dean Veltry wasn't listening. Sheriff Earl Nichols opened fire. Six rounds zipped off into the cave. Gus and I took cover, diving behind the statue halves. But before the sheriff took his seventh shot, the dean's fingers shifted in form. A bundle of elongating, razor-like ribbons pitched forward and split right through the sheriff's throat. The middle-aged lawman gurgled for breath until his knees buckled, and he tumbled down the stairs. The sound of him falling was clumsy and short-lived, thirty years of service discontinued.

I stood still, speechless.

"What do we do now?" I then managed to whisper to Gus.

Gus, shaking, looked at my arm.

"But I don't know how to use it yet."

"Of course you don't." Dean Veltry's voice boomed. He came to the top of the stairs inexplicably fast. He stared into the mist. His skin was gray, steely and shaved clean. He appeared renewed and was even more striking than usual. He wasn't handsome like Mr. Kraft had been, but his size and stature contained the same mind-bending symmetry.

"Your brains are filled with gray matter," the dean said didactically. "Do you know what that means? It means that you, teenagers, are unformed." He took a couple of loose steps in our direction. "That your heads are filled with smoke and mirrors. Your personalities, everything you think you know about yourselves, is the work of phantom matter. Doesn't that...frighten you?"

His upturned eyes grew white until they were nearly indistinguishable from circles of pale stone.

"You're impulses masquerading as personality. You gather fascinations to replace self-definition. For instance, Mr. Mustus. You have an unusually capacious brain for your age. I know you think it came from your father, but it is our opinion that your mother's mind is comprised of components far more robust. Which is why we had to take her from you."

Gus's lips tightened.

"I know it's hard to understand, this business of abduction. But if you had gone on living beyond tonight, you'd have noticed that your intelligence is a trapping, not a boon. That once the phantoms were cleared from your brain, you'd have to fill in the gaps yourself. What we're doing is trying to preserve clarity. When you're too young, you're useless, and when you're too old, the phantoms return, and you start forgetting who you are again."

I struggled to my feet, and the dean, as if just noticing me, guffawed.

"Ah, the flutterer. I almost forgot we were talking about you to begin with. What can be said about a creature like yourself? Here you are, at the precipice of demise, and I can see you still think someone will keep you from it. Like your father. Poor man. Bad man. Head filled with shadows. As I ate his heart, I must say I found its determination to keep beating admirable. It fascinates me that someone could think it possible to end up on the right side of things without changing his biological definition."

"You." I felt my arm vibrate with fury. "It was you beneath the bay. You killed him."

"Well," said Dean Veltry with a sideways smile. "When you start to see the world as we do, killing becomes a form of mercy. I thus prefer saying that we released your father from his suffering."

"Bullshit," Gus said. "You're a thief. And a butcher."

"You can't understand what he's doing down here. You can't know what sort of love it takes to create life. It is love that saved your mother from bleeding out like a slaughtered animal, Eberstark. Useful beast that she is."

"Stop talking about her."

The dean laughed.

He reared his hand. Even though he was feet away, his arm seemed to elongate as his fingers found my jaw. I felt sharp, hot pain at my cheeks and realized almost immediately that he'd cut me. Sticky blood oozed down the side of my face followed by searing pain.

"You don't even deserve to complain." The top of his head seemed to be cracking open. Little white feelers began to slip through. His fingers grew long and sharp. The gray flesh transitioned into strands of rimy, serrated metal that hung down to his feet. "Silence is virtue." He straightened his fingers. When he did so, the metal strands joined together and went rigid so that it looked like he was holding two wicked swords. "Silence is the end." He drew his arms back. "May I preserve your voice."

We felt a thump beneath our feet. The ground rumbled a little, and the dean, with a look of blithe amusement, turned toward the source. In front of Myers High, right before the front doors, stood Gus's Crow Seraph. But not the same one I remembered. Taller now than the first floor and bulging with circuitry, armor, and muscle, it was as if, over the last week, it had grown to take on parts of our imaginations, straight from the illustrations we flipped through in the Sword Star Origins' handbook in which half-human, half machines loomed taller than three normal men. Its mechanical wings stretched toward the sky, and its eyes blazed blood-red. The paint Gus had applied was diminished, replaced instead with an armored suit of red and white. And there was now a beak in place of what had been a human mouth. The feathered plumes that erupted from the helmet curved behind it in golden arcs that ran to the heels of its boots. It drew a sword from a sheath at its side, a thick, double-edged thing. When it held it in front of him, it burst into flames. The beak opened and shrieked horribly. I knew now that this is it what I'd seen above the front entrance, still as a statue. I also knew now that these were the eyes Gus was seeing through whenever he blacked out.

"Gimmickry at its best." The dean sneered and pointed at the

Crow Seraph, dismissing it with a downward gesture. "Is this yours, Mr. Mustus? Did you chance upon the blood of one of my kinsman like the murderous flesh-boy that you are? It's not entirely unimpressive, I'll admit. But it is against our laws. Both of you have committed unspeakable crimes. Your sins are intractable despite your ignorance."

Gus gawped at the Crow Seraph, then almost smiled. I felt my own arm surge with activity and restrained an impulse to scream.

"You're going down, Dean Veltry," Gus growled. "And after that, if I graduate valedictorian, I'm dedicating my speech to your wasted corpse."

Dean Veltry began to laugh again until his laugh turned into something inhuman and wolf-like.

"For your crimes against us, Gus Mustus, I was only going to deliver you to the dark. But this insolence is too remarkable to ignore. When I remove your head, I will make sure it lies next to your mother's." He lifted his sword arms. "So that when she wakes to face her purpose, your lightless eyes will greet her."

He took his arm and heaved it toward Gus, the razors slicing in the direction of his throat. Gus tried to duck away but couldn't be expected to match Dean Veltry's speed. The only thing that saved him was a *clink* of resistance. The Crow Seraph, using its wings to leap through the air, crashed down right before Dean Veltry, putting the sword up against his own. The flames from it seared the dean's eyebrows, so with his other bladed arm, he attempted to slice upwards into the Crow Seraph's chin. But the dream creature predicted the blow and back-circled, removing a huge, fat-ended plasma gun from its belt. With it, he fired three pulses into the dean's gut, three orange, radiated ovals that liquefied his flesh.

The dean stumbled backward, smoke hissing from his abdomen.

THE SILENT END

The wound had gone straight through, and its edges shimmered with Murje.

"It thinks," he said. "It is just like me."

A few tentacles wiggled on top of the dean's head.

"It thinks. It is alive."

His entire face split in half. A blob of flesh and metal erupted from inside, until the force and size of the surging mass overtook and inverted the man himself, sucking him somewhere inside. The creature grew and grew, making wet, kiss-like noises as the body spouted limbs and the stomach solidified. Metal and bone and muscle twisted into a grotesque organism, into a six-legged boar. The tusks were comprised of piping, and exhaled black smoke. Each of the limbs were made out of a sack-like mesh, reminiscent of vacuum cleaner bags. At the end of each one were a series of razor-sharp, curved claws that clicked against the concrete. The eyes were hollow and deep. The mouth was slithery, broad, and filled with teeth. Splotches of lichen-like growths attached themselves to its stomach, rump, snout, and lips, and a greasy tongue salivated.

"The big one," I said, remembering what Father said.

Though its imposing form was now dwarfed, the Crow Seraph drew up his sword. The boar creature's back rose to the second floor of Myers High, bigger than what Mr. Kraft became. Black smoke snorted from its tusks. The Crow Seraph leaped fearlessly into the air. Opening its beak in a shrieking cry, its wings carried it upward. It descended on the dean, its sword raging with green flame, but the adversary was too large, too quick. With deadly adroit, the boar creature reared up and snatched the Crow Seraph out of the air by its right foot with its front claws, swinging it into the first floor of Myers High. The Non Entity slammed through the brick and took it apart is if toppling toy blocks. Dust and sediment crumbled around it. My throat dropped into my gut, and Gus, he seemed to actually be injured, falling to his knees and crying out. The Crow Seraph quickly recovered from the rubble and shot back toward Dean Veltry with its sword and gun ahead of it, its wings drawn in and its boots blasting with rocket thrusters at the heels. Plasma erupted from the gun, and the sword crackled. But the boar creature was stronger, faster. It reared up on four limbs as the Crow Seraph flew toward it. When it arrived, it took the creature by its wings and threw it into the ground. The boar then pounced on the Crow Seraph, pinning the wings of Gus's dream creature under its two front claws. Roaring, it began to pull them apart, tearing them from the shoulders.

"Eberstark," Gus screamed. "You've got to use it!"

I stared at my arm. "I don't know how."

"You do!" Gus cried out as the hog creature tore off the Crow Seraph's left wing, tossing the appendage onto the front stairs where it flapped desperately like a fish out of water. "Trust me; you do. You're smarter than you think you are. Just stop looking at yourself through other people's eyes, and remember you're worth something for fuck's sake!"

"But I'm not!"

The dean began ripping the right wing from the Crow Seraph's back.

"You are! You don't need to live up to anyone's standards. Your mother, your father. You just need…to fucking be!"

Without so much as a thought, my arm ripped through my puffy jacket with a monstrous squelch. I looked at it for the first time, eyes reaming at the magnificent and horrifying maze of choral metal veining up my flesh. The marine creatures on Mother's charm bracelet—starfish, octopus, jellyfish, and seashells—proliferated from shoulder to fingertip. Their colors were divergent and beautiful. The octopus, whose mouth was clamped on my shoulder, was comprised of a red, rusty metal. Its two watery eyes buzzed with electricity. Its tentacles unfurled into mellifluous strands that swayed in the breeze. The starfish, of silver-yellow hue and fixated to my knuckles, had stretched its front appendages to form the mouth of a cannon. Silver, gold, and bone-white shells collected around it to reinforce the hull. Within the cannon, in the soft underside of my fist, I felt the thump of a wet, muscular membrane. Small, silver jellyfish were imbedded like nodes in the flesh of my bicep and forearm, connected by vein-like tubules. As I walked forward, the octopus' tentacles wrapped around my chest and waist, thickening into a sort of armor. The tip of one formed a loop around my right eye, and a glossy film slipped over it like a lens. Through it, I could see the world sharp and clear. I heard the gradual whistling sound within the cannon as if it were a battery charging and brought it to eye level.

"Holy shit," said Gus.

As the boar creature got ready to gore the Crow Seraph's stomach with its tusks, I clenched my fist. A wet, whirring sound built within the cannon and from it shot a silver orb. It rushed forward. As the boar creature prepared to gore the Crow Seraph with its tusks, the orb landed just below its right eye. We heard a sizzling sound as it burned right through, burrowing somewhere inside.

At this, the beast turned to look at me. Its gaze was half-blind and confused. It raised its mouth into a toothy smiled and roared, "*Unnnnnnnformmmmmmed.*"

As it turned back toward the Crow Seraph, its body seized. It wobbled backward before settling on its haunches. Its head rattled, and the mouth opened in thin-lipped anger—an expression I could see the dean himself making. This before more than half of the head exploded in a flash of white, silver, pink, and blue.

The creature stepped sideways, disoriented and clumsy, before tipping on its side. Only a small section of its head, half of the jaw, and a gooey scaffolding of neck remained. The Crow Seraph, lifting itself from the ground, finished tearing the right wing from its own body, casting it to the ground with something like disdain. It picked up its sword, reignited the flames, and turned toward the boar beast. Cawing, its eyes blazing red, it drove the blade deep into the neck cavity. With a vicious upswing, it then sliced the beast's stomach in half by its width. The cauterized flesh fell away in a shimmering pile. Surrounded by metal and dripping caverns of Murje was the dean's rearranged face and body, mutated as Mr. Kraft's had been within his host. His waist was folded above his head. His tie dangled between his eyes. His lips, scrunched below his nose, trembled.

"Flesh-boy," he begged. "Mercy...for the defeated."

The Crow Seraph brought its sword back to finish the job, but Gus yelled, "Stop."

The dream creature dropped his blade and cocked its head curiously.

Gus trudged up to Dean Veltry's face. The smell the thing was giving off was terrible, a combination of smoldering flesh, blood, and metal.

Gus felt at the crumpled folds of Dean Veltry's suit. Finding the breast pocket, he wiggled his hand inside and, clinching, withdrew a silver blade. The dean's penknife, mounted with a likeness of Mickey the Bullfrog.

"I can get her back..." the dean's lips sputtered. "I...I can help...

just don't…don't…feed me to the…sssssilence."

Gus took the knife and jammed it into the dean's throat. There was a moist, gasping sound, and red fluid sputtered from his lips. I could see his steely eyes flash with shock, knowing that someone like Gus, warm, intelligent, nearly invisible, would be the one to relieve him of his breath.

"I'll get her back myself." Gus twisted the blade.

He then left it there as he stomped away, toward the Crow Seraph, wiping his hands. Out of breath, he stood before it.

"So you're my Non Entity, right?" He seemed content now, saying those words.

The Crow Seraph, with red eyes in a perpetual diagonal slant, nodded. The only revealed skin on its face had an orange hue.

"Gus." I looked toward the entrance to the catacombs. "I think it's time."

Gus turned his back to the Crow Seraph, closed his eyes, and seemed to concentrate for a moment. The creature's armor then began to open up, separating down the middle from the neck to shin. Pistons depressurized, and I saw it was creating a human-sized depression within its body. It was filled with circuitry, harnesses, and tubing. Gus, pausing to look back at me and nod, prepared to step in. He climbed upward awkwardly, securing his arms and legs into place with a natural knowing he fell into easily. Slowly, the armor began to close around him with the same series of pressurized movements. For a second, he wasn't visible within. But then, an elevating mechanism lifted his body skyward. The Crow Seraph's face rotated to the rear of its head, and Gus, or something like Gus, appeared in its place. It was still my friend staring down at me, but the contours of his chin were more severe. He had a well-healed, X-shaped scar across his cheek, and his eyes glowed pale blue. A green glass visor fell over them, and he took a step forward.

"Gus?" I was a little wary. "Everything okay in there?"

"I am fine." His voice, though still his, was now deeper and synthesized as if through a computer. He and the Non Entity had merged. In a way, it was exactly as how I'd imagined a Demigod would look in real life: half-human, half-machine, tooled for war. I felt a leap of terrible excitement just witnessing it. "New directive is to retrieve the mothers along with Corporal Navarro. Are we clear, Grunt-sweat?"

I almost chuckled at the last part. 'Grunt-sweat' was taken directly from the Sword Star Origins' handbook as a term commanding officers used for new recruits. He made a series of heavy, deliberative steps toward the stairs leading below Myers High.

"Are your ears full of wax? I asked if we are clear."

"Uh…yes, sir." I saluted him with my Murje-enhanced arm. The Octopus' tentacles coiled tight around my chest but loosened intelligently so I could breathe. "Clear as day."

"Then proceed with caution," the Gus Seraph boomed. "Resistance is anticipated."

TWO

WE WEREN'T SURE WHAT TO do about the bodies of Sheriff Earl Nichols and Deputy Stapleton. There was also the matter of a gigantic pile of flesh that had once been Dean Veltry reeking and festering on the Myers High courtyard. We quickly realized we were under too much duress to do the honorable thing. After pulling the bloody corpses from the stairs, we laid them on the courtyard and began our descent.

I discovered a lever at the bottom of the stairs. Upon pulling it, the statue halves rumbled shut above us, and we were immersed in darkness.

The tunnel awaiting us below was barely tall enough for the Gus Seraph to walk down without hunching over. Since his wings had been ripped off, it made things easier, but he was cutting it close. After walking a while, I felt increasingly cut off from the world above. The Gus Seraph had a high-powered spotlight on his chest that shone into the darkness ahead. But even with its reach, we could only see so far. Every time I turned around, I felt like a barrier of night was sliding up against my back. It was liquid and thick, swishing between our arms and legs.

"How far do you think this goes?"

The Gus Seraph swiveled its head. "Depth unknown. Current directive recommends silence to better assess the environment."

His voice echoed down the chamber.

"Talking helps me feel less afraid," I whispered. "We both know things aren't right down here."

"Define right."

"Opposite of wrong. Like someone's expecting us."

"Define someone."

"Damn it, Gus, you know what I mean."

"It is recommended you keep your cool, Grunt-sweat. We are entering enemy territory without sufficient intel. Better to observe prior to engagement."

"This Grunt Sweat thing is going to get old quick."

After a few more minutes of walking, we caught a blip of movement. Gus brought his armored boots to a halt, and his visor produced a surveillance laser scan. A blue sheet of light flooded over the cavern, searching for movement.

"Nothing there," I said.

"Your assessment is false."

We cautiously approached the spot where we'd thought we'd seen something. I shined Gus's Maglite over it, and a ripple of static filled the Seraph's visor, analyzing. In the wet were a series of footprints. Each of them had four oval-shaped toes and long, skinny digits.

The Gus Seraph blared. "Footprints like these suggest amphibian origins. Lithobates catesbeianus."

"Goddamnit. Quit it with the 'directive' shit. What are you talking about?"

"American Bullfrog is what I am talking about, Grunt-sweat. And do not question my reconnaissance, or I will put you to work in the Tiferius fields for sixty cycles."

"You're just a big nerd."

"Define nerd."

"I'm not going to define nerd for you."

"That is unfortunate."

"It *is* unfortunate."

"Affirmative."

"Will you stop it?"

"Request denied."

After a few more minutes, we caught movement again. Except this time, there was more than one shape in the shadows. The Gus Seraph withdrew his plasma pistol, holding it before him, poised to fire. I rose my arm as well and concentrated, hoping the next shot would come more naturally.

"You have three seconds to reveal yourself before I toast your ass," the Gus Seraph said to the stranger in the dark. "Three, two, one."

A creature hopped into the light. The Gus Seraph didn't fire but held the target in his sights.

Sitting there silently was a frog. A large frog. Maybe two feet tall.

"What the hell." I looked up at the Gus Seraph. "It's a frog."

"Erroneous. Scans reveal multiple bogies. All with biomorphic tendencies."

"Bio-what?"

"Life forms possess biological anomalies uncommon to amphibians.

Are larger than normal. Chances of genetic enhancement likely."

I watched the frog stare at me with glassy eyes. The bubble below its mouth blew and deflated, but it didn't make a sound. "They're quiet."

"Latent gular sac."

"Again, what?"

"The frog is not croaking, Grunt-sweat. This is unusual, do you not agree?"

As he said that, I saw another frog hop into the light. It was a little bigger than the first one and looked at me with its callow eyes. Another frog followed it. And another yet again until we noticed the entire passageway was filling up with them by the hundreds. When they hopped, they barely made a sound.

"Shall we blast our way through, Commander Crow?" I asked.

"Affirmative, Grunt-sweat. Keep your fire level, and leave no survivors. We cannot chance triggering alarm."

I lifted the cannon, but before I could fire, something dove at my legs, and I went flying on my back. Gus, too, was sent smashing into the ground. It was then I knew that the frogs weren't only in front of us but behind as well. They swelled in number, overwhelming our bodies in a swell of slippery green. I felt myself being lifted off my back. I tried to fire my arm cannon; an orb emerged and exploded a smattering of bodies into blood and skin, but it wasn't enough to inhibit the invasion. The creatures swarmed beneath me and collected together into one undulating organism. That organism then began carrying me off down the tunnel, gaining speed but not making a sound.

"Gus!"

I saw the Gus Seraph leap to its feet. He withdrew his flaming sword and set an entire herd of the creatures on fire. He crushed them against the walls and smashed them beneath his boots; his plasma pistol thumped off a full round. Fire and blood and plasma surrounded him. But his rampage faded into the distance as I was swept into the deep.

THREE

I COULDN'T SEE A THING. EVERY time I tried to get away, I was forced viciously back atop the raft of giant frogs, hurtling me down a river of silence.

"Stop," I tried to plead. "Let me go."

The creatures' rapid leaps made less noise than drizzle on a pond. I fired off my canon a few times and felt the octopus on my shoulder doing something to crunch a frog or three in its slithers, but their numbers grew as we traveled, as if they were constantly emerging from holes in the ground, clinging to the host organism as we sped along. I hoped that Gus was having better luck.

My eyes caught a drop of light ahead. It was so small, however, so insignificant, I wondered if I was being wishful. I was traveling at such a ferocious speed I feared I'd pass by it in a blink.

As we poured past the light—a small hole in the ceiling, it seemed—a hand shot out, and breathless, I found myself grabbing it. It pulled me off the frogs, and I dangled, kicking my feet. Looking up into the dim hollow, I saw a face covered in green mucus, gritting its teeth and grunting. I almost screamed but then noticed the black eyepatch, the slime-slicked shaved head, and full lips.

"Pull, Eberstark," Lexi whispered. "Quick."

Shoving my shoulder against the lip of the cavern, I squirmed inside. Lexi fell backward as I came toppling in, then scrambled out from under me and came to her knees, flashlight strapped to her head.

"Come on." She didn't even pause to comment on my arm. I couldn't keep from staring at her. She looked like she'd been swimming through scum. Her body, clothed in a tank top and overalls, was slathered in a yellow-green film, some of which gelled together in clumps around her ears and chin.

"What the fuck are you looking at? Move, now."

I scrambled into action, following her as she climbed down the tunnel and turned right into another one. I heard a pattering sound behind us—the frogs, they were crowding into the passage. Lexi's flashlight revealed shadows at our rear.

"Faster!"

We arrived at a circular, metal gate, already opened. Lexi jumped in and pulled me through before slamming it shut and fastening a metal latch. We then watched as a deluge of oversized frogs flooded up against the gate, so blind in their purpose that they pushed their bodies as hard as they could until some began to split apart between the bars; blood and ichor and organs slicked through, flooding around our feet.

"This way." Lexi crawled around another tunnel to the left. My right arm crushed up against the walls and took out chunks of it whenever I moved.

We came to another circular, metal gate; Lexi opened it and, when I was through, locked the latch. We were at a crossroads. Another gate stood ten feet away, and between it and the one we came through was a hole leading straight down.

"Go."

I nodded and looked over the hole. "Just jump?"

Hissing, she shoved me in.

I would have fallen straight down, but the octopus on my shoulder shot its tentacles into the wall and added resistance, drilling into the stone to slow my bulk as I neared the bottom. Lexi jumped right on my shoulders, however, and we fell the rest of the way, crunching onto a cold, stony surface. We got to our feet, breathing heavily. Lexi shone her light around frantically for more signs of movement.

"How did you find me?" I panted. "How long have you been down here? What happened to—"

"Shh..." She gestured around us.

A skin-like material crawled across the walls and ceiling, vast canvasses of red flesh that bunched up, forming polyp-like growths. Some of them pulsed and flexed. Within the skin were little bits of household wares, the shells of toasters, tape recorders, coffee grinders, spoons, extension cords and grizzled camcorders. When I listened close, it was as if the room itself was breathing, exhaling slow, raspy bouts of wind.

"I came from down there." She took me to the edge of the room and, though it was hard to identify at first in the dark, showed me a hole in the wall. It was pillowed with red flesh, soft, alive. Lexi shone her flashlight through. It wasn't as much a hole as it was a window, leading into a cavern below. "From that."

In the clearing was a machine. A pod. A glassy case secured to the top had been opened like a lid. Inside was a bed of sorts but one that I'd never want to sleep on. It looked bony and wet. Beside the pod was a small consul with a series of ruddy indicator lights on it. Some of them were blinking. The walls were covered in the same flesh as elsewhere.

"What is it?" I whispered.

"Something to keep me in, I think."

"Keep you in?"

"I got carried here by the frogs, just like you. That was a while ago. I can't keep track of time in here…I think I've been drugged…a few times. I was down in that room, half-asleep. And then…something came for me. Something horrible, Eberstark." She looked around, as if that 'something horrible' might hear her. "It tried to pick me up, put me in that thing. Thankfully, I don't think they drugged me well enough, so I woke while it was stuffing me inside. Somehow…I escaped. I don't even know how—I think I stabbed it. And maybe I ran around for a while until it lost me. I ran around more and found myself right back where I started. I noticed there was a room. I climbed up inside. It led me to the tunnels…There's a whole lot of them here. I'm thinking they're air ducts. It's easy to get lost." Her one eye blinked with delirium. "How long have I been down here?"

"I don't know." And I honestly didn't. I didn't even know how long I'd been here myself. "Not long, I don't think. Ten, maybe twelve hours."

"No." She looked befuddled. "It had to be…it seemed so much longer. At least a full day. Maybe even two."

"But how did you know I was coming? How did you know to find me?"

"You hear when things move in this place. It sounds crazy, but you do. I could hear the frogs—they don't come unless they're bringing someone—and they bring more people than you know, Eberstark. And maybe not just from Mossglow… This place goes deep. Deeper than we thought. When you think you're going forward, you're going down. And when you think you're going backward, you're going down."

I explained to Lexi what had happened since she'd been taken. I told her of Gus's mother, the Crow Seraph, Dean Veltry, and my arm. I told her about the Hat and the mint and expressed hope that the Non Entity would be able to find us here.

Lexi touched at the silver jellyfish on my arm. She tapped one of them with her finger, and it wobbled in response. "It's beautiful."

"Oh, uh, thanks."

"Don't thank me. That comes from you, you know. It all comes from you. Just like the Shepherd came from me."

"Lexi." I looked her in the eye. "I'm so sorry. About your house. About the Shepherd. About everything."

"I'm tired of your apologies."

"I just can't stop from thinking…if only we had known each other better…if we'd been friends longer, we might have been able to… We might have had a better chance."

She reached out and prodded the tentacles of the octopus on my shoulder and watched with almost child-like glee as they shied away.

"Eberstark." She gave a slime-drenched smile. "If nothing bad had happened, do you think we'd even be talking to each other?"

"I think so."

"You really do need to grow up."

"That was harsh."

"Friendship can be harsh. That's how the good stuff's built. From really bad shit." She wiped her hand over her head and removed a swath of mucus, flinging it to the ground. "You can't count on honesty when things are going well. You never know if someone cares about you until the sky falls."

We heard the almost inaudible pattering sound again, somewhere in the tunnels. Lexi, she seemed more attuned to it even though she'd only been here a short while.

"We've got to move," she said.

"Where?"

"To him. To the man in the mirror. To the end."

"But what if we can't even make it that far?"

"Then the sky falls," she smiled before climbing out the window. "Come on."

FOUR

CLIMBING DOWN THROUGH THE HOLE in the wall, we entered the room where the pod machine was stationed. It resembled a scaly cocoon, a capsule where something could undergo metamorphosis. A massive cable ran from a notch at its front. It was comprised of sturdy metal and was secured to the ground every fifteen feet with steel clamps as it wound ahead. A scent surrounded me that was as repulsive as it was heady. It smelled like rotting meat and freshly baked piecrust, of day old vomit and fresh coffee grounds.

We followed the cable as it twisted through a cavern whose entrances and exits were numerous—a porous maze of stone. We felt so small and lost. I imagined we were walking through a fossilized beehive. Guided by the cable alone, we could barely see ahead of us. With every step, our eyes grew murky. The skin covering the walls, the biotic material infused with the most obscure household items imaginable—internet routers, can openers, candelabras, egg whisks—

seemed to be pumping out a disorienting haze.

"Shh." Lexi put her arm across my chest to halt me, much in the same way Mother used to when making a sudden traffic stop. She made her best effort not to squish her glopped up Chuck Taylors against the ground and cupped a hand to her ear.

"Listen," she mouthed.

I tried to hold my breath. At first, there was nothing, just stillness, until from that stillness came the quiet sound of chewing. Lexi dimmed her flashlight to a low, near untraceable glow and motioned for me to follow her. I tried to keep my right arm still as I moved, as not to make a sound. When we sidled around a column of rock, we saw a shape crouched against the rear end of a cavern. It was twitching and made slurping sounds. From the back, its naked flesh was knobby and riddled with lumps. Though we couldn't see its face, we discerned that meat slurped through its lips, taken from a corpse at the creature's feet. Long patches of stringy, slick, black hair dripped off its skull, and its shoulders rose high and bony like a cat's.

We continued to go quietly to avoid attracting it, every movement an exercise in stealth. I tried to pretend nothing was there. Pretend that before me wasn't a demon in the dark. But my arm couldn't maintain the same composure. As it rubbed up against a patch of wall and scraped it too hard, I heard the creature snarl. Two black eyes turned toward us.

Lexi flipped up the frequency on her flashlight, illuminating the creature's face. From the waist up, it could have been a woman with scarred, knobby breasts and ostrich-like eyes. But from the feet down, her legs were like a bird's: long, leathery, and taloned. Her mouth dripped with yellow effluvium, her nose was a hole in the middle of her face, and in her stomach were little bits of silver, like threads of fishing twine had been sewn into her abdomen.

She howled at Lexi's flashlight. I thought she would pounce right then, but instead, she decided to turn toward me. She licked her lips and saw something in my eyes. Something she found delicious and heinous. Bending her strong bird's legs, she leaped, turning her heels forward, making for my throat. The talons spread, filled with torn ligaments and blood. I put out my hands in defense. That's when the tentacles from the octopus on my shoulder reacted. In a florid display, two of them caught the creature by her ankles. A third caught her neck and wrapped tight, crunching bone and muscle. Her arms reached for my throat. Her grimy teeth continued to snap until her back straightened and her glassy eyes went blank. The tentacles loosened, and the creature slid to the ground. Lexi's knife was protruding from the back of her skull. She removed it and stabbed again and again, opening gashes on her back. I stood away, watching her do so, taking a strange pleasure, as if by killing this creature, she was killing other, less grotesque creatures as well.

Lexi then kicked the corpse to make sure it was dead and, upon confirmation, removed the blade. On it was something that wasn't quite blood but wasn't quite Murje either. It was black and viscous, like motor oil. Taking my shirt, she used it to remove the fluid.

"What was that?" I prodded my neck to make sure I hadn't been slashed.

"Something that's been down here for a long time, I'm guessing."

I backed away from the creature. I didn't even want to look at it, stepping out of the way from its oily fluids as they pooled around my feet. I returned, shaken, to the cable. "Why do you think he's doing this?"

"Who's he?"

"You know. Mr. Blue? Thomas Hellwidth Myers? And not just him…but Mr. Kraft. Dean Veltry. There have to be more. He must have a reason."

"If he didn't, would it make a difference?"

"I think it would."

"Not for me." She shook her head. "To tell you the truth, I hope this guy is a fucking lunatic. I don't want have to think that someone could actually justify creating what we…what we just killed. I'd prefer a sociopath any day of the week."

"And if he's not a sociopath? If there is a reason?"

"Then people are even worse than I already thought they were." She followed the cable into another tunnel.

FIVE

WE CONTINUED TO FOLLOW THE cable. I explained quietly what the Hat had said about crafting the pistol and tried to keep in mind that, as Lexi had experienced, time seemed to pass differently down here. You misplaced your body, your sense of direction. You didn't know if you were heading north, west, or south. You got lost in thoughts of this underworld's vastness and all the creeping things throughout it. You thought that if you disappeared, if you got snatched off in an instant, your body would be claimed by a rival universe.

As Lexi had also observed, you knew whenever something moved down here. As time passed, it was as if I could feel footsteps with our fingers. The entirety of this lair, this maze of stone and skin and garbage, was ruled by silence. Every whisper we made was carried across the quiet like motes of sound in an abandoned opera house. And somewhere along that trajectory, it was pinned down and executed. I remembered the words drawn with Mrs. Duncan's blood. The words that told us to stay out of the silent end. This place tried to make us forget that we could speak.

We knew we were getting somewhere when we saw a second set of cables. They were identical to the ones we were following and appeared to our right when we emerged into an open area. A third set stretched out into it from a tunnel to our left and beyond that, from another tunnel, a fourth. Lexi adjusted her flashlight's brightness and found it wouldn't burn as high as before. The darkness here was savage. It might as well have been eating her batteries. But when she shone it above, we were able to see we'd come into a new domain. High above us was a ceiling of asperous rock. So high that the light was barely able to reach. Twenty feet before us, trapped beneath the ceiling, sat a large, domelike structure. The cables, it appeared, were leading from a multitude of tunnels at our back, so many, maybe sixty, maybe more, one of which, near the middle, we'd come from. They all converged here, on this stone landing, and, collecting into one tangle, they disappeared into the dome, into a massive, upturned rectangle carved into its front.

"Is this it?" I asked Lexi. The dream creatures on my arm rattled as I shook with fear.

She was quiet as she stared into the entrance to the dome. I saw that she was now hobbled, two bends away from a hunch. She was worn down. Not having her Non Entity to rely upon was hurting her. Though she tried to pretend otherwise—for what else could she have done—she was missing a piece of herself.

"I think so." Her hands shook. "I wish…I had a cigarette."

"Smoking is a class 9 pollutant and should be avoided at all costs, Corporal."

Lexi jumped a full one hundred and eighty degrees, withdrawing her knife and crouching to the ground.

"Gus," I gasped, running to the Gus Seraph, who'd emerged from a tunnel only three away from the one we'd come through. He'd been gliding inconspicuously on thrusters under his boots. They reduced their fire, and he landed on the stone with a soft click. He was covered almost head to toe in frog viscera. "Am I happy to see you."

"Gus?" Lexi looked at the Gus Seraph with watery eyes.

"Affirmative, Corporal Navarro. Reporting."

On the verge of expressing glee, Lexi's expression soured.

"How come you get the fucking super suit?" She looked him up and down. "My truck comes alive, fine, but you get a giant robot? I want my money back."

The Gus Seraph brought his fist before his chest. "In the eyes of the Imperium, all men are rich."

"Well if that isn't a load of bullshit," said Lexi. "What's more important is that gun…" She pointed to the Gus Seraph's plasma pistol. "Does it work?"

The Gus Seraph produced the sword from his back, and flames roared up its expanse.

"My armaments are at premium function."

"I guess so."

"We should not dwindle. We are nearing the directive and possess the element of surprise. The longer we wait, the more the enemy can prepare."

Lexi cracked her neck side to side.

"If I die in battle," The Gus Seraph puffed out his massive chest, "Then I will know with certainty I was alive."

"Correction," said Lexi. "If you die in battle you won't know anything at all."

"That is your opinion, Corporal. And only your opinion. It is mine, however, that monsters must be killed to maintain the integrity of human discovery. If we do not fight them in our hearts, they will overtake our minds. If we fall, we fall defending the future of enlightened thought. If we die..." the Gus Seraph paused. His lower lip folded. "We show them they are not invincible. And if they are not invincible, they will reconsider the character of future adversaries."

"That's easy for you to say in a robot suit. I'm just a girl with a knife."

"Just a girl with a knife?" I laughed.

Lexi turned to me. "It's not funny."

"Of course it is."

"Back off, Eberstark."

"Don't you know how many people are terrified of you?" I said. "The answer is everyone."

"I concur," said the Gus Seraph.

"I'm not scary."

"Even without that knife, you're more powerful than a legion of tanks as far I'm concerned."

"You have grit, soldier," said the Gus Seraph.

Lexi looked at us for a moment before coughing and turning away. "Don't think just because I've got fight in me doesn't mean I'm not afraid."

The Gus Seraph took out his plasma pistol and jolted it back so that a blazing red cartridge fell smoking to the floor. From an iron utility belt on his waist, he took another rubicund rectangle and fit it in, cocking the gun to readiness. He then turned and handed it to Lexi. In her hands, it looked like more of an assault rifle than a pistol, but she could wield it. "We should stop wasting time."

"I think you can forget about the Hat finding us down here, Eberstark," said Lexi, evaluating her new weapon. "Wherever here is…"

I closed my eyes, tried to concentrate. Tried to find the Hat somewhere in the ether. Perhaps there was a distant flutter of something but little more than that.

SIX

WE ENTERED THE DOME. THE second we passed inside, my thoughts melted. The light worms, as Gus had named them, began crawling at the corners of my eyes. A rattling sound battered my ears, and I felt as if my brain wanted to break free of my skull. For a moment, it was as if I was above the ground, staring down at my own awkward body. There was dust and dark; a red light emanated from the end of the corridor. I saw Lexi put a hand on my back to move me along, and I wanted to tell her I wasn't inside. No, I was far away. I was at home, in my bathroom, holding Mother's hand, watching her blood funnel down the drain. I was watching as the ambulance roared up the front lawn. Then, I was somewhere else. Somewhere even further away. And young. Very young. A child on a playground in elementary school in Cleveland. I was telling a first grade girl named Kim that I liked to collect shards of glass. That whenever I found a shattered pile on the ground, I took a piece and stowed in it a hole I dug, right beside the tarmac by the wall ball court.

"Can I show them to you?" I said to her. "I have a lot of colors."

I was telling the truth. They were blue, and green, and sometimes red. I didn't even think about how sharp they were. That when I showed them to Kim she'd run away crying. That she'd tell the principle later I threatened to hurt her. That I'd sit in his office and tell him it wasn't true, that I thought the glass was beautiful, that I was careful with it and could be trusted. But the principle didn't believe me. He called my parents, frightened them half to death. He told them that I needed to train myself to stop liking sharp things.

With a rush, I was awake again, back inside my body. It was like Gus had said about the Murje blackouts; I couldn't understand how I'd moved my legs while gone. We continued to trace the passage of the cables through the entrance regardless, as if I hadn't left to begin with. I occasionally touched them to keep myself level.

"Are you okay, Gus?" Lexi noticed that the Gus Seraph had slowed to a stop. He had his hands on his knees.

"I…am…okay. Do…you…feel…the…cold?"

"Yes." Lexi exhaled hot breath.

"Good…to know…I am not alone."

We continued down the corridor leading through the dome. Eventually, the red light grew brighter. Nearing it, I realized it was the end of the corridor. Though freezing, it looked like we were walking into the mouth of a furnace.

"Weapons…ready." The Gus Seraph pulled out his sword and set it ablaze. "Use caution… We are here foremost…on a rescue mission."

"We'll find her, Gus," I said.

"I hope…you are correct…Grunt-sweat."

What came next was as Edwina had described: like nothing created for or on Earth.

We exited the corridor, emerging into the gigantic underbelly of the dome. Our bodies turned the color of blood, and my eyes couldn't take it. Everything was murder. Everything was anger. To live down here, one would have to learn to forget other colors. Thankfully, the octopus on my shoulder took two tentacles and looped their tips around each of my eyes. Two gel lenses squiggled across their edges, and a moment later, I appeared to be wearing protective lenses. The red light dimmed. It didn't go away but became easier to bear, fading to a fuzzy orange. The Gus Seraph did something similar by adjusting his visor. Lexi was the only one who had to bear it alone. Her face tensed, and she swallowed her breath before opening up her eye wide to stare into the source of the glare above.

"Lexi?" I said.

"I'm fine."

I looked up as well. The redness was emanating from a large, pulsating, heart-like organism secured to the ceiling. It could have been a jewel for its color and luster, a gargantuan ruby, but there was something organic about its composition. Beneath its glass-like surface rushed a tide of life. Glistening shapes formed and dissipated like the Murje I'd seen in the back of Father's bunker only in vibrant red instead of blue. I saw coils of crystalline sinew twist into objects I recognized. I was afraid to look at them even if they weren't at all frightening. I ended up looking anyway. I saw Father's face in the red, rage-filled and sad. I saw Mother's face, lost and deprived. I saw Gus and Lexi and Mrs. Duncan. I saw an umbilical cord being snipped from a newborn's belly. I saw Charlene Poughkeepsie's ragged teeth and Jesse Maroon's springy fists. I understood what Edwina had meant by something not meant for this world. As when I observed the Murje in Father's bunker, inside this object was an intelligence so complex its language was impenetrable by a consciousness like mine.

At the object's bottom was a cylindrical buffer; three black cables fed into it. Each one came from what looked to be capsules or tanks. There were three total, arranged in a set with one in the middle. They were shaped like bee hives and composed of a skeletal-looking material, something between skin and shell. Small, circular port windows were stationed at the front of each. In the tanks that flanked the middle one, I saw dark shapes shift within. Amorphous limbs flailing through magmatic fluid. The cables that ran from the organism above shimmied, as if pumping its blood into those tanks. The cables we'd followed to arrive here in the first place twisted off to our right, into a depression in the earth where sat a generator, humming with power.

"Dangerous reflective surface located," the Gus Seraph said.

Not knowing what he meant, I followed his gaze. He was looking behind the tanks, at a flight of stairs that led to a carpeted platform. On that platform sat a pair of thrones. Two tall-backed chairs whose tops almost rose to the organism on the ceiling. Above them on the wall was a gaping mirror bordered with ornate bronze. I hadn't noticed it before, but it was the only object in the room that didn't seem to be touched by the red, glaring light. Its surface, cool and dark, was of the deepest marine blue. The sort of blue that was almost black.

The dome itself, I realized, the entire structure that housed this machine, this Living Artifact as Edwina had referred to it, was covered in a pulsing layer of skin that climbed up the walls. And worse still, beginning behind the mirror, was a spine of abominable dimensions, a long strip of sectioned bone that arced along the dome's circumference. I was inside something's body.

"Corporal Navarro," the Gus Seraph said. "Are you functioning at full capacity?"

Lexi was transfixed on the gigantic organism above.

"Corporal Navarro?"

"Lexi," I said. "What's wrong?"

"I...I see." Her eye was glazed over.

"What do you see?"

Her lips and teeth arranged into a big toothy smile she'd never have condoned normally. "My other eye."

She pulled off her patch. Holding the fabric in her fingers, she then let it fall to the ground. She looked up into the red with her gray, sightless pupil, and it turned pink. "I...I can see again." Tears came to her eyes.

"Corporal Navarro," said the Gus Seraph. "I find this development suspicious. Remember the original directive."

"You don't understand what this is like. I can...I can..." She started to shake. Her hands convulsed. She dropped to the ground and began to seize, her entire body jouncing and jerking side to side.

I ran to her side. "What do we do?"

"I am not a licensed medic," the Gus Seraph said in a panicked robot voice.

"Lexi!" I tried to keep her head straight as she shook. "Lexi, are you okay?"

"She is fine..." A loud voice echoed throughout the dome.

Gus and I jumped to our feet, weapons at the ready. The Gus Seraph scanned the room with his visor.

"Activity in the tanks, Grunt-sweat, but voice origin is multidirectional. Unverified."

"Non Entity," we heard. "Non Entity. Non Entity. Non Entity. The voice of the dream creature. Sin against our kind."

"Who are you?" I looked around the room. There was a blurry, white haze in the mirror above the thrones.

Lexi got up from the ground, groaning, and stumbled to her feet. She blinked wildly, as if trying to force something from her eyes. The Gus Seraph helped her retain her poise. She covered her right eye with her hand. Then her left.

"It's fascinating." The voice echoed throughout the chamber. "The concept of meeting someone face to face. In my experience, humans tend to think that if you look a man in the eyes, truth will be revealed about him. Window to the soul and all that superstition. When really, the eye reveals as much about a man's intentions as a dream reveals your future."

"What happened?" Lexi picked up her eye patch. "I could see. I was sure I could see."

The voice was calm, salient. A stormy sort of reasonable. "I am so disappointed in my security apparatus. First Reed, then Edward, then Faustus—how did you manage that one? Each fell to little more than smoke and mirrors. Dream pistols and urge bombs. I know now I should have taught them to see clearer. To not think themselves invincible to our own tricks." He paused. I saw the mirror grow gray with the silhouette of someone inside. "Regardless, it seems as if you were able to escape before I could introduce you to the wonders of my enterprise. All of which, I assure, will serve your sex rather well."

"My sex?" Lexi said. "Who the fuck are you, man? What are you talking about, my sex?"

The voice sniggered. It was a petulant, rodent sound. "I apologize. Your wit reminds me why you were chosen. And it's been a long while since anyone's come down here unexpected. The last person who did without my permission was my dear wife more than century ago.

Which is the reason you're here as well whether you know it yet or not."

"Where is Mother, alien scum?" the Gus Seraph bellowed. He held up his sword and took three steps forward. Hot breath erupted from his mouth.

"Soon enough, sinner. Now that Ms. Navarro has arrived, we can finally begin."

"Begin what?" I said.

"It sounds as if you've already decided that I'm a representative of all the world's evil. The devil in the deep. When if you only knew, flesh-boy, what I go through to ensure the workings of an enterprise, then you might speak differently. Your mother, for starters. You may think I just devoured her. Strung her up and cut her throat like a pig in a butcher's box. But no, I am not nearly so simple or cruel. Don't you understand that I plan to use her? She is part and parcel of my next great leap."

"Are you saying…my mother is alive?" I nearly croaked.

"Don't think I don't know who all of you are," the voice continued, dodging the question. "I've been inside your homes. I've seen you at your worst moments. When you've got your pants around your ankles. When you're crying yourselves to sleep. It's what I've learned to do. It's what I was taught by my friends here, in the beautiful universe above your heads, who showed me how to enter glass, to inhabit sound."

"You kidnapped our mothers," I said. "You killed Mrs. Duncan. You killed…my father."

"Doesn't sound like the work of a beautiful universe to me," said Lexi.

"Sentiments echoed and amplified," said the Gus Seraph.

"Oh," said the voice. "If only I could claim to the contrary. For yes, there is something about humanity that drives me to violence. It was when I discovered this amazing machine, really, that I began to understand why men kill. You'd think it's because of power or wealth, but really, it's because of meaning. Men want to know why they've been born into a body that dies almost as quickly as it lives. They want to know why the universe is cruel and why love is destructive. Those are the type of men that brought me down here. The type of men that drove my sweet wife to betray her nature and defy me. The type of men that made her steal my treasures. The type of men that made her drown herself off Goon's Cove."

"Your wife killed herself because she knew you were corrupt, alien scum," the Gus Seraph said. "You are the one that affected her derivative. Her skeleton speaks for itself."

"Her what?" For a moment, it was as if the entire dome trembled. Lexi and I gave the Gus Seraph a look that insinuated he should put the card he'd just played right back in his pocket. "Despite your intelligence, I'd caution you, Gus Mustus, against evoking my dear wife's memory. Especially since your mother will be used in her reawakening."

"Look, Mr...Mr. Myers, right?" I asked. "The only reason we came down here was to help the people we love. We're not looking for a fight. We just want to know—are our mothers...are they okay?"

"You called me Mr. Myers... Do you know how long it's been since I've thought of myself that way?"

I saw the figure in the mirror brighten for a moment, a phantom rediscovering its earthly form.

"It's incredible when you realize that who you've become killed off who you were. It's the noblest act of murder on the planet."

"We just want to know where they are," I said. "That's all."

"If that's all you want, then I think I can indulge you. All you need to do is look up, Mr. Eberstark. Read the writing on the wall."

Slowly, we all did so. The Gus Seraph used his visor to scan the room, and in a morbid series of seconds, the three of us came to understand what the voice had meant. In the flesh that covered the walls, captured and cocooned like tiny flies in a behemoth spider's web, we saw faces. Bodies. Perhaps a hundred. Perhaps more. Heads and feet dangled downwards, scum-slicked hair like spools of mold. Women, countless women, girls, too, sleeping inside a living nightmare. I couldn't believe I hadn't noticed them before. I must have taken them for more of the creature's clutter, strewn throughout this maze of junk. I saw that they were mostly concentrated above the mirror, turning its backdrop into a tapestry of tortured flesh.

The Gus Seraph activated the rocket thrusters on the soles of his feet and slowly began to lift off.

"I'd be careful about that, Mr. Mustus," said the voice. "I don't want to spill your mother's brains on the ground, but if you fly up here, I will end her in an instant. She's not as important as some of the others, and I do enjoy displays of discipline."

The Gus Seraph came back down to the ground.

"Why are you doing this?" Lexi asked. She didn't have her eyepatch on, and the Gus Seraph's plasma gun was at her side. "All these women…stuck here. You're feeding off them. You're surviving by stealing their lives away."

"No…no…I'm doing nothing of the sort. In fact, I am giving them a new life. An evolved existence they will enjoy at my side."

"How?" Lexi gestured to the women above. "How will this become life?"

"Lexi Navarro. Your sensitivity, though you don't acknowledge it, is enduring. It is why you were considered to contribute to this enterprise. Gus's mother very well may be used, but we didn't need her like we needed you. You are special."

"But I don't belong to you. None of these women do."

"You are correct. They belong to my wife."

Those words echoed throughout the cavern. As far as we understood, what was left of Thomas Hellwidth Myers' wife took the form of old bones and rags at the bottom of the Horn.

I chose my words carefully. "What do you mean, your wife? Isn't she… Hasn't she passed away by now?"

"I was not always the moral creature I am today." Gray shapes continued to flow through the mirror, the rise of an arm, the pale oval of a face. "My wife, she was all I had when I came to this part of the country. I was small-minded then like you, Mr. Eberstark. I looked at my life as short and painful, a limited number of seconds to produce a bit of success before I crawled into my coffin. But discovering this chasm changed all that. The artifact proved how stale and filthy our own world is. That should we learn how to speak a more complex language, we could create a more complex self.

"But my wife refused to follow me in my pursuit of higher meaning. The so-called monsters you've slaughtered in your streets…if you only knew the gifts I gave them. And more importantly, the gifts you took away. Granger. Kraft. Veltry. Oh, poor, troubled Veltry. He was just like you to begin with, you know. He was worse than you, come to think of it. A flesh-man dying of a terminal disease when his father plucked him from Crowstone Heights years ago. You wouldn't have recognized him from how sick and emaciated he'd been. He would have been six feet under by now if I hadn't offered him renewal. Renewal that turned him into a handsome creature. And so loyal too. If not for his and Kraft's faithful service, I'd have been unaware that people such as yourselves were attempting to destroy all my good work. He even told me that you children, along with your father..." I shuddered, "...discovered something beneath the Horn. Something he'd not been able to identify but whose presence frightened him. I dare inquire as to what it was you uncovered in that abyss, but since you've arrived at your final moments, I'm not going to pretend it matters."

I thought of what had happened to Father. "Dean Veltry was a monster. And he deserved to die. Just like you."

"Everyone deserves to die, little piggy," said the voice. "Why do you think I've lived in the darkness for so long? We've been enacting this process for years. Not too many have heard of it, even in Crowstone, where the cults gather, they don't know the details, but there are those who are familiar with old histories. Families whose respect for life runs deep and are willing to offer up their sons and daughters for the opportunity not to worry about disease."

"Okay, fine," said Lexi. "But what does any of that have to do with these women? With your wife?"

"Every time you talk about my wife, Ms. Navarro, I want to murder your friends a little quicker."

We went silent.

"But since you belong to her now and not me, I suppose you are owed a word or two. My wife, she could not abide the idea that I had discovered something so useful. For her, the earth she walked upon, the ugliness above with its factions and races and religions, was all she required to remain happy. It was naïve, of course, even ignorant. But our allegiances were so strong that they drove us apart. All I wanted was for her to if not join me, then entertain my vocation without constant admonishment. But no. Edwina was too attached to her seaside and sunlight. So attached she attempted to break me away from my discovery. To convince me I'd gone mad. To remove me from this new world below, where quiet is lord, and sound is sin."

The voice paused. I saw now a face in the mirror, a blurry, white face with hollows for eyes. Its mouth, it was frowning in an arc so sharp and grim it almost looked like Melpomene, the tragedy mask I'd learned about in Mrs. Duncan's class.

"Though it was not my intention, we fought often. She claims I did harm to her—physical harm—but I knew that her mind had created a conspiracy against me. Women are prone to thinking that a slap to the cheek is akin to abuse while at the same time, they long to be tamed into submission. That is why she stole something from me, so that I would show her where she truly belonged. If only what she took hadn't been something so important, something that couldn't be replaced, she may have enjoyed a different end."

"What did she steal?" I asked. It seemed as if the voice, the voice of what had once been Thomas Hellwidth Myers, didn't know about Edwina's notes. I exchanged knowing glances with the Gus Seraph and Lexi. These creatures were as blind as they were perceptive.

"Ah, wouldn't that be darling if I told you," the voice said. "But there's no need for me to carry on with past tragedies. Rest assured, dear Mr. Eberstark, that what she took from me was both precious and dangerous. She spit in the face of our lasting love together. She took it with her and left me note that said she'd be taking her own life off the coast of Goon's Cove to pay for her sins. In trying to take my passion away, she destroyed her own life. My love, my life, my infantile goddess."

"So what do you mean that I belong to her then?" said Lexi. "She's already dead, right?"

"Yes!" the voice bit out into the air. The entire cavern rumbled.

"Dead as Earth's future. But that's the miracle of this Artifact, Ms. Navarro. This gift from what gods birthed even the almighty. With it, I improve upon life."

What looked like two hands in the mirror rose upward, as if pantomiming the act of prayer.

"I started small. With frogs, pigeons, ducks. I'd combine them with iron or straw or even each other. I'd watch the results of my experiments and record their outcomes. As time went on, I'd have fetched for me new technologies from the surface, anything that could be used to strengthen my pursuit. See what happens when you combine a man with a piece of modern technology—unrefined steel and a sack of sulfur. See what happens when you combine a frog with a grasshopper and then combine that creature with barley and milk. I gradually realized that I could kill disease in such a fashion. That I could mix human beings with the materials they loved to produce, the materials that gave them the illusion of eternity in order to bring to life the dream of a deathless universe. How beautiful it must sound to you now as I tell it.

"The only problem with my pursuit, however, is that as one whose human roots still remained, I felt alone. It's one of the trappings I've never been able to escape, this longing for…connection. So I recruited those who could be thought to keep a secret. Residents of Crowstone whose allegiances to the Artifact go back as far as the mines went deep. I combined men with metal and metal with glass. I combined band saws and axes with crows and infant deer, growing a small squadron of loyal devotees. We didn't love each other, but camaraderie can be fashioned from lesser emotions.

"As time went on, I learned my capacity for this science grew. Grew until I could simply combine humans together…though that process was far more delicate than others. I learned that if the combination I offered was not cohesive or bonding that it would produce nothing less than a monstrosity, typically with suicidal tendencies. That's why I set out on my latest pursuit. I thought the reason Edwina had not been able to trust my methods was that I couldn't show them how safe and effective they could be. In order to prove my point, I would have to recreate Edwina herself."

The voice ceased. Lexi, the Gus Seraph, and I lingered for a moment on the words.

"So effectively." Lexi gripped the plasma pistol with her hand. "You've abducted countless women and girls, terrorized our town, and put yourself into some crazy mirror contraption so that you can recreate a copy of your dead wife?"

"My wife," the miry voice growled. I saw a form flash to life in the mirror. Two wide maniac's eyes, a flair of raven-black hair. "*Will* be brought back to life. She will not be a *copy*. She will be recreated to perfection. Just like she was before—even improved. The only difference this time is that she will know I was correct. That my work was not for nothing. And she will sit beside me, to hear and cherish my whispers. Together, we will develop a new world. I have spent years compiling appropriate data. It turns out recreating a person is far more difficult than I'd once thought but not impossible. You only need adjust the ingredients correctly."

"Well." Lexi shrugged. "I'm sorry. But that's just stupid."

"Uh, Lexi?" I said.

"No. It is. You're going to take my life and their mothers' lives and other mothers' and children's lives just so you can entertain some psychotic fantasy? A psychotic fantasy, by the way, that can never be realized. Do you want to know *why* that is?"

"Corporal Navarro?" the Gus Seraph said.

"Because *you* were the one who turned her away. You were the one who drove her to mistrust. You were the one who didn't know her to begin with, and you *are* the one who doesn't know her even now, almost two hundred years later. And I'll tell you another thing, pal." Lexi put her eye patch back on. "She told us to come down here in the first place. We found her body—in the Horn, motherfucker, not in Goon's Cove. Because why? Because she lied to you. Because she was looking to end your ass, and she gave us the tools to do it. You're not trying to recreate your wife…"

"Lexi, please," I said.

"You're trying to create someone to reflect your image. I mean, for shit's sake—you live inside a mirror!" she crowed. "You're a reflection of yourself—a goddamned joke, haunting teenage girls at home and driving middle-aged women to suicide. And if you do somehow succeed with this bullshit plan, if we all die down here, crushed by some bloodthirsty, thirty-clawed hellbeast, then I promise, when you put me into that witch's cauldron you call a machine with all those other ladies, no matter what happens, no matter how small of a piece of that creature you create I happen to become, I swear to God." She spat. "I will ruin your ass."

The dome rumbled.

"Ah, shit," I said.

"I assume you were not trained in diplomacy, Corporal," said the Gus Seraph.

"You are correct, Captain," said Lexi with a salute.

"In the tank before you," the voice said with an added edge, "are the most recent products of my alchemy. You may know them. Actually, I'm quite sure that you do."

With a steaming hiss, the middle tank's door opened. The ones at its side seemed empty now. The arcane stuff of their transformation had been transferred to the center.

"Ready your arms, soldiers," said the Gus Seraph.

Lexi pumped the pistol and pointed it at the tank's door.

The creature that came from it had to duck down to squeeze out its terrible bulk. Steam enveloped its fleshy, white form, rising above it in a sulfuric cloud. As the moisture cleared, two long, thick legs emerged into the bloody light. They unfolded to almost half the height of the dome. Its feet were shoed into what looked to be pointed clogs, and the knees caps raised to sharp wedges. On top of the legs sat a short, thick torso and chest. Both were clothed in a metallic version of what I realized, immediately, was Charlene Poughkeepsie's red tracksuit. I would have recognized the outfit anywhere. The red, zippered up Aviva sweat suit. The only difference between it and what the creature wore was that it could have been comprised of palladium.

Its stomach bulged out fat and far, and the head…the head was a yin-yin of ugly. Unlike the other creatures I'd seen, this one seemed to reflect its human hosts. And because of that, we could see it was made up of not just one host but two. I could see Charlene Poughkeepsie's sadistic smile right alongside Joe Ross' incoherent grimace. A set of pigtails topped the otherwise bald bone of its scalp, and a wolf's snout erupted from its center. At the elbow of its left arm began a large shingling hatchet, and at the elbow of its right arm began a serrated, metal hook.

I noticed as this creature stepped before us, towering over our shoulders in this dome of madness, that this was everything I'd hated about high school. That before me was not just a monster created by a machine beyond our understanding, but a monster out of my darkest imagination. Suddenly, I felt as if even Mother couldn't protect me. That even with a powerful entity wrapped around my arm, I wouldn't be saved.

"Charlene Poughkeepsie and Joe Ross," the voice said. "Whose parents, and their parents before that, have maintained steadfast allegiance to the silence. Though you mock my genius, you will now understand how small your dreams are. Lexi, you will follow your glorious destiny. And as for Mr. Eberstark and Mr. Mustus? Your screams will die beneath the earth."

"Eeeeeeeberstark," the creature said. Half of its mouth rose in a wry smirk. The sound of its voice was something in between male and female. Something high-pitched that was reminiscent of Charlene Poughkeepsie but tinged with the blunt masculinity of Joe Ross. "Do you think we should hurt him, Jooooooooe?"

The other half of its mouth twisted in confusion.

"Hurt...hurt...hurt..."

"Fat boy, Eberstark," the other half snarled. "Time to pay yourrrr dues, piggy. Time to pay your duessss."

"Oink oink," the other half of the face said.

"Oink...*OINK*."

SEVEN

I REMEMBERED MY FIRST DAY AT Myers High.
I came into the cafeteria from a door that led outside to the courtyard, where on a nice day, you could sit on the grass and gaze from a distance upon the waters of Goon's Cove. It was cold even for early autumn, and I'd not worn a warm enough coat. My hair was mussed up from the wind. I could feel hundreds of eyes on me.

Trying to slip quietly in line and grab a food tray, I attempted not to notice the gap that was made between me and other students who didn't want to associate with a new kid whose looks weren't sterling, whose chubby cheeks were frosted pink, and whose scraggly facial hair stained his top lip.

After I retrieved two squares of tepid pizza and an ice cream sandwich, I scanned the cafeteria for seats. Most of the tables were taken up, but one at the very end, in the corner beside the lone Myers High vending machine, was nearly empty. All save for a scrawny boy

THE SILENT END

with dark skin, wearing a button up shirt.

I sat down at the opposite end of his table. He barely looked up at me, eating a slow and distracted lunch. He dipped a tater tot in ketchup and, upon examining it, set it back down. He was reading a book whose cover featured a horde of men with swords fighting aliens. It was hardbound with the words, *Sword Star, 2nd Edition* emblazoned in industrial steel lettering.

I watched him read, trying to pretend I had something to preoccupy myself with as well. I took one of our brand new *Eberstark's* coupon books from my backpack and opened it. I went through the pages—fabric softener twenty percent off, two for one cans of baked beans. I did this, of course, until I realized how stupid it was. No one was interested in groceries. Not even Father.

"Hey," I whispered, but he didn't hear me. I took a bite of my pepperoni pizza and leaned forward.

"Hey," I said a little louder.

"Oh." The boy glanced up briefly from his book. His eyebrows raised. "Hey."

"You play Sword Star?"

He looked up again, this time a little more interested.

"Yes," he said as if it was obvious. "Why, do you?"

"Hell yeah," I lied. "It's my favorite game."

"Really?" He smiled a little, folding the book closed and placing it in front of him. It clapped shut, and I inhaled the smell of paper and glue. "Who do you play with?"

I froze.

"I mean, um…anyone."

"No, no." He giggled and shook his head. "I mean, which race do you play with?"

"Race?"

"Like Human, Xeno, Lorque, Dwarf, Gelding…"

"Oh, race!" I smiled nervously. "Uh, Human. I play human. Yeah."

"Me too! I think they're the most effective in tower defense campaigns, which is what the tournaments focus on. Though I've always been partial towards Galdars from an aesthetic standpoint. I like the way their speeders look with those bifurcated cannon mounts." He snorted happily at the thought. "Hey, what's your name?"

"Eberstark."

"Eberstark? I've never heard a name like that before."

I scratched my head. "It's my last name. It's what people call me."

"Why?"

"I don't know. I guess because I don't like my first name that much."

"Cool. Well, Eberstark, I'm Gus. Gus Mustus."

We ate our respective meals for a moment, me inhaling my pizza and him futzing with his tots.

"You want to make a game happen?" Gus asked. "Like a match?"

"Uh, sure. When are you thinking?"

"Maybe this weekend. I'm trying to get ahead on my Bio homework, but no guarantees."

"You already have homework on the first day of school?"

"Oh, no." He shook his head. "Not *homework* homework. I just tend to read the textbooks for the semester during the first week to familiarize myself with the material."

"You do what?"

"You'll be more prepared when things come up at a later date even if you don't understand them at first. My dad taught me that trick." He smiled proudly. "He's an academic."

"A what?"

"Oh, an academic. You know, like someone who works at a university."

"I don't even know if my dad went to college."

"Well, it doesn't really matter in the long run." He ate the tater tot. "Hey, watch out!"

Someone knocked against Gus's chair as she passed by, almost causing him to spill his ketchup cup. I looked up at the perpetrator. It was a girl with an eyepatch and long, dark hair hunched over a load of books she carried in her arms. She practically ran out of the cafeteria and disappeared into what I'd come to know as Myers East without a word.

"The nerve of some people," Gus said. "Like we don't live in a society. I swear, you'd think some people were raised without basic ethics. I'm glad I picked up Spinoza this year before I started school. For where I'd be now without that, I do not know."

"Yeah," I laughed uneasily. "Ethics."

I looked at Gus. I wanted to know where he learned about stuff like ethics and how he knew about people called Spinoza, who I assumed was some Spanish chef. I even wanted to know how he talked like he did. I wanted to know all those things and more until the ground began to shift.

"Gus?" I said.

"Hey man. Everything okay?"

The cafeteria wavered with heat as if it had turned into an oven. I tried to keep my feet on the ground. The tables warped, and Gus's body began to stretch. My pizza bent in half and flapped into the air like a cheese-covered bat. I didn't know where I was going. I didn't even know where I was.

"I'll see you this weekend, Eberstark," I heard Gus say. "Don't forget to bring your *kiiiiiiiiiit...*"

Something in a remote part of my consciousness told me I was in the middle of a Murje black out. I couldn't find my way back to my body, to the dome, the red light. That hooked arm attached to the Charlene/Joe creature could be sweeping toward my throat. All I saw in the air before me was a pair of lenses. Black and thick. They became sunglasses. Ray Bans. I could hear the sound of drilling, earth-rending coils dredging rock, and I felt my body nearing a presence far greater than my own. I imagined I was soaring through the skies above Mossglow. I saw Myers High and plummeted toward it then past it, toward Goon's Cove, where I penetrated the ground. My body impacted the surface like a depth charge, and I was powering through layers of earth. I heard my friends' voices. Heard them pleading. Heard them telling me to get out of the way. But I couldn't reach them. All I could see were the Ray Bans in the chaotic air before me. I reached out with both hands, fingers reaching, until finally, diving forward, I took them in my hands.

I returned to my body with a fearsome jolt. The monster's hammer arm was coming down above my head. The Gus Seraph was running for me, and Lexi was tugging at my arm. I lost my breath and saw the end of all I'd been. All I could think about was that day in the cafeteria when I met Gus. The day I first thought I could be someone other than who I was.

I closed my eyes, hoping it would be over quick, but felt nothing. I opened my eyes again and looked up. The creature was staring at the ceiling, at what looked to be a drill, an actual drill, plowing through the top of the dome.

"It's him," said Lexi.

"Who?" said Gus.

With a *boom*, the Shepherd, in the shape of a tank with a spiral of metal at its head, pounded through the very top of the dome, right next to the Living Artifact, and hurtled through, crashing down atop the Charlene/Joe creature. It landed right on its shoulders, splitting the gangly thing's body nearly in two from throat to groin before embedding itself in the ground. I suddenly felt like I could move again and opened fire, the silver orbs impacting the left part the body. Gus, with his flaming sword, ripped apart the right.

At the base of the creature's spine, exposed to the air, was a tangle of human flesh. Charlene and Joe folded together, wrapped in each other's arms and legs. Their heads touched at the side, melded at the cheeks, and their lips and eyes were jumbled. Murje dripped down their chins.

"No," they screamed, sobbing and crying. "No—this wasn't, wasn't, wasn't supposed to happen."

Lexi marched up, removing her knife from her back pocket.

"We didn't mean to," said the lips that belonged to Charlene—long, thin, filled with tiny teeth. "It, it, it…wasn't what we thought. They said we'd be st-st-strong. They said we'd live long. They, they, they, they said it would help the town… P-p-please don't hurt us. I'm…I'm scared."

"Sc-sc-sc-scared," said the lips that belonged to Joe Ross.

Lexi seemed to take pity for a moment, but then something else, something darker, took over.

"No!" shouted Charlene as Lexi, beholding to the promise she'd made the night we went to back to the cave, took one of the girl's ears in her fingers and, with a grunt, sliced it off. A flash of eggy blood squirted into the air.

"It hurts!" screamed Joe Ross. "It burns!"

Lexi then took the ear and, with a grimace, stuffed it into Charlene Poughkeepsie's mutated mouth. "Chew."

Joe Ross screamed, and Charlene spit up blood and flesh.

"Finish it, Eberstark," she said.

Nodding, I stood before them and brought up my cannon. I felt a moment of hesitation, not wishing to end anyone's life, not even Charlene Poughkeepsie's and Joe Ross' regardless of the torture they'd planned to put us through. But what these two were now was beyond saving. Not human, not Collector, not anything but disrupted flesh. Taking a deep breath, I leveled the canon at them, at these former specters of Myers High. The orb pulsed from the muzzle, and their screams ended. Their delusions defused.

The Shepherd, looking beyond banged up with its drill lodged in the stone a few yards behind the beast, opened its hatch. Smoke hissed from inside; flames flickered within. A hand appeared on the rim of the hatch, and I saw a bone-white fedora. With a leap, the Hat in his seersucker suit emerged from the Shepherd and landed before the stairs leading up to the throne. His suit was unblemished as always. He was enraged—I hadn't seen him like that before—and in his left hand, he held an object of thrilling beauty. An object that steamed with gaseous light. It was Edwina's pistol, yet it looked brighter than before. The grooves in its barrel now revealed movement shuttering inside, like a fan beneath a grate. And where once was an empty gap now shone a white-hot cylinder.

The Hat stepped up to the mirror, to the ghastly figure shaking within. He held up a piece of paper in his hand, taken from his notebook.

Jig's up, fuck-o. You've had too much ice cream.

"What are you holding in your hand, Non Entity?" the voice snarled. Calm had left it. It was scared.

"I think you know exactly what it is, Thomas Hellwidth Myers," I yelled. "Your unstable element. The doomsday device *you* created."

"And since you are alien scum," said the Gus Seraph. "It is high time you know that your beloved wife is the one who led us to its location."

"She sure does love you," said Lexi, aiming her pistol toward the mirror. "Enough that she asked us to kill you. And not only that but to bring your entire 'enterprise' to an end. Isn't that just the tops?"

The Hat lifted the gun up and aimed it above him, toward the organism on the ceiling, whose undercurrent of life now whirled with activity.

"If you do not drop that weapon right now," said the voice. "I will release all of these women to their deaths."

The Hat let the gun fall to his side and dropped his head to his shoulder.

"That's a good piece of nothing. Now, drop the weapon."

The Hat, nodding, set Edwina's pistol to the ground. We all took a deep breath.

"Now, come toward the mirror. Slowly."

The Hat obliged, taking two steps up the stairs before stopping.

"Closer."

But the Hat didn't move closer. He just looked into the mirror. To where a ghostly apparition curled its fists. He then turned to me, Gus, and Lexi. He raised a hand and waved.

"Hat," I said. "What are you doing?"

He didn't respond. Instead, he crouched on one knee.

"Ah, I see," said the voice from the mirror. "That's a good boy. Now, which one of your friends should I have kill you? Leverage is a mighty element, isn't it? If you have enough of it, you can wager against the world."

The Hat didn't move his legs, but he put one hand on his fedora.

"Now, this is just getting ridiculous. You stupid creatures and your etiquette. I don't need your hat. I need your life."

The Hat, without hesitation, removed the fedora with a click and set it on the ground. He aimed his head at the mirror, revealing the darkness inside him. At first, it was dormant, a pool of black in the emptiness of his head. But then, it began to leak out. Strands of blackness whorled out toward the mirror, stretching into tendrils that looked like smoke.

"What are you doing?" The man in the mirror was panicked. His face contorted in anger. "I'll drop them all—I'll kill all of you!"

He was making an attempt to pull at what looked like levers behind the glass, but the darkness emanating from the Hat's head penetrated the surface and gripped the man's wrists. A wrestling between two kinds of smoke then began, the man behind the mirror yowling as the darker tendrils encircled his body. The Hat himself pulled back as if wrangling a bull, yanking the man toward the glass.

At first, Hellwidth's body slammed against the mirror with a dull clunk. The Hat dug his feet into the ground and pulled harder and harder still. They went back and forth, the man in the mirror screaming hideously. A moment later and accompanied by a slurping sound, a form came kicking and screaming from the glass. It didn't look human. It didn't even looked solid in its form. It looked like musculature, like a collection of veins drained of blood that only formed the shape of a human being. The tendrils of darkness continued to drag the creature down the steps. It wailed and spit, snarled and dug its fingers into the stone, trying to stave off the inevitable. The Hat swung his head back, wrenching the monster toward him until, with a howl, it was dragged inside the Hat's head.

"No!" it screamed. "No! I won't go in there! I won't go back!"

Its hands reached out for something to grapple. But it was no use. Its feet disappeared inside the Hat. Followed by its legs, torso, and chest, all snapping and breaking. It tried to grab onto the sides of the Hat's face but relinquished in one last, squirming flail. A moment later, it was inside him.

The Hat put his fedora back on and turned to us.

Scribbling a letter on his notepad, he held up the following:

Your dreams protect you more than you know.
Don't ever relinquish your right to sleep.

A second later, his body grew white-hot with heat and, standing peacefully with his hands at his sides, the Hat exploded.

"Hat!" I screamed as the body boomed apart.

Left behind in the sizzling aftermath was a man. A nude man whose skin was the color of Styrofoam. Thomas Hellwidth Myers. Or what he'd once been. The same man, I began to think, I'd seen in the photo with a woman, perhaps his wife, in the basement of Stumart. His eyes were crazed, and his mouth was empty of teeth. His scraggly hair was matted to his head. His nudeness revealed how bony he was. He was shaking and covered in a rime of moisture, like babies when they're born.

"What the hell?" Lexi coughed, fanning smoke from her eyes.

He turned to look at us. He seemed confused. Even stupid. The

Gus Seraph raised his sword, and Lexi took her plasma pistol to his head. I, too, aimed my cannon as he looked at the glowing gun at his feet.

"Don't you even fucking think about it," Lexi said.

But there were no words that could have convinced him against what he did next. Thomas Hellwidth Myers' skeletal fingers reached for Edwina's pistol. He then picked it up and aimed it at us. It seemed like he was trying to speak but couldn't .

"Lower the weapon, and you will increase your chances of survival, villain," said the Gus Seraph.

The gun continued to rattle in Myers' hand. I tensed up. I had no idea what would happen if he fired.

"Just hand it over," I said. "We can talk about this like human beings."

"Like…human…beings," he managed to say. His voice was tiny, disparaged. It sounded like a toddler's voice.

He looked at me, opened his black, rheumy eyes, and drooled. He then took Edwina's pistol, aimed it at the Living Artifact, and, with a howl, fired.

EIGHT

WHEN HE PULLED THE TRIGGER, the air blazed white. The Living Artifact could have been smashed by a gigantic fist. Its hard, ruby-like exterior swelled inward with a round, knuckle-like force. With a crackle, it then ruptured. Fluid gushed from within. It hit the floor right on top of Myers with an impact so gargantuan we were all flung from our feet. The red, gelatinous mass of material began to shimmer with electricity. We saw Myers' body for a second, bathed in the red. At first, he seemed enthralled until his skin melted away. It was only a second more before his bones disintegrated.

"We have to get out of here," Lexi screamed.

"We have to get our mothers first," I screamed back.

The Gus Seraph, with a cyborgian cry, surged to the ceiling, flying frantically. Lexi and I ran up the stairs toward the mirror, trying to make out faces in the wall. Meanwhile, the red fluid from the Living Artifact was swirling around the room. It moved like it was alive and was growing in size.

"There are so many of them," Lexi said, looking at all the women. She was crying. "We can't leave them here!"

"Lexi," I yelled. "Look!"

Hanging about ten feet off the ground, right beyond the top of the mirror, embedded in the flesh of the wall, was Mother. I knew it was her even enwrapped as she was in skin and slime. I saw her nose, her lovely, crooked nose, her darkened eyelids, all like mine. My heart felt as if it would rip from my chest, grow fists, and beat the living crap out of me.

"Let's get her," Lexi said.

We climbed atop Myers' tall tyrant's chair. I boosted Lexi on top of my shoulders so that she arrived just about at Mother's foot. She took her knife and, as carefully as she could, flexed her feet so that she could reach the flesh that trapped her. She began slicing.

"Hurry up, Lexi," I shouted as, looking over my back, I saw the engorged alien element growing, rippling with static electricity.

"I am!" she screamed. Black fluid from the skin splattered our faces as she cut.

The Gus Seraph came soaring down from the ceiling. His eyes blazed with tears. In his arms, he held his mother. She was covered in a black fluid as well and looked to be unconscious.

"We must evacuate the premises," he commanded.

"We know, Gus," Lexi yelled. "Little help?"

From Gus's visor singed a tiny laser beam that finished cutting Mother from the wall. She fell from her perch, and I caught her in my arms. Nearly all of her life had been drained from her. She'd been trapped in this stasis for such a long time. I wondered if she dreamed now. Or if she'd even be able to wake up. Who knew what evil things had been pumped into her system to keep her in this state?

The mass was erupting now, the ground shaking. I knew that at any moment, the dome would cave in.

"How are we going to get out of here?" Lexi yelled. She watched as the Shepherd was consumed by the red tide. It lurched spasmodically as if to resist its death before melting into metal glaze.

The Gus Seraph spread his arms and legs. "Hold on tight."

Lexi and I clung to the Gus Seraph's legs. In each of his arms, he held the mothers. His rocket thrusters began to lift us off the ground.

"But what about the rest of them?" screamed Lexi. "We can't just let them die down here!"

But the choice wasn't ours to make. The flood of death swept towards us. It seemed to be killing everything it touched. The leftovers of the bullies were consumed, as were the tanks, the cables, and generators. The Gus Seraph powered upward. We felt our stomachs sink. We rocketed through the hole the Shepherd had drilled through and rose up through layers of earth. A flood of red rose beneath us. The Gus Seraph continued to rise.

"Quicker," I squealed.

The Gus Seraph opened its mouth to scream, and a second later, we felt fresh air on our faces. We whizzed out of the depths, careering above the beach of Goon's Cove. The hole had been dug right on the shore. We kept on rising and rising more into a murky Mossglow afternoon until we turned and banked inland.

"We made it," Lexi sobbed. "We're alive."

As we flew past the Cove, however, toward a stretch of green between it and Myers High, the Gus Seraph's rocket boots began to rupture. They sputtered at first until their burn was lost. The armor, it began to come apart. I noticed at that point that my arm was doing the same, the jellyfish squiggling from my flesh and popping off into the air.

"We're going down!" The Gus Seraph had begun to sound a lot more like just Gus.

"Hold on," Lexi yelled.

We plowed into the grass.

The Gus Seraph was able to keep the mothers safe as he landed. The second he set them down, however, the rest of his armor toppled off him like an outfit ten times too big for his body, leaving what looked like a pile of trash at his feet. The highly mechanized parts of his suit now were now little more than plastic pieces of a what could have been a Halloween costume. The octopus on my shoulder, using the last of its life to keep Lexi and me from injuring ourselves upon landing, crumbled into sand, and the cannon on my arm broke apart into pieces of moldy driftwood. All that remained was Mother's charm bracelet on my wrist.

The ground shook, and we saw a fountain of red emerge from the hole we'd come through on Goon's Cove. And then a louder shake still as it sank back into it, and the entire beach began to collapse. We found ourselves at a safe distance as we watched the shore disappear into the earth. A jagged cave-in then crumbled along the beach, toward Myers High.

"Oh no." Gus's normal voice had returned.

Myers High crumbled to the ground.

"Well, high school *is* terrible," Lexi said as each floor collapsed upon itself, raising a mountain of dirt and dust.

"I hated high school before I even knew what it was," I said.

"But how are we going to graduate?" Gus was teary eyed.

"Let's leave that worry for tomorrow, okay?" said Lexi.

As Myers High crashed into the ground, level by level, the last part to collapse was the roof. The one part of the building none of us had seen. On the very top, hiding from view, was indeed, as the rumors went, another statue of a frog. It was similar to the one at the lee of Myers High, where we'd traveled into the silent end. But unlike its twin, its mouth was closed, and its eyes were filled with terror.

PART FIVE
FRENCH TOAST

EPILOGUE

FRENCH TOAST.

It's been a long time since anyone's made me French toast. It's been a long time since anyone's made me anything, and when I wake to sounds and smells coming from the kitchen that aren't disgusting or dangerous, I almost want to cry.

Mother isn't a domestic type. It was one of the things she and Father used to fight about, her inability to "maintain a home." Funny that I never really knew what that meant. She likes to work hard and doesn't see a kitchen as a woman's rightful place. But if maintaining a home means knowing how to put clothes on my back, keeping food in our stomachs, and being generally awesome, then she belongs on the cover of one of those domestic values magazines.

I run downstairs. As has been the case in the days since Myers High collapsed, outside, we are experiencing a nice day. Of course, the mist isn't gone. The mist will never be gone. But it is better now. Thinner. You can actually see sun in the morning, and by mid-afternoon, if you're lucky, the wind carries the clouds out over Goon's Cove, and a blue sky opens overhead.

It's been a couple of months now since the silent end. All of that darkness and quiet feels like a drug-induced vision—not just for Gus and Lexi and I but for the entire town.

Gus's mother woke up soon after the collapse, almost as soon as the debris cleared. Her eyes shot open, and she began screaming. When the school crumbled, the ground opened up all across Mossglow. Parts of Graywood Forest were sucked into craters, and Goon's Cove was practically laid to waste. People were killed. Houses toppled in the Lowers, and a section of Crowstone Heights slid into the sea when a cliff broke off. Emergency crews from around the state were immediately dispatched, and hundreds of our citizens were rushed off to Ozark Medical for emergency treatment. There was so much chaos that few could provide a coherent account of what had happened. It's not like earthquakes are common in our part of the country, and the damage areas were unusual.

The trenches formed the shape of a spiral. Investigations were carried out at a later point but didn't find anything but a large honeycomb structure beneath the town's surface. Nothing that once lived there survived the fallout from that night. Soon after came the strange red flowers. The ones with faces on their petals…

Gus's mother awoke early the next morning and checked out of the hospital. She had memory loss of the previous two days and cloudy recollections from the weeks before that. Mother's recovery was a slower process. I stayed with the Mustus family at night, picking away at take-out Chinese food and passing time with Gus. Marshall was fully revived by that point, snapped out of his trance. Not at all distant and quiet like before, he became quick, energetic, and eager to engage with others. He challenged me to a game of chess and, when I told him I didn't play, insisted to teach me that very night. After the silent end collapsed, he came to remind me a lot of Gus.

A lot of things changed after the silent end collapsed. People, they moved faster. They talked louder.

I continued to come back to the hospital only to see Mother sleeping quietly. Sometimes, she whimpered as if having a bad dream. A week later, she awoke. The first time she opened her eyes, I was sitting in a chair right beside her, flipping through *PC Gamer* magazine. Our eyes met, and I burst into tears, hugging her so hard a nurse eventually had to pry me away. As she did so, we realized that Mother wasn't hugging me back. She could barely move. She definitely couldn't speak. At first, it was as if she couldn't think either. But over the next week, she started pointing and making sounds with her throat. Soon after that, she was gesturing. Eventually, she uttered words.

"M…Morrison?" was the first thing she said. It took me a second to understand what she meant, until I realized she was asking about Father.

Teary-eyed, I explained to her what had happened in the Horn. After that, I decided to tell her everything else as well from the day she disappeared to the moment she awoke. I told her about evil penumbras, and Murje. I told her about monsters and the mass on Mr. Kraft's wall. I began telling her about Mrs. Duncan when she waved her hand at me to stop. I would have understood if she'd have wanted never to think about what had happened to her down below the surface again. Later, she'd tell me that she couldn't recall much. That the previous months had been a long, sad, now-forgotten dream.

Before long, she was speaking in full sentences. In a trend that worried everyone at first, she also launched into random fits of laughter. Huge belly gusts I hadn't heard since Cleveland.

We returned home and went about our daily lives. Or at least tried to. Odd types began coming around the house, slick smelling men in button-down shirts and blazers, asking questions about Mother's whereabouts for the last year. The two of us adapted a story that involved problems between her and Father, causing her to stay with her sister in Seattle. It had only been coincidence that she arrived the day before the earthquake with the aims of sorting out her old life. After discussion with the Mustus family, along with Lexi and her mother, who were also receiving these unpleasant visits, we adopted alibis. It wasn't that we were afraid of letting others know about what happened below the city. We just didn't think they'd understand.

The second step in Mother's reentry into the world was to establish control over Stumart. She began only a month after she was discharged from the hospital but had so much energy she worked six days a week. She doesn't get sad anymore. Or at least like she used to.

After working at Stumart for a few months, she made the decision to sell the store and move to Colorado at the end of the year, where some of her family lives. Not just because of what happened in Mossglow but because she applied and on her first try got into the law school at the University of Denver.

"Honey," Mother calls out to me as I land on the bottom of the stairs come down the stairs. I hear plates clinking in the kitchen. "Breakfast!"

I stop for a moment and peek into the kitchen, watch her lean over the stove. For a second, whether I want to or not, I can't help but think about Father.

Though his name was the first thing that came out of her mouth after she awoke from her sleep, she can't seem to say it anymore. I don't bring him up. Practically every time she runs into someone from town, someone that used to know her, she tells the same story of a dysfunctional marriage. And whenever someone asks about what happened to Morrison?

"He died in the earthquake. The only thing we found of his was his hat."

The answer tends to work and is at least partially true. The hat was found after the quake in the wreckage of Myers High but not by me. It was Ronald Peterson, of all people, I saw wearing it down at Tinos one night. After bribing him with a new set of Siege Hornets, I was able to convince him to give it back. Apparently, he and his father went scavenging near the quake site and have a whole host of things stashed in the hoarder dungeon they call a basement.

The hat is all we have left of Father now. Though Mother tries not to talk about him, sometimes she hears a creak in the floorboards upstairs, the normal groans of a normal old house, and she worries. She doesn't like to speak about the silent end either or the night terrors she has from time to time. She is home. She is alive. The past is dead and gone.

Mother is already piling the French toast in a steaming heap atop a large, white serving plate when I arrive.

"Morning," I say. She doesn't respond. She just pulls two glasses and a mug from the cupboard. The glasses she fills up with orange juice and the mug with coffee for herself.

"Can I have some too? Coffee?"

Mother sets down the orange juice in front of me. "Sure. But you can get it yourself."

I pour myself a mug and add cream. The coffee is an Italian blend that comes out of a silver can. It's all she buys now, and she drinks a lot of it, as if she can never be awake enough.

I put the half and half back in the refrigerator and return to the table.

"Bon appetite." Mother smiles and opens the Saturday paper in front of her. As she scans the headlines with one finger, her other hand forks a piece of French toast onto her plate, which she then drenches in syrup.

I take my first bite and make an "Mmmmmmm" sound.

"Glad you like it." She flips through the paper. It's the *Mossglow Sentry*, delivered now to our house daily. *The New York Times* also comes on Sunday, and sometimes, we get the *Wall Street Journal*.

"Hey, kiddo." She points at an article. "Did you see this?"

She lifts up the paper so I can see the headline.

MORE MYSTERY FLOWERS DISCOVERED BY EARTHQUAKE SITE

"More, huh?" I say uneasily.

Below the headline, alongside an article, is a color photograph of an exotic-looking, red flower. I almost turn my head; looking at those things still makes me wobbly in the knees. Its stem is green and normal-looking, but its petals twist into elaborate shapes. Shapes that look like faces, women's faces. Some of them grin, some of them glower, some of them grit their teeth or gaze sadly downwards. The faces are so detailed and haunting they are impossible to look at without feeling unsettled. It's partially because of them that the men in button-down shirts keep returning.

"And apparently it's just as large as the last ones they found," Mother says. "Ten feet tall, can you believe it?"

"Did they find this one around Myers High?"

"Yep. And another near Goon's Cove too. They've been finding so many of them during the rebuild that they're thinking about placing the new high school closer to the old Hinterlord factory. I guess that would make more sense for the bus routes. It was always such an inconvenience, trucking everyone out to the Cove. And the weather there…don't even get me started. Always cold. Always wet. No proper place for a school."

After what we've been through, it doesn't surprise me that whatever evolved from the remains of that alien machine would exhibit anything but unusual tendencies. But I can't look at the faces on the flowers. Not after seeing them on the wall.

"Anyways." She turns to the next page, to a story about an ongoing proposal to merge Mossglow with Ozark County. "Are you heading off to your tournament soon?"

"Yes ma'am." I shake bad thoughts from my head, fork my third piece of French toast and drown it in syrup. "Pick up's at ten. We've made it into the finals. Looks like we might even take home an Obsidian Tower this year."

"I don't know what you're talking about." Mother sips her coffee. "But as long as you're not smoking cocaine, that's fine."

I look at her. We are at home. Safe. Our entire lives ahead of us. And even if an occasional glint of darkness blooms in her eyes, the moment passes.

An hour and a half later, Gus Mustus shows up at my front door. I am running a little late, hopping into a pair of jeans in my bedroom.

"Hey, handsome," I hear Mother say downstairs. "Decided what school you're going to yet? I know my good for nothing's taking a semester to think about it, but to be honest." She lowers her voice as if I won't hear. "Maybe you can convince him otherwise? What else worthwhile does an eighteen-year-old have to do but study?"

"I couldn't agree more," I hear Gus say.

"And your mother? She's well?"

"She's great."

"And your father?"

"Just finished his book."

"I'm sure you'll it won't be long before you're doing the same thing."

Before I leave my room, I look at Father's hat, Grandfather's hat. I keep it on the dresser next to my windowsill, next to Mother's charm bracelet. The bracelet I put on, but the hat I just touch, pinching the rim and taking a deep breath.

We wave goodbye to Mother from Gus's van. The trunk is already packed with Sword Star paraphernalia, our entire human army with our Thunder Tanques decked out in a coat of Sandblaster Yellow 6.

"Did you finish the new Seraph?" I ask Gus.

"Kinda." He puts the car into drive. Though it's only been a couple months since the silent end, he looks to have grown. Not taller, but thicker. "I don't know. I just couldn't bring myself to finish it off."

"Seriously? How are we going to enter the tournament without—?"

"I'm fucking with you, Eberstark." Gus sarcasm is more common to Lexi than himself. But then again, we've all borrowed parts of each other since Halloween. "Of course it's finished. Check it out."

Gus nods to a plastic case at my feet with six compartments. I pick it up and examine the Demigods. Though all are as detailed as they were months ago when Gus finished them, the new Crow Seraph he's taken to the next level. With a basecoat of yellow, he used plaster to simulate little pieces of skin, which he then painted green and overlaid with tiny streaks of red blood. The sword blazes brighter now than ever, and I notice something peculiar in the face. It looks a lot like Gus's own.

"Nice work."

"I upgraded my magnifying glass. And my mom bought me an entire set of new brushes after I got my acceptance letter."

I marvel at the last part of that sentence. "Brown. Man. I thought that place was make-believe, like wizard school or something. Didn't you get a scholarship too?"

"Partial. It's something at least."

"Hey." I put my hand on his shoulder. "You've done more than a dumb fuck like me can ever dream of."

"Look, Eberstark. You are a fuck, but you've really got to stop with the dumb stuff. You're applying to college next year." He pulls out a piece of paper, folded in half, and hands it to me. On it is written the names of multiple schools from San Francisco State to some local community colleges.

"You have to stop listening to my mom," I say.

"Just look at some of them. It'll help when I start bugging you in September. All you've got to do is apply. You'll get in. And then, you and me, we'll conquer the world."

The first stop we make is by Ajay Kapur's house, a nice, somewhat spare Upper Thicks townhouse the color of a green tea latte. He and Ronald are waiting outside, holding lock boxes that contain their Galdar armies. Ajay looks at the van with a dour expression as we roll up—we're running a few minutes behind. Ronald inhales a king-sized Snickers like some sort of jungle snake as they climb into the car.

"How is it at seventeen you get to drive?" says Ajay as he buckles his seatbelt.

"Eighteen in a month," Gus says.

"My parents won't even let me get my permit."

"No, man, you don't get it. That's *a good* thing," says Ronald through his chocolate-filled braces. "Once you get a license, you're officially registered with the government."

"So?" says Ajay.

"So? So after that, you can kiss your vital organs goodbye."

"That's stupid."

"Not according to my dad. He says that the government is developing an organ delivery enterprise with foreigners via anti-aircraft drones. You know, for rich Europeans mostly. There are a *lllloooooot* of wealthy people that need new spleens, and when it comes to Uncle Sam, it's all supply and demand."

"Ronald," Ajay says. "For the love of Christ, shut your mouth."

"Whatever, man. What do you think happened to Sheriff Nichols?"

"Will you shut up about that, Ronald?" said Gus. "He was killed in the earthquake.

It was a tragedy."

"I don't know...I heard that when his body was recovered, it had been torn scrotum to sternum. Doesn't sound like an earthquake to me. Truth be told, my homies, I think this whole thing was a false flag operation. Probably so some German millionaire could get a new heart."

"You're fucking insane."

"Just don't come to running to me when you're walking around without a pair of lungs."

"So don't drive then. Use a bike instead."

"Nah. Most bikes in this country are built out of Chinese lead that's known to lower sperm count."

We change the subject toward the tournament. We talk about strategy and how we'll avoid the same brackets so as not to have to play against each other. That way, with luck, we'll take home enough accolades to make us on the radar in the state circuit, subsequently allowing us entry to national Cons next summer, where the big boys play.

We're about to exit the Lower Thicks and get on the highway. From there, we'll travel down past Ozark to Corvallis, a place none of us had ever been before. Since Myers High collapsed, people are traveling more. Tourists stop through Mossglow on their way north, hoping for a dramatic ocean view. Our residents take trips to the big cities down south. It's almost as if we're easier to find now. As if we've reappeared on the map. The haze that kept men like Gus's father on the back porch has dissipated.

Just when we're about to leave the Lower Thicks, Gus slams on the brakes. Ronald's lock box almost tips over.

"If any of my Zepps are cracked, you're paying for it."

"We forgot Lexi," Gus says.

"Shit, you're right." I turn back toward Ajay and Ronald. "Nobody say anything to her, okay?"

"Just hurry up," said Ajay. "I don't want to be late."

Gus checks his Casio. "Even at this pace, we're going to be three hours early. I wouldn't worry about it."

Ronald eyes us suspiciously. "I wouldn't be surprised if we got attacked by vampire goats on the way down."

We pull up in front of Lexi's house about ten minutes late. She's waiting on the front step, smoking a cigarette that she extinguishes in an ashtray beside the doormat. The second she stands up, her mother, Pinky, opens the front door. I'm surprised by how the woman looks at first, taking her for a much different person than before. With the sun out and a little bit of warmth in the air, she looks softer, happier.

She's wearing a cream-colored sundress and is tapping a pack of cigarettes against her palm.

"Eberstark, Mustus." Her voice, unlike her demeanor, hasn't changed a bit. "You two look good. One is less fat, and one is less skinny."

"Thanks, Mrs. Navarro."

"Both of you need haircuts though. You look like drug addicts."

"Enough, Ma," says Lexi, coming toward the car.

"Bring back milk." Pinky closes the door.

"Yo," we say she gets in the van. Ronald and Ajay, not used to interactions with the opposite sex, flash insane smiles as she sits between them.

"You guys almost forgot me, didn't you?"

We all shake our heads.

"You almost forgot me. It's okay. I understand."

"I'm insulted you'd even think that," says Gus.

"Yea," says Ronald. "We didn't forget you. We just almost didn't remember you."

"Goddamnit, Peterson."

Lexi begins to chuckle. "It's okay. I don't even know why I'm coming along on this greasy nerdventure. Apart from the fact that I find it interesting. Like, from an anthropological perspective."

"Don't lie," says Ajay. "You're genuinely curious."

"Just make sure to explain what the hell is going while we're there, okay? And don't let any of your disgusting Pokémon handlers hit on me. I'll cut a bitch."

"We've got your back," I say.

We drive onto the highway leading out of Mossglow. It's our first time being on it together. Gus is nervous about maneuvering the road and stays in the right lane, maintaining a slow pace even as Ronald jeers. "You drive like my grandma."

There's a little darkness building on the horizon, a gathering of spring thunderclouds overshadowing the sun. We're driving right into it. Gus turns up the radio a little. It's playing something soft and melodious. Classical music. I realize I kind of like it.

"What is this?"

"Schubert. The Unfinished Symphony."

"Who the hell is sherbet?" says Ronald.

"You're an idiot," says Ajay.

The clouds are pregnant with rain, and we speed toward them. Though it's dark ahead of us, we're still where the sun is. We're crossing a border between day and night.

"Hey, Eberstark?" Lexi says. "Did you see that story in the paper? About the flowers?"

Gus makes a noise that suggests we shouldn't talk about too much about that in front of Ronald and Ajay, but it's too late. Ronald's on it. "Oh yeah, the flowers. I think they were sent here by aliens. Why do you think the government's covering it up? Because it's the beginning of an invasion. First, you trick everybody into being like, 'Oh, look how pretty these fucking things are.' And then, it's like, '*GRAR*—you're dead!'"

Ajay scoffs. "It's probably a hoax. Some pranksters trying to make a big to-do."

"Did you just say, 'a big to-do?'"

"What about it?"

"I can't believe I'm your friend."

"I don't know." Lexi's eye turns toward the storm. She's wearing a new, forest green eye patch. "I think they've been here all along. That the earthquake just brought them to the surface."

"Interesting theory," says Gus.

"What do you think, Eberstark?" asks Ronald.

"Me? I don't know. I think that maybe…they're alive."

"Of course they're alive," Ajay says. "They're plants."

"No. I mean, I think they're alive in the same way that we're alive." Ronald blinks at me. "What?"

"I mean." I crack open the window. "You know how when you sleep, and you have a dream…either a really good one or a really bad one…you call out sometimes?"

"Yea, okay."

"Well. I think that's what the faces are. I think the flowers are dreaming."

"That's stupid."

"Hey," says Gus. "Enough about the flowers. Let's concentrate on the tournament. Eberstark, are you thinking we should start out with our Techno-Lorques or Engineers?"

"Either one." The clouds are drawing nearer, but I'm not scared. I'm with my friends. And when you're with your friends, you can do anything. In some situations, you can even understand what it means to be happy.

"Come on, Eberstark," says Ajay. "You can't just say 'either one.'"

"Hey guys." I look down at my stomach. I notice, for the first time in my life, that it's not as large as I imagined it to be. That I'm chubby, but that could change. Change is the most constant thing on Earth.

"From here on out," I say as Gus changes lanes and the rain begins to fall, "don't call me Eberstark anymore. Call me by my first name. Call me Nathaniel."

ACKNOWLEDGEMENTS

The Silent End was written during a challenging point in my life. Though I'd begun the story years earlier, it almost got shelved, only to be dragged out of the drawer shortly before signing with my agent and finished within a series of tumultuous months thereafter.

I have many to thank for the book's survival. The Beanery in North Berkeley, for starters, whose genteel staff tolerated my presence for six months as I scared away customers by grunting in a corner. Nick Sharps for making big introductions. Victor LaValle, Sean Beaudoin and D Foy for their words and insight. Tim Marquitz, Joe Martin, Ragnarok, and M.S. Corley for combing the knots out of my sentences and creating a cover worth weeping over. To Jacob Magraw Mickelson for charting Mossglow's map. To the beta readers of Small Vino, Ben Korn, Cristina Garcia, and the great shepherd of this project, my agent Dara Hyde. If it wasn't for her, this book never would have seen the light of day. To my wife and dearest love, Melanie, who supported me through the cyclone that accompanied *The Silent End* and stayed with me until the clouds cleared. And lastly, to my mother, gone for five years now. Every word I write is an attempt to return her to life.

ABOUT THE AUTHOR

Samuel Sattin is a novelist and essayist. He is the author of *League of Somebodies*, described by *Pop Matters* as "One of the most important novels of 2013." His work has appeared in *The Atlantic, Salon, io9, Kotaku, San Francisco Magazine, Publishing Perspectives, LitReactor, The Weeklings, The Good Men Project* and elsewhere. He has an MFA in Creative Writing from Mills College and an MFA in Comics from CCA. He's the recipient of NYS and SLS Fellowships and lives in Oakland, California.

www.samuelsattin.com